Wipe-out

Wipe-out

◆ ◆ ◆

D N Foster

ISBN: 151876181X
ISBN 13: 9781518761812
Library of Congress Control Number: 2015917773
CreateSpace Independent Publishing Platform
North Charleston, South Carolina

After the sickness – thing was, one of the things was – once you'd survived – you never had any more idea what was going to come up next than you had in the crazy world before. Our "safe" world we were so sure about...

At least – I didn't...

Note to Readers

(E A Harris – Transcriber)

Hello future person. (I wonder who you will be?) This is a brief note from Beth. (You will discover who I am as you read on).

This is to explain to you that Eli wrote down her story by hand in a project book at the beginning. That was because we had not sorted out reliable power for computers, printers and all the things like that. It was also partly (substantially) to get her started. To give her something to do – and us a bit of peace. However; I must not start to tell the story over again myself. (Not here at least).

We did not dare to comment on Eli's handwriting. This was no more than fair really.

Fortunately, because my own is so bad that I can struggle to read it myself, I was able to decipher hers. Consequently I have been able to transcribe all her writings from before we managed to switch her to using a laptop.

I should maybe explain that, despite what Eli says about her education, we have had to do very little to assist her text. Ben often helped her out while she was writing. Richard (and to be honest, myself) may or may not have helped out a little: we did get yelled at a lot.

Having, as her transciber, read every word I am aware that some passages might shock while others might offend. The reader should use their discretion. Eli's writing is about her life experience through appalling times: when she has found the strength to express herself she has pulled no punches.

So here is Eli's deciphered story: almost entirely in her own words, in a legible form and with only lots of crossed-out sections and blobs omitted.

Beth

Box 1
File 1

◆ ◆ ◆

1 – 1

I SUPPOSE I COULD START with my good pal, Bodger... Crazy dog... No, that isn't right, not fair. He wasn't crazy – not exactly... Might be he had a whole load more sense than a lot of people. Got to laugh... He could look a buffoon... But, if you knew – you'd be extra careful then...

It was people that were dim-witted. I mean, if Bodger could fool them that easy...

He wouldn't attack people, he wasn't a bad dog... And, if you did deserve a bite – well – he would have warned you – which was okay so long as you weren't too brainless to know it – to see it...

Somehow, I don't know, it's so much easier to begin with him... Some place to get me started...

Anyway – I'm not sure if Bodger did ever bite anyone. Probably not. Slobbered a load – for certain... That was more than enough to make people run away... Probably better than any bite. (He was fussy about flavours anyhow).

Like a Rottie he would hold a hand... Held onto my leg or the seat of my pants more than a few times... When he figured I needed to behave myself. Kept me from getting myself into trouble.

Anyhow, with other people... That should have had more sense... I mean – a seriously big dog coolly standing there staring at you, taking one small step at a time – towards you – rumbling... That should be enough to give anyone the message.

Bodger didn't growl... Not unless he wanted to warn me, or Greg, about something – get our attention like...

I suppose that means I should explain Greg...

He's dead of course. Like most everybody... He was one person I would so very much have liked to have made it through... But then – hardly anybody did. Did they?

===========

So – here we are – "surviving" I suppose you'd call it... Well; I guess that it would be accurate to call us "survivors"...

Seems to me that we had to survive before. That was just called "everyday life" though – wasn't it? Yeah, for a whole load of us "in the West" it was easy compared to the majority of the world – mostly... Our lives just didn't always seem so fantastic...

We didn't have a clue!

Now? "People who didn't die" might be a more accurate description. Is there a word for that? I don't think so.

People that are muddling through... Staggering from one cock-up to the next. "Muddlers" maybe?

Thing is... Okay, it was awful at first, everything was dreadful – *horrific...* But it isn't so bad now. We're kind of getting used to the idea that we have so much to learn – and we find out the next issue when it slaps us in the face.

It helps a lot if you don't think about what happened "The End of the World" as we knew it... What that was like – or any of it. So I'm going to skip over what happened...

The important aim is to keep going forward – make sure to – keep going...

Yeah well... You could say that that's what I've been doing all along... Sort-of... On the whole...

I left home, our Estate and the Village. I left pretty quick – well, with no Mum, Bodger and Greg gone – there wasn't anyone to stay for was there? Only one decent set of neighbours (dead). No friends on the Estate (dead – probably). Friends I had at college – all dead as well weren't they? Probably...

"Probably"... No I didn't go check everyone or everywhere... Didn't have the energy.

Those I did see were – *gross*... Disgusting...

Wasn't many people I didn't like enough to want that to happen to them. Not even the snotty-pants in the "Old Village" the other side of the hill.

Huh! All their money and their attitudes – didn't stop them getting sick did it? They died as horribly as anyone...

Going raiding for food is bad enough, without having to break into your neighbours' places. Once the power was gone... Not that, that – nor the freezing cold – is any excuse...

How am I ***ever*** supposed to write about any of that????????

Like I said... I'll skip-over that...

1 – 2

So – anyway – Ben said that I should try and write about the good times, the good things. Said that I should write about what's – what *was* – important to me... Give myself something to remember what it was all like by...

How am I supposed to write? I'm no writer...

[I went off on one about this here – but we're going to leave it out... For now at least...]

So – Ben says ("Ben says") to just write down what I think – as I remember it. Maybe begin with a few big events... So – okay... I guess that would be the sort of suggestion both Mum and Greg would come up with – have said... and I want to remember them – whatever happens.

Trouble is... It's all still so close... Thinking about them too much gets me weeping – again...

Loads of people have this "hard" image of me... *Bollocks!*

===========

I've been told to step back and explain a bit... Told it will help...

Who's Ben? Where are we? What happened?

You want a list of people? Who they are? A cast of characters?

Where are we? You don't know?

Um... Actually – I'm not too sure about that last one myself... *I know my way around! Right!?*

We're in England. Right? Somewhere south west – sort of. What's it matter anyway? It's not like there are a whole load of people left to have "distinct accents" is there... Yeah, yeah – so we all have recognisable voices... And *where* are they from? More-or-less all over the place...

Like my Gran used to complain – "the TV has killed all the wonderful local dialects".

Accents? Don't ever get her started on "TV Scouse" or "TV Geordie"... And "East End Mockney"... She *was* a real Cockney – not that you'd ever have known it... A load of her generation were taught "elocution" (even though that crap was going out of fashion) – and DO NOT get her started on that!

My Gran was great though – fantastic – especially when she went off on one...

So – anyhow... The "Big Event" was going on four years ago now...

How am I supposed...?

"Just" write what happened...? Like? "Just write what happened"????

Well that would be what this is supposed to be all about wouldn't it? Except – far as the "What happened" bit goes I thought you said I should write about "nice, happy memories"?

Alright!

So Ben is one of our group, we all live (happily ever after) in a big safe valley... And you'll have to read this to find out what happened and what was good and nice... Some of it after "what happened". Okay? Happy with that? How about letting me get on and write? *Without keep looking over my shoulder!*

One more bit – while no-one is looking... Me – I'm Eli. Not the regular spelling "Ellie". I got a short version E l i – but it's said that way... Shortened name for a short person.

Okay – so my Mum didn't believe you had to use all the letters people said you had to... Leastways – that's what she said... I sometimes wonder if she accidentally spelled it wrong when she did the forms? Whatever – she'd never have admitted to that.

So now you know how come I'm stroppy...

It's in my *jeans... (Innit?)*

My Mum didn't believe in wasting time or effort. I've kind of got that way too... Last few years have changed me (changed all of us). I had to get tough, practical – get real...

So now a load of people call me AK. I have the reputation. Some people say I'm hard. (Not near me they don't). This new world – you have to be tough. Events that happen – you can't go running off whining, looking for counselling and compensation.

Yeah – so I'm strong. Take my story and you'll get some idea why... Way I see it – I have to be... Okay – it's going to colour the way I tell my story – I can't be who I was back then... Probably wouldn't want to be...

===========

Okay! So – the "nice stuff". Not the gory, the gruesome or the grotesque – we all know about that already... Don't we just! Except someone said to write this for history – so Dani would understand – and her kids...

Alright! I'll *do* the nice stuff!

Yeah, fine Ben – except a lot of it was crap – crappy... Don't suppose you'd have liked my life so much... Seen it as "fun"... But – I can't honestly blame it all on you can I? It couldn't all be your fault could it Ben?

I suppose you had a nice life – before... Maybe that would be what makes you so sad – or angry – sometimes now... Must have been so nice for you... Not that I really know... Maybe we should get you writing?

Huh! He's pushed off now!

Now isn't so bad... Lots of ways it's a whole lot better than it ever was before... No stupid exams and qualifications and crap like that...

What's on the "curriculum" now? Everything you need to know (like yesterday) about how to survive. (Funny – that doesn't include Shakespeare or Harper Lee).

Now – well, now – if you can do something useful – get stuck in (not make a mess of it) – that *is* all the exams and qualifications you need... Load of other things about you – well – they don't matter anymore do they?

Could be good if everyone looked at it that way...

'Course – some things about you matter – everybody has to be checked out... You can't simply go and trust anyone... People learnt that... Round about the time they woke up to the fact that there aren't any police to call and/or organisations to claim from.

Well – there's hardly anyone at all is there? Money's no use. You could look for billions – what good would it do you? Nothing to spend it on.

Anything and everything there is – well – you can just go get it – no-one to stop you... Least – not if you're careful – go somewhere there isn't anyone...

Ummm... And so long as you have some way of getting there – and the hell out if you need to...

Got to go careful of course, that's real obvious – never know who might be hiding – who might be making a claim... Some people want to make you pay for everything – even just travelling in "their patch". *(Stuff that!!)*

Okay – so how're you going to pay with no money – or all the money in the world – and no value to it?

Ben (he's an accountant – was) says that we've gone back to a "barter economy". He means that if you've got something and can keep hold of it, then anyone else that wants it has got to have something you want to swap for it... Like the ability to let you stay alive when things get rough.

There was a time when things were more rough than they weren't rough; but they have mostly quietened down now. The arseholes that want to play dirty have (at last) got the message that it is not a good idea... *Definitely* not good around us.

People have settled more – given up wandering around asking everyone "WTF happened?" or "Who's going to come and rescue me?"

I am so, *not* like that!

To be fair; no-one here in the valley is... From all the different places we come from and are many pasts we are all workers. That's how come we get along okay.

I guess, no I know, I was lucky. My life before wasn't so magical but it taught me to stand on my own two feet – people around me taught me... I owe them...

I miss them...

The "improvement" explains how come I can sit here and write this... (Despite a total cock-up). What went on (and can kick off again any time) is how come I have an automatic on my belt and my rifle in easy reach.

(That's, not to mention the dogs).

Like Mum always told me "When the truck's a metre from hitting you isn't the time to be putting your bike helmet on". (I *so* knew better than to ask her what good a plastic helmet would do against a truck – she'd have locked up my bike – solid – fast).

Actually – my Kevlar's next door in the kitchen (I've been evicted for grumping too much)... *But* – I *am* wearing my armour – of course... I am *not* going through all the aches of getting used to wearing it again! No way!

Yeah – so I'm a girl – Ben says I'm a "young woman"... And Beth always agrees with that – says I've "grown up fast"...

Did I have a choice? I got shot at!

How unreal is that?

I figure that's when I properly woke up to my situation – to how things are now.

Wasn't hardly doing a thing. Quietly walking into town, looking around, enjoying the sunshine...

You know – it's not the least like all those films the boys watched. None of all that darkness and creeping around...

Nothing like that! You're away from home; it gets dark – you better be in somewhere safe – somewhere you can close the doors, shut yourself in – and shut out anyone wandering around...

Other side of that... You go wandering about after dark – you better be good at ducking real fast. REAL fast.

And, either way, whatever you do – don't let any light show – or smoke...

That was how Ben and Beth found me – well – not smoke – the smell... Of cooking! *Not* me! ***Watch it!!!***

Everyone keeps mega-clean now... Because we're all freaked-out – *terrified*...

Anyone would be – after – what happened... You're looking at this – then you know what that was... Bet you're terrified too. You're a liar if you say you're not!

===========

1 – 3

NOW RICHARD "SUGGESTS" I DO a "time line" – to provide the historical bit... ('Cos I got stuck again).

Let's see...

Trying to write this from memory (so I won't keep bothering them) is sort of difficult. So much has happened. Great chunks of it seem like hardly yesterday – many of them, things I'm not going to let myself think about. Lots of events are all a vague jumble...

Okay, so now I've finished yelling and cussing... Before she went back in "her" kitchen Beth said... "How about working out at least the start of a timeline?" Yeah – maybe I can do that....

So how about you stayed and helped me work it out Beth?

Right...

Going to try to start at the beginning... Like I said – *what* was the beginning?

In my mind it goes back – probably many years. It doesn't make sense without Mum, Gramps, Gran, Greg and Bodger. They would be where I come from – or the who, the closest people... They gave me the skills to make it through... Wasn't that anyone knew what would happen. Nobody had clue-one...

Wasn't "Survivalist" and all that crap they taught me... They had a lousy view of all that "theory"/waffle in books and on the telly... What were the odds we'd get stuck in a jungle or on a polar ice cap anyhow?

Survive "behind enemy lines"? What lines? Exactly <u>who</u> is the enemy? Or – going to be? You were going to be more likely to have to survive on a motorway if patchy fog set in.

[How come so many "sane, mature, responsible adults" drove like crazed idiots regardless of the weather? Mum said they hadn't switched their brains on... <u>What</u> brains???]

And explain this... Back then... How did you ever figure out who was going to drop you right in it? Straight in deep poo in your ordinary, everyday life... My life wasn't just between school/college, the police, trouble in town, miserable gits in the Village and Donuts on the Estate... There were "global executives" making "strategic decisions" – so Mum got made redundant – again... Big City Bankers... Well... Do I need to say anything about them?

Right...

What happened? Richard's precious "time line"?

I'm not very clear on whole loads of it. Apart from not wanting to ever remember the really horrible events, I've no idea how much is my memory or what I've put together since – maybe with bits of other people's story added into it... They say that witnesses are unreliable...

Anyhow... Far as I can tell (*sort of* remember) things started happening late December...

1. College finished a whole week early before Christmas for some weird reason. That was okay though; because those of us that had figured it out had got jobs shelf stacking in the big stores for that week. (My "rep" was cleaned up enough by then. Could be that Greg helped out a touch as well – again). The big stores must have loved it... I wonder if they had arranged it?

   [Okay – this is definite – I know I had the job – worked my arse off...]

   Would have been sensible of the stores... Christmas shopping was nowhere like sensible – as always... It was mental! Right up to Christmas with all the usual blur and fuss – people buying way-too-much and having rows and shouting matches about how much things had cost and "Who's going to pay all the cards then?"

   With "Christmas" starting in September – how come there was always that insane rush in the last week – or two?

   Naturally all that fuss and bother was *way* more important than everything going on out in the real world – anywhere beyond the shopping lists, family events and parties.

   [Come to think of it... There were some odd times when the supervisors and managers went into unusual meetings and came out looking a bit weird – maybe a tiny-bit freaked... Some products, even regular stock items, ran out. We got told that there'd been an "IT Glitch" and not to bother about it. Well, it was hardly surprising or unusual. We just repeated it to anyone that asked. More unusual that we got told...]

2. Then Christmas was the usual spooky dead-quiet everywhere. Everyone would have stuffed themselves solid with all that food they had carted home – and then crashed out to let it wear off.

   There was no snow and it wasn't too muddy so I was able to get over to see and feed Bodger, no bother. Greg was away working like he always was at a time like that.

   [Christmas/New Year – that sort of time – we didn't dream what other sort of time it was going to be. <u>Couldn't</u> have imagined the nightmare...]

3. Between Christmas and New Year I mostly crashed out – apart from seeing Bodger. Hardly bothered with social media, texting or any of that. Barely glanced at essentials.

At some point, when I wandered by, Mum remarked about the news on the TV. There was something going on in Africa – and maybe China or someplace – and that it was *"Awful!"*... But I had essays to catch up on because of hanging out at too many parties when I wasn't stacking shelves – so I didn't bother to pay any attention. (Didn't listen at all to be honest).

Same, "same-old-same-old". Exactly when *wasn't* something awful happening in Africa? There was a whole industry around "giving to help out" about awful things happening in Africa... And every advert break had a couple of appeals to "help" (send a fiver) to Africa – or for stray donkeys or abused kids. How much of each fiver got to the kids, the donkeys or Africa? How much went to the TV advert makers and the administrators' expense accounts? I *wasn't* the only one asking.

Anyway – we had all basically tuned out – to the "awful" and to the news... The "Media Experts" had a name for it -"Charity Fatigue". What did anyone expect? It was so like teachers droning on-and-on telling you a whole load of garbage you didn't want to know.

I've got nothing against Azerbaijan or Patagonia – but – how exactly is a bus crash in either country "news" that affects me? Wouldn't something about good work being done to help donkeys at home have been a tad more relevant?

It had all gotten to be blur-noise in the background – like the God-awful Christmas-music over-and-over in the stores... Didn't anyone *ever* think to be a teeny bit different?

(Gramps used to complain that when a street beggar made a nuisance you could at least get the police to move them on. They'd arrest the organised/criminal ones... You didn't get pestered by beggars in the theatre or cinema. In the pub you could make them show their licences – or kick them out... But the "charities" had gotten to invading our homes – every damn twenty minutes... He reckoned it was yet another harassment of old people that no politician was ever going to have the balls to do anything serious about. "It's for charity" was like some sacred mantra...

Gramps protested. "*What* happened to an Englishman's home is his castle? You can't keep the buggers out!")

4. So. The damn essays were doing my head in and I was trying to get some sense out of a text war between Sophie and Angela about New Year's parties – that'd be like – which one to crash and who did or didn't know who was and wasn't "BFF" with who... (Couldn't ignore that trash of course).

   It all seems so – pointless – now... It all seemed – well a load of crap to me if I'm honest... I wasn't anyone's "best friend forever" or ever likely to be, that I could see... But – well – you sort of had to go along with a load of bullshit – or you really would be out on your own... I'd "been there and done that" way more than enough with school... College was a fresh start...

   Even with millions and millions of people you still had to watch that you didn't end up a "Billy-No-Mates" and ignored by everyone...

5. Then Mum was saying '*Oh-my-God* they've got *It* in America... Oh no – Mexico... The Yanks are going nuts about the border...'

   "It?" What? I've got essays still to do. When *aren't* the Yanks going nuts? My lousy pay is short. Greg's away again – gone tearing off on some sudden extra job. *Must* be crucial. Mum said he had a big escort of blue lights *and* sirens out of the village... Police outriders... Never, ever, saw that any other time... Was hours before he texted me. Now <u>that</u> was seriously freaky... Probably should have woken me up. I'd got to feed Bodger though, make sure he's okay... There'd never be enough time...

Little that I noticed – the US border guards seemed to be more trigger happy than usual. All the "Be nice to illegals cuz a TV crew is filming" had been totally replaced by "See 'em – **Shoot**".

The media made a total switch to "Defend the Border!" The so-called "Bleeding Heart Liberals" vanished completely from the screens... Could be that, that too should have got my attention...

It didn't.

Then again – knowing what we know now – any effort to keep the sickness at bay made sense... We'd probably have done the same – if we could... Once we did begin to pay a fraction of attention the "Sod Off Scotland!" brigade at college reckoned we should get the Italians back to rebuild their wall.

Seems it wouldn't have made any difference though... Some people are thinking that It (the unknown whatever-it-was) must have already been here –somehow waiting the right conditions...

6. Right away college started back early because we had ended early... Totally regardless of everything going on in the rest of the world, the term strolled on completely as usual. As far as I know all of Britain chugged on as usual... Pretty much...

I suppose, maybe, it did that all round the world – more-or-less – until it was way too late...

Wasn't even as if the bus crashes happened here was it?

Okay, so, there were a few more things not appearing on the shelves in the stores... But the TV confirmed that it was an IT problem. They didn't mention the idea of not panic buying. There wasn't a sugar shortage after all. There was still plenty of booze and crisps – and post-Christmas Sales... (That started before Christmas?)

I'm told, mainly by the conspiracy-theory-geeks, that the people "explaining" weren't the usual retail pundits but government clones... They reckon that was suspicious at least... But then – they would...

I could still get any extras of Bodger's preferred cans and kibble, though. Mum simply switched choices like she always would... So I wasn't the least bothered was I? Don't think I even noticed.

7. First day of term we all still looked mullered from the New Year's piss-ups we'd been on.

Only difference was a whole rash of posters – on about every door – both sides – laminated, colour A3 copies (what did that cost?) – about washing hands properly... Some of the mature students decided that the Government must reckon that it had to be a flu virus. The anatomy and physiology course people declared that it would have to be a "gastric flu"... And looked smug.

Well – that was the first real change we noticed – took us a day or two to pick up on it... Well before we began to wonder where all the Chinese students were – and then some of the East African ones. (Weren't so many of them to miss).

Those of us whose hangovers or guts weren't too bad kept on stuffing our faces in the cafeteria as usual.

That was mid-week – start of the year – and damn cold... So everyone that might have noticed and paid a bit more attention – like the "Anat & Fizzies" – was saying that we wouldn't get the virus because it was all happening in the countries that were having their summer and nice and warm – like we were – *not...*

A load of us huddled around in our coats hugging Americanos (cheapest out of the machines) – moaning – didn't give a toss. We wanted to know *when* they were going to get the heating on. They *knew* when the term started... Didn't they?

I suppose I assumed (like probably everyone) that if the Yanks did get it – whatever the mystery sickness was... Then it would be in the South – Florida, California, Texas Louisiana... We all knew our American geography from all the mega-storms and school shootings they were always having. We all, every one of us, wished that we were there, in the sun – topping up our tans... ("*Not* getting shot at!" – was the joke).

Someone wondered if the cartoon character actors in the resorts would get the shits... Some clown said that chucking up in one of those big costumes would be disgusting... The silly Donuts got into which suit would be the worst or best to do it in... Available space, "dump doors"... Imaginations went loopy.

I thought ***"What?!"*** and tuned straight back out... (Still writing essays)... Until the crowd were taking the piss about quarantining all Americans. America had shut its air-space – again...

And why? We weren't hearing the least thing about what all the fuss was. No-one was reporting "from the scene". No-one was saying what it was – not the least description. Nothing about what symptoms to look out for... Just – "Wash your hands like this" and all that crap – over-and-over again... So – naturally – we ignored it all.

Well? No-one was even starting to appeal for donations in the ad breaks were they? Clearly it couldn't be anything serious...

Okay -- so it wasn't like we didn't care about them – whoever it was (exactly) that was getting messed around. We could feel bad about what was happening... What *was* happening? No-one was being clear...

Thing was – the USA especially – were the biggest, most powerful country on the planet – yet they were always saying "Why us? Why doesn't anybody love us? Why'd they all hate us?" Truth was – most of the time no-one anywhere gave a toss about them – so long as they kept their noses and their armies out of our lives... And kept sending aid and movies...

Reality – the bottom line was that no-one on the planet, any time in history or anywhere *ever,* gave much of a toss about anyone in the next village let alone people the other side of the planet. Okay, so family and clan modified that a bit – and "charity" I suppose... But the significant thing was that anyone and everyone shouldn't be being a threat – or be doing a whole load better than we could ever hope to...

Aah... Right... That would be more than enough to totally piss everyone else on the planet off about the Yanks... They had so much... They could do so much... Worse – they *kept* sodding telling us! "Their World" and "Their Way" were so fucking wonderful... Worse – they had armed forces big enough to go stomping round giving it to everyone they decided needed it.

But... Hell! Even a whole load of "disaffected" Yanks hated their own system – their own government at the least.

Their police just seemed to be insane... What we saw on the news...

Everyone in the rest of the "poor, benighted world" should want that? Want that imposed on them?" What single Yank would ever have accepted that imposition – accepted it even being suggested???

Except – they already had it didn't they? It was "all their own great invention".

But their movies??? What "impression" did their movies give about America? Either all saccharin or bloody murder and mayhem... So, not-a-good advertising campaign... Oh yeah – and a heap of porn...

Not that all of the "porn" was so bad... Much better than "Human Reproduction" in school ever was! At least you could get a good laugh from it! Not to mention – "turned on" by the nice stuff... Plus – you could turn it off... Which you couldn't do with a droning teacher...

I'd always rather watch the good sexy porn than endless rounds of Murder, Multiple Murder, Serial Murder, War, Counter Terrorism, Spies, Aliens, Zombies, Bank Robberies, Muggings, Prison Breaks, Torture or Mutilation... Or any combination. Who thought up all that blood-and-guts crap??? *Who* decided that that didn't need censoring and was "marketable"???

Maybe the problem for all those (probably very nice) Americans – was that when they tried to see what it was about them that "everybody hated" they looked in a mirror – like looking for a zit... They should have tried to see through the eyes of non-Americans. Okay – so not at all easy – but at least give it a go... They'd get more answers to their questions than from a mirror... Er... They might get a few bullets too... Whatever – they've always got Cruise and Drones...

Always had...

8. Meanwhile...

Different people will tell you different stories but I was extra busy and not looking around much. I was still scribbling frantically and Greg didn't seem to have returned. His texts were extremely short – and few. I *did* notice that.

Normally he'd have kept up a commentary-come-check-up that all was well.

Shows how crazy-busy I was – I didn't fully pick up on that... (Didn't make a connection). As usual, New year had screwed with how long texts took anyhow.

It did mean I had a bit extra to do looking after Bodger (getting a fresh load of cans and opening them) – I just got on with it. That's how things were... How we were – get on with life... I loved Bodger anyway. The extra walks gave me time to think – and clear my head some.

9. Odd change – weirdly – people around the village had started to get all freaky about anyone "wandering about" – so except when Bodger saw them off I had started to run into hassle that had never happened before... Different hassle – much more aggressive – and from people that would normally just look down their noses at you but not have the balls to begin to get near.

Maybe I heard some muttering about "There'll have to be rationing if it goes on." in the village shop. They tried to get more sniffy than usual about serving me – but I just opened the door and let them see Bodger sitting there waiting for his treats. There was never going to be any arguing with that...

10. Then suddenly – it seemed like the mystery bug wasn't bothered about warm weather. It was showing up in Europe – and Russia too... So even I noticed in passing that the TV was talking about "precautions" and more "how to wash our hands properly"... Like they hadn't told us that *every* time there was a panic about a flu pandemic... That *never* happened,

    That was – the Friday... End of the first week of January...

11. As I was leaving College someone was announcing vague possible restrictions – "maybe"... And "check the web site" before coming in Monday. The College would text those with a mobile... Like that meant *everyone*... But they went on as if they didn't know that and kept on repeating a number to call and check – saying we had to be sure to write it down... Like we couldn't simply put it in our tablets? *If* we could be arsed? We had jobs or parties to go to ... *Friday?* We all had matters of our own to get away to... (Like preparing the latest assignments – not).

    I was *so* relieved that I'd got my essays in and no-one had fussed... And I was *so* totally knackered!

I headed home, planning to go over the far side of the village to feed Bodger on my way, then double back and maybe get some chips on the Estate as I neared home... And then swiftly go to sleep...

Sleep! Felt like sleeping right through till Monday... Check my texts etc then... *Everything* else was going to have to wait some more.

Although I had noticed that bits of the internet seemed to be messing up – or plain vanishing – but then they did that some days anyway...

12. Then it – whatever "it" was... Well – we finally got it here in the UK didn't we?

    Crazy Toni's chips were never that bad... Never managed to take out the whole place...

13. Saturday morning I was a bit worried that I hadn't seen Bodger. When I didn't get over to see him early I'd have expected him to be thumping the door. Thought maybe he was inside Greg's place as there had been a light on – but Greg hadn't come out... I didn't want to disturb him if he hadn't long got back from whatever the sudden big fuss was... Plus – I honestly had been all-in exhausted.

    So I'd decided that if Greg was home Bodger would be okay and I would leave it until the morning... By the time I'd got over the ridge to the top of The Green where I could see the house, I was all-but falling-over-knackered. I sent him a text... Greg that is – brilliant as he was Bodger would more likely have swallowed a tablet than – well – you can figure that...

14. Then it... It... Well – we totally got sick didn't we?

    More like It got us...

    Not clear what I saw of Saturday...

    Sunday... Never happened.

    Neither did... Like everyone that made it through – I have no idea how long...

15. I could almost say that when I woke up ... *Everything* was fucked-up... Mum was writhing in screaming agony – I think I had been...

I don't know anything clearly... They say it was different for different people – except that most of them/us kind-of melted inside – and we all wished we would *PLEASE* STOP being.

Being – conscious – semi-conscious – was *the most* horrible physical experience I have ever known – anyone has ever known. One thing that it was not – was a mere tummy bug. Not even a gastric flu! Everyone started vomiting and pouring liquid – we (Mum and me) didn't start with the shits (unlike most people) – nothing that good... My whole existence was one infinite howling to be empty – to stop being full of fire...

It was a disgusting way to die.

16. But...

    I didn't die...

    That was the creepy, freaky thing... That was more terrifying than the sickness...

17. I ran away. Is the truth. Mum was dead – there was no sign or sound of life anywhere around us on the Estate and, when I could get over the silent village, Greg was dead – Bodger had vanished...

    The first rush of texts, e mails and all that had long dried up – well before that. No idea if we'd actually lost all that by then...

    I suppose that I sort-of figured out what that meant... I don't know... I have no idea where my head was at...

    So – I... Ran away.

I don't begin to know why I ran. I've tried, tried and tried to figure it. It was so not the sensible action to go for... I guess that I had no real idea of what I was doing at all. How could I? How could anyone?

----

18. Umm... Okay – going back a bit – to before I lost it and ran...

I've got no idea how many goes it took for me to wake up properly. To sit up – half sit up – propped against the wall... How many times I kind-of wondered where-the-fuck I was and what-the-fuck had happened. I didn't recognise my own home...

About all I knew was that I hurt and I was a mess. I couldn't tell where I began and ended and where the pains and mess did...

19. Wasn't just me – *everywhere* around me, everywhere I'd been was – *disgusting.*

I am *NOT* describing that!

The mess that was me was still alive though. That morning I finally surfaced with the sun shining on me... My face felt like I'd fallen asleep with a face-pack on and left it too long so that it had set solid – and then been ripped off...

While I was out-of-it things had gone wrong at the other end as well... You want to know about that? The blood – and having to push parts back inside?

Like I said – a disgusting way to die...

20. A disgusting way to find you're still alive – sort of... Sort of alive...

I didn't seem to have made as much mess as Mum and (when I got to see him) I didn't look as ghastly as what was left of Greg... He looked like half his face was ripped right off...

21. I'm messing up the order of things here... Not surprising. There was a bit *[of time]* while I got myself moving again. Time while I tried to figure out what was going on, what had happened, what I should do... I managed to crawl next door and bring back food I could keep inside – and took their little car... Don't want to think about that... Wasn't nice...

22. I think that the power going off on the Estate was what got me moving more. I think that I kind-of thought that it would be an ordinary, short outage like we sometimes had on our side of the ridge. After a day there was no sign of it coming back on though. (Somehow the posh side – the village – never seemed to get cut-off... That was "such a surprise" wasn't it?)

23. So I figured that Greg's place – and Greg of course – would be okay – the sensible place to make an effort to drive to... I guess that I'd been shutting out that he hadn't come looking for us... So – I know – I knew – that if he could have he would have been there long ago... I simply wasn't letting reality in... I couldn't...
    I'd got some strength by then. I wasn't so completely battered and wrecked... Not quite...

So that is some sort of time line – as one person saw it...

For me it was nearly a non-event. Huh! I wish it had been! I **wish** it had **never** happened... Like we all do...

But then... Probably I would never have met Danny... Then we wouldn't have...

So... Take a deep breath... (*Do not* fall apart). What next?

===========

1 – 4

So – ANYWAY. I'M SUPPOSED to be writing about what was good. I guess it was natural to start with Bodger...

He was the BEST "bad dog" you could ever meet. He terrorised the whole place – both sides of the hill – both the village and our Estate. I mean – like – everyone was half (at least) frightened of him...

So – he was big – about the size of a Mastiff, no, half way between a Mastiff and a Bull-Mastiff – but – *UGLY!* And he could *DROOL* – when he wanted to – he'd figured out that people totally hate drool – so he could kind of turn it on or off like a tap... *DISGUSTING!* And it was *sticky! YEUK!*

It meant that he could make people go away real easy though... He'd do that stand-and-look-at-you thing – and if you didn't get the message and go away because of that – he'd start to – slobber... *EUCH!* Made some people actually gag.

Didn't do it to his friends though – or around little kids – if they weren't nasty they could do anything with him – he'd no more than slobber a little bit, like a warning, if they didn't stop when he rumbled a warning... Never bit a kid. A few claimed he did – which was drastically ridiculous – as they didn't have any bites... But then – donut liars trying to make out a case can be fundamentally stupid can't they?

Anyway. No-one was ever successfully going to make trouble about Bodger – because he was Greg's dog... Greg would have said that he was Bodger's can-opener... Which was sort of my job as well... Not that he couldn't crunch his way into any can of dog food – or beans – he fancied... (House Rule #1 All beans must be locked away out of reach!) He could get a drink of beer when he wanted – which was most days...

God! I haven't had a properly cold beer in... Don't know how long...

Mustn't think about that – I'm supposed to be writing...

Okay. So Bodger being disgusting isn't exactly a nice idea – but it was fun – and could be a real laugh... (Helped if you were up wind...)

People, especially town people and people with big cars and lots of money, thought they could ignore him and, if they saw me, be rude to me...

That was *so* wrong. You don't ignore nearly eighty kilos of muscle – that can move faster than you're ever going to run – no matter how "stupid" you think he looks – A big, healthy animal that has jaws big enough to bite your tyres – unless you're in a big four by four... And he could rip the lights off of those – for fun.

(I'm talking about Bodger Richard! Eighty kilos! *I* was hardly ever more than half that! Shove off! Stop laughing! Go *away!)*

So? What about the police? The dog wardens? Huh! *Laugh...* If they weren't scared of Bodger – they *were* terrified of Greg...

Greg... Okay... Time to tell you about Greg...

He was fucked-up. Big time. No joke – and I'm not being mean or horrible... It's simple fact... The first fact to tell you about him – because of what life had done to him... He never told me much... But if you had any brain at all and took the time to look – well – you could see. He'd been hurt – more than hurt... Things piled on top of each other...

I guess we're all like that now.

Now sad looks and things that no-one talks about are part of the way things are – but then...

He was extra good at not letting it show. I – was probably privileged that he let his guard down (at least a bit/sometimes) when I was around.

But I did know, almost as soon as he arrived, that he had triple glazing for his bedroom. I saw it delivered – when he had all the windows replaced right after he bought the place.

That was the Hermitage, the Hermit's house, that Greg bought after the old man died. From the outside it looked pretty run-down when he got it. That was how-come I was lurking in the overgrown garden...

I don't think I've mentioned this... Before I got to college, before I met Greg... Well – there was a whole load of stuff... I'll get round to that...

Anyhow... Before he moved in Greg had a load of work done. You'd expect that wouldn't you?

Okay... So, now we're back to a whole different world... The "Time Before"...

Greg's Snooty village neighbours were pleased – at first. They liked him "improving the tone" and all that bullshit... Badgered him about "landscaping the garden", calling in "experts"... One's they would recommend of course – probably hope to get a kick-back for themselves out of it – or a discount on their next job.

Greg's place, the Hermitage; that's my name for it... Bodger's place... No... The <u>World</u> was Bodger's place – wherever he chose to be.

Anyhow, if they'd got it, it would have been a massive job – a real earner... The house was big, one of the largest in the village. It was one of the oldest as well... Probably Edwardian originally. The garden had overgrown into a real jungle that all but buried all the outhouses.

All I knew about the Hermit, the old – ancient – gentleman that had been there forever, was that he barely ever appeared outside the house.

For years before Greg, there was all the usual kid's bullshit about the old man being a vampire and all that sort of thing. Fine by me. It gave me the idea of hiding away there – so long as he wasn't one of the living dead.

"Gentleman" turned out to be the right word for him though. He had respect – was respectful. He gave me space and peace. That was generous of him.

That was a whole load more than anyone else – except Mum and Gran *[and next-door]* – at that time. There were a whole load of people that crowded their wants on me whenever they could – whether it was teachers or drug pushers... If they are the "extremes"...

The drugs never stayed outside the school gates. *[Didn't know that? Get real!]*

They and everyone in between (that actually saw me) all wanted to gain from me – one way or another.

So, once the Hermit hadn't sucked all my blood, the garden jungle became like my sanctuary for most of a couple of years – before Greg arrived.

That was, had been, a good time though – an exceptionally good time so far as my life had gone up to then. I don't suppose that it sounds so much – but – I had some peace, I could be myself and do what I wanted – and do it my own way. I was away from the bullies and bullshit. No-one was pushing me to be this and do that... Well – not for most of the time – all the time I could slip out-of-sight and be forgotten by people... Forgotten by the stupid system – both ends of it. "Crime" is as much part of the "System" as the "Law". You don't get one without the other... They NEED each other. *That's* for sure!

===========

I have no idea how Mum and me came to be on the Estate – that's down the south slope – on the other side of the ridge from most of the "old" village. Years later (when I got reason to look) it turned out that we were almost as far as possible from the Hermitage/Greg's place right over on the far north side – on the far bottom end of The Green.

The Estate got plonked down on its side of the ridge sometime in the late sixties. The usual kind of scattering of bland, supposed to each be slightly different to be interesting, chuck-up-and-run boxes. Most of the people got dumped in as well – moved out of manky old parts of Southampton or Portsmouth as the Town Planners got round to clearing up the mess after the Second World War... Leastways – that was the version I heard.

It wasn't the best of estates and it wasn't the worst. "Right to buy" had actually done it a few favours. Near all of the fences remained original but the semis had gained their bits of independence and pride – clear signs of declaration that the new owners were on their way up... At least before they got stuffed back down again. I don't think that any of the up-and-down-pairs in their strips ever got bought by anyone – not even developers or property companies. They weren't so bad – but I'd guess that the legal crap was just too complicated.

We arrived well after the first crowd though. Even well after they finally got a line of shops, a pub (closed as much as it was opened), a school (closed 'cos the building was unsafe) and a garage (opposite the one road from the "main drag" down the hill into the Estate... Closed by the price of independent fuel) – in that order... *"Way to go!"* on the planning!

The Estate's tiny surgery got "relocated" into a massive "state-of-the-art" (leased by private owners) place... In town (of course) – two bus rides away (of course)... Right when they stopped giving the old people (like our neighbours the Spicers) free bus passes (what a surprise)...

They turned the surgery into a betting shop...

I don't think Mum ever knew why we couldn't ever be accepted by most of the Estate people... If she did – she never told me... Gran didn't either...

Gran would quietly back-hand any kid she caught giving me hassle – and any adult come to that. Gran was real "Old School". She was a true Cockney and proud of it – not that you'd ever have known it... Like I said – she'd got *"elocution"*. It didn't help any that she sounded like them over in the village... Not that any of us were bothered what shit attitudes anyone had.

My Gran was great – *superb* – though – especially when she went off on one. People were frightened of her for sure. She was *terrifying* when she kicked off...

Maybe people knew some reason? Maybe Gran warned them off? (She could be petrifying – easily).

I'll never know now...

School was **crap**.

I was "new". I was "behind". I was "different"... Different accent, different words (even cuss words), different intonation, different clothes – from different stores... Different trainers even... I never "fit in"... (Being fair – I never, ever wanted to "fit in". Never saw why I should make myself a clone). I didn't know the tribal divides – not even the boundaries and nuances between Town, Estate and Village... Not that the Village ever bothered with subtlety.

Add to that, I'm sure that a load of the teachers had attitude about me even before I arrived – everywhere I landed up. I don't see that I can have had a reputation, not much of one, for the first few...

I was all the things that mean no-one will ever pick you for a team – or – when they get dumped with you – will ever include you in the game... No teacher can actually do a thing about that... Not without making it worse.

Like – you got kicked some more when they weren't not looking... But – they always managed to look quick enough when the kid yowled... After I smacked them one...

So. I was "trouble".

My family was "trouble".

After Gramps died Gran could rarely visit. Mum had to work. Low-paid, temporary, agency most of the time. Keeping up as best she could. Keeping OFF Benefits. My Mum was proud. My Mum was a real hard worker. My Mum was skint and knackered most of the time... Getting child care for after school was a real problem until I was older... I did know it. I really tried to keep out of trouble – there at least...

So. I didn't want to be "trouble" – for her. I wanted to be left alone. No kids. No teachers. No-anybody...

Eventually, approaching my twelfth birthday, with summer holidays coming up, I got the idea of disappearing into the Hermit's place. No-one ever went there. None of the neighbours, hardly even the Postie or , fought their way to the front door. The back was near impossible.

Except – I wasn't small – I was tiny. Plus – I moved on from gymnastics to Kodokan judo (*ju yoku go o seisu)* – so I was always lithe with good muscle and poise. I could get places without trace that no-one half my age could get.

I practiced vanishing. I had reasons to not leave a trace.

Loads of the time most people looked right through me anyhow... Unless it was their job (keeping it) to see me.... Or, unless they wanted to use me for their schemes... So I'd developed skills of getting around unseen. If I'd wanted I could have burgled every house in both the village and the Estate... Much of the time no-one saw me. (Apart from Mum and Gran and the Spicers).

===========

Well, I wasn't breaking into the garden – trespassing probably... It was easy for me to get into the back. I never broke so much as a twig. (Would have shown up wouldn't it?)

The sheds ("outbuildings") were nearly all solid brick with tile roofs, windows and solid doors. The single wooden one, a double stable and garage, was sagging in the middle and leaning to one side and end. Anyone could see that was dangerous. I kept well clear of it.

Of the rest all but the toilet were shut up tight – almost a relief – apart from the one that became mine. It was almost like it was waiting for me. First time I looked I only tried the door. No joke – I was *shaking.* I never even peeped inside.

Things were getting bad though – and the holidays were close.

I'd had – I don't know how many brushes with the plod. I'd been caught several times – and taken home a few times. If I'd not gone out the car window (advantage of being small) they'd have taken me to where Mum worked once. So the Social were sniffing round.

There was "stuff" okay? Things I'm not proud of... Not necessarily... Let's "discreetly" say "Not things that anyone now might expect..."

Worse... There <u>is</u> worse than the law and the Social... Some "do-gooder" idiot plod went to the Village Vicar about me – and his prissy wife came sticking her beak in.

I did *not* want Mum ending up in prison – nor Gran. No-way I could have stopped an eruption or two if that kept up.

So – frantic – I made a third visit and looked inside the hut. There'd been no sign at all that the house door at the top of the garden had been opened. No sign of any movement in the jungle since I'd last been there. I reckoned there was no way anyone usual size could have got to my shed without leaving some trace... Except of course someone like Greg – but that was over the future horizon – somewhere I couldn't imagine – or fear.

Through the dusty glass I'd seen a table and armchair – maybe the top of a straight-backed chair as well. I'd not dared try the door more than to check it wasn't locked – in case it squealed... When I finally had to risk it the hinges stuck a bit – and then were gloriously silent. Not the least squeak... I was in...

I was out! The dust was diabolical! I tumbled all the way back to the pony field at the back – trying to hold my breath and keep quiet.

Got taken to the nick in town that night. Stupid plod shouldn't have tried to grab me should she? I wasn't big enough to achieve a full throw – but I definitely gave them a surprise – or two... Took three of them to keep me still. No way they could say that I was fighting them though – I tickled them more than I punched... Confused them silly. When they finally got me back to the nick, they couldn't figure out anything sensible to charge me with. Well? I was tiny, especially next to three gorillas, sober and no-way stoned... I even gave them their cuffs back.

Gran retrieved me. I thought she was going to nut the Desk Sergeant in the last seconds before we left. I'm certain they were terrified of her. I was. What made it worse was that she never said a word about it all the way home from town... But – she didn't tell Mum.

Risking any vampire was less terrifying than that. Loads less terrifying. So I got a dust mask, quietly oiled the shed's hinges and began to tidy-up – leaving the windows so they didn't show.

The Hermit let me use the hut – my hut. He was so good to do that. Poor old man was tall and so skinny – always wore a suit and tie – always looked smart. The few times he came near – like when he changed the light bulb – he left a gentle waft of some expensive cologne. When he changed the bulb he must have about flattened himself against the other sheds to get through – he left hardly any sign that he'd come through the jungle.

Okay, I was feeling more confident by then, safer, so I hadn't looked so closely – but he'd made hardly any mark at all. Yeah, I was slack – I didn't spot the clean glass for a day or two is the truth. Apart from me no-one, except Greg, ever got to the shed with less trace... Bodger could – when he could be arsed – ***if*** he could be...

===========

So how come I got bullied? Why does anyone get bullied? They "don't fit", maybe they "look like a target"... What kind of shithead goes round looking for someone they can bully? What sick little need do they have that makes them think that bullying is going to be a good thing?

Bigger question... What kind of pathetic moron follows a bully? They're the seriously pathetic, sick creeps. Those creeps that support the bullies... That is "such a cool and tough thing" to do isn't it? Haven't got the balls to do the bullying themselves... So they suck up to some arsehole that needs to prove themselves by being mean to someone they see as weak and vulnerable...

Small and different doesn't equal weak, though. They had to be immensely thick to not learn that for ages and ages.

Was it because I had no Dad? Plenty of other kids had that. Maybe who he was? Did people know? Would they, could they, have kept that a secret from me? Even with Gran in the background?

Was it because I was small? Blonde? (Sort of blonde... Gramps called it "Muddy" – it was always changing – still does – with the sunshine...) Anyhow... Who knows?

Was it only because I didn't fit in? Didn't want to fit in... Not that I ever could have done... Genius logic that would be – not letting someone fit in and then persecuting them for not joining... Wouldn't have made any difference if I had wanted to in that case would it? If I'd got in I'd probably have been crapped on – made the butt of every joke... I've seen that – seen poor pathetic kids (and adults) living with that warped "acceptance"...

Me? I live my own life.

We kind of got dropped into the Estate when I was four. Right off I knew there was something different – not right. We got reactions. We got hostility – not a lot – but definitely some attitude – toward Mum at first – from other "adults". People that didn't know us...

You can figure that we "jumped the queue" somehow. The place definitely had its clans and tribes. It had its pecking orders. More than one family reckoned that their kin were next in line – there'd have been nastiness whoever got in. I expect that our interruption of the expected feuds was just another motive. If we'd been East European or refugees we wouldn't have been more or less unwelcome – political correctness and the law would have muted the hostility though. It might have died down – sometime.

I know about this now – I was too young then. Looking back I recall times Mum had the police round. I don't know whether they'd been sent or she called them. Beyond that... Kids learn attitudes from their parents. Could be that, when Mum saw the adults off, the kids still got the idea they could take a pop at me.

Mum and me never fell conveniently into any category though. Like I say – I have no idea what the background was. In my head there is just a dividing line between before and the Estate. Almost like I never existed before we landed up there. When we arrived we didn't fit – so we were no-one's specific responsibility. There was no (relevant) net for us to fall through...

Truth is – that was just as well... From way back before Gran and Gramps we were the kind of people that sorted our own affairs. Back in London – and wherever on earth a few generations before that – there was a long, long society with its own supports, its own ways – even its own laws... Social Services and all that were not much different from the law... Except that they could be milked for cash by those smart enough – those without such a strong moral culture.

No way I'm saying that accepting support and benefits (*if* you could actually get any) was wrong of itself... But – it put you in debt to the system – "their system". The totally de-humanised system in which you were hardly even another statistic – except for your NI number and tax code. You had to submit yourself and fit in just like at one time you had to go to the "parish" to get help. You had to accept their judgements on you – and fit in – fit in how they said...

Question – was having to keep in good with the parish neighbours that you knew – and who knew you – better or worse than having to fill in totally standardised forms for nine-to-five office workers that sent them off to be input into a computer by nine-to-fivers that you never ever saw?

The Welfare State was good in some ways – but – it was Middle Class, with Middle Class values, Middle Class perspectives... It was probably bad enough for anyone Middle Class needing benefits – but it just crapped on everyone else... Said that we weren't good enough just as human beings but that we had to jump through their hoops to prove that we should be helped out.

One thing the Welfare State *never* was... They told everyone that it was "free". Like hell it was! Everyone in work *paid* for it. Like education – we paid in our taxes. Neither of them was ever free.

Being a lazy, scrounging scumbag is just plain being a parasite. (No way that we put up with any of that now). If some money-man in an executive office has shipped all your factory's machines off to some other country and shut you down, then there's a fat lot of good blaming you for being out of work, though. It wasn't exactly your choice was it? And were those top-executive's wives all hard working wage earners? Did their fannying around with coffee mornings count as genuine efforts to provide for their families?

Yeah, I'm a tad biased... Did you notice that? Right from a little kid I saw my Mum slogging to keep us afloat. Working God-awful hours – and getting dumped out on her arse by the agencies if she even mentioned shit working conditions...

That was another thing – a lot of the time – you had to put up with illegal conditions – or at best "just legal" a whole load of the time – just to stay on minimum wage... On which you were supposed to have a pension plan, life insurance and savings... (Not to mention your own house with a 42 inch plasma TV and the kids all in the latest trainers...) And – if you did actually achieve any of those – they counted against any benefits you might get... Terrific! Real "caring society" that was... And that was what socialism achieved!

We were not the only ones. I know that more than two thirds of the Estate were in the same position many years... And every single worker or benefit claimer had to sort getting from our outer-orbit into town for work or the next interview... By bus? You think? Most of the rail line got closed decades before. The bit into town ripped up and the other end only left in for some freight – until whatever that was closed down.

Mustn't be bad people and use those dreadful polluting cars of course. How shocking! The government would have to stick some extra taxes on that...

Whatever... I said that our falling through the net was just as well... It really was – because we still knew we could stand on our own two feet – and not become nailed down by of the system. The system could make good people into useless drones. For all the media and politicians ranting hardly a single skiver ever got properly sorted. Like law and crime, the system needed them – if only as "examples" to bitch about.

I <u>was</u> lucky though... We fell outside that.

Okay, it made it tough. It meant that I had to fight... At least I knew that I could fight – even should fight...

Fact was, and I accept this, neither Mum nor Gran could be around all the time. I <u>did</u> try to keep out of trouble. I do <u>not</u> like bruises! No way was there any need for me to go looking for trouble – arseholes came looking for me. I was <u>not</u> going to run. I was not going to try a long way round to avoid them. I was never skulking or submitting. It <u>was</u> genuinely necessary for me to stand up for myself.

So – I fought back. I wasn't bothered if I lost out. <u>No way</u> I was letting anyone get at me without it costing them. I would get bruises, a bloody nose sometimes – but they always got as many whacks as possible from me. It was usually less than I got. Frequently they reckoned that it was reason to have another go at me some other time... (*What* brand of stupid was that?)

Some complete PC arsehole reckoned that if I didn't fight back the "difficulties" wouldn't arise and the children (never called them what they were – <u>bullies</u>) would leave me alone. (Don't remember if it was a teacher or what). Well... If they ever had to try it for real they'd soon learn how crap that idea was. Maybe they were one of the creeps that supported a bully – so that they'd not get bullied. That's real heroic isn't it?

Stupid shithead reckoned that it was my "second punch" that started the fight. Reckoned that if I didn't respond it wouldn't happen... "Just walk away..." Yeah? Exactly how do you "just walk away" when some bully has you cornered? How do you "just walk" anywhere when a gang has you surrounded? When they keep coming looking for you?

When Gran heard about it she demanded "So, by fighting back when Germany attacked Poland – then we started the Second World War did we?" She took me to identify the woman – slapped the arsehole – who got all flustered and wanted to find someone to complain to... Gran told her that she should "Just walk away"... Meekly.

Long and short of it... When I had to I would fight. I wasn't letting anyone get away without at least one bruise for their bother... It was hassle though. I didn't want – I didn't need – all the bullshit.

Richard's just got himself clattered by Ben and Beth won't let him eat with us tonight – because he got smart mouthed and made a crack about me sitting here writing "on the benefit" of the rest of the Valley working.

Like I want to be stuck here??? Like he doesn't know how come?

I am NOT explaining here! It embarrasses-the-fuck out of me! He's just lucky I couldn't reach him myself – and I'm not going to shoot him – 'cos Beth would make me clean up the mess – regardless. Pillock!

"Conservative" he said in response to my charm. "Not Tory..." Got his shin kicked and a punch in the groin from Dani (she's learning still) for being a clever-dick. I can't imagine where she'd have picked up the expression "fucking fascist" from.

Given that his right-wing business buddies were so keen on the "sovereignty of the country" and tired of it being "milked white" by "benefit scroungers"... Then why did the geniuses ship their production out of this country and buy-in foreign products and labour? Could it be that the money they squirreled away was just that teensy bit more important to them than their national values?

So, just in case you were wondering, I don't like politicians of either end of the scale (scale of bullshit. lunacy and plain-old-stupidity). And most of them in the middle...

School itself was always a pain too... I couldn't see what they were on about, why everything had to be exactly as they said. Just suck-it-up – don't waste time with questions. Learn the answers and tick the boxes in the tests. They just kept chucking more and more stuff at me – not giving me time to get my head round it properly. Loads of bullshit. Of course the kids pick up on that too. None of the "equality" propaganda works. Doesn't matter what any "educationalist" says – the kids know who's smart and who's "thick". You're already a target, plus thick... You're stuffed.

So, when they'd given up on me I gave up on them... I went and found different hassle other places... Not that I was looking for bother... I was just very good at managing to wander into it...

I got myself a whole alternative "education"...

Result... It made sense for me to find a safe hideaway for myself. Like it made sense for me to fight. Around school and the Estate the not-so-tough kids would spit at me and call me names but all the time I was taking on the hard kids they wouldn't risk getting close enough for a smack in the face. Other places... Well – they were a different matter...

So – that was my wonderful world... Until I got my Hermitage hide-away and hassle couldn't find me... And again – until Greg appeared.

===========

Long before Greg... Using my hidden ways from home to the Hermit's I'd got sorted about dogs hitting garden fences with a bang, barking and snarling at me... Most of them I made friends with – helped by a few chews and things. Bit like men – fill their tummies and their minds cool down...

Minds? Yeah well – I'm not saying a word... ('Cept it's said that they keep them outside to cool them down...)

I suppose that all meant that I had some ideas when I needed them. In some freaky kind of way I almost got trained for making it through on my own after the sickness.

===========

Moving into the garden very slowly, I was terrified of the Hermit. You can imagine – the kids had all sorts of stories about him – a whole pile of viciously gory ideas about what he would do to anyone he caught... (That was a real encouragement – somewhere the other kids wouldn't to go. Not even for a dare).

School fights and "street-cred" didn't figure in it. I had no real idea what I could be walking into. I was frightened near silly at first... But – I realised that he wasn't doing anything to me – even though, after a bit, he must have known I was there...

Then he put the new bulb in the light – cleaned the window and changed the curtain – so I sort of knew that he didn't mind... Although I hardly ever saw him and he never spoke – never made any communication with me at all...

He must have had a real struggle to get in and do that – now that I think of it – because he'd hardly done any damage to the jungle to get in – then out again... He must have been extra careful... Was one of the ways he was kind – considerate. He didn't scare me off and he never made it obvious where I was either.

The fact was – the first weeks when I crept in to hide – there wasn't any electric – or I didn't spot that there was – so I couldn't have a radio on. (My phone was bust again wasn't it?) Yeah – there could be batteries or a wind-up – but I knew any sound would tell the Hermit I was there – and I was arse-clenching afraid of that... Which was the same reason I didn't use earphones – because I wanted to be sure that I would hear if anyone started to try and creep up on me... Even if that would have been near impossible for anyone not tiny to fit in through all the overgrown plants... I did reckon that the poor old sod would have to struggle so hard I'd have ages of time to run for it.

Anyway – I was perfectly happy reading... Reading quietly and uninterrupted for a change. I could take my own time and enjoy it. No fuss around me, no teacher deciding that I wasn't paying attention to their yammering. No lesson changes. No kids... The place was dry, out of the wind, peaceful... I could get into the books and absorb stuff – I *loved* it.

The outbuilding did have some spiders and creepy crawlies at first but they don't pull your hair, punch you or spit at you do they? They don't ask you stupid questions and stop you concentrating... They don't praise favourites for dead-easy questions anyone would know anyway and try to make you look ignorant to impress the whole class...

Anyway, when you get rid of the creepies a lot of the spiders go hunt someplace else... And I got to quite like some of the regular big spiders that sat there by their webs and waited for lunch to come to them. Maybe that taught me something? Like the Scottish King – whoever he was. Robert-the-Coltrain or somebody.

Maybe...

No-one now will ever know why the Hermit was alone, why he wanted to be so alone – but, I wonder, maybe he recognised someone else who needed somewhere to be – somewhere they would be safe? I owe him.

Later he was kind and put a little electric heater in there for me. I could still be cold – but at least I didn't freeze.

===========

Then, about the second Easter, he died. They – I mean "*they*" – relatives – (SO NOT "family") – the vulture-scumbags – made a fuss about it. Like it was his fault that no-one noticed for a couple of weeks...

It was a time when "they" (Different – "school-they") were making me be in classes all the time – or they'd prosecute Mum. Getting at us – not the arseholes that bullied me. So I wasn't there to see what happened to him – or when... Although I don't have any idea what I would have done – what I *could* have done.

I was there, though (hiding in the bushes) when his relatives came – crashing and smashing around – arguing about who would have what and complaining how little there was that they wanted... I still hate them. I can see why he didn't want to have any contact with them!

But why were they so... *What* were they? How do you describe it? They had no care at all about him. Their whole aim was to grab everything they liked, sell the place fast and grab the cash. They whined that "He hadn't maintained the garden to a sufficient standard to help a quick sale".

One good thing was that the contents of one of the other sheds, that they broke into, scared them off – they never got as far as mine. The estate agents never did either.

I was glad of that. The jungle – and strange noises coming from it (wonder what could have caused them) put people off... The estate agent people loathed coming on the place – helped by me letting some tyres down when they parked in the not-so-clear drive to the original garage built into the extension on the side of the house.

In the end the Hermitage stayed unsold all summer – which was terrific – no-one remembered to turn the power off – and I made sure to not use too much so that a bill shouldn't remind them... I was beginning to get smart – and I already knew a whole lot about bills anyway...

===========

1 – 5

EVENTUALLY GREG SHOWED UP... His first look around he absolutely frightened the "pomposity" out of the snotty estate agent woman. I nearly laughed aloud – after I'd got over the shock and fright that he obviously knew that not only was the shed being used but that someone was there and watching him... That freaked the life out of me – before he clearly didn't do a thing about it...

Plus, he didn't touch my few remaining bits but closed the door firmly and went off toward the house to freak out the woman – who had finally started to complain and try to find him... She shrieked when he "found" her! I loved it!

But – while he'd not said or done anything about me, I was frantic what would happen next.

Soon as the old man died I knew my hide-away was threatened... The idea of it all being ripped up and made tidy had me out-of-my-brain for ages. I overheard neighbour talk about demolition and new houses.

When all the renovation work started (before I knew for sure who'd got the place) I couldn't figure out what to make of it or what to do. I couldn't pretend that whenever the buyer decided to do what they wanted with the garden that, well, then the place wouldn't be the same any more. They wouldn't want me around... Certainly they'd want my shed – that's "my shed" – their property... So I would want to – that would be, have to move on... I guess that I desperately held on – for a bit – because I had no idea at all what to do.

I couldn't think of anywhere. The old train station by the north main road (one-time level crossing) was being refurbished into a designer house (with a mountain of money thrown at it). On the other north road (lane) the old goods station was empty – but, while it was easy enough to get in, everyone knew about it... Wasn't any use for parties or "illicit activities" any more... Not that either was what I wanted. The security people had long ago given up and moved on but the police kept checking it out fairly regularly – and I *did not* need to have any run-ins with them... I'd managed to break contact – I wanted to keep it that way.

I desperately needed somewhere quiet – like the Hermit's place had been.

Anyhow... Around the Village I could hear the snoots muttering and trying to decide whether to complain about the "disruptive" noise of the work or to approve because he was "bringing the place up to an acceptable standard. And about time too – yadda-yadda ". He would, *"of course"*, be getting rid of the trees next – Leylandii they called them – or "weeds that should be banned".

Those trees were massive. They blocked out all view right round. Seemed like the Hermit had planted them when he thoroughly got into being on his own... And from then on he simply let them and all the bushes in the garden grow wild. That suited me fine.

But now that the Hermit was dead and the house sold – to this new person. Whoever it might be... I didn't know who exactly or his name at first, of course... Nor if he'd move in or what...

It was all ending. My whole private world was about to be destroyed...

For about a week, maybe two, I froze-up... I had ***no*** answers...

And then I heard the buzz-saws. Five or six of them – like some insane band gone total.

===========

By then I was fairly sure Greg knew I was around but he hadn't reacted... It was like we were both pretending...

He could move quieter than a cat – much quieter than me when I was trying my hardest (back then) but he always made some noise when I was around. (It took me forever to figure that he knew exactly when I was around). Leastways – for those first days – as far as I know he let me know he was there... Maybe? It could have been? (Can never know about that now can I?) Whenever he did I just froze and watched. Sooner or later one of us would back up – but – I never went on in while he was around – not when he was in sight at least.

Greg said (later) that I was a huge relief to him – first because I knew how to be discreet, patient and quiet – and second because he straight away reckoned I'd be good for looking after Bodger when he was away working... He also said that, third, he was "reasonably sure" that Bodger wouldn't eat me – not at once anyway (Cheek!)

Of course – with all the Hermit-being-a-vampire stories and national scaremongering always in the papers and on TV – I was more worried that Greg would eat me – or "something"... But – he looked okay – and the Hermit had been okay...

I even (sort of) wondered if the old guy was still hanging around (as some sort of ghost) and watching out for me... But – you never can know about ideas like that can you?

Anyhow... I knew how to handle myself didn't I?

So (before the buzz-saws) I didn't know what would happen next and seriously had cause to worry. At least he hadn't touched my few bits still there up to then. On the other hand – he hadn't actually said anything, that I'd heard, about buying the place.

School interrupted the important business of my life again. They woke up to the fact that I was one of their statistics and that I wasn't going to pass any test – so far as they knew. I would mess up their score... They couldn't have that – so they got on my case again.

That meant I wasn't able to be around the Hermit's for several days. Mum was watching me like a hawk – there was no way she was ever going to let them take her to court or get the "Social Arseholes" involved... So I wasn't so much grounded as "locked down". She made a big effort to find the money to drive me to school...

It wasn't ever school's way to let you simply learn is it? You *had* to do it their way – or not at all. Didn't matter how much their precious way didn't work for you... Only thing that mattered was their head count and meeting their targets.

Yeah? So I do have a thing about it. I'm *not* stupid like their "system" said I was. Ticking all those multiple choice boxes never did me any good... But I can figure out how to do stuff – really useful stuff – like maintain a gun – for myself... And not shoot myself while I'm doing it... Now *that* is *properly* useful!

===========

Yeah, so – right... Getting to it...

I heard the howl of the saws...
It bugs me now – even now...
There is *no way ever* of mistaking *that* sound!

Everything since – and it *still* bugs me... My world, “my” little safe bit of the world – was being – ripped – destroyed... It would be gone – forever...

Mind you – the whole village heard them – Sunday morning. We heard them right over the ridge in the Estate...

I instantly *knew* what it was. No way anyone but Greg would kick up that kind of racket around the village – and there weren't enough trees in the Estate. My world was wrecked! I locked myself in my room and tried to bury my head under the duvet and pillows.

Mum got a bit frantic after a day and a half. I hadn't done that for a long time – not since I'd found my hiding place...

Naturally she thought it was school and being locked down. She wouldn't have wanted bad things for me... She didn't, couldn't, know what to do. I couldn't tell her of course – and there was no-way that she knew where I went... Where I'd been vanishing to.

She can only have known that I'd found a way of keeping out of bother... I wasn't getting bullied and the plod weren't fetching me home from fights – my grades (when I was in school to get any) had got better – and I wasn't looking like I lived rough, I didn't have a whiff of smoke or booze about me and I wasn't being moody and obnoxious under her feet all the time.

I couldn't go looking, of course... Couldn't go and see my haven all ripped out and replaced with decking and water features. Whatever the latest fashion was.

Until... Well – once I got myself on terms with disaster and emerged – I had to shift my arse to keep in clear with Mum and school.

The weather was foul so I was forced to hang-out around school. (Getting there and back on the bus was another story...)

So, anyway... More than a week of being miserable later, I was queuing in the Estate chippy for a mess of chips, fritters and curry sauce.

[Loved that – haven't been able to get it – since... Well, you know since what...]

There was one of the cars from "over the hill" parked with "Mummsy" looking terrified and clutching her mobile in case she had to call the police to come and rescue her from the evil kids that hung around the shops bored out of their skulls (as always)...

Two kids up from me were two girls about my age. The different stores that their same-image came from meant they stood out as "Village Girls" like cat mess on a new carpet. Plus completely failing to do "street cred" – as they would. They didn't begin to know how to mimic properly – and their posh-school tones kept creeping out...

Then they were suddenly on about "That *awful* new man" how "*So peed* off" they were. He looked "***so*** fit". (Yeah – like he could have been as much their Dad as mine). More crap about how he "seemed to have sufficiently adequate standards..." (Real "street cred" *that* was, wasn't it? Came straight from their parents – with excellent, unintended, "imitations" of them...) But – "After all that *totally* inconsiderate noise and disturbance he'd caused..." Apparently he wasn't re-designing the whole place the way they said he should...

I was thinking "What disturbance?" I knew exactly what noise. (I was *so* glad that I'd got all my books and most of the rest out in time).

Before I could learn more they got shoved along with the queue and jostled about until Crazy Toni yelled at the crowd of kids to behave or he'd gut them all with his fish knife. (Same old, same old).

The "other-siders" changed to talking ponies, kittens or fashion after that... But they'd got me wondering... Maybe the new man – still didn't know his name by then... Maybe he hadn't wrecked everything...

So I got my greasy slop wrapped up (and a skew-eyed glare from Crazy Toni for wanting it in a bag) and legged it down around the rear of the Estate-school ruin, up the hedge to the cemetery, through the bottom of the vicarage garden... (Dodged the *crazy* vicar's wife).

The rest of the way, out-of-sight behind the backs of the posh houses on the east side of The Green, I stayed round the field hedges. That got me to the lane behind the Hermitage...

Diversion...

In the boom before 2008 they'd built the New Road with its expensive new "detached houses" with double garages,... Laws to do with ancient trees with preservation orders on them meant that it was halfway between the back of The Hermit's place and the old line of the railway – which was sort of two thirds down into the valley. You could see right over them into the bottom land from Greg's attic.

Because they built lower down a space was left and that became the pony field... As no-one knew what else to do with it, it sort of got rented out to keep ponies in... Which it would be with that name wouldn't it...? (DUH!)

Nuisance –the big cars and horseboxes were dangerous twisting in or out... But none of the new people were bothered about a skinny kid like me – that's if they saw me at all...

Who kept their horses there was always changing so I was nothing more than part of the scenery. They probably took it that I was a feral villager like some of the fat moggies from the posh houses on that side of the hill...

If they'd figured I was from the Estate they'd have freaked and demanded the police helicopter came over to track me down. As they never did that, they must have assumed that I was supposed to be there...

Anyhow, the ancient hedges were so enormous and un-kept that I could easily stay out of sight inside them. My route to the Hermit's was invisible to most people – so long as I stayed quiet and patient.

The "Old Guard" rejected this fresh batch of intruders almost as much as they did the Estate. So the "incomers" probably took it that I wasn't going to talk to them either... Always supposing that they did actually see me – before Greg and Bodger were around.

The one person that did ever see (react to) me was the mobile farrier... That came in massively useful... Way, way later...

Only people that Greg wanted to be un-noticed by ever ignored him. *No-one* ignored Bodger – not unless they wanted to get slobbered.

Got to laugh! He had this way of sneaking up behind people, absolutely silent – then he'd wait patiently until a bare hand or arm relaxed down toward him – then – **SLURP!** *Brilliant!* Of course anyone in shorts or a short skirt never stood a chance... He could get them easy, simply by strolling by... Would stick his big cold nose in the back of their knee – and slobber as they went airborne. I'm talking about Bodger. Not Greg!

If you weren't around you'd know when he'd done it – you could hear the yowls of shock and horror right across The Green.

No-one *ever* ignored Bodger twice.

Diversion End.

===========

1 – 6

WHERE WAS I?

Back at the Hermit's place – to see what had happened to the garden... Greg's place now – well – the "stranger's place" around then. Didn't even know for certain who had bought it – maybe who for... The agent had called out for "Mr Parks" or "Parker" but that didn't mean anything for sure yet. The window-men I'd heard talked about "Greg" wanting this or that... No help to me at all.

That evening I could still get in from the field lane. I mean easily – before he completely changed that part.

He'd left my shed untouched! I stood there and cried – wept... (Quietly. Hugging my bag of fritters and chips).

The trees all round the edge of the place had been cut short – about eight feet short across the front – and about twenty feet "short" round the rest. The jungle had kind-of had a haircut – sort of neat paths through it to the other sheds and outhouses but still a jungle in between – except my bit – you still couldn't hardly see the front of my shed – you had to duck down and wriggle under to reach the door... Which did have a coat of fresh paint on it...

That stopped me... Stopped my heart I think...

Which was as well – because he was right behind me... Only time he ever made me jump (except in fun). I'd have cleared the trees before they were cut if he hadn't grabbed me.

No-one else ever got hold of me without getting lashed-out at... Other than family of course. (Wouldn't have dared with Gran... Wish I could say the same about Mum...) The way he did it... He could have tied me in knots no bother... Quietly had his hand on my shoulder, though... Firmly – more like steadying me than actually holding... Calming.

"Hello Miss Corbetts..." That *shook* me. Nobody *ever* called me that – not even the stand-in Desk Sergeants. I was *always* "Eli"... When I wasn't "her" or "it"... Blood pounding in my head I fought to think how he knew that. How could he? Anyone?

While I was still shaking and gasping he told me the deal... I kept my hut if I kept an eye open for him – that was all. Discreetly watch out for anything – odd – or different... Except... Did I like dogs?

Well – I sort of did... So long as they weren't too big and the arsehole kids on the Estate weren't trying to get them to bite me.

I was still about bricking myself so all I could do was a tiny nod... He knew – I *knew* that he knew – that I was looking for a way to run for it... Get out of there and never go again – fast...

"You got chips there?" He got right out of my way. I could have gone – strolled away – no problem... So – naturally – I stayed...

Mad Toni's chips were excellent... Better with a good brew of tea... And doorsteps. Mr Parkes taught me the insanities of mixing chilli sauce or Piri-Piri into mayonnaise or ketchup right then...

Pretty good start.

===========

I got the job looking after Bodger lined up – with payment – so he could sack me if I was rubbish at it... Told me that Bodger was a Chihuahua... Yeah – right! Like I was ever going to fall for that...

Still – I got to keep my hut – with a water pipe added so I could brew tea – kettle, microwave and toaster. Luxury. Plus real opulence – I could use the old outside toilet – all cleaned up and squeaky clean – no spiders or moths...

And – maybe – there would be some other jobs – "*proper*" ones – for me when I finished school... Times to fit round college – so long as I did my college work...

Hey! Never thought it through before... He assumed – no – he sorted me – that I would be going to college... I'd *never* have gone... Would have been straight on the dole... He – stitched me up – kind of... But – well – that was okay... Sneaky – but – okay... It was – well – just – just part of the way – the way he helped me...

I *did* think one hell of a lot about his knowing my name... It told me right off that he must have checked me out... And – that he'd made no fuss about it... Not gone to the police... By my reckoning he'd have chucked me right out if he'd talked to the local plod.

No – he'd Home Office checked me... That's a different matter – that I had no idea about...

Also – he called me "Miss"... Not taking the piss but respectful-like.

He didn't seem like a perv or yeuky, though... In fact – I almost fancied him – almost could have – except he was *much* too old – and – kind of sad... He always had this, like, background sadness about him... Sometimes, when I got to know him, I'd catch him looking like someone had taken away his whole world...

I knew from the start that the sadness was something to do with why he had the strange windows to all the main rooms. (Couldn't see in them – even with the lights on inside). When I got the job of cleaning house I learnt the triple-glaze was so that people didn't hear when he woke up screaming... His bedroom had sound proofing. Nothing freaky-weird like the media would have jumped to conclude...

Except, like I said, he was fucked-up...

I could tell when he was bad... Didn't need to see him. Bodger would lose his smile – such an absurd smile – now you can call *that* "stupid" – 'cos that's how it looked – all lop-sided, wonky – and trying to be friendly... Terrified the total crap out of most people – they guessed that he was working out ways to eat them. He'd never do that, though – unless you could tin them first.

Don't *exactly* know why the police and that were scared of Greg. After a couple of run-ins brought on by the Old Guard the local plod avoided him like their lives depended on it – I guess their jobs probably did. I soon knew it was something to do with his job.

His job was also why he needed me to look after Bodger. Greg would vanish for days in his big four-by-four with the black windows. (Later Mum figured out more).

All Greg ever did about things like that was smile – quietly.

There was no-point anyone being nosey – unless they wanted their collar felt... By real-spooky plain clothes in unmarked cars...

===========

So... I was supposed to be explaining Greg...

When he arrived – in the Old Hermit's house...

Did I say that it was right over on the other side of the old village from us on the Estate? Down at the north end of The Green, just before the land began to drop down more steeply into the valley that side. When I eventually got into the attic rooms I could see right over the Pony Field, the New Road houses and the top of the tree lines where the railway had been. Then over the river with its bridges and to the slope up the other side.

Anyway...

Even before he bought it the neighbours especially wanted "the New Man" to chop down all the big fir trees around the whole place. "Wanted him to..."? More like said he was going to "absolutely *have* to..." They were fanatical about those trees...

(And, yeah... Notice that they took it for granted that the buyer would be male... Even the "posh" women were doing that. Not protesting at the very least...)

Before the sign changed to "Sold" I heard them pronouncing that the new owner would "have to seriously improve the whole property – beginning with the appearance of the trees".

The usual sorts of self-appointed committee would cluster to discuss the things *he'd* have to do. They had me worried that they'd start poking around. Even before I'd fully accepted that I was going to lose my hide-away, that spooked me into shifting out – before they maybe shifted from the front to the back... I was half expecting them to start doing some chopping down and clearing-out of their own.

Turned out that I needn't have worried... I didn't see it but Greg got the police on them... Said there were people trespassing and acting suspiciously... I'd love to have seen what happened – but only saw the horde of Law going screaming up our side of the ridge. (Had no idea what for at the time).

It wasn't the usual local plod that came. From what I saw it was armed-response and plain clothes (definitely *not* the local CID)... I should have caught on... The Village should have caught on...

I did hear the snoots huffing and puffing about it. Seemed like they didn't like being very thoroughly turned over and having to prove their identities. A couple of the more pompous (mouthy) ones even got cuffed.

I'd absolutely loved to have seen that!

Later, they kept on bitching. "That was no way to behave! He could not expect a sincere welcome, if he was going to begin like that. He would have to meet certain standards."

Yeah? Like letting them trample all over his property? Be shoved around? Cow-tow to their petty "standards"?

Soon as Greg moved in the snotty-noses still tried to make him fit in.

That was *never* going to happen – if he'd brought Bodger right away they might have seen that... Yeah – might have...

Trying to make Greg fit into their little world – all their little rules. Huh! Hilarious! They had *no* chance!

Before they got the message they almost walked themselves into the garden again... The front one. Told him they'd come to "discuss plans" for his garden and recommend "their" garden designers. That went nowhere – fast... Strange thing was... How politely he did it. I'd have told them... Well – guess...

It cheered me up loads that he did it though... I'd been a bit worried... Would he turn out to be another pain-in-the-arse Village-snoot? I'd kept my sanctuary – but what was it going to cost? No way I was going to be his wage-slave or dog's-body...

One good development though – not one of them ever said a word about me being around... Couple of years and more and they'd never noticed me... Says a whole lot doesn't it?

Next the snoots wanted – well – they *expected* to know everything about him, intended to put him in their little social boxes. Greg was definitely "not forthcoming".

He'd asked me to keep my eyes open hadn't he... So I did... Heard the snoots – Greg called them the "Old Guard" – discussing his suitability, trying to decide which committees he should be on. What would he be suitable for? What beneficial experience did he have?

Greg's "experience"? They'd have freaked if they'd begun to guess...

Then they were onto memberships... whether he would afford their subscriptions – was there any reason he should be "Black-balled?"

Had to look that up on the net didn't I? You can imagine what I was expecting – and wondering what would happen if I didn't warn him about their plans...

They got stuck then – right ahead of panicking. Greg's "track record" was a real problem for them. Seemed like he didn't have one – not one anyone could get hold of. He "had no network" and there "seemed to be no-one to vouch for him". (Had to look that up too...)

I'd expect that any trying to search his background got blocked. Might easily have got a nasty response. He told me right off not to try to pirate a Wi-Fi link around his place – but he put in a line for me as soon as I was looking after Bodger... Astounding – 'cept he did need me to look after him.

So – back with the Old Guard... Greg could obviously afford the high price for the house and a load of work on it – the rumour mill said he paid for everything with cash – up front... So then they started dreaming up explanations – and "problems" about that. Like – how come he had so much money, how come he didn't use any local traders? Especially no-one they recommended – who were all *so* good...Then there was "Who does he work for?" and "Why *doesn't* he have a profile? *Everyone* has a profile".

Even those with connections, and some of them had real-serious connections, came back stone-walled. The more persistent ones ended up warned off... Which, naturally, only made them try to dig harder. *So*, *not* a good idea. It took forever for them to get the message.

But he *would* fit in. They were sure of that – on their side of the hill of course... He would have to...

Yeah. Right. Like he ever suggested that he wanted to fit into their little world.

===========

Like I said, Greg cut down a few trees at the front – himself with his mates... (You know what that did to me) They took some right out – so he could get his big, black 4x4 truck into the new separate garage – that he had fitted out with automatic doors – and big CCTV signs. All new gates (powered) and new paved driveway that side as well – left of the house as you looked from the front. It looked very smart – delighted the neighbours – until he didn't bother to do the other (old) side with its wooden gates, uneven concrete and old-style wooden doors in the garage under the extension's bay window.

He said that it "simply didn't need doing" – but I'm convinced that he didn't do it just so as to piss them off – because they "expected" him to and were so damn nosey and condescending.

I guess that was more "life-skills" training I got from Greg. If you wanted to get one of "those looks" from Greg? Then you only had to stand there in your smart (never got dust on them) "gardening" clothes and say something like "Well. It's coming along. It's nice to see an improvement". Things like that were certain-sure to set him off being awkward...

I guess that's a lot why we got along so well.

Not that I'm *ever* difficult or awkward or *anything* at all like that... Although, these days, I'm told that one of my "looks" can be "a bit frightening"...

What got through to me, *really* had me wondering, was that Greg was *always* polite. It didn't matter what was going on. Polite and quiet. He had this subtle poise. Not the in-your-face or bullshit confidence of some lecturers nor the "cred" of street and Estate donuts... Greg never tried to "own" anywhere like the snoots or club doormen did. From near the start it had me thinking. It changed my ways – even before he began to teach me things.

So much of that has worked for me getting here – and works now. Any kind of confrontation, any sort of in-your-face... People don't expect a cool, calm response... It throws them.

The 4x4 crewcab was his work. A "www – all the rest" thingy on the tail – that if you tried it went direct to a password page that shut your computer down if you didn't fill it in right, straight away... And the truck carried special labels on it – that the Motorway Police and Fire Brigade knew about – he said... And – no – the Snoots couldn't stop him keeping it there... Completely failed when they got pissed-off at him and tried going to the Council... He wasn't using the property for "inappropriate business purposes"... But... Maybe some of the snoots were using theirs? Prod at Greg – and you got poked back. I loved that.

That was after they tried, with the Neighbourhood Watch, to make all sorts of bother for him... Which started sometime after the trees business when he showed up one Sunday morning on his big, black, rat bike... *Oh! That bike...!*

I wonder if it's still there? Wouldn't try to go back though... Just keep my memories of that springer and his other terrific bikes. (Only ever got to ride pillion... Penalty for being short. That's the only real gripe I have about my "stature").

So... Here's something that tells you a whole load... Mum never, ever, even began to warm-up about Greg letting me ride. Anyone else – she'd have gone off like Krakatau.

Meanwhile... On the Great Day...

All in black leathers, welder's boots, gauntlets, matt-black helmet and goggles, Greg rode right up to the church gate – while the vicar was still at the front door smarming and smooching all the old (white haired or bald – and that's the women) Old Guard. All of them straight-backed and so-so-polite in their latest expensive clothes strolling in to be seen... All smiling "quite so" and politely delighted to see each other. (All slagging or shagging each other the rest of the week...)

(I am not slandering anyone... You get to see all sorts of goings-on when no-one sees you... Okay – so it only proved that they weren't any different from the Estate... Whatever they liked to think).

So, Greg arrives with this luscious deep rumble. (Livid stares from all the snoots). He turns off, takes his helmet off still sitting on the bike and calmly looks around...

Flash-of-a-smile to me, then (HORRORS!) he heads on through the gate.

Out of nowhere Bodger appears – like some ghost dog materialising... I think half the congregation – well – I'll let you imagine what they were doing... No-one hung about outside the church for a moment... Don't know what good they thought being in there would do.

That was the first anyone saw of Bodger. First I saw him anyway – and I reckon I'd have been first...

Showing no sign of seeing any of the fuss Greg finished talking to the vicar at the big door and went in. (I was appalled – but thought, maybe he was aiming to wind them up – got that wrong)...

I was well established around Greg's place by then... In my shed – in among all the shrubs and trees – and other outhouses... And a massive new triple garage/workshop he was building across the back...

You should have seen that bike! Degenerate/Gorgeous! So great I had to risk edging closer for a look right then... Wouldn't have dared to breathe near it – not with the massive dog laying there – coolly panting and watching me – all sort of "chilled" – like he knew I had respect – for the bike – and him...

I guess he already knew my scent – must have done – but I didn't think of that right then.

In a couple of minutes one of the Parish Committee people came out. One of the OG of course – full three-piece and tie despite the heat. He took a couple of steps through the gate before he settled for backtracking and staring over the wall from a safe distance.

The *gentleman* glared hard at the bike and Bodger for a couple of minutes – until it maybe dawned on him that he wasn't going to shift either of them that way – gave up and took his phone round the other side (toward the war memorial at the top of The Green).

Guess he reckoned he'd be safe there... Didn't so much as look-right-through me. I mean – I didn't even exist to most people my side of the hill did I? I wasn't going to be an object that someone important like him would notice was I?

Not when he had something "truly outrageous" to bitch about.
Didn't take long and he went back inside.

Not much later the law showed up (urgent with blue lights – but quiet – it was Sunday after all... Wouldn't want to upset the OG's church scene...) The first one got out (all in his hi-viz, stab-vest and equipment belt) – tried to check the bike – the tyres or something – and got slobbered...

Copper was practically screaming! You'd have thought he'd run into a terrorist cell... (Got to get my breath for laughing – even now).

Driver had more sense – stayed where he was. I was disappointed by that – he looked quite fit – despite being a plod.

Quick-smart the police dog van showed up... (Quietly)

I knew her... Far <u>too</u> well. She'd been "not-on-my-case" the Easter before I disappeared myself. I'd known something was screwy when I *wasn't* getting any attention – all the other plod were making sure her Spaniel dog got *nowhere* near me. With school, the Estate and town my life had been trouble enough. I had *<u>not</u>* needed anyone reckoning I was grassing.

So this woman was one person that *did* see me... Now she clocked me before she'd pulled up. I knew that look – "person of interest"... Regardless she'd not seen me for months. No-one to stop her checking me out this time... She parked near the gate and went straight to get twitchy-nose out the back...

I knew I was clean... Sparkling... Even though I'd been out all night... Greg had made it crystal, that there was the least sniff of using, he'd bounce me out of the garden in a flash. <u>But</u> – I also knew that Greg would fight my corner if she tried to fit me up... I was set for keeping my shed and he wanted me around... I could so see that Bodger was going to need some keeping an eye on... Tidying-up after... Serious brushing – disentangling... All frequently.

Anyhow... Soon as the van door opened Sniffy was at his cage door bursting full with zeal... Until he saw the big dog quietly staring at him. Bodger didn't deign to lift his head from his paws. Sniffy got some-kind-of-telepathic message and had an abrupt change of mind. His usual maniac enthusiasm instantly evaporated. He went flat – totally submissive. Flummoxed his boss... But, in her interest in me, she'd forgotten she was supposed to be there about Bodger. Until he strolled over and sniffed her.

The *look* he gave... Disdain. Didn't slobber her... He turned around, paused, farted and sauntered back to the bike.

She got into one with her colleagues... *What* was the problem? *Why* all the fuss? A major drool put her off her thought of checking Bodger out.

Meanwhile the new Tervueren bitch in the van's other cage went demented – barking, whining, scrabbling to get out... Something plod woman had clearly never seen before... Distracted her from the others and Sniffy. She got all anxious about welfare – and opened the cage...

ZOOM! Bitch was off to Bodger like a missile. Practically knocked the woman flat.

You should have *seen* the plods' faces! None of them had a clue what to do... Bodger was no-way a dog you'd interrupt... And neither was his new friend at that moment.

Bitch didn't get rewarded with her ball to play with – didn't seem to bother her much though... I'm damn certain she was smirking as she curled up contentedly back in her box.

Glad I didn't see any puppies – not if they were half as ugly as others he produced... I guess that dogs aren't so different from humans – some ladies see something special in an ugly rogue... And Bodger definitely qualified...

So – having "done the deed" Bodger peed on the police van, slobbered everyone (except me) and lay down by the bike for a nap. After a bit of red faced discussion the police decided that he seemed to be "docile" and "no risk" and buggered off – discreetly...

When I told Greg about it – much later – he reckoned that "the bitch must have fancied a bit of Wuff". (GROAN!!!)

===========

That morning I so had to wait around and see what happened next. During the excitement, when no-one was looking, I'd made myself comfortable across the road in the back-garden hedge of the first of the old cottages. I vanished myself as normal – and waited.

Don't know what they do in those church services – but they take an awful long time about it. I dozed off in the sun.

It had been an early morning the night before – which was why I'd come over to the village shop – didn't use the Estate shops, except the Chippy. ("Other stories"...)

I figure everyone else had left before Greg came out – clumping like a troll in his big boots – and looking very chuffed with himself...

I should have seen where Bodger vanished to when Greg started up the bike but I spotted the vicar and the verger getting into a tizz in the porch. They had quite a row – I'd guess at something about Greg from the arm waving and pointing. So I missed what Greg did – except that I could hear the bike go down the east side of The Green past the old school, turn the corner at the bottom and – I suppose – go into his front garden.

My head was *banging* then – so I went and got some bits and pieces (and watched *all* the time) in the village shop.

Got home to a right row with my Mum sometime after lunch. (Hers – mine would have been breakfast – if I *could* have eaten...) She'd given up grounding me and all that around then. Figured it was more complication than it was worth I suppose...

===========

I wish – wish that I'd not been such a cow with my Mum... You simply – foolishly... Well...

I suppose you figure you "have a right" and that they'll always be there – and then probably they'll *always* be having a go at you – like – that's all you know about life isn't it?

Like – Mum was always there, always your friend, always on your side – was how it *was*. That's – how you expected it to be... Then you wanted to do things and she said "No", you couldn't do them – not at all – seemed like she meant "never – not-ever".

But your friends (huh!) "contemporaries" – loads of them (all competing of course) – were doing them, allowed to do them – least – that's what they *said* – probably lied – on both counts... 'cept the silly-fool ones that got caught, stoned-off their heads, vomiting-smashed or pregnant... or Overdosed... I guess that you could call any of those "proof" that they did – did do something...

Kimberley kind of achieved the last – got herself a massive down off some bad E and put herself in front of a train – made such a mess... They said...

Gross!

That put me right off screwing around with drugs.

Couple of years after she did that, when I told Greg about it (part of convincing him I wasn't trouble) he said "Yeah. I can see how it would do that.' Naturally, I thought he was taking the piss. Then he said. "Bet it put the train Driver off drugs a bit too..." I hadn't thought about that up to then... Don't want to imagine what it would have been like for him (or her I suppose)...

(Some people topped themselves – with what happened with the sickness – or after... You didn't stumble on that – unlike me – you're damn lucky).

So – what was I saying?

Yeah. Mum and me...

It was always just Mum and me... (Even with Gran in the background – and Gramps at one time...) Doesn't seem so bad now – got a whole new "sense of proportion"... Greg always said that was something we all got – at different times as we got older – saw more – had to deal with more crap... He said a whole lot of life was crap – or crappy... I guess he'd seen more than enough...

I said that could be in his eyes – didn't I?

Oh – maybe... I wrote a different bit – something I thought of – maybe I should put that in here...

===========

(Bit I wrote the other night when I couldn't sleep and didn't have this with me – next...)

First time Greg brought a woman friend to the Hermit's house (somehow I still, always, call it that) I got – well... First I got all upset – then nosey (couldn't do a thing about that of course – Bodger wouldn't have let me anywhere near with a moody on) – then I got all angry and righteous... How *dare* he! He'd broken...

Well – he hadn't broken anything real had he? I mean – a friend can shag whoever they want... Like I've always insisted I can... So – I got to feeling totally foolish – until Bodger came and flopped down and stared bleakly at me – I don't know – maybe – like he felt left out, shut out – too?

All clearly ridiculous. I wasn't a virgin, wasn't a "good little girl" – hadn't been for – Yeah – well – we don't need to go there... 'xcept that a whole lot of it was a BIG disappointment...

That was way more effective than any morals or law...

I had *hormones*. Right? Doesn't matter what social/moral panics and witch hunts there have ever been – humans are coded to reproduce. They've evolved that way over millennia. Trying to legislate against nature is like trying to stick prohibition on gravity.

Sure! Protect kids from bad things – bad people especially... But for fuck's sake do it practically! "Prohibition" makes unwanted pregnancies... And abortion is NOT contraception!

Anyway... Talking of now – the Sickness made all that kind of irrelevant didn't it?

There are still scum around – the freaks that think rape is okay... We have practical rules now though... We shoot them. Get the right one – for sure – problem solved... And we don't waste food feeding them in prison.

Someone stitches an innocent person up? Well – that's murder... We shoot murderers too.

[Strange how knowing what we do about false witness affects what people choose to do...]

Meanwhile – back then... The mega-*stoopid* thing? I'd have sworn blind that I'd never, ever, ever fancy Greg – and, if he'd fancied me (even if I had guessed he did) I'd have called him an "Old Perv" – just because he was so much older than me...

Which – which was so, *so* ridiculous in its own way... Because he was superbly fit. I mean – so, okay, his hair had gone white in places. (Because of what made him scream in his sleep I suppose – now). But he was seriously well built, all muscle – well – he would be – he was a soldier wasn't he...

(**Duh!** And that would have had a lot to do with his screams... Sometimes I get way-too-close to even begin to see the obvious).

Anyway... I should have, like, at least seen – something – something beyond his age... Except it was... Well – he was, like, from a totally different world. He was *older* than my Mum! Least – I think he was – he certainly looked it... He – had this – kind of sadness about him – like he'd seen too much. I didn't know what for the first months...

In those days – I mostly reckoned that he seemed old – at times... I know different now of course...

We've all-of-us seen <u>*way*</u> too much now. Haven't we?

So? Why did I get mad when I thought he was shagging someone? Jumped to a conclusion of course. Turned out Stephanie was one-hundred percent lesbian... Greg had to tell me that because he laughed so much at me jumping to conclusions and sulking... He'd do that – not get mad at me – like I'd have expected...

I could have *died* when he coolly asked me "You fancy a quick shag then?"

Still not entirely sure if he meant it... Was probably winding me up... That was never exactly difficult to do for him... When he wanted – but – he was never nasty or mean with it.

Talking then though, that day, he got serious next. He said something that is so true... Problem isn't jumping into bed – it's always the getting out after – what happens then? Where do things go next?

I had to think about that... I'd achieved some completely messed-up entanglements of my own by then... I got all quiet – which – truth told – was half 'cos I was frantically embarrassed, half working out what to do if we did go to bed (how the hell did I know what to do? He'd know so much... More than me any-ways) and half trying to work out if he meant it – and – another half – what if he did? What then...?

I sat there, desperately trying not to look stupid – nothing I could do about feeling it. Not a thing! Couldn't work out what to say or do next...

Then, cool as cool, he said "We could get round the out-of-bed-after problem..." (Completely serious face).

Like a mug, trying to act all cool, I said "Yeah? How's that then?"

Greg laughed – chuckled... "We could do it in the middle of The Green – liven the place up a bit..."

I thought I was going to ***die!*** I've never – well – laughed so much... Was part of it... He could be such a...

Yeah. Well... Guess I'm going to leave this for a bit... Tears make the ink run don't they?

===========

1 – 7

WHERE HAD I GOT TO?

===========

Mum and me...

Well – I never knew my Dad at all, did I? Can't say I actually hated him for it... Just – I don't know... It was plain mean not being there – not ever there – no way – not a thing – nothing at all...

No explanation ever... "Taboo subject" – without that ever actually being said.

So – I guess – I'm still pissed-off about it...

Seems a bit – pointless – now... He's probably – almost certainly – dead... Like most people.

I mean – what would be the chances? I think I'd be incensed if he was still alive... If – somehow – he did show up...

Would we recognise each other? I've no idea what he looked like way back then... Except – the genes say he must have been blonde and short... So not Mum's side of my heritage.

Mum kept any pictures of him she had locked up. I've no real idea if there actually were any... Is that weird? They'd have been years old anyway... I didn't think to look – when I got out – started moving... Ran away...

Wasn't thinking clearly then anyway – don't think anyone was – I reckon everyone frantically wanted to get away from the – the horror of it...

No-one much thought that escaping from one lot of horror would probably (actually, definitely) mean another, tiny-bit-different, mass of horror... Seemed like endless horror – at first – until we got used to it...

It's astounding what you can get used to...

Things like the big wars and then Bosnia, places in Africa, Syria – all that – you could always reckon that somewhere, someday things would return to the way they were – if you could somehow get there – then things would be okay – get to be the way they were – like, how they should be...

It took time for people – for me – to work out – it isn't ever going to be that way at all with this business...

There aren't going to be any helicopters coming over the hill dropping emergency supplies and leaflets telling us where to get help...

If there were – leaflets and all that – no-one would believe them. They'd probably go the other way... Get away – fast.

You ever see that Mogadishu-Total-Screw-Up film? (Lots of the boys loved it). The start of that? Where the helicopters can't shoot at the bad guys? Well – we all of us know that anywhere there's a lot of good food or useful material that could help us it will mean at least potential for danger. A high risk of people ready to shoot at the least thing. Some arsehole that wants to stake a claim – say that the whole pile is his and demand that everyone else pays for tiny bits of it.

Guess how I feel about that...

Doesn't matter what anyone tells you – people were traumatised – terrified-crazy for quite a while... Before we started to get ourselves more sorted out.

Now, well, things are more sorted – doesn't always mean that they're good every way or all the time. Even without arseholes making trouble people everywhere are still jumpy...

The sickness was bad enough – hellish-awful... But – people since that are a much worse problem.

Good thing though, things have quietened down a lot now – around us here at least.

You'd <u>think</u> there had been enough dead. More than enough!

You'd <u>think</u> people would want to get on and help each other...

Yeah. Right...

My Gran said that "Thatcher started everyone being selfish "Me! Me! Me!"..." Whoever "Thatcher" was... Must have been a real cow...

Anyway – Greg laughed at that and said that she was "No more than a medieval baron in drag – same morals, same principles, same selfish greed – same "example to the masses"". He totally lost me when he compared her to Churchill.

Okay – so even I was never going to get away with not knowing who *he* was. *(I <u>do not</u> mean the stupid dog in the adverts... <u>Watch it!)</u>* I still don't know about Churchill's "aristocratic perspective" and "broad vision of history"... But I can see that you want someone more than a grocer's daughter to understand the economy of a country... You have to make things – you have to "add value" – not just sell "commodities" round and round in circles... Even I can see that! (Could see it when I was a little kid too). Service industry is great – until the served re short of cash and figure that they can do it themselves – or just find cheaper labour...

Make things! At least grow things! Most of all don't chuck away all the knowledge and skills while battery-henning people in call centres and offices. We are so stuffed for skills and knowledge now! We don't have a clue!

Alright – turned out we got stuffed by some freak, unknown disease – but – what would have happened if there'd been another big war? How would we ever have been able to make enough of our own steel for ships, tanks and even guns? We were shipping so much of it in...

Now... Well, there's tons and tons of stuff just laying around... But there's no way it will last forever. Then what?

So – did this "Thatcher" person smoke cigars and drink loads and loads of booze every day? History loses me most of the time... It's all so long ago.

I remember now – I thought of something about "Victorian Morals". Greg said "Oh. You mean shoving children up chimneys and beating your children and wife – so long as the stick wasn't thicker than your thumb... Yeah. Wonderful times..." He roughed me over (playfully) when I said he'd remember them.

Central heating solved the chimney problem – and made a fresh one for us... Even in the posh land of the Village snoots there was never a complete stop to exploitation of domestic labour... The Estate probably did outclass them for domestic violence... I definitely saw some around town.

What is wrong with people??? Why can't they achieve for others what they want for themselves – someone to be nice...?

God! I wish I'd had sex with Greg! The once maybe... At least – been extra nice to him – some special way... (Not that I'd have known how to do that... Nor how he'd have felt about it...)

He was so – lonely? Was that what he was? I knew that he could get sex – sometimes – when he was away... I realised that he never did with anyone that came to the Hermitage... No-one except his closest friends ever came visiting. Most of them were men anyway – and the last thing Greg would have been was Gay.

Does that mean I was a close friend? That makes me cry again...

Anyway – since we're talking about Greg – and sex again...

One day, a few months in, he said that he didn't know how to relate to me... Of course that was *horrible.* Way, <u>*way*</u> too "serious"... But – well – I didn't know how to relate to him – except I wanted to – a bit... I'd never known anyone like him... He – he always "saw me" – *always* related to me...

Suppose I'll have to explain that...

I was so quiet. (Yeah – me – I *was.* It was like my protection...) I'm little, very little – and very, tremendously shy... Well I was – before Bodger and Greg... Even with the "issues" that meant I had to vanish into my sanctuary...

Yeah, I fought back all the time – no way that meant I was brimming with confidence. I simply never saw any other way... I really did work on not getting in fights. I know I never sound like that – but I did. I tried the Judo principles – but – when it came down to it I often ended up having to fight dirty – punching. kicking and gouging for all I was worth. Doesn't matter what they did in the movies – when you've got six or more idiots wanting to knock you about for entertainment – you just hit them every way you can.

By the time the sickness hit us... Well I was still shy – just able to handle it better – a bit more coolly. That was – before Danny and...

So, anyhow..

Except when I was being a rebel at school or with Mum I would not be noticed – like I wasn't there – like people looked right through me – except any stinking bully of course... Like, because I didn't have a Dad – I didn't exist... (That was how I thought it). Or; like I was a soft target...

<u>*Fuck!*</u> It makes me so *fucking angry!* I can see why all those Americans would get so angry and go killing people... Just the built-up frustration of knowing that no-one sees you – no-one gives a toss – except when they want to have a go at you – or get something from you...

Except – now that about everyone has a gun – or several – many people have quietened down. Knowing you can get shot goes a long way to helping you be polite and reasonable.

I don't want to kill anyone – except I have to...

Even when I kicked off at school all they ever said was "Oh, it's just Eli". Didn't matter what I did – I suppose that if I'd set fire to something... You make it about property – about <u>money</u> – *then* they take notice...

Yeah – I did notice... "IT's just Eli"... I was an "IT" to them... Not a person... Still – looking back at it now – at least they did notice that I existed – a bit – although it was merely "nuisance value"... Seemed to me that a nuisance should have had some better kind of identifying tag than "it"...

Okay... So now people notice me – call me "A K" – and not because I'm some famous writer...

Wonder what happened to her? Could have done with some magic to get us all out of the shit... Or maybe some wizard now to solve the mystery and tell us what-from-hell it was...

Back then though...

They might have sent me for "counselling" (Blah-blah-blah) or to some special "unit" for "disruptive" pupils...

All I wanted... I don't know – didn't know then... I simply wanted to have some; some – value... And not to be different – <u>not</u> "thick".

That was it (I guess). To actually matter... To be something – no "some<u>**one**</u>" – not just a "unit" to be processed through the system... More than a thing that messed up their score.

Greg gave me that... Didn't uselessly talk about it. He didn't give lip-service to the meaningless, PC-latest-bullshit. I <u>knew</u> that the plain fact that I was, that I existed, *mattered* to Greg... He'd listen to what I thought and what I felt. He <u>bothered</u> to watch out for how I was feeling... I wasn't another valueless blob in the machine... He'd go raging if I pushed it – pushed being "nothing/unimportant". Frightened me sometimes – but Bodger wouldn't have let him... Amazing... Bodger would have stopped Greg if... And he adored Greg... Wow! I hadn't really connected that...

===========

Okay – so I made the page all of a mess crying on it... Again.

So – brace myself – be tough... I suppose – did I love him? Greg... Don't know. What is love? What does it feel like?

Greg said once that "You don't ever properly realise how painful pain is until it stops". Well – I *damn* well know what he meant by that now! Maybe love is the same? When all you have is a massive great hole left that nothing ever, ever, ever is going to begin to fill... And you never realised that what was there was – there – part of you... Part of everything you did.

Is that what love is? That doesn't start to explain what it feels like...

I asked Greg what love felt like. His reply? (He made me *mega* curl-up). "What does sex feel like?" Rotten sod grinned *all* over his face. I'd already told him I'd "been" with some people...

Yeah – right... What there was of it...

I will <u>never</u> believe that there's a single kid that doesn't have a whole load of questions about sex and all that goes with it... Except, probably, the crap side of it – like fucked-up relationships. Our bodies change right? Everything we've known goes squiffy. We get hormones – and zits. We get a whole rush of – all sorts of weirdness we've never known before – and nobody explained to us – not that we could ever explain it – either before or after...

However does a nice, sensible, sane female body go from thinking all males are yeuky-slimy-toads to the most attractive beings on the planet? Hormones have one hell of a lot to answer for!!!

When beginning to find out about sex, especially all the first steps, is so often so *completely* crappy – <u>*why*</u> do we ever keep trying it?

Alright. I can't tell if I was lucky. (Can't can I?) My first couple of times weren't bad – not bad like some girls said. (Could be they made it up to make out they'd done it... Repeated lies they'd heard... Much like some of the boys). I've no way of measuring it have I? Maybe I was extra lucky...

It was all the "social complications" that followed after, that messed the whole thing up in my eyes.

Of course Greg laughed about the question and said "It isn't all it gets hyped up to be... But it can be more than that – *that* is the damnable thing about it..." Then he leered sideways at me and added "Whatever "it" might be". He could drive you crazy! He *would* drive you crazy!

So – one day (a bit later when we'd established ourselves – safely) he answered some of my questions and explained a load of ideas about "extra things" – touching, taking it slow, oral sex and more – and how, if things worked superbly, you could get an absolutely massive orgasm that went on and on forever... And how that was extra good – the best (almost) for a man – if you (the woman) did that. Of course I said that I did all those things.

Yeah right...

Reality was – I was figuring hard as I could how to remember it all for the next time – whenever that would be... And wondering what *exactly* were the special things to do... And how to do them... Get them "done" to me...?

But I did ask him – "Okay? If that's not the best – what is?"

His answer? "After – when you can simply be together – no need to say a word – no need for any action – bit like that stupid song "just be there – forgetting about the world". His "singing" (if you could even *begin* to call it that) was *awful* – *diabolical*... Don't know what song he meant...

But – I have kind of known that "forget about the world" thing – a bit... When it's so special to be with someone – and no need to talk. Yeah. That *can* be good.

(Helps if he doesn't fart).

You know – I can so clearly picture Greg talking about all that – more than remember his exact words... He looked – sad –wistful... Then of course he would pull a face... Protecting himself I suppose – I know about that too as well now...

(Would help if I didn't blub all over the damn page...)

Some bastard shoots your lover – you get splashed and hit – with – bits of them – yeah – you could say that makes you "wistful"...

===========

1 – 8

Yeah – well – I learnt a while ago that throwing things at walls doesn't help...

Wasn't really "a little bit" that I knew that good feeling was it...? But – all of that still hurts way-too-much right now...

So – make some sense of all this...

Where would I begin?

===========

One thing that Greg taught me that has definitely proved useful – value myself.
And another... How and where to kick a man to stop him – fast. That proved useful before...
So – anyway... Back at the start... (Where was that?)

The very start? I got born – prematurely – but – I made it into the world – tiny then – tiny now... Against the odds...

Someone said that more than ninety nine in a hundred people were killed by the sickness – everywhere... Maybe so many as nine hundred and ninety nine in a thousand... At least – as far as anyone knows – it was everywhere.

I guess that being a survivor now is against the odds as well...

Probably the first sign that anyone had of the sickness was that the systems crashed – phones first of course – texts, internet, tweets – then everything else fell down around them... Should we count that as a start? Wasn't the same everywhere. Some countries fell apart quicker... First ones to get hit I suppose... Should we have seen it as a warning?

Wasn't like "SARS" or Ebola or any of those emergencies. (I'm sure I'd never heard of some of the things people talk about now). Of course – all those things happened somewhere else; they were someone else's problem – far off countries (poor ones) that didn't have all the science and technology we had.

We were totally damn confident that we'd get so much warning. Nothing could touch us – not for real... We <u>knew</u> so much. We'd always have time to get on top of it... A few thousand(s) in third world places would die – but – it would never get to us – because we'd do the research and get ahead of it.

Except – we didn't did we?

We were *so* complacent. *So* Cock-sure. We saw things like the net not working as an inconvenience... A pain-in-the-arse. We moaned about it... How were we supposed to get our essays done?

Go to the College library and get real books out? You think? *For real?*

Yeah – like that was <u>so</u> going to happen... We were *totally* pissed-off!

We were <u>seriously</u> *inconvenienced!* That was <u>not</u> tolerable! There'd *have* to be compensation...

That was just us students. The blur on TV was all kinds of people bitching about "lost contracts" and what were people "over there" doing about it? *What* was the government doing about it? You'd have thought the whole thing was some gigantic I-T glitch... I guess that'd be exactly what we all did think... Probably even the government...

No idea what it was or how fast it, the sickness, was going to be...

Not a clue...

There isn't anyone to get all that I-T up and running again. It hasn't been a "turn it off and back on again" job. *If* there were tech people they wouldn't have enough time. Simply finding enough food, fuel and shelter takes about everything – plus watching for any threat. You have to keep an eye open and be ready *all* the time... Problems, danger, can be in so many different shapes and sizes – the craziest things.

But – I'm supposed to write about "before"...

===========

Don't get the idea that my Mum wasn't a good Mum**.** ***Don't dare!*** Mum was **terrific** – but she couldn't do everything and be everywhere could she? She did all she could – and a whole load more than a lot of other kids' Mums did – ones that had it a whole load easier as well.

There was still so much prejudice. So much casual, unthinking *bigotry*.

No-one bothered to asked why a Mum (or a Dad) was on their own. The stinking politicians – who were so much into "multi-culturalism" saw no problem about promoting the "family unit"...

Yeah? And so aren't a kid and a parent a family?

Anyone who wasn't a "proper-married-two-parent (male and female) unit" was fair game for any arsehole MP, Councillor, media editor, moraliser or "expert" – even a plain civil servant (aka "government lackey") to slag off whenever they wanted a "cause" – especially to justify cutting any benefits or tax breaks (for ordinary people) that were left... Or when they figured it would get them elected or promote their cause.

I never heard any politician come up with a "multi-cultural" perspective on that!

They didn't begin to think that they were discriminating – like they say that people never thought twice about using the word "nigger" a long time ago. Single parents were fair game for any *shithead* politician or *shithead* news editor to snipe at... They did whole programmes on it – casually slagging off people they knew nothing about – and cared about less.

So? Queen Victoria was a single parent wasn't she? No-one ever got snotty about her getting pregnant over-and-over again before she got to be single. How "responsible" was that?.

Then again – they reckon she was useless at being a Mum – and hated babies... She should have practiced a bit of "safe sex" then shouldn't she – instead of shagging her passion-man like a bunny... Gran said that maybe if she hadn't spread her genes, ideas and class-culture so far around Europe we might have not had two World Wars...

(Gran going on about it is why I remember that bit of history).

Yeah – and no-one ever whined about royals "living off the State"... But then – they "owned" it didn't they?

Uh! Couple of the "never-worked-in-their-lives" families on the Estate went around like they owned the world – or like it *owed* them everything... *Arseholes* everywhere...

To be fair to Queen Vic though... It can't have been just her... Not just the politicians and media discriminated. People, lots of people, bought into slagging off single parents – with bugger-all real knowledge and less concern about actual people. Like with Hitler and the Nazis – Or Stalin or Mao – the prejudice and insanity of one or two leaders couldn't have significant effect if people didn't go along with it.

Not even McCarthy... No one man, not even a political party, can run the whole show... Not without people buying into what they can get out of it... Accepting it at the least... Maybe buying into not getting a kicking – or not getting sent to a concentration camp... People giving tacit acceptance, if not approval, by accepting that it's better for them to ignore their neighbours being dragged off in the night... Or – worse – in broad daylight in a "democracy"...

Someone said something like "Evil can flourish when good men do nothing".

That's why I'm so obstinate, why all of us here in the Valley are so belligerent.

Could be that all of us here in the Valley – and the groups around us – are a bunch of anarchists at heart? Should that be nihilists? People starting completely fresh after the whole business got swept away...

Was that possibility what was so fascinating about the idea of "Apocalypse"? Dump the whole screwed-up mess and start over?

Again – we hadn't a clue how soft we had it – nor how complicated not having that world would be...

Anyhow...

Long before the sickness struck, probably talking about all the wars, Greg said that nature had to cull the population somehow... And we humans, with our selfishness and conflicts, were by far the most efficient way of doing that... World Wars basically did it on a bit bigger scale than usual.

Well – I reckon we probably were the best at it – *until* the sickness came along... Could be that just happened because there were too many of us? Maybe?

===========

No way I can write about the end of all my old world... I suppose that was an "apocalypse"... Our world ended...

It – that – and everything with it – is all far *too* raw – much too close... For now at least...

But – how things are now – how we are, how we manage – or not... That all comes from back then – before...

It wasn't surviving that made us what and how we are... It was where we came from – mainly our people...

===========

I suppose that I get my fighting nature from Mum. Like I said – she was an excellent Mum – fought for me every way... Okay, so I got bullied and all that crap – she couldn't be there for me every second – and I did know I had to do things about it for myself – and I *did* know that there were people, official people, that *should* get off their arses and do the right thing... It was so much easier for me to do my own thing... Most of the time...

At least – "doing my own thing" seemed to me to be the way to go... How was I to know any different? How was I to know how crazy it would go?

At least my sanctuary got me away from things... I coped – in a way...

Until Greg came along... He made a huge difference... Showed me different ways of doing things – ways that got me into a load less bother. That was good.

(I know that he "intervened" a couple of times as well – discreetly – well – almost discreetly... I'll get round to those stories...)

Yeah so – "if I'd had a Dad" and all that... There were plenty of weak and totally pathetic-useless Dads around – so – okay – I know that that would have been no guarantee – could have been a whole lot worse...

In me you could call the "fighting nature" plain "being bloody-difficult". Maybe getting myself born too soon kind-of started me off? As if!

Hmmm... I was always jumping into things too fast – like I leapt to the idea that Greg, or whoever, would wreck the Hermit's place.

Must say this for Mum, she fought everything and everybody to keep us going – to keep us together – and as safe as she could.

Of course – I didn't appreciate it... Wish I had, now – *"of course"*. Fat lot of good that is.

By the time I was eleven I was bunking off at every opportunity... Yet another change of school. Back then I couldn't quietly sit out of the way on the bus and get no hassle like I wanted to. When I reacted and I kicked up the lousy regular driver would blame me, say it was "always me"; say I started it and kick me off... The git told the other drivers I was bad.

Of course the other kids soon got wise to them chucking me off – so they set about seeing how soon they could get it done. Shits!

Didn't seem that anyone would ever listen to my side of things – so it was better for me to disappear some more. Being round the house was difficult – I couldn't always know what shift Mum would be working. Then there were too many nosey neighbours... And I didn't want to lie to the nice old people next door.

Hanging around in town had all sorts of problems – drugs, shoplifting and gangs at one end of the spectrum and "businesses" and the law at the other. Everything was set (kind of). They called it the "status quo"... Definitions, rules – the "System"...

Practical, simple answers that worked with me as a human being – an individual – didn't exist in the "System".

I was sick of it all long before the Easter of year seven. Didn't want to be sick of life... Never "self harmed"... That was one good thing...

Eventually, once I was twelve, just before the end-of-year, with the horror of summer coming up, I sorted my shed. I could disappear and read in peace in there.

One thing I could be good at was reading – leastways – when I could take my own time – no stupid kids or teachers to bother me.

It never crossed my mind that I was kind of soaking up the information like a sponge – ideas and more ideas – about everything I could quietly get on and read at my own pace. I loved it. I could go back over it as many times as I wanted – until I got it straight... Couldn't usually do too much or else I'd get a headache. Frustrating – because I'd be getting deep into something interesting when my head would go and split. But, I could get done way more than I could ever do at school.

It was far worse at school... I thought that was all there was to it... No one asked me why I got moody. No-one official even bothered suggesting to test my eyes, not even for ordinary vision.

Gran and Gramps gave Mum the money to get me tested for dyslexia... When I was very first at school... Good idea – in principle... But – when that came up negative no-one looked any further. My family didn't know – and no one in the "education system" could be arsed... Certainly wouldn't spend any money... The system defaulted back to tradition... I was "Lazy", "Idle" and – "Difficult"... Working on towards "Disruptive".. So? How about shutting up and leaving me in peace? You keep poking any animal – most times – it'll fight back – or – bugger off...

My family... Well... They knew as little as I did... We all dealt with the chaos around me... The chaos we didn't realise was being created by the System – not just created by me...

I didn't know it then – but it seems like all the pages I dumped in my head sort of got mixed up – and then sorted out... Bit like making a cake – chuck all the bits in, stir it up like mad – let it cook for a bit – and the splodgy mess comes out as a proper cake... Well – brains are splodgy messes – leave them to it – they sort something out... They must do...

What changed all that?

Once we'd got a bit established Greg figured another thing out... He reckoned that the green "jungle" light in my hut helped me to read. I told him he was nuts of course. Like I would have a clue about a thing like that. He insisted I read in my hut and again outside in the open in bright sunlight...

(Greg could "insist" very effectively...) I had to admit – it was much harder outside... So what?

I had found it much easier to get learning into my head in my hide-away?

What? Learning? I was just reading, looking at pictures! Yeah?!

So... Had I learnt nothing from all that effort?

Course I had learnt! I'm not stupid... (Whatever school says...)

"Fuck what school says!"

That shocked me! Some real-serious adult saying that?

Greg gave me a lecture on how I was never stupid and never to even begin to think I was... And then got back to his thing about me finding it so much easier to take in stuff in my green-jungle shed...

Yeah. Could be it was easier... *SO?* No pain-in-the-arse teachers nagging me. No grotty kids or shitty bullies.

He said he'd come back to them later – BUT – I could read it quicker and understand – faster – in my shed?

Of course I could! I said didn't I? "There were no stupid teachers or other kids there!"

Was that the only difference?

Yeah! (I'm *steaming* by this time).

Really? ... What was the lighting like at school?...

I just glared at him.

What was the lighting like at school?... Said with one of those "I'm going to be a pain-in-the-arse until you give me a proper answer" looks.

Yeah-yeah... Bright. Tubes. So what? Didn't mean a thing...

I wanted to go off on one... Was he saying I was some kind of freak? But I knew Greg would no way stand for that – even early on like it was. So... I sulked. Thought it was a load of bollocks... Except – Greg changed the light in my shed. Massive great floodlight. Fixed it so I couldn't turn it off – and I didn't dare smash it – like I would have with anyone else.

So – he proved it. Then he got it all organised, with Mum, for me to be tested. Through everything that's happened I've kept hold of my coloured specs... Now I have a hard pouch on my belt for them. You wouldn't know they are coloured unless you looked closely – but they make so much difference for me. It's so totally crazy – but once I had them I rapidly caught up at school. I was doing alright at College. I'd <u>never</u> have believed it – but it was happening to me. And I didn't get headaches at school any more. I'm using them now while I write.

Once I was sorted, just after New Year in year ten, I caught up like crazy... Really got on well... Helped of course by having Greg lurking in the background – although I never really figured out just what he was up to at the time.

Let's just say that Greg could be "persuasive"... He, near certainly, "influenced" some attitudes toward me... School and then college admissions.

Then again... It's little more than a century that we've had so much education – and that hasn't been in much of the world... If brains couldn't sort things out for themselves – get to understand cows and sheep or cabbages and wheat... Humans would never have survived at all would they? Okay – so they stomped around not doing things the best way for – centuries and centuries... But they didn't pollute the hell out of everything with their chemicals did they? What was so educated and clever about doing that...? For *millennia* people *knew* that it was <u>stupid</u> to shit on your own doorstep...

Well... Most people did...

===========

But – that was all way down the line from when I first copped off from school – because school was nothing but hassle for me.

You could say that I ended up sort of "self educated" – it isn't so impossible – it's happened throughout history. How could the first people to learn things have understood even one thing before there were teachers if they had to be taught by someone that already had all the answers?

Then again – look at all the dogmatic claptrap that was totally bolloxed-up for centuries because the "wise teachers" had made it all up and were spouting absolute bollocks... Get Mum or Greg going on that and about religion – BIG MISTAKE! You'd be there for hours...

Or, of course... You can go for the option of being good and only memorising all the correct answers with no understanding or ability to use the "facts" at all – except to regurgitate it for your next government/political latest bullshit new tests.

{Good word that "regurgitate"... Greg taught me that one}.

I'm totally mixing things up of course... Mum always did her nut at the teachers – long before we were joined by Greg – only he kind of always did it more quietly – but – more devastatingly... No teacher, lecturer or even the Principal wanted Greg to show up for a "quiet little chat" with them...

Naturally – right from the start I learnt what I could read – and that was what was written so that it made sense to me – "making sense" does help – a lot. I spent hours in my shed, whole days, reading and reading... I could enjoy that. Thoroughly enjoy it – kind of especially when there was rain pouring down...

The summers of years eight and nine my shed would get sticky but not all sweaty-horrible like school. No crowds of noisy, smelly people and stupid bells going off to tell you "STOP! Go do the next thing"...

In winter I'd wrap myself in loads of layers and have my favourite hat... Except when there was snow of course. No way I could have got around un-noticed then – but school shut if they saw a snowflake on the forecast on the TV so I could stay at home – no bother.

Before Greg sorted me with a good laptop and connection I used to make like I was going to school – but then slide off, go to the big library (before they closed it) and then circle back to the village and my hide-away. I've no idea how much stuff I waded through like that...

I've no idea if the librarians believed my story about getting stuff for projects. There was one good one that kept an eye out for me and suggested things for me to look at... I suppose she must have guessed. She would buy me a coffee sometimes if I showed up when she could take a break. In fact she was neat, she'd ask me questions – sensible ones that made me think before I answered – about the books I'd taken back... Jayne got her friend helping me when she couldn't. (Not sure how much she knew).

Huh! Jayne had me sussed. But I always kept the books clean and dry and got them back on time. (Didn't want any letters to home did I?) Hey! She was cool... Even though she *never* got my name right... Always called me "Francie". Maybe she was covering for me? I never sussed she was checking me out... She must have figured me out – and she didn't shop me to the school or anyone... Well... I suppose you could say she mentored me... I owe her...

Late summer or early autumn, after the Hermit died, Greg finally settled in and then provided me with internet access exactly at the right time. Later on he gave me a Kindle. That was good. (Said it was a spare he had... Yeah, right... But I was so not going to argue was I?)

Another fact Greg showed me – sometimes (as well as having favourites and being sarcastic at others) the "expert" teachers make the lessons extra complicated – to show how *wonderfully* clever they are... Arseholes!

That's a lot like some of the total donuts that want to lead groups now... "Geniuses" that are convinced that they know exactly how everyone should do everything – their way...

So... (Sod them!) My numbers were absolutely crap. I could count my money and knew when I was being screwed over, though... I knew any deductions should be made – what were legal and what was thieving from me. Of course I didn't make myself popular by fighting any crap like that... Screwed them by saying I'd go right to the media if they fired me. Asked them how they'd feel if some shithead pulled a stunt like that on their kid...

These days I can count how many morons are shooting at me – and how many bullets I have... How many they've loosed off... And there are some very simple sums I can do real fast when I've got to figure that situation out.

I can, I *do*, work out how many ks or miles a truck is doing to the litre and figure if I've got enough to get home... And that's a load more than a lot of the boys can do – or (being generous) what they stop for a second to think to do... Proved by how many times the silly sods run out...

===========

1 – 9

Meanwhile... Back at "then"...

By the time the second Easter of the Hermit's garden came around things were getting more-and-more difficult. Some education-department-bureaucrat noticed that they were always a few statistics short – and I was always one of them.

Like I said – that meant I wasn't around when the Hermit died.

Mum had been in consistent work for a while. Long hours that helped pay the bills but left her knackered most of the time. It had to be easier for her for me to be out-of-sight and at least not in trouble...

Until the system's computers detected me – or – the lack of me...

Mum got a better job though – permanent. The extra money sorted getting me to school. I still didn't want to be on any smelly bus at all... Didn't want to be in school way more... And their sudden "concern" for my "progress" – yeah right – *concern for <u>their</u> shitty government/political tests... And <u>their</u> targets...*

It was like being some special kind of freak-prisoner that had to be watched all the time... Like **D**eath **R**ow.

But when I could get to the Hermitage again I dug out an old bike from the bushes...

(So this was about four months before Greg showed up. Right?)

I didn't know what was happening or who would be buying the Hermitage yet so I was dreading that I'd piss someone off and get done for stealing – except that it was a real wreck.

Even when I totally oiled everything it squealed its own "audible warning" (which was probably a good thing). I had to get whole new wheels for it from my savings – and a really solid chain so that no scum-bag at school would chuck it in the river with all the shopping trolleys and junk...

Of course the teachers and the secretaries got on my case and interrogated me where I'd got it from. I fought straight back and pissed them off by demanding "What fucking business of yours is it?" Of course (after they'd so carefully *not* corrected me) they said that they were concerned for my safety... Got much more pissed and huffy at me when I said that I supposed that a pupil/statistic being splattered by a truck would *major* fuck-up their government/political targets.

They started in on Mum, said I had to have proper lights, a helmet, High Visibility and all those things. Mum said "Yeah? Who says? You say she's got to have it – *you* can pay for it". Don't know where they suddenly found the money from – but they did... Fair play – I've got to give them that...

Would never have admitted it to them – but the lights were superb – those zappy bright LED ones. Must have been worth more than the bike – which meant, naturally, that I had to cart them around with me all day so they didn't get stolen or smashed up.

Aren't kids so wonderful? Still, the bike was so battered anyway that it didn't look like it could have much more done to it... And – the Head did say that I had to park it right under a CCTV camera... So – I have to give some credit for that – even if none of them ever spotted that it hardly had any brakes...

Wasn't Greg got me the bright gear. Much too early on for that. I'm not sure how much he was around by then. I think he had still only begun to buy the Hermitage. The "For Sale" sign was gone – had me totally freaking out. I wasn't sure it was him buying the place. But I had to keep in school and the ride took a load of time and energy...

It was easy going into school (and later college) in the morning. I started with the long drop down from the Estate on our side of the ridge before turning nearly a right angle west – once I was over the river bridge – and past the smelly sewage plant.... Lousy brakes made that bend interesting... But the plant really encouraged me to get it right! Next came a bit of a helpful rise to the junction into the main drag... That helped me jump off before I crossed the main drag side-to-side by the shortest way. It looked stupid – but nowhere near as stupid as getting mashed under the wheels of a truck would have done.

Okay, so I was still useless at learning and convinced I always would be – but I was excellent at the practical... And didn't give a shit what any smart-mouthed arsehole wanted to jeer at me... So long as they kept their face out of reach of my fist.

Anyhow beyond the "Junction of Death" there wasn't much uphill along the bottom for most of the way to the edge of town. Spring and Autumn you had to watch out for the sun being low behind you – overtaking drivers, coming the other way in a rush don't look for silhouettes. Doesn't matter how bright or flashing you are when you've got massive rays of sunshine on your back. Mists didn't only chill but added to the "excitement". I got expert at swerving. I learnt which other places to absolutely NOT dive into the hedge.

Apart from the Russian Roulette the going was easy though. If I wanted I could free wheel most of into town fast... Could be frightening...

Which meant...

End of the day was a **slog**. After the junction the climb up the last kilometre and a bit – felt like a couple of miles – was ***brutal***. End of most weeks I had to get off, get my breath and then plod it. It was only how much I hated the bus that kept me doing it – even in the rain.

Fog and snow (couple of years on) – well – thank God (or something) Mum banned me – well before Greg threatened to cut my bike into little bits if I used it over to his place when the weather got atrocious. (Like with Mum – sometimes I totally knew when he meant serious business – no argument... In fact – he didn't make threats – just warned me – anyone – what would happen... I do that now... Uh! I've got way, way ahead of myself...)

By the first winter at college, when we got the year's first awful weather (later, after I got the good bike), Mum had moved to a job in town. We'd go in early for her and I would stay in the library after classes...

And by then I was sort of attached to a group that at least helped a little to keep me out of bother – or, at least, made me less visible. Being in a bit of a crowd did seem to keep trouble away from me – except for Anton of course...

Hold on! all out of order – again...

===========

There were all sorts of goings-on before college – and Anton... Like near causing a few crashes riding round the big kink in the stone wall at the church graveyard our side of the top of the ridge, between us and the village. Like sweating more over my exams to at least get into college and keep the job Greg was giving me while I was going to be there. Sweating more over that than I did climbing the hill in summer...

Ummm... Other events.. Like – er – losing my virginity and thinking I was in love forever with Gerry...

Soon got myself sorted round that though. Both bits of that... The first bit was "terrific" – the second was crap – stupid crap... Not sure what it taught me... Except, maybe, that good sex has no essential connection to emotions... Not the "in love" kind anyhow.

So... Well...

I'm not going there now – leastways – not yet... Too much information. Far too much...

But – Ben said to write about the good things... Like meeting Greg. Said about that – with Toni's chips – before... (Actually... Some of the sex was pretty good... Could even be better than fritters and chips with spiced-up mayonnaise...)

And meeting Bodger of course... He was SO ***special***...

Yeah? So *of course* I'm crying again! What you expect?

It was terrific though. There was never any question with Bodge – he accepted me – nearly like no-one ever did...

Anyway – with Bodger (more than the bike) I was able to stop sodding about going all round the back ways (unless I wanted to). I could ride straight up round "Smash-up Corner" past the church gate and over the hill to sort out his food – and clean up... *All* dogs are messy!

We'd go for great long walks all along and over that far side – he'd "get out" and come over to meet me. More like drag me up the last of the hill full of impatience... It was amazing how seeing him near the pub on the hill road, waiting between there and the church at the very top, would give me a huge lift and energy...

All the riding, walking (trying to keep up with him) and the rest meant I got fitter and fitter. Didn't make me any bigger but it definitely got me in good shape...

Maybe that helped me survive?

Definitely meant that all the great food Mum cooked didn't turn me into a vast hippo-blob – like it would have done otherwise.

I *needed* all the calories in those chips! *Right?!*

Pity being fit didn't mean Bodger and Greg made it through...

I'm going to need a mop if I go on like this... There's near a puddle of tears round me...

It's good to cry though. Cry not weep. "Letting it all out" is dangerous – when it isn't plain impossible. There has been too much – far, far too much. I think we all know that.

Far as I can tell no-one here in the valley has been brainless enough to say any of the old stupid platitudes... We occasionally get bruises – not the kind from a full on punch though.

It was moronic enough before to tell anyone grieving to "not keep it in"... Now you could get shot for it...

"Not keep it in"? The danger has been, can still be, of getting swept away by it... If you're not careful.

This writing must be being good for me. I can at least start to talk about this.

Bodger took me off on the most fantastic walks... I don't reckon anyone ever "walked" him.

It was a good thing I was small and could scramble – because the one thing he had *no* idea about at all was what kind of space a human needs to be able to get through... Could be he wasn't bothered – figured that I was still with him anyhow when he – we – finally emerged at the other end of a tunnel of bushes... I've no idea what went on when he was out with Greg... Didn't notice that before... We never all went hiking together... No idea why not – it didn't happen... Strange – was plain how it was.

So (before that) with all the cycling – when I first had the original, dreadful, old iron bike – it was a pretty surprising I woke up with the screech of the chain saws on the Sunday morning...

I gave myself the few days from hell fretting about what had happened, what would be left, what I would do next...

And then the thing at the chippy happened – and I met Greg – and then I met Bodger... And then... Then so much – and so many things...

And if I go on like this I'll never get this written... Get "release" with a good cry? Get soggy more like!

===========

Anyhow... (Got my act together)... Riding home one Autumn evening in the last year of school – all glowing like a lemon and flashing like a Christmas tree so that Mum wouldn't make me go in the car or take the bus again... I wasn't watching my arse so much... Probably thinking about my mate Bodger...

One of the Estate boys, Carlton, from the year before mine, (that I kind-of knew around town) wanted to have a go at me. I was well aware he wanted to "make a name" for himself... (Okay, so – old scores from my days in town... There were some dickheads that were out to get me – any way they could – short of killing me – or attracting the Law...) I knew that they wanted to "teach me Respect"... All that pathetic bullshit. What they meant was "bully fear into people"... Small-time, small-town "terror"... No different from political or religious thugs – anywhere or any time.

His brother had a wreck of an old VW that he'd spent a load on tarting up. (Like it hadn't been shagged five owners before he got it). So that evening they sneaked up behind me with no lights and Carlton leaned out and shoved me off – right into the ditch...

Didn't matter if I shit myself with fright – I was soaked – and last year's nettles still sting – in your face...

I just about stood up to wrestle the bike when a big, black 4x4 pulled up next to me. Someone checked me out, told the Driver "She's okay" and they zoomed off. With a spotlight right in my face, I couldn't see a thing of them.

Greg told me later that "whoever it was" said that they could see I was "basically alright". Some nonsense about all the swearing and cursing I was doing... Me? No idea what that could have been – must have imagined that...

Next thing the truck took off – but the lights went off – which right then I thought was weird... Was a long straight there so I saw – They swerved Carlton straight into the hedge... Into a thick oak.

I heard the crunch and could see a bit – at a distance – and, although it was getting dark, the truck's work lights suddenly silhouetted everything.

The car's passenger side was mangled in the hedge, so the only way out was into the road... Soon as the first yob appeared the door got flying-kicked shut. I heard that double bang much louder. Carlton's brother had some *massive* bruises... They both had – before they got home.

I guess that "someone" phoned the police and told them the car had "run off the road"...?

So... The thing I was sort of figuring – was – did I have some sort of "Dark Protector" looking out for me. What I could figure – right away – was that the Police didn't do any looking around... I guessed they were glad to have the chance to get the two of them with baggies of weed – again. Easy statistic to help meet their targets.

No-one around the shops believed a word either of them bragged about – about the police beating them up but it being no problem – "'Cos they woz so hard". Permanently Numb more like.

Next thing I knew there was a decent bike in my shed. Not new – Greg said that would have attracted attention – not least from the plod – but much better than the old wreck. With gears that worked! *And...* Good Brakes!!!

Made my life a whole lot easier – and my bum a load firmer... I thoroughly got into cycling... I actually got into how I looked – nothing "girly" or over-the-top... That was *never* me – but I did like what being extra fit did for my shape – even when there was so little of it.

Another thing... The idea got about that there was someone a whole lot more "stroppy" than my Mum or my Gran around. So – anyone that wanted to make life unpleasant for me had better be prepared for a ton of shit to land on them.

===========

Around the time of the Carlton business Greg was starting a massive run-in with the local plod – started by the snotty Parish Council or Neighbourhood Watch... All Old Guard, like you'd expect. Could have been all those questions about "no profile" and where his money came from. That and the expensive truck and his bikes...

I know that he slapped them all down – that someone did – probably to do with that "www" thingy on the truck... But I didn't begin to imagine then how or why he could do that... I was busy being relieved that he was okay with me – that I'd not only been able to keep my sanctuary but that it was improved. He gave me new tins of paint and brushes and cleaner – called it "self improvement" – *smirked.* Plus I could be "achieving" my jobs. Greg supported my learning – so long as I got stuck-in. Not only the eyes thing but he helped me about numbers, maths and all that.

I guess I didn't trouble to think about what work he did... All I was bothered about was that he wasn't pervy in any way and he wasn't one of "them" – not an OG snoot. He wasn't like anyone I'd ever known... But that probably hadn't sunk in immediately.

If I'd known what he did... I'd have run miles if I'd had *any* idea... I'd still be running. When you know – what he was – what he did...

Of course no-one in the village had any idea. Don't suppose any of them cared – so long as they could make him fit in. They'd have wanted to make him their "poster-boy" and run coach tours to see him if they'd figured out who he was before he made such a total job of fucking-them-off

Everyone over on the snotty side swiftly gave up reckoning that he could be made "respectable" and got into moaning and muttering about him.

Thing I never got though – he got on well with the vicar – and the piss-artist, artist that had a mess of a place on the west side of The Green. (He's a different story – he was ultra-*creepy*).

Naturally no-one in the Estate gave a shit who or what Greg was. For most of the Estate, he was no more than another one of "them over the hill" – even though he used the Estate Chippy quite often – when it hadn't had another fire...

Greg would arrive at the shops on one of his bikes, clump into Crazy Tony's like some visored machine-man, silently order with a note and the cash, stomp out and leave. He would queue like an impassive robot. The kids were *totally* in awe of him. If I hadn't known him I would have been too... I put on the right face of course – or there would have been bother...

None of the kids had got to hear anything clear about me and the ditch – Carlton, his brother and <u>all</u> their mates had got the message to stay <u>well</u> clear of me and that filtered out.... Toughing it out, they made the most of the law busting them... Though I know the brothers got a thrashing from their Dad.

Important thing was – like I said – all the Estate kids got the idea and backed off from around then... Was helped a whole load by Bodger of course.

Until one evening.

We all heard the Rat-bike of course – but Kylie was well into having a go at me. She'd started sniping the moment I walked round the end of the shops

– nasty, vicious stuff. She had to keep it down a bit because of the smaller kids around and the parents (who did absolutely nothing as usual). You wouldn't call any of it "innuendo". Then again, she wasn't bright enough for that.

Bully? She would have liked to be – wanted to be "Queen of the Estate"... "Trend setter" in fashion – which gum to chew this week, which strong brew to glug – and (of course) which drugs... A charmer... Liked to think herself hard – especially once the real trouble moved away.

Fashion? Well... She wasn't fashionably obese. That was some kind of good... Never meant that her display of thighs or cleavage were going to be tasteful. Maybe the Estate boys thought that looking like a news-rag tart was the high-standard?

Okay... We'd had more than a few run-ins... I did not go looking for her though. Avoid her? What d'you expect?

She wanted to get at me about being small, having no tits, not using a yard of make-up... She blinked too hard she'd have taken off – except there was no way her bras made her aerodynamic...

Yeah... I took-the-piss... Big time. (There's a surprise!) She would try to slap me – I would kick her wedges from under her... Wasn't my fault she slopped drink all over herself... Silly cow got caught nine times out of ten.

Neither she nor her Mum got the message from either my Mum or Gran... Police? You think? For real?

The pathetic war went on – and on...

Truth was – she needed me. She needed a "hate figure" she could big herself up against. She needed an "outsider" – a target. She simply chose the wrong one – and was way-too-stoopid to ever see it.

Thing was – that my situation had changed with Greg coming on the scene. She had to be moronic to even dream of extending her hate campaign to him – to "me and him"...

That evening... New/modified me – I behaved – joined the back of the queue outside Tony's and said nothing. When she kept at me she did have the marbles (or Pavlovian conditioning) to stay at arm's (and leg's) distance – plus a bit. Not that it would have done her any good – I was always fast.

Okay, so it was still unusual for me not to kick-off instantly. I was hungry though so I didn't want to get banned by Crazy Tony... At least – not until I'd got my grub... Then I might choose to get the bitch if she was stupid enough to still be around.

I would have given her some if she got in my face again – regardless that Sheridan, her idiot boyfriend, was loitering with their little crowd of heroes. (Yeah, I'd had fights with every last one of them over the years).

Odd thing was – that (maybe for a first time) I didn't just get mad. Maybe I felt something – something new – like – disdain. Early on as it was in my new life, my new friends were already giving me a different perspective.

I have no idea if any difference registered in Kylie's tiny brain. She *must* have heard Greg's bike coming, though. There was no way anyone wouldn't have recognised that... In fact there was quite a bit of shuffling and checking for escape routes going on, well before he even came into sight.

Greg parked up as usual, started to get off as usual – then paused. He took in the face-off and the way the usual hang-around kids were gawping – gobs open...

For them some "real action" was breaking the boredom... An "event" to catch on their phones and post on-line. Something fucking-stupid!

The spectators included a few of the adults (Huh! "Big Kids") half watching out the corners of their eyes. "Discretely" and not-actually-noticing, of course...

Greg put the bike on its stand – exactly as always... But then – he paused, looked around, kind of summed up what was going on by the way people were standing and the looks on their faces.

Somehow even the slowest ones got the idea that it was best to put their phones away... Anyone who hadn't already known that I was connected in some way with Greg must have caught on fast about then – linking the shit Kylie had been saying to the way her eyes suddenly widened and flickered fast from me to Greg and back several times.

The "adults" were suddenly extra busy making out they hadn't noticed a thing... The kids were half silly-giggly and half *"Oh shit!"*...

Then Kylie decided to start in on Greg – shouting really crude stuff at him about his "shagging little kids" and worse... STUPID!

Wasn't like the movies. Well – there were no saloon doors – but – it did go *so* quiet – no-one daring to breathe.

Maybe for the first time Greg took his helmet off. He put it ever-so-carefully on the saddle, turned and started toward the queue – not looking at her or reacting in any way...

I don't to this day clearly know what went on... Kylie (insanely) decided to shift from me into Greg's path. Scowling – probably trying to put words together in her brain cell – got right in his face. Gobbing off. Greg stopped, didn't say a word – didn't react at all... He just stood there... Smiling – pleasantly... Looking straight in Kylie's eyes... Relaxed. Cool. Smiling.

Stupid girl must have been insane. She backed up then, clawing her fingers she suddenly flew at his face – which wasn't there...

Somehow, with no sign of doing a thing, he'd tripped and accelerated her. Her screech changed to a squeal as she smacked down and belly-slid on the gritty pavement. Doing that in her skimpy, sleeveless top with her cantilevered boobs was *not* a good idea!

Could it be that Sheridan had a scrap of gallantry in him? More likely felt he had to do something for his cred – or got shoved into action. He flew at Greg's back – and over it.

All that I saw was Greg duck.. Sheridan cart-wheeled and landed without any break of fall with the most horrible thud... I never saw Greg actually touch the idiot. No-one did. If it ever was on CCTV or a phone no-one ever used it – no-one at all.

That was logical... Sheridan suddenly flat on his back, stunned, was petrifying – more than that. I was convinced something must have been broken – maybe his neck. He'd really smashed down hard – only just missed where Kylie was sprawled – howling about the mess she was in.

Greg, apparently unaware of anything unusual, adjusted his bootlace, straightened and carried on toward the queue.

Suddenly she was up and after him. She tried a swipe at Greg – and near got her nose busted... You should have seen the state of her face – all swollen and black eyes. She more jumped onto his elbow than he hit her though... Well – his elbow kind of happened to be coming round into the same place her nose was...

The queue had totally broken up – so Greg just went past quietly and got his fish and chips – like nothing had happened.

Still wobbly and rubbing his neck Sheridan dragged Kylie away before Greg came back out.

Greg never said a thing about it to me.

No–one *actually,* even vaguely, mentioned it around the Estate – although everyone knew near instantly of course... It produced a few smiles. Somehow even Kylie got to keep her mouth shut – as if all the kids didn't know that...

Only difference that night – Crazy Tony probably did a bit more business than usual...

Oh... And I got mine free, "On the House" – with a big smile at me and a sweeping black-browed, squiffy-eyed glare at everyone else.

It made my life far easier from then on – including on Greg's side of the hill. Even Kylie managed to get the idea to avoid me.

I wasn't making a big fuss that I worked for Greg (never did especially) but no-one was idiotic enough to risk walking into a confrontation like that... Well – almost no-one.

I didn't say about it... I didn't, ever, see or hear a thing... Really I didn't... I haven't written this...

There's no way I'd suggest that Sheridan or Kylie might have been in the tanning shop before I got there – no way anyone might have noticed any oddness about their pupils... After all – no-one ever bought anything other than an orange-tan there did they...?

A different business... (A little before Kylie's stunt).

Before Bodger arrived... It must have been very soon after Greg moved in... You have to expect, with an "Estate" and a posh village... Some numb-nuts is going to reckon that anyone new moving in is going to be good for a break in and burglary. You knew who, the police knew... The Pope knew who it would be, I reckon...

Greg didn't know who... I don't think he was bothered.

I do not know what he did – and I never, ever want to know what he did... Nothing got stolen. The police were never involved.

I do know that he had some friends in the SAS and SBS and I've heard (on the TV round boys' places) about how they train people – with interrogation... I do not want to know what happened... But two Dickheads found ways to get right out of the Estate soon after Greg arrived... And they never came back.

What crime we had shot right down. Kids and yobs coming in from other places causing any kind of trouble stopped. Mr Spicer, next door, reckoned the whole place had become like "Steepford". Didn't mean a thing to me but Mum liked it – and said she definitely wanted to get to the sequel... So – it must have been some old film.

No amount of squawking by the Parish Council and Watch could keep the previous two whole days of fuzz sitting on their arses in a corner of the closed (old village) school up at the top of The Green beyond the war memorial...

What sort of combination was that? School, war memorial and church? Education, the "Glorious Dead" and religion...

Greg reckoned that there was nothing in the least "glorious" about getting dead because some officer fucked up – the equipment was crap – or the intelligence was crap...

Was no-way he didn't have respect – for the soldiers that got wasted – for mates he'd lost – was still losing...

One time he told me (quietly) that he'd "rather have a Chicken Korma and a cold beer with people that understood than all the eulogies."

Remember he'd told me that perspectives change? As you get older, you see more? Well, I'd been here a while, doing some of the work I do now, before it clicked... Those "Officers that fucked up"... Greg was a Captain... I never caught on to the pressure he had on him.

I wish I had. I wish I could tell him...

The coppers and the OG Muppets were totally pissed about the cut-back! The (their) Watch people wrote to the local paper saying that there was "... a <u>severe</u> lack of appreciation of the problems caused by *those people* of the Estate that had been imposed on them since the seventies. Blah, blah, blah". No way they were ever going to be pleased that there was practically no crime around us from then on.

Well – who *didn't* get nicked for drunk driving and where the class A was, is another story...

But on our side of the ridge what little serious trouble there had been around the Estate moved out – or kept an ultra low profile from then on.

"Robot" could have been a good nickname for Greg... He'd have hated it in one way – but – I'm certain he played up an image – when it suited him. Only when it suited him though... Most of the time – well – you probably wouldn't really take in that he was around... Strange – but – not strange... All his mates were like that as well... "Discreet"... AKA – *"scary-as-fuck"*.

===========

Soon as Mum found out about me looking at Greg's jobs she checked him out (of course). Can't have found a scrap she'd worry about – else she'd have ripped him to bits and banned me from going anywhere near – the kind of ban that would totally achieve me not arguing about it...

And don't think that all that toughness about Greg would have stopped her going for him – if she'd decided to... Okay, so –- I've got a reputation now... You never met my Mum!

She just kind of gave me the nod that she wasn't going to object... Except – she did say that he "wasn't the kind of man she would want to get on the wrong side of"... Very circumspect for Mum... And I'd never known anyone she wouldn't face off and crack into if she decided to. Mum was never someone who didn't "call a spade a bloody shovel" – as her Mum said. (*Huh!* She should talk!)

Mum eventually figured out who he was. Once you got that, it was obvious how come he knew the Special Forces people... Mum's okay – Mum was okay – before...

Shit! Don't think I'll ever...

<u>Anyhow</u>... Mum figured out that he was some hero from Afghanistan. His wife and kid got killed in a car wreck on a roundabout somewhere close to London while he was out there taking IED things apart to stop their kids and villagers getting killed...

The press tried to make a big thing of it of course... I think they got warned off... Actually – I'm sure they did... Pity they weren't "warned" about a few other things...

Anyway – Mum didn't need any warning. She'd have had a crack at any media that showed up herself. She was *superb* my Mum was...

(AAAARGH! That fucking word "was" again!!!)

Mum reckoned that if he wanted a quiet place in the country with no hassles he was about entitled to one.

Greg certainly made sure he got some quiet. Me and Bodger could come and go from the Hermitage without any difficulty – but I'm damn sure no-one else could without his say-so. Not even his friends. He kept the Hermit's post box out by the front gate... And that got a covert CCTV on it...

So... I have no idea how to explain this... Back then, right away, I was able to see that same – indefinable thing – in Greg's mates – and – although I wouldn't have admitted that I let myself think it – I knew it was in Greg. All of them sized things up – made decisions – but didn't feel that they had to tell anyone – didn't do a thing – not unless they decided to...

Somehow they also communicated what they weren't or were doing without visibly talking...

Back then I could kind-of detect that... But I hardly had any real idea... I just knew something was there – even without his sorting out Carlton and Sheridan... Or – the rest...

Greg – had this – confidence? I could never have described what it was. Don't have a clue... It was somehow, like, more what he *didn't* do...

Okay – he could play-act... Put on an image – like outside the church that morning Bodger appeared... He put that on though... I have no idea how to explain it...

Kylie and Sheridan *must* have been loaded. The crowd knew that Greg wasn't putting on any act that time – partly because he took his helmet off – but more in the way he quietly moved... The "peaceful" way he didn't do anything...

Anyone that wasn't jacked-up would have known that Greg was giving the option of running away or getting smacked through the pavement...

They must have both have been totally off their skulls. Even Kylie wasn't that stupid – normally.

===========

I just realised... I never actually told Mum about the jobs with Greg. I'm definite she never knew about my Hermitage sanctuary before Greg... She'd have banned me from that for sure. (I was younger and no-one could get close to the Hermit).

Only possible thing would be – Greg must have gone and seen her...

Which must mean – he'd found out who I was – where I lived... That is *so* weird!

Hey! He checked me out! *The cheek!*

Durr! I should have known!

Wake up me! Of course he checked me out. He knew my name and all that... (Creeped the hell out of me that first meeting...)

He made me report my income – and put me on his expenses for his tax... He would have had to – had to do both... He told me that he got me some kind of "CRB check"... I never risked asking – but I think he got Mum checked as well... Could be that he had to...

===========

Thinking about this... About those days... (Snivelling now). I've only now realised – Bodger *never once* slobbered Mum... Don't think he slobbered in the garden – definitely never in the house... He liked Mum... So – I *knew* that... But – he – respected her too...

Great-Hairy-Mutt ***slobbered*** me!

He even drooled at Greg a few times.

However did that dog work things out?

He didn't like Anton – wouldn't let him near me... No slobber though – not for Anton... Bodger went flat, ears back and watched Anton's every move – like he *prowled* Anton – flat, on his belly – watched until his car was out of sight... I should probably have got the message.

Now I think of it – wake up to it – that was damn frightening...

Greg gave me a "job induction" before I started.

I thought he was winding me up when he told me I had to do it. I no-way told him to piss off – although he probably knew I was thinking it. I kept quiet because I still dreaded losing my shed – and didn't know him much by then.

It was okay though – practical business ... Like what meals, when and how much for Bodger. Never to leave the gate open. Bodger could get himself in and out with an implanted electronic thingy.

It was all obvious – like all inductions – yawn, yawn, yawn... But next I had to watch a "boys'-film"... And when I scowled and made a big yawn – he made me stand up to watch it – and comment on what I thought.

What!? Nearly did say "piss off" to that – but... Bottled it up. I'd got this far – got clearance from Mum...

Over the next few weeks there were films I had to watch... That thoroughly pushed it with me. First off, I reckoned he was testing me. Then I woke up to he was telling me something... Something significant... How he thought, what he valued – even something of how he saw life... It did make me think. I did get into it... Once I paid attention – once I knew I had to – Greg was definitely serious about it.

So – okay – I'll admit it – I also watched other "boys' films" that Greg "suggested"... And not only because he'd given me the laptop "so that I could watch them in the shed – and not under his feet in the house – or (accidentally) lose the disc on the way home"... He had me well sussed from the start.

He cheated of course. He'd had his own daughter hadn't he?

He only ever "suggested" excellent films though. (Had to admit that – eventually). A major, famous Japanese director. Amazing! To have eyes like that! To have the imagination! Incredible! Greg was right – the pictures were so beautiful (ignoring the gory bits) you didn't need the sound – or to know the words.

So I watched those especially over and over. Even the gory bits had a beauty about them. I was fascinated – the vision of them was so much better than all the films I'd seen before. Greg's films gave me ideas about how to sort things in my own life. For a start, to maybe not resort to smacking someone in the face as soon as they bugged me...

No-one had ever suggested that to me before – I don't think – not even Mum... Well, if they had... I'd never heard them... But – Greg showed me another way – an effective one.

Mum did tell me to try to not get into (so many) fights. Though she encouraged me to make damn sure that I won any I did get into.

Except for family and the Spicers everyone told me I was wrong and bad and nothing-but-trouble. I got told I'd spend most of my life in prison "the way I was going"... Gee! Thanks! That *really* encouraged me! No-one listened to my side did they?

Well – not until Greg – and Bodger – of course.

Okay – so Mum listened (I'm sure she did) – but – she didn't have answers – not like Greg had – or Bodger...

Greg said that he thought Bodger was some kind of Oriental martial artist – the "unarmed – use the enemy's strength" kind... He didn't look "Oriental" – more like someone had put a dog's face and bum on a Kodiak bear. His feet were *enormous!* Did I tell you he was black? All over – but, kind-of, mottled – like he needed a repaint.

===========

1 – 10

So – I HAD CAUGHT up and done good enough to scrape into college.

"Lifeskills" they called it. They meant – "Catch up on what school didn't do..."

Greg laughed and asked "Exactly how are they helping – running two separate words together?" I never got my mind round how he argued with everything the system did but got himself into the army – and didn't get chucked straight out... He said it was about him taking a tank apart – but I reckon he was winding me up about that... If he did do that, you'd expect him to have got thrown out – fast... Except he'd have probably put it back together better – he was always like that...

He put a tracker thing in my new bike – with some weird battery that didn't need replacing... Didn't know about it until much later – wasn't creepy – he was simply making sure I was okay – and that if anyone stole it – they would regret it...

I guess I was like some sort of replacement family for him – although he never said – and would have denied it – wouldn't have wanted to "put that on me"... Wish I'd realised...

Of course – I suppose – it meant that he knew who I was seeing and where I was hanging out.

I loved that bike. It was freedom to me – and it kept me fit – wonderfully fit... Which, starting college – with all those new, different, boys about...

And some of them were definitely fit...

So – of course – they got all the obviously fit girls – that stood out... Like I did – NOT...

Colouring my hair and "accidentally" bumping into some of them did no good... But – third division... Goes with third division – second if you get a bit lucky... (Wouldn't have dared to think that around Greg – he'd have gone *totally* ape-shit at me).

(Mum said my Dad was "Premiership" – but I didn't want to know about that. If he was so wonderful... So I blanked all that – except for hating his parents some more – because Gran said it was them that split them up... Another story...)

Didn't cop-off behind the "Construction Industry Department" – AKA "brick-laying barn"... But – I did give myself a real panic. (Not being careful enough one time – *only* one – learnt that lesson fast... Is all I'm saying)... Greg spotted I was freaking out... What did he do? Started a regular supply of condoms!

Should I explain? Maybe? Yeah?

Naturally there were comments – around The Green at least. "Unknown Older Man" – "Young Girl"... "No track record". (Again). The constant moral panic in the media. The "All men are impending rapists!!!" CRAP!!! Two plus Two makes ninety five... *Arseholes!*

I've no idea what, if anything, Greg did about it. If he did react he probably made any trouble boomerang back on the idiots. I know Mum and Gran had at least a couple of face-offs apiece. Gran probably landed a smack or two even if Mum didn't. Gran had this "Honi soit qui mal y pense" thing. You had to be stupid to look at Mum or me funny when she was around. She'd bite the head off anyone.

So... There were bad things that went on – extremely sick, disgusting things at times... But – there didn't need to be, shouldn't have been, a whole culture of fear whipped up by the media, the politicians and people-with-a-cause. There were a number of incidents, whole corrupt plots even. Yes there were a number... But they were in the setting of a national population of millions. They weren't in every other house and on every corner.

What did all the howling and crying achieve anyway? Police forces, social services and even hospitals all managed to completely miss obvious signs anyway. That's *completely* miss – or *ignore* – them...

If no-one official sorted – or could be arsed to sort – the bullying around me... Well? What surprise should there be about worse stuff?

The trouble was "Happy Speak"... Police, schools, social services and hospitals, all had government targets to hit (or massage-the-hell-out-of). The requirement was no-way ever for truth and sorting any real problem.

The statistics had to show "Positive Outcomes". Both Gramps and Greg said that it was like "Happy Hour" in Vietnam... The military feeding the tame media total-bullshit to keep the politicians happy – and the money flowing... According to Gramps and Greg it was the same kind of "acceptable information" approach that got a friendly village napalmed in Vietnam and a bunch of kids-in-care groomed and raped in England.

So – Greg wasn't some evil monster – any more than the Hermit had been. It was sick to even begin to suggest... Probably a sickness in society... A culture of induced fear.

Then you could add to that – Political Correctness... Much like religious bigotry. Any disagreement, just the least question – no matter how sensible... That was like blasphemy. Any questioning of the "experts" brought on howls of righteous-protest... There could only be one-true-creed...

Didn't matter one bit what the truth was on the ground... So Rotherham and other places happened. There was abuse in "Care Homes" and foul stuff that went on in Ireland – done by the church... All that crap got hidden, accepted – and only sorted out when a brave few forced the system to stop looking the other way and massaging its image.

I got off light... I dropped out of school... But I only became "of interest" when I became "a problem"... There was only attention because I fought. The attention saw me as the problem – rather than "vulnerable" – "at risk"... (For all their talk).

I had to be sorted by the system, in the system, in the system's way... When I started being "wrong" for the system – mainly screwing-up their statistics... Potentially messing their next funding...

I'm not complaining – not for me at least – I got through it and out of it... There were others were no way near as lucky... Abused kids, self-abusing kids, kids that became smack-heads... Kids that died – or lived some kind of death...

I got lucky.

I got my garden hide-away...

The Hermitage garden and my shed were my place – my sanctuary... It was where my life was – simple – stable... Like it isn't now – hasn't been since...

Screw it! You know since what!

But – again – you could say that I got lucky... That life – that "experience" went to putting me on my feet – with my own brain – my brain switched on – thinking for itself... Kind of training for what was to come...

So – anyhow... Long before the garden – Mum made certain that I knew the facts – and the consequences... Gran – well... Gran more than believed in speaking plain – about that... Said that "*No-one* in her family acted like a cheap slapper". No problem about enjoying myself – but do *not* be cheap – *not ever.*

And that was well before any hormones got started, making their efforts to drive me silly – like they do with all humans...

Greg? He was – cool... Cool about all things like that. He expected me to be responsible – to take care of myself – to *respect* myself...

Amazing really... It was all – amazing... All of them – Bodger included – gave me a real freedom... Gave me standards too... But – <u>none</u> of the usual "You must... Blah! Blah! Blah!" No, none of that. They gave me self respect. <u>That is so amazing!</u> <u>*So important!*</u>

Self respect and self confidence make it possible to achieve – to learn for yourself... Giving any kid those sets them free – to – to do that thing the stupid system claimed it wanted them to do... To achieve... That it tried to shove down our throats... Being able to tick boxes DOESN'T mean you're an achiever...

Uh... I've kicked off again...

Anyhow – having a decent bike – pushbike – <u>not</u> being "a bike" – meant that it could be fun cutting off the main road and going round the lanes to get home. It didn't usually take much longer (Bodger wouldn't have put up with much lateness)...

How did he *always* know which way I was coming home? Maybe he gave up on waiting on the main hill and switched to the side lane (the one that came in past the village hall) when a bit of time had gone by. I tried extra oiling the new bike so it wouldn't make the least squeak when Mum suggested that he heard the bike... Greg got a slap (not so hard) for saying Bodger heard me wheezing... I did *not* wheeze!

(Bodger ate the only pack of fags I ever got once I knew Greg – then he vomited it back up over my feet... Kind of persuasive...)

On my bike or with Bodger I loved wandering around. Sounds mad – but I discovered that I lived on a planet – a whole world – outside... Also learnt about getting soaked through by rain on a hot sunny day of course – joy of living in England. Couldn't let it take me out of college of course – although it did make sitting inside, steaming, more of a pain some days.

I almost took up jogging... Almost...

===========

Soon as Greg had the back gate security-wired I had a PIN to get in – and an alarm de-activator thingy as soon as I got inside. Greg was very serious about his precautions. Passed it off with a "Well, if you've got mates that can set it up..." But I always knew not to go being nosey.

The back way in – that had been a small hole in the Hermit's hedge – got to be serious with CCTV – the works (infra red). It let me get in clear of the new big garage and workshop... That I didn't go poking my nose in.

There were things about Greg and his work that were seriously spooky – and frightening... Things I never asked about – but – sometimes he'd vanish in a cloud of dust out of the village – with black, black-windowed cars front and rear of him... Not just two cars either... Hardly "covert"... He'd laugh about that – say it was his pals winding up the locals.

Those cars had blue strobes in the front grills though. Never had them on around the village (Greg would have done his nut at that I reckon) but I saw them out on the main road once. They were shifting hard – with sirens on the whole time...

That was years before the big event I mentioned before – when he vanished for days, just before the sickness struck...

I know he killed people. Had at least killed people before I knew him. I don't think he still needed to do that...

He never said... But that was part of his job wasn't it... And; the only time I asked – he– looked sad... Only said that if someone, anyone was trying to kill you – then fighting them seemed the reasonable thing to do...

I never worked out if he was sad that I asked... Or...

Now I've got some more of that "life experience" I know that raising things like that (pushing them) is behaviour we all avoid as much to protect ourselves as to not "offend" someone else... At *least* as much.

Of course – you can't actually ever win with any situation like that. Maybe it's best to let things lay – sometimes they'll sort themselves out for themselves later – sometime...

Then again... Some things never sort themselves out – do they?

===========

Anyhow, Greg made sure I spent time in my shed and did my studies. That always came first. Then Bodger – I wasn't ever, exactly, sure that he waited outside the door for me to go walk with him or he was keeping me in doing my assignments...

Then came cleaning – although that wasn't so much. Greg was pretty tidy – mostly – compared to a whole load of men... ***[Richard!]***

Wasn't a whole load of time left to hang out with Greg and his mates – but – somehow – I'd get included. That was – *amazing!*

Sod it! Time to blubber again...

===========

Start of the second year I started to get serious with Anton – wasn't his real name of course – but he was a cookery student (he hated that tease – what did he expect?) He reckoned a "chef" had to have the right name to be taken seriously.

Mum said he had to be able to cook – without setting off the smoke alarm – and he "could do the fucking washing up himself. Neither of us were his fucking skivvies!"

I was stunned!

Mum would swear and have a go a bit, sometimes, but I'd never heard her have a go like that – not at home – not at some (potential) serious boyfriend that I'd actually brought home – although, come to think of it, he might have been the first – that she was supposed to know about at any rate...

She must have known – she wasn't exactly a perfect kid herself was she...? Not that I'd have a go... She made sure I knew about contraception, the pill, protection, Chlamydia and all that – the last bit was *monstrous*. But

I got the idea alright. I didn't take any risks... Although I might have done –a little – if Anton hadn't...

Who did I run to? Who listened to my tale of woe? Bodger of course! I still laugh at that... But – I still reckon that he'd have chewed Anton up and spat him out if he had found him. That oh-so-ugly mutt had so many expressions. I'm sure he understood me...

I dumped him. (Anton *not* Bodger). Me! Little me! I actually dumped someone...

What choice did I have? She was a ***big fat slug!*** And *he* thought it funny! Said she was a "contrast".

I gave him a "contrast" to think about – right in the canteen in front of a huge crowd – a big long kiss – then a kick... I was so glad Greg had taught me precisely where the kick a man... For "self defence". Never told him I did it though...

Anton was hobbling around for days... Donut should have known better – NOT boasted in front of everyone. He totally did not have two women "begging for it".

Didn't matter that it had been quite a time since the troubles I had in town that pushed me into the Hermit's garden – but I still had a whole-lot of reputation... (Maybe helped by the odd "minor" incident...) People had not forgotten what I was like at school – before. No-one was going to shout about it – but everyone from the Estate knew about Greg.

[Fact was – it was probably Greg delivering me for my interviews in his truck that scared College into not rejecting me right off... Even when I'd worked-my-arse-off and caught up in the last terms at school... Actually... The second delivery-for-interview was the only time I ever saw him in uniform... He meant that much for me to not be messed about].

Anton had to be mega-up-his-own to even dream of messing me about like that...

Slug should have had more self-respect! Might have poached the idiot from me – but "begging for it" as "#2"? For *real??*

I'd have way-more-than kicked him if he'd stuck *that* on me!

Okay – so booting Anton got me in front of the Principal – but my tears were real, genuine... And at the time she was being divorced by her cheating husband... So I got away with it on grounds of "emotional distress" – or a "crime of passion" as she called it.

Didn't tell her that I was crying because I'd tripped over my bike and bashed the hell out of my elbow and ribs...

Of course, after that I changed my look – again.

I'd long since given up on the start-of-year bright blue hair that had completely the wrong effect – and covered it with intense black. (*And* managed to change my pillows without Mum noticing).

After Anton, making the change from sultry deep black to my natural, erratic blonde was never going to be easy. (Like, Mum was cool and never said word one about the whole thing). (Umm... Maybe she "never noticed" the sheets either?)

Okay – so going that far at college was crazy. I *know* that! We do it though. Right? Even the boys do it. (Did it).

No! I did not go from the original blue to Goth – nor Emo... Just slim, sexy and very, very cool... I hoped... Black tops, sharp jeans (show off my bum) and high healed black boots... It did look good... Wasn't only me that thought so. I glowed when Greg smiled and said "neat".

Bodger wasn't impressed – at all... Greg said it was the scent of the dye – was probably killing Bodge's nose... He got used to it though – or the pong wore off... Bodger that is...

I *had* figured that Greg's automatic security meant that I had to tell him what I was going to do before I showed up looking totally different.

Actually – I liked that look. (Except the boots – they were rubbish – and useless on the bike – had to keep switching to trainers).

The blue phase and then the black were a whole lot better than before them. I hadn't so much chosen grundge at school and around town as become it – kind of a protest at people never seeing me, never taking any notice. I wasn't a mess, was not dirty. Mum would have chucked me in the shower and scrubbed me down... I dread to think what Gran would have done! Would never have happened though – I even kept my room tidy – always... I hate not being able to find what I want quickly.

So – anyhow... Medium-cut, black hair back to berserk-mermaid-blonde... *How* was I going to do that fast and not spend months looking like a zebra? Simple! Shaved the lot. Great protest.

Great for sitting around not being recognised for a day or two – so long as you can take the lies you hear about yourself from two-faced-bitches that smile and say they're your friends.

Three of them... Okay, so it did hurt – but it wasn't like I wasn't practically expecting it... And most of the others that vaguely made a group at least didn't agree with them – didn't get stuck in or encourage it... So it was useful to covertly know who was saying what, before I put on a wig and arrived back in planet college.

Yeah, okay, so I did dress like a boy those two days. I wanted to see what it would be like. (Made my tits hurt – although there was never so much of them).

Freaked everyone out with a bright violet wig first... Mum went cross-eyed, Greg choked on his coffee – Bodger – stole it and killed it – definitely dead.

So I did what I'd always been going to do (says she) and went – cropped...

Yeah, well... I gave up on the prickle of wigs when Mum said I had a face like a constipated horse.

Anyway – cropped is sexy... I *know* that. (That comes later in my story).

Stayed with the black tops and jeans – hadn't got the spare money to do anything else – and both Greg and Mum would have been on my case if I'd skimped on meals – Bodger too probably.

(Sold the boots).

Never knew if it was Anton or the Slug set me up for revenge... I started to get bullied again – by their crowd... "Accidentally bumped into" and things said – at first.

I kept my fists to myself – behaved "nicely" for a change... I'd pushed it way out beyond the edge already – and was shit-scared I'd get chucked out – which *would* have meant losing my jobs and my Bodger-Rights.

So, when their pushing and shoving wasn't working, they started to have a go at me on the phone and then the net – more and more nasty... My new college "girlfriends" didn't ever properly stick up for me.

Some friends! Much of the time they more got out of the way as soon as they thought they saw the least imagined problem coming. I was fairly sure a couple others of the group started to believe some of the things that got posted – at least.

I didn't want to mention it to Greg. I had some idea what had happened to the burglars – stupid maybe – but I didn't want that to happen to the bullies at college... My trouble came from arsehole-bullies – but I didn't think they were as scummy as burglars...

That wasn't Greg's view though. He reckoned that bullies and thugs steal people's freedom and self-worth. That was when he'd spotted that I'd skipped a few days at college... Didn't ask me... He saw – he would... He noticed details.

In fact he didn't react at all – except silently look... Look sad – and then Bodger was looking sad... I thought "Uh-oh! What's going on?" Bodger couldn't actually tell me could he? So I had to go and ask Greg.

"You tell me..."

Yeah? Well I should have expected that shouldn't I? That was how he would do everything like that. He called it "Looking at things sideways".

All I told him was that I had a bit of bother at college. Well, that was all I meant to tell him – but then a whole load of it came out – all of it. Especially about Anton and the Slug. (Greg had noticed that I'd dumped him – of course).

I expected Greg to piss me off. He didn't take the Mickey, wasn't nasty or clever about it, though. His response was. "Yeah that would be the sort of crap that happens in life – often from those you least expect it... Welcome to another bit of life".

If he'd said "welcome to the world" or "adult life"... I'd have been exploding mad at him... But, while I was thinking about what he had said he added "So – that's one screw-up done with... You going to let it spoil your day or move on?"

So, okay... I'd had my vengeance on Anton with the kick – but – experience had taught me that sorting out the bullying was a different matter. Bullies are shitty little cowards so they never work up front – never give you easy evidence to justify your reaction.

I told Greg this, he agreed. Even by then, that was a bit of a surprise to me. I expected him to take the usual "adult" line – which was ridiculous of me – of course...

Anyhow. He just said "okay – I'll see if I can help..."

I was a bit worried by what he meant by that. More than a bit – I had visions of him or his mates "sorting the bullies out"...

I was fed-up with the hassle though. So, as he was seeing things at least a bit like the way I did – well – I risked it (as I saw it then) – I showed him some of the crap they were mailing me and posting.

Greg got me scared – he went quiet, some kind of strange quiet... Then he asked if he could borrow my phone and my pad for half an hour or so – and my passwords... Way he asked me – there was *no way* I was *ever* going to say "no"...

I've said before – I never definitely knew who or what Greg was... It was never right to stick my beak in. It took me a while to figure out the little I do know.

I got myself into college and faced off or ignored the bullies as much as I could. None of them vanished or suddenly had bruises. Nothing much changed... Except we started seeing a couple of maintenance guys – who seemed to always be around. Wasn't clear what they were doing, who they were or anything – they just somehow always seemed to be around... They usually seemed to be doing laptop and electronic stuff...

I probably should have guessed...

Ali told me that one of the College Security guys (one of the arsy ones) tried to check them out – she told me because she'd had a run in (or three) with him – so she was laughing herself silly at the way they'd seen him off... Said he went a sick shade of green and then white – decided that he had somewhere else to be...

I didn't think it was that funny. She had been in the guys face for nothing anyway...

Then one of Anton's mates went screaming freaked at his tablet – ranting and raging that it had stopped working. *"How the fuck was he going to get his course work in?"*

Truth? I didn't think much of it. Probably thought that he should have charged the thing.

Day after I reckoned I was right – it was obviously working again – and he was only doing his nut about it because his tutor gave him a hard time for being late... I did smile – his tutor had told him to "Get your act together, stop making pathetic excuses and make sure the thing is fully charged". So all I thought was "Donut!"

Next – him and his mates went into a huddle and started setting something up. I figured they were maybe sending crap to his tutor – probably nasty and malicious – but they kept sniggering and taking looks at me.

Okay. So I had more than half a mind to go over and smack him in the face – if he was being that obvious about taking a shot at me – and proud of it in front of his pals... But – well – Mum always told me to never lower myself to their level. Plus – I'd pushed things to the limit already...

So I stayed quiet – waited for my pad to bleep... Maybe I'd be able to get evidence and get him caught. Get his collar felt at least... Thinking – for a change...

Didn't happen. Instead he suddenly started squawking again. All his mates leapt around... Then they totally went berserk... All their phones and pads started to go off... Everyone in the place was looking at them. They all went demented... They started yelling at Anton's mate to *"Turn your fucking thing off!"* Seemed like it was feeding them all a virus... A programme that was chucking out <u>everything</u> they had – wiping them clean... And – his pad *wouldn't* turn off – and theirs wouldn't either...

Well... College always did tell us that we should back up everything we worked on properly... Guess who hadn't?

Those idiots thought they were so smart! They were so good at photo shopping porn pics with my face. (Didn't manage to get the size of my tits right did they?) About eleven of them lost all their work. **<u>Stupid!</u>** All the nasty stuff about me was infected... A *very* bad idea to open any of it.

I've no idea what message they got sent before their devices got wiped. Anton and his mate took a sudden massive drop in popularity – got both eyes blacked – probably a few more bruises too...

Nothing changed – apart from Anton and the arseholes left me <u>well</u> alone... The digital crap stopped. I think things happened to a few other phones and devices... But – there was no way I was asking around...

Actually – I know... You recall that a couple of the girls that were supposed to be my friends seemed to be dodgy? Well – their phones died as well – after they suddenly ran themselves up appalling bills.

One or two of the brighter boys sussed out that things went wrong when the creep tried to have a go at me. Hard to tell – there was no clear sign... Except – they would look at me – before they shied away like I had an electric prodder on me...

Weird – I'm sure Greg had it done... And those odd maintenance guys had vanished as mysteriously as they had appeared. I know that Greg knew some seriously bizarre I-T and electronics people... Well – he would, wouldn't he?

How do I know for sure that something weird connected to my hassles happened? Apart from the knobheads leaving me alone and the trouble stopping? Sam – my about-to-be *ex*-mate – complained at me that Anton had given up his course and left because of me – and I knew that he would never, ever have done that without he had to...

And she had the cheek to tell me he left right before she was going to get off with him...

You could say – we had a bit of a row...

Then I noticed a few odd things... Including the Principal looking at me funny every time we crossed paths... None of my lecturers changed much though. I still felt that I had to work extra hard to get decent grades... Harder than any of my mates I hung around with... In fact I was convinced they gave me a harder time to get work done – and that played into my desperation to get everything sorted over that last Christmas...

So... Well, I guess I'll never know now will I?

You think I should have asked Greg? If he'd...? What had he...? <u>No way!</u> That wasn't the way he was. He wouldn't have looked surprised, wouldn't have reacted in any way... I simply knew that – well – that he looked after his own... And – yeah – it was special to me.

Without ever a word being said – I belonged – and I knew that I belonged... It was a big thing in my life – enormous.

Anyway... I hadn't got up to so much with Anton. (Hadn't reckoned he'd be two-timing me but I did think he was more concerned about his poxey soufflés than anything else rising as excited as it should). Approaching Christmas though I was getting a bit – "edgy"...

There was at least one quite fit boy at the store – shelf loading in the dry goods section... Wouldn't you know it? He had a boyfriend.

Couple of others were alrightish – except one reckoned himself *way*-too-much and the other started to get spots... Ghastly, bad, *yeuky* spots... ***UGH!***

So – it seemed like not such a bad thing that I was too knackered to bother much anyway. Couple of party nights out I fell asleep. Dopey buggers with me didn't notice the second time – so I had to get a cab home on my own... I was *not* impressed.

I did know that I was, like I said, getting "edgy"...

That's all you need to know about that... Because then "it" happened...

No! Not that sort of "it"... More's the pity. (Was happening anyhow). I mean the BIG "IT".

===========

1 – 11

I SUPPOSE THAT NOW EVERYONE has about accepted that we will never know what on earth "it" was.

Right at the start – if there was any real "start" that anyone around me now knows about – there was only vague wooliness. We didn't really pay any attention at all. First we might have noticed (if you could call it "noticed") was soon as College started term, really soon after New Year...

I said about the notices on all the doors – that we took no notice of at all... We were all good potty-trained citizens of the sanitised-to-death West. We'd been force-fed hygiene in TV ads from birth. We knew how to keep clean – exactly how crucial it was... Like looking perfect so that we would win the perfect soulmate... Blah! Blah! Blah!

The first real reaction was when the clone on the TV in the cafeteria said, all cool and collected, that the Government had "everything in hand". Naturally that got a good laugh and loads of shouts of "wankers!"... Which turned out to be about right... The "government" – whoever they were – died as horribly and quickly as everyone else...

<u>What the fuck was it?</u>

<u>It *wasn't* anything *anyone* knew about.</u>
That could well be about the most we can ever say.

Some people say a virus – and others say that's stupid – the "morphology" or whatever isn't right... Then they have big arguments... Because, when it comes to it – they do <u>not</u> know. Not any of them. Not even the very few scientists that are still around. <u>*They don't have a clue.*</u>

Me? I don't think that it makes any difference – so long as the damn-evil thing doesn't come back round again – but there has been no sign of it doing that – anywhere... So that at least is good. I can live with that...

That's nearly a bad joke...

Like the one about all the ads saying that the latest "Super Improved Product" killed 99% of all known germs... Clearly what got us was that one percent bastard... Damn thing must have been lurking all the time.

First off we all made jokes. It was easy – *"It"* was woolly vagueness. <u>Everything</u> was conjecture. No-one was reporting definite events. There wasn't even any film. Of ? What? It was all happening everywhere but where we were – Asia. Africa... None of it was anything like the endless, pointless speculation about what the effect of referendum results would be. No-one remotely suggested that it would be anything like a problem – let alone the mega-disaster the "democratic decisions" would bring down on all our heads. (Bullshit!)

One new thing we did learn... When it's a real 100%, total fucked-up DISASTER... Then the politicians, pundits and experts do not hang around to say word-one... They leg it.

So – naturally – "back then" the first thing everyone did was joke about any excitement the TV squawked about. So long as it wasn't affecting us – our course, our potential results... To everyone the bits of fuss the College started to make looked stupid.

That was all in the first week... Like I've said – we were complacent – all of us... Not only college – "us mere kids"... The whole of the West – the "First World"... We had the science. We had technology. We would sort it...

Yeah.

Right.

Problem was...

No-one had told the sickness that.

Someone ("They" – the government – or whoever) *should* have *told* the sickness that... About how sodding-clever we were. About our science... About...

Maybe they just didn't get round to doing that... Didn't get the time...

It began. It hit – maybe a couple of weeks before we – "our world" – had any idea about it... Once we got it, It was all over in another couple of weeks.

It *can't* all have happened that fast of course... All our surviving "experts" <u>state</u> <u>*that*</u> – catee-fucking-gorically... That is *so* <u>*not*</u> how it works...

How come so many survivors are fucking-experts?!?!?

Go tell the sickness! Tell it to back up! Give us time!

Better still... Tell it to just – <u>FUCK OFF!</u>

I've a big confusion here... What was then, what was after and what we have learned and/or figured out since. I don't think anyone will ever sort out the muddle of that.

It could be that the one thing everyone agrees on is that the authorities were hushing things up... Someone *must* have known something – or should have known...

I *have* wondered... Where did Greg suddenly rush off to...? What was that about?

Except – I *know* that if he'd known anything in time he would have warned me.

As far as anyone can tell though – no-one ever had any real idea of what was happening – it looks like no-one that went looking was coming back with any clear information...

Seems that nobody ever connected that "no-one coming back" thing with – "There is a reason they don't come back". It probably was something like sensible, if they had no "data", that it made sense (some sort of sense) not to get people worried... After all – it didn't seem like it was a flu virus...

I did hear a rumour that someone, the USA probably, sent drones to look around. Those came back – contaminated probably... All they showed was empty streets – maybe a few dead people – like a sci-fi movie... Rumours are no use though.

Then again... There were spy satellites... But I don't suppose they could have told anyone anything useful. What "intelligence" can anyone get out of absolutely-bugger-all happening? Perhaps Greg went tearing off because someone wanted a conference? I guess that the military must have been going ape-shit. "Nothing" is way, way, way worse than stuff happening...

Systems started crashing as well... Paranoia must have sky-rocketed. What terrorists could have been doing it? Yeah... That would explain Greg's departure.

But? His coming back?

I ***know*** he'd have warned me if he'd had reason...

Whatever...

It was all, miles too outlandish to us. "Us ordinary people". Even when we did begin to get some idea that some freaky event was happening. It was all "somewhere else".

For everyone there was always so much "news" about crap going on around the world. This one didn't seem to have any good/useful/exciting footage of guns being fired. There might have been loads of dead bodies – but they'd increasingly been censored out of the sterilised media. No-one would risk claims for upsetting anyone's sensibilities... Unless they wanted donations or to claim some kind of moral high ground...

Most of all – there were no definite reports of a <u>single</u> British person involved... (Most disappointing for the editors and pundits). So – if nothing else – that last would have pushed it all way down the pecking order of exciting "news" things happening.

Government... They're "in charge" and they're "in control" aren't they? Usually the PM rushes around having emergency COBRA meetings and saying significant-important things to the media... No politician was going to want to stand up and say "We <u>don't</u> have a fucking clue!" – not ever. No wonder all those that could scuttled off as fast as possible. Even the tame media got to commenting about "empty chairs" and the impossibility of getting any hard facts... Just before they began to vanish too...

Anyhow – for us – in college, busy ignoring the rest of the world, we were way more worried what marks we were going to get on those essays. Frantic about having them in on time...

All the tutors were kicking off about those stupid essays, assessments and all the rest – how "absolutely essential it was to be prompt". Like it would be the End-of-the-World to be a minute late...

IF anyone in college paid any real attention to events outside, it was probably about what effect they could or would have on our exams and course results – <u>they</u> were by far the most important thing in our tiny little world right then – the absolute limit of our horizon.

Of course we had to be a bit careful around some of the foreign students – not just to keep out of bother with the "thought police" but – well – we did have some feelings for them. What (<u>very little</u>) we were hearing wasn't nice – not nice at all... It can't have been good for them losing all their different social media links like that... We knew that – know it now for sure... It happened to us – later...

No real idea about them though. I wasn't just "pre-occupied", I didn't actually know any of them personally – but – well... It could be it was a good thing that a whole load of the video-on-line systems (from anywhere) conked out very quick... There might have been a whole load of extraordinarily disgusting material otherwise...

Wouldn't have helped any to have pictures anyway – as we were to discover...

Naturally there's conspiracy theories about the government (or somebody) deliberately blocking all of that – so that we wouldn't see what was going on... Some guess it was malicious and others reckon it was to avoid panic.

Like anyone would have wanted pictures of what happened??? For real???

Then again... With the speed that it hit and what it did to us I guess that we'd never have got to make any "documentary"...

YEUK! Who would want to have that? Even for scientific research! It was way too DISGUSTING.

Anyhow... We had a good laugh when America shut its borders – including to its own people that wanted to get home... We said we should put all of them in quarantine... I think everyone joked and laughed at that...

[Okay – just in case some American does ever read this some day... We weren't being nasty. Right? You gotta do that "look at it from our point-of-view" thing...

Biggest, most powerful country in the world – never been invaded... Yet "you" went near hysterical every time you even thought something was kicking off... Only – yeah – of course... This time "something" did... Big time... But – hey! We got it too... So – alright... We'd had practice... Europe was always getting invaded and occupied, Britain got Blitzed... We got through it by having a laugh – even at the most horrific...

Anyhow – if you can't take the Mickey out of your friends... People you have a "Special Relationship" with...]

Then we got it – or – more like – *It* got us...

BAM! I think some people never got home from college... From a few texts that got through before things started to collapse... On the Saturday people started asking "hav u sn xxx?" and "W R U? Sposd meet me".

Messaging like that wasn't so unusual. It made a change from some of the bitching... But it didn't stop – and people didn't know where others were – or didn't reply ... Which got into slagging – except – people didn't respond to that either... Well before the system crashed... That should have been creepy...

But I was only on the edges of it (got cc'd in to a lot). On the day I stopped bothering. Only saw it briefly in a haze as I went down... Later, when I crawled out, most all of that had crashed.

It took me ages to figure that out. I got the idea about the time I got the strength to move around much. When I dragged up to a window – maybe the fourth or fifth time – I started to get the idea that no-one was coming because no-one was doing a thing – at all... That was at least a couple of days before I could get out – go next door for food that I might keep inside me – and later go look for Greg... Days later... I think...

Early on I kept going through what was still in my pad and Mum's phone looking; expecting, wanting – something, *anything*, from him... Didn't want to start to think why there was nothing... That was before I got mad at it and smashed it.

I was – more than disappointed – more than hurt – got furious – and got pissed – completely, totally pissed – on everything that we still had around...

Greg hated me getting out-of-my-gourd – so it was some kind of stupid fight-back...

Maybe the alcohol saved me?

Nobody knows... Nobody ever will... I don't think we ever will...

I do <u>not</u> want to write about this next bit... I'll do it short – a minimum...

===========

No matter what anyone comes up with – it was NOT a known thing. No-one ever began to have any idea what symptoms to look for – until you got them – **WHAM!**

That was it – near exactly – one minute you were there, basically, apparently, okay... Nothing different (except you were petrified by then). Then your insides exploded – like a fire-monster was in there that couldn't get out – so was raging around breathing flame and giving you hell...

Not nice...

Thing was – we've figured out – the reason that there were never any details, there were no reports... You saw it – you got it... Probably already had it... You died.

Except the tiny number of us that didn't...

Maybe a bit like radiation? Except that wouldn't work for all the places in the world that had no source... Nothing to leak or explode... And a whole load of radiation symptoms never showed up. Plus – the statistics – survival rates – are all wrong... Completely. Like everything else about what happened is all wrong.

There isn't even any explanation why some of us didn't die. Are we all some kind of freaks? There's far more than enough people running their own, personal, guilt-trip hell... You can guess what I think about that! (I'm told that I should be nice though...)

Anyhow, it does look like it was in the air... Although no-one ever saw any clear thing. Nor did anyone smell or taste any obviously unusual thing. Weird. You'd have thought there would have been something...

Anyway... (Stop waffling...)

When I fell out of my room Mum – well... She was in an ***awful*** state... Okay – I'm not going to say any more about that...

I wanted to stop her agony... Maybe – maybe – kill her... ***<u>That's so fucking-awful...</u>***

I know now that a lot of people that didn't get killed felt that way... No-one says (no-one I've met anyway) – maybe some of them did kill people... It would have been kind...

There was a point where I wanted someone to kill me... I didn't have the strength to do it myself –not because I didn't have the courage... Just not the strength... So, I didn't have the option.

I think that if I had had the strength – I would have done it... They reckon that some people did... I'm not going there – you hear the most grisly stories... Many of them too horrible for anyone to make up...

Some things you see... Some we fell over... (We've *all* learned to look where we're treading...)

Even before – no sicko would have made a horror movie as bad as all that – they couldn't have done... No-one has a mind <u>that</u> sick... *<u>I hope!</u>* I've seen some diabolical sights... We all have... No-one talks about it...

Anyway... It didn't kill me.

One morning the sun shone into the bathroom, woke me up and I wasn't dead... Wasn't too pleased about that at first. I ***hurt!*** All over... All inside...

And I was a mess. You put all the stupid drunks pissing themselves and throwing up, all of them in the world, together in a heap – they would look attractive compared to how I found myself...

Is that enough of a picture?

It sounds – sort of like – nothing – like nothing happened to me... But how the hell would I ever begin to explain what it was like to anyone that hadn't been through it?

Anyone that got through it... *You* don't need any explaining – do you??? So – well – it was bad – bad enough... But, when I found Mum again – I was glad she was dead...

That sounds *so* ***awful*** – so *very wrong* – but – the last way I'd seen her (don't *ever* want to think about that) and the state she was in... (So much more don't want to think about that)... Well – like I said – anyone else that got through, has got this far – would need me to say no more...

One thing (from all that) that none of us that made it through realised – usually not for a long time... Seeing all that death – and wanting to do something – and wanting to just-stop-being... All of that – created a dreadful loneliness in us. It doesn't show. It's down deep... Mostly we never see it in ourselves... Because we don't look.

Wish I had thought to grab a nice picture – out of an album or somewhere –a good memory to keep; to remind me...

I got out – ran. Didn't actually grab anything at all. I'd been learning to drive...

That didn't happen at once. Couldn't have done. I was way, way too weak. Before I could open the front door it took me days to stand up holding onto things.

When I could get about – and had near run out of food I could keep inside me – I went next door, the Spicers, to get food (supplement powders) originally... By then I expected they were dead. I was right of course... Horrible mess. So I took their car – just to get back home...

Later, when the power went out and I began to freeze, I used the car to head over the ridge... That sounds wrong again... Wasn't anything I could do for them... Their little car was about what I could manage...

Went to see Greg – terrified all the way... No-way admitting it to myself...

All I could see – climbing on something I'd dragged against the wall, looking in his front hall beside the old garage doors – was Greg slumped against the hall wall... I had no key, hadn't brought it – hadn't thought – didn't want to think that anything would happen except he'd be waiting at the door for me – ready to carry me inside and make everything right...

How totally sodding feeble was that?!

I must have nearly broken my hand banging the window – but he never moved...

Don't know why I ever thought he would. He looked wrecked – like he'd been in a car smash – all one side of his face torn up and bloody... ***Uh!*** Wish I didn't recall that!

I don't know what I did then... Well; not properly... I have some idea what I must have done – what happened next – before I had my head on again – had it on a bit at least...

Bodger hadn't shown up – I – imagine that I finally sort-of concluded what that meant... There was no way he wouldn't have come looking for me long before that anyway... Maybe I was aware that there had been no sight or sound of dogs round the Estate – for days – and that never happened – ever – before... The tiny bit of moving around the neighbours I had done hadn't set a single dog barking... I was aware of that.. It freaked me out.

Then seeing Greg... No Bodger...

I must have gone crazy... Grief or...? Fear maybe?

Next I knew I was some place down in Devon or somewhere. Car had run out of petrol – and it was dark – night-time that is... The place was – Silent... Dead.

===========

Box 1
File 2

◆ ◆ ◆

2 – 1

In some ways the amazing thing was that I had got there – Devon or wherever – wherever "there" was – in one piece – without even stalling or having my instructor need to grab the wheel... Or – stomp on his brakes... There's a LOT to learn! Okay?

But – kind-of realising all that – it sort of crashed in on me that, in the whole journey, I hadn't seen a sign of one other vehicle – not on the move... And – probably – not one single person...

Even at Christmas there was some traffic, the odd person about – getting away from the family or the tv – or headed for a corner shop... There would be dogs – there would be background noises...

The big thing in my head from that moment when the car stopped is – that there was absolutely nothing... Like there had been for days...

The drone of the little car, its rattles and road noise, had been some sort of reassuring... Until it stopped...

I'm sure my mind was shutting down at that time – keeping things out – protecting me. It was all *too* much – way more than *too* much... And – the odd thing was – I was clear that I wasn't dreaming... Although, of course, I should have been.

I'm sure that I had realised that the Estate had been silent. No one had moved for days – maybe weeks... No-one complained or fussed when the power went off... Did I register that? Must have done. I had seen the village – seen Greg... I guess that , somehow, my brain wasn't letting it in... Wasn't "denial" – more like "shut out"... "Don't *ever* let it in..."

All the street lights were still on around where the car stopped – and the traffic lights all working... The car had actually given up while I sat at a set waiting for them to change... One of those weird lights part way round a roundabout – I could have thoroughly blocked things up.

So, naturally, the first thing I thought was "Oh no! *Shit!* I'll be in the way here... There'll be trouble... When the police come..." I'd already had enough hassle with people questioning my driving lessons – because of my size – because I "looked far too young". *(Muppets!)*

So – trying not to cry too much – I did the obvious thing... I ran away... Some more – on foot.

It sounds stupid, now – with that wonderful good view you get into the past – but it took me a while to work out that there weren't any police for me to be in bother with – there weren't any drivers – other drivers...

It didn't take far for me to run out of breath so I leaned on a lamppost for a bit... Sliding down it into a heap... Where I suddenly grasped that I hadn't been sick – or dumped – for the whole journey – which was excellent... Should have cheered me up a whole lot... Except – I was ravenously, ferociously-painfully; hungry...

I did *not* want to put any food inside me. My mouth – it still felt like it was all burnt up by acid... That was the only time I ever seriously wanted to go on *[different]* acid – something – something to send me on a long-long trip out and away from there... Maybe heroine – opium... Just go – drift away...

So – I started to walk – round about when the birds began to wake up. I walked – slowly – looking – I didn't know what for until I saw it...

I must have sat on the step of that cafe for a couple of hours. It was cold – but not freezing – and at least there was no wind – or rain... Then I sat a bit more – muttering that their stupid sign said they should have been open by now. *Why* weren't they? Where the hell were they?

After a bit I graduated from pissed-off to raging. I was thirsty. *Awful* thirsty. I wanted a drink – didn't care about my mouth or throat any more...

I got up and kicked the door... It swung open so hard that it hit the wall, bounced back and shut again... As a result I saw the sign that said "Stiff Door. Push Hard". So I did – got in – and found the water tap...

===========

I was terrified when I woke up – or came-round – naturally. I didn't recognise the ceiling at all. The last one I could recall was my bedroom at home – that had seemed to have swum around a lot in the last – I didn't know how long...

Some sort of car suddenly rushed past outside. I leapt up, went dizzy – and hit the floor again. I got good at hitting floors – because of gravity at first – later encouraged by idiots shooting – absolutely anywhere near me – If I could hear it – I learnt to drop flat *FAST* – not wait to figure out where it was coming from or where it was going. Doing "technical work" like that is much better done from where you can't be seen.

Right then at the start though... When I woke up – I knew I was scared – should be scared...

Looking up I figured out what sort of place I was in – a cafe – wonderful... All I needed to do then was to vaguely work out why... Which took me a while – together with recalling that I had, somehow, got there (wherever I was) from home...

When I worked it out I felt kind-of pleased about my driving. I'd never driven so far or for so long... It got a bit spoiled by realising that I'd run out of petrol, didn't have any idea where the car was, had no money, no things with me (no licence) – and no idea at all of where I was... I hadn't got my tablet – I couldn't contact anyone... I wasn't scared any more – I was fucking terrified!

What got me distressed and frantic then, was realising that I hadn't been able to contact anyone – and no-one had contacted me – for – days – *many* days – probably more than a week... My whole world – kind of – spiralled... My world, no world – nothing I could imagine – was like that – ever...

I howled...

Yeah? So I repeated some stuff? Had to figure a few things out just a bit more than once? You saying that you didn't? For Real? You got it sorted right off? And... What you say your name is? Santa Claus?

Anyhow... The howling didn't have any effect. No-one came to tell me to be quiet... I went and curled up in a ball in a corner – under a table... That didn't work either...

So – after a bit – I started to look around, began to think about food as well as water. So I dared to look behind the counter in the rooms in the back... I could still hardly face eating – only started slowly – nibbling and swallowing slushy goop – cautiously. It was at least a day before I managed to cook... It didn't look any good before it landed on the floor – via my insides...

To get rid of the vileness in my mouth I guzzled water. With the pain I passed out – hitting the floor – again.

===========

I must have been in Cathy's Cabin for a few days. Eating nervously, sleeping; trying to figure out what to do. Never asking what had happened. I totally did *not* want to know. I wanted to obliterate that whole thing. As much as I could I spent my time sleeping and keeping warm...

Lucky for me they'd left background heat on. Because the power had been out on the Estate I was wearing, leggings, jeans, 2 Ts, jumper, fleece body-warmer and puffer jacket. Finally shifting my butt to go over the hill I'd still (stupidly) expected to get greeted by Greg – taken into the house – and safety... (Brain just rejecting that he'd not already arrived in his shining armour). So I only had trainers... Good ones at least – you don't do serious dog walks in rubbish – but not proper hiking boots... (Okay, one excuse was that the weather stayed dry... Fat lot of good excuses are!) Idiotically I'd left my gloves in the car.

It wasn't long, even before it got through to me that I was on my own, and one thing I did do was light one of those bottled-gas heaters – and put it on full blast... I warmed the back room because I needed to clean myself up. (No-way am I explaining that!) I wasn't thinking I was going to be stopping there any time before someone came along, found me – and probably shipped me off to the nick... So my wash was pretty fast and nervy. Potty trained, reverting to normal, making sure I'd got a clean hanky... If... When, I was getting nicked I wanted to have some shred of dignity left...

I'm not clear how I eventually concluded that, at least for now, no-one was coming in to open shop – or stock take – or anything...

I was so lucky there were two full bottles in the furthest storeroom – and I knew very well how to change them and not blow myself up... That was – maybe – kind-of therapeutic... Was something in all the mess that I did know how to do.

I mean – no-one had ever taught me for this – for anything the least bit like this – this "nothingness"... Not even Greg... Though – truth – if he had... Well – honest – I'd have written it off as "boy's daydreams" – probably – certainly...

But – could be... Some things he'd said – or done... Well – that had somehow lodged in my brain – somehow...

Even some of the crap at school and in town probably went some way to preparing me for what was about to come... Would never have thought it – especially not then, when it was happening... We never know what weird good results might come out of even the worst crap...

Hey! Odd thing... I've got some kind of recall of Gramps telling me that... Some time when we were driving round in the van...

I guess it was there in the cafe and about then that I figured out that "something had happened". Sounds ridiculous – except – I know it got most people like that... It was all too – un-natural. "Unreal". Plain "not possible"...

After a while on that first day the quiet and no-one coming to ask me what the hell I was doing was a bit of a clue – that and the almost dead silence outside – there wasn't a single dog bark.

All that sounds kind of "mega-stoopid" I guess...

Okay. So I knew what I had just been through, what I had seen; what I had done. (Run away – I was so *not* feeling great about that). Beyond that...? Nada. Blank.

I would never say what anyone else did (that's their business) – but sorting myself, my thinking, clearly figuring what the hell had happened <u>and</u> what it meant... What it was going to mean... That <u>so</u> wasn't a process I achieved in a hurry... Didn't manage to get started for ages, not even when I found the TV remote between the microwaves and got my first dose of in-a-loop official-government-garbage about "staying calm" and "solutions being found". The first I paid attention to, that sank in, at least...

I didn't connect the dots right away... That area was like one of the islands with power. It seemed natural that the lights, the TV and everything worked... Regardless of the power having gone out at home and even in the village – it would have freaked me out way more if they hadn't... Crazy... But it took so long for the obvious to sink in – for me to focus properly on things, on the way they were – just basic, obvious facts – stuff that we take for granted now.

Thing was – apart from being beaten-up-inside and stunned silly – and the dead bodies – "of course"...

(Helped by the warnings of stench I'd managed to actually see very few bodies by then. That early-period the reek was so bad that it easily got way past the mangled state of my nose – it was in my mouth and throat. UGH! I *tasted* the stink! *UGH!* Not one of us ever wants to go there again).

Thing was, until you got hit by that, everything appeared *exactly* the same as it always did... No-one had set off any bombs. There'd been no monster, ravaging storm, the skies weren't full of fire and smoke... There were no invading gunships, tanks or soldiers... No rioting mobs. Not even one zombie... Like I said – it was so like Christmas after lunch. (Okay – yeah – maybe it was missing an odd zombie wandering to the local open-all-hours...)

I managed to turn the TV on, kind-of by accident. Frightened the life out of me! Thought that someone had finally arrived, soon as I heard the voice. *Yeah – well... Was a good thing that I'd come from an expedition to the loo... I was actually trying to find the right plug for the micro-wave... When I figured it out – and got my breath back* – I thought the TV was into some stupid history programme or some "post-apocalyptic, sci-fi" nonsense. Maybe, at an extreme, it was news about riots some place or one of those films about "impoverished estates" and "gang culture".

Then-again...

Why'd those films *always* jump to the conclusion that the "apocalypse" would immediately result in the collapse of law and order, violence and mayhem???

We were all far too busy with Christmas and New Year to pay any attention to even local things going wrong. (So long as they didn't inconvenience us directly. Even then most of what anyone did was bitch at the store staff – like there was anything they could do about it).). As most years a whole load of people weren't at work for the whole week or more. With the maniac buying spree no-one was exactly likely to run out of food were they? The "After-Christmas Sales" had near-all ended back in November – for what sales there were everyone was maxed-out anyway.

Once the sickness struck – we were way too shagged-out for any of that "disorder" bullshit. If we could have rioted about anything – it would have been about possession of bog-rolls and bum-ointment.

It took a while to begin a few drunken parties – for the few that could get together and who chose that option... Right at the very-start I don't reckon that anyone kept even spirits inside them long enough to get tipsy... Experiments in little-and-often were the rule...

No-one was running about the streets. No-one looted TVs or games... Any dashing about headed... Yeah, well – you *know* where...

Me? I spent the whole time striving to keep the little I ate inside – and wondering what I was supposed to do next... Not even my "street education" had prepared me for where and how I found myself.

So, once I landed in the cafe, the TV was freaky – and more freaky when I'd only found about three or four scattered and fuzzy channels with the same drivel on all of them. It seemed more weird that loads of channels weren't working – not a single tele-sales programme – no superbly fit, suntanned, blonde Yanks enthusing about how many pounds they'd lost in a couple of hours of easy/exciting/invigorating workout. Many were just blank – some no more than a hazy flicker... At least that was a weirdness I could recognise...

On the few channels that worked... All that way-out-of-date "keep calm" verbage... What did they ever think it would achieve? I reckon it would have more likely put the shits up everyone when it was new – when (maybe) people believed that government waffle – like way, way back in history... If there was ever any truth in that.

Last thing you need when you're terrified and the brown-stuff's clearly, totally hit the fan is some po-faced clone droning on about "calm down" and "everything is under control".

Ummm? Hate to be fussy... But – like – what – *what exactly* – is... "Under control"??? Whose control? *Where* are they? Why don't I see them – *anyone...*?

In all that verbage there was nothing to tell me what to do, how to do it... Why I was here... What I was supposed to do... No hint of what I might do next...

Yeah – "Keep Calm". What else? What next? Carry on with – *what* exactly? Excuse me while I go ***scream...***

Got to laugh actually – Greg would have done... He'd have said that "When a ton of crap is whizzing around your ears at speed – you do tend to notice that everything is not quite so under control... No matter what someone fifty miles away is telling you – about then is an *excellent* time to bugger-off someplace else".

We agreed – had agreed – if it's official and going round and round – you totally know that everything is screwed – and they don't want to admit it... Like the moment the Prime Minister announces that he absolutely-to-tally-supports some moron politician... Soon as that happens you know the idiot is screwed – he or she is gone...

Greg might have figured it, what was going on, straight away. Someone like him that had seen all sorts of crap – been in all sorts of chaos – had got through it – had their act together.

I've never met anyone (least, not anyone I believe) that says that they understood what had happened and got straight down to sorting things out. Events like that didn't happen – not to me – *not* where I am...

We all felt that – the "this can't be real" – whether we admitted it or not.

Flooding, massive storms, high winds with drastic reports "from the scene" (with some Muppet asking people "how do you feel?") Yeah. News-events like that happened... To *someone else* – *somewhere else* in the country – or in the world.

Mum and Greg both used to yell at the TV "How'd'you think they feel?!" And a whole lot more. I agreed with all they said on that. So much "on-the-scene" wasn't "News" – it was *fucking ghoulish.* It didn't need re-peating a dozen times either...

What-the-hell good did it do, the PM and Leader of the Opposition turning up? Gave them photo-calls and sound bites for sure... Wasted a whole load of people's time fannying around maintaining their security... How much of their "concern" and promises of support (no real cash fig-ure ever mentioned) ever really produced anything tangible – that wouldn't have happened anyway? Weren't they supposed to be busy running the country? Seemed like they could always drop everything and dash in front of the cameras as soon as the wind rose about fart level.

(How come the flood defences only ever became "priority" *after* the event? Wouldn't it have been better to spend the time making a law prohibiting building – "developing" – houses in water meadows? Those places are near useless to us now – simply rotting away. Near everything in them is contaminated...)

Anyhow... (From what I've learned in the years since)... When it came to it there soon ceased to be anyone on the TV telling us what was happening, asking how anyone felt or explaining what a virus was with lots of sexy diagrams. Once it came here – to Britain...

Once, you could say, "The shit hit the fan"...

Okay, before the TV waffle stopped, (well away, in the background for me) they had the usual parade of "experts". (Glance at telly, while walking between microwave-in-kitchen and my room, barely register and tune-back-out). Not that they could ever say much that was sensible – with absolutely nothing at all coming back from the places as they got hit... "No News" suddenly became "absolutely no information" – and that was *not* "Good News"... We just didn't know it yet...

It was astounding how fast the politicians not in the government vanished... They hardly stopped around long enough to say that it was all the government's fault, that *they* should be doing more about it...

Then anyone in government and other public figures that could bugger off did so – fast. Especially the cranks that wanted to stop all immigration and send all foreigners back – they disappeared – pronto. Maybe that should have given us a clue? Didn't take long before there was no-one at all explaining what-the-hell *was* going on – abroad...

Then, soon as it "came ashore" here...

In no time at all there was no–one telling us that whatever-the-hell-it-was had wiped out most of the population of this or that town, city or – of – everywhere...

Okay, so, I personally missed most of that... But it doesn't matter how many people you hear it from, nor how many times... You simply can't begin to get an idea of that – not one that sticks in your mind – fits inside your skull – or around it – it's *way* too big to fit in...

No idea about anybody else – but – for me... It's never been a matter of making some sense of the numbers – or anything "logical" like that... Most of the time I've been way too busy keeping all the questions out. Much too occupied *not* going frantic-crazy with worry... Worry about what? There was, there is, too much – impossible much – to worry about... Get your head round it? Stop your mind exploding... *Imploding...*

At least I'd stopped worrying about essay deadlines and grades... That was for definite. Didn't actually seem to help much though...

In a way it was made easier – by the fact that it was all *totally* impossible... None of it was *really* real... This *wasn't* my world. This *couldn't* be my world.

In my world we went to school/college. Yesterday was much the same as today and tomorrow would be the same again. Parents went to work; yesterday, today and tomorrow... Unless there was a holiday – and that meant a whole load of fuss – last year, this year and it would again next year... Chances were the biggest change would be that the council altered the day the bins were collected... We complained that life was routine – boring...

Except you didn't *ever* begin to moan that around my family or around Greg – NOT if you didn't want an "interesting" thing to happen to wake you up...

What was going on – now – couldn't be for real...

Weird... I'm sure I wasn't afraid. Fear didn't get hold of me... Don't know about anyone else... In the last few days of actual world TV there had started to be reports of towns, and cities, going "Off the network"... "Off grid" or (the official favourite) "Having a few, minor, technical difficulties"... "Normal service would be restored – very soon..."

Yeah... Right...

People tell me the "official calm" was there for sure... (Part of the unreality of it all – as things really got going). Maybe I do recall hearing something about Boston or Seattle – as I chucked my guts out the first time? It couldn't be real for whole cities to stop talking... I think I only heard the lists after... Vancouver, Edmonton, Perth... Duisburg – wherever that is... In Europe... A rash of places from Spain to Russia... Before they censored it – then things got vague...

We had the protection of the Channel and the North Sea...

It's agreed that Dunfermline proved that theory wrong... I'd bet that's one "first" the Scots *didn't* want to claim... They'll have blamed the English and London. Seems that Colchester was next. Maybe followed by Keswick – then Hull. Absolutely no pattern or logic to it that anyone can see... Sounds like they began reporting places again to tell people where to stay away from...

What I saw... We maybe had it well before any of them... The Village and Estate were simply much too small for anyone to notice... I do *not* want to think about the things that I saw for real...

Big question... How could that happen? Happen like that?

No-one has the least idea... To be exact... Loads of people have theories... NONE of which add up.

No-one agrees whether the police or army ever took action – whether they were definitely instructed in any way. More likely everyone was just trying to get home – back to their families... That was screwed up fast by ASLEF stopping work – saying it was much-too-dangerous.... They were probably right... A coach gone off the motorway when the driver collapsed made a mess – I'm told... I do not want any proof of that.

They said to not go to hospitals... I think I recall that myself... Could be I saw it between bouts of chucking up. We would have been able to go? I couldn't have phoned for an ambulance – or anyone... You <u>do not</u> want to know why not...

===========

I've got myself turned-back in time from Cathy's place though...

Some of the time in the cafe this last stuff was charging round in my head. That is, would been – what I knew about any of it... And that was allvague, mixed up and confused. Bits I remembered... Couldn't put together. I <u>know</u> that we must have got hit very early.

Ummm... I got diverted by the idea that it was all too much... When it began it was too-much. It was "too much" as I struggled to begin to recover and to understand.

Having got myself into a totally strange place <u>did not</u> help at all...

I'm certain I wasn't the only one that didn't start to think <u>*(panic)*</u> about food and clean water for some time... My excuse? I was in Cathy's Cabin wasn't I? I stayed warm, the lights were on. There was plenty of food and water there... Bottled...

In fact the tap water was clean – and the loo flushed... With what my guts were still doing that really meant a whole lot – the smell alone (diabolical enough to impact me) would have driven me out otherwise... And the electric was still on – so the freezers and microwaves were good...

I <u>*freaked*</u> when I looked in a mirror... Or, just happened to see myself. I guess I'd somehow unconsciously avoided doing that until then... I *know* why. What looked out at me was enough to make me faint again – except that I was fed up with adding more bruises – I always seemed to hit a hard edge – or two... So – I sat down and cried for a bit...

Maybe that was the first time I cried?

If it was – it was more like with shock... It was not grief, mourning or any kind of reaction to all the "loss"... That didn't come till later... Much, much later. There was no-way any of that could happen... That was not "too big"... That was monstrous – dangerous – overwhelming – impossible...

So...

That first morning – eventually – I made myself a *very* weak coffee (black of course – heap of sugar) and sat sipping it at a table in the deepest corner trying to figure out how I was going to explain everything to the police – when they came – after the owners called them and said that I'd broken in...

It was like waiting outside the Head's Office not knowing what they were saying to Mum – or when the eruption back at them would come... Or if I would be in *real* trouble – if she agreed with them...

Except – of course – Cathy didn't come... Nor anyone else... No-one came for their breakfast. No-one came or phoned for sandwiches for any local offices – or a garage or some place. No-one came for their lunch... No-one did the things that everyone is supposed to do in a cafe... Except I put the hot water machine on and checked-out the fridges...

No-one called the police about the intruder... The police didn't come. There weren't any police – or anyone... Anyone at all.

And those few loops on the TV kept going round and round...

After quite a bit of sitting dazed I got up and made myself some sort of mush to eat – from what I found... Did I say about that?

First off I hardly dared to eat at all – went looking in the back and found a toilet first – which was just as well.

I think that I kept a first bit inside – at least long enough to get some use from it... Softened stale bread – nearly dried out – but <u>not</u> green-furry – doesn't matter at all when your mouth is wrecked – so long as it's not gone hard. No way you're going to eat crisp breads or crackers – not at that stage... Unless you soaked them into a disgusting mush... That was calories though. I had to get what I could inside... We all did, didn't we?

That was the beginning of my relationship with tin-openers...

While there was still power anywhere I got a fabulous new rapport with blenders. (Before I got wise to keeping totally quiet).

Anyhow – then I slept a bit. I couldn't stay awake – and I ached all over – all through... Felt like mangled-hell.

Wasn't a thing I could do but sleep. The journey must have caught up on me. I had no energy left. So I curled up on the floor where I reckoned I would be least seen.

Second time I woke I made myself eat a bit more – and thought it could be Sunday – until I saw their opening times chart – which led me to thinking there must be some reason no-one had come to open up... Maybe they'd been arrested... No, not that... Murdered? Abducted? I started to frighten myself...

Spooked myself with "my-real-world" reasons... Reasons from before – reasons the detectives on the TV would have worked out... Didn't let the "real-real-world" reasons in... That was much too dangerous... I guess I kind of floated for a bit.

Shoving food inside – HURT – then I had to hope it would stay inside – like it should...

Okay, so survivors know *all* about that... But, person from the future – reading this as "history"... (*Good grief* – me writing "history". YEUK!) Anyhow – you should know – not just my guts – everybody's guts – SCORCHED. Felt like they'd been run over by a truck, burnt, run over again, melted down – and had a few other disgusting things done to them for good measure. Drinking water SEARED.

And *you* see if you can ever achieve chucking your whole guts out without any of it going through your nose... Once stings enough...

===========

But – then – a bit of sense drifted in from somewhere... I stuck the TV on again... And saw the same old loops... Began to recall...

And to recognise that I hadn't heard a single thing going on outside – anywhere... That it was all – freaky... Weird... Was I stuck inside some sort of dream?

I knew I'd not gone deaf – I definitely heard myself cursing when I cut myself opening a can – being impatient and trying to prise it wide instead of cutting all round. That lesson I got real fast. (Should have known it!) I heard the can hit the floor and the spoon crash in the sink...

Had I been in an accident – maybe – driving the car? Was I stuck in a coma?

Bruises I had, blisters in my mouth and sores... More sores... You survived – you *know* where they were... *Exactly*. I could *definitely* feel all that for far-more-real than I ever wanted – or ever want to recall... And all that told me that "this is no dream"...

I finally edged to the front window and peeked out...

I can't say why I crept forward cautiously and tried to stay hidden while I peeked... It wasn't because I'd sneaked in... I guess I kind of "knew" (maybe deep down) that there was no-one to be frightened of... But that was exactly what I was screaming-inside-fucking-afraid of. I figure the back of my mind knew only too well what the front of it was rejecting...

I wonder... Maybe I would have been happy to see a bunch of zombies lurching around... Probably have been ecstatic! Someone to go lurch with...

Nothing. No-one. Nothing at all. No more than an empty street... No problem... Someone would come along soon... I wouldn't have minded seeing a copper coming to arrest me...

Half an hour – an hour... I had to drag a table closer to the window to sit on...

Fell off that – the next time I dozed off...

===========

I have never had the kind of patience that kept me sitting there waiting for someone to show up... I don't think there were even any birds flying around...

Except it wasn't patience at all was it...? It was – increasingly – fear...

So much fear, so big – I didn't know what it was.

Paralysing was one thing that it was. So much that I had to make myself get up and go to the loo... And then to eat and drink on the way to the front again – except that – at least stopping there – in the loo – and then behind the counter – at least they meant that I didn't have to return to watching – watching – no-one... Nothing...

I don't think that I actually asked myself "what do I do?" for a long time – probably days... I sat there watching – going to the loo (at least I wasn't chucking up) – eating – taking small drinks...

I think that it was when I began to figure things out a bit that I got adventurous and tried cooking... I said what happened.

My cooking is *not* that bad!

Before; in our old world – with all the traffic, planes, TV, games and everything... Who would ever have thought that utter silence could be terrifying? I don't think you ever got that in a film – not even the sick, horror-garbage... Not days and days of – nothing... Nothing...

Sometimes (there in the Cabin) the diminishing numbers of TV clones (as the channels failed) were a relief from that – for a short while... At least I could scream abuse at them –when my burnt-out throat let me.

I've no idea what woke me up to how quiet everything was – much less the fact that I had got used to it... More to work my brain around.

Quiet until I heard a motorbike go screaming by the cafe.

Before I could get up there was an almighty crash... Never before heard a sound like it – but – when I left the cafe a few days later – when the food was running out – I went the opposite way from the noise... I didn't want to see – I didn't want to know.

===========

I did figure (when I let things sink in a bit) – that I had some significant questions to answer – like where was my food coming from when I'd used up what was there. Even with the little I was pecking each tiny meal I knew that would happen. At least I got that bit right... I did think about water – and put some bottles by in a bag – along with a tin-opener and a couple of spoons.

All those "post apocalyptic" and survivor movies and games the boys spent so much time watching or playing – I don't remember them ever walking around three-quarters-dazed trying to figure out where-the-hell they were going to get even one bite to eat and not get into hassle... (Not even meet a stupid zombie to bite them). It took a <u>very</u> long time to truly sink in that there was hardly anyone to get into bother with...

So eventually I got my head on – woke-up to reality... A Bit...

Weird – I relaxed then...

Just before some arsehole shot at me...

That was some days, many miles, several broken windows, a nasty cut on my arm and quite a bit of food later... Along with a load of other events...

Maybe I should say that I finally sussed it out – that in the tiny number of people still around a percentage of them were still going to be arseholes... Ordinary ones, stupid ones, bad ones and – the <u>complete</u> kind. Even really nice, well meaning and happy – arseholes... So there would be worse than hassle – there'd be real danger...

I gashed my arm going through a window. Nasty and dangerous – on the inside of my forearm. (Still have the scar). No idea how I missed the arteries. Surgical Spirit was how it didn't get infected... Was how I bit through my lip not screaming...

Never mind that I totally confirmed that you can't stitch your own arm (do *not* ask) – I'd begun to think that I was getting it down – had it sorted...

Yeah, yeah... Stupid every time. That's always when you relax – just enough to seriously fuck-up and/or get caught out by the obvious – that you totally should have seen coming/avoided. Nine times out of ten that's how the police caught anyone... No fantastic sleuthing – the idiot they were after just got too confident, relaxed – got sloppy... Okay, so maybe it was only eight times out of ten... Eight and a half...

I at least thoroughly cleaned the gash and was keeping it well bound and covered up... That was initially due to getting lucky with someone's excellent first-aid kit.

Sorting that and finding enough food, I got so I could also figure by the smell and/or sound of flies what rooms not to go into because there would be rotting stiffs in there... Some things I did learn fast – faster... Wasn't just the original decomposition – however long that took... I so was not making a study of that! All the mess set things rotting didn't it? Seemed like even man-made fibres had their own ways of going yeuky. Flies were bad enough – those great "recyclers" of nature – slugs... UGH!!!

Smells with a mangled nose? So? Survivors do not need an explanation of how that works... You don't know? Lucky you!

Those few lines are about so much – so many days... The transition from stunned and clueless to beginning, only beginning, to have some idea – via realising I'd have to break into more and more places, figuring how to (preferably without injuring myself) and what to get once in there... Learning how to not fall over, chuck up or both because of what I did find...

I suppose that starting again, living, keeping on – is what we do – sort of natural...

Programmed maybe...

When it comes to it – I don't think we have any idea what else to do...

Anyway...

When you've hardly ever heard a real gun (definitely not one near you) it's sort of weird... I heard a strange "*WIZZ*", the air did something peculiar and, almost at once, I heard a bang... Yeah, yeah... I'm supposed to have known WTF it was... Like, right away. Really? You did the first time? I bet! I just bet! The feeling that some enormous bug had just zapped by you wasn't something they ever digitally achieved for you on your couch was it?

So it all happened three times more, while I'm standing there thinking *"WTF?!"* and gawping around for some sodding great-big fly. I had to see a flash, and then another, to go with the noises, before I thought ***"Oh shit!*** *Someone's shooting at me!"*

So what did I do?

I yelled ***"Fuck off! Don't fucking shoot at me!"***

I was a *bit* angry at them – people ***are not*** supposed to shoot at you in this country.

Which they did – and didn't...

That is – they stopped shooting at me and ran away... Then I hit the pavement – again – fainted properly this time.

So I was laying on the pavement when I woke up again and heard someone yelling at a "fucking moron" that he must have missed "the tosser" so that they had "got away"... Which sort of encouraged me to slide under the van I found I was next to and stay very, very still until I reckoned that they had absolutely, definitely; for certain – gone away.

I'm from "an estate". I'd had all kinds of trouble with school and bunking off. I had hassles in town, had the attention of the local constabulary... And a few other things... I'm supposed to have been "street wise" and "tough"... Yeah, so I can tick the boxes... No arsehole had ever shot remotely near me – away from me even – before that. It was just as well the donut was a *totally* crap shot. He probably had his eyes shut. Not that, that would automatically mean he would miss me. The pillock could mean a warning shot and then have hit me.

Anyhow... It's like I said... That woke me up – a bit...

Tough, "streetwise" kid? I fucked-off out of there. As fast as my little legs would take me!

The first bit of any street wisdom – for anyone with a functioning brain cell – is to know when to be somewhere else. Preferably *before* the shit hits the fan.

===========

I guess that I've jumped ahead some more there...

===========

2 – 2

YOU DON'T NEED A DAY-BY-DAY account – You're not going to get one anyhow! Not least because I don't recall it all – and I don't want to remember a whole load of experiences. Not ever...

Leaving Cathy's Cabin was a hell of a step for me. It was quite a nice place. I wouldn't have minded working there – if Cathy had been alright – there was a picture of her – I reckon it was her – on the backroom wall – and she looked okay...

Least – I began to let myself think that "when she showed up" she would "understand" and be okay about everything...

But she never did "show up" did she?

I wonder – what it was like for others – when they had to start to step out – maybe what it was like for you? Ghastly? Petrifying? I don't think that there can be any single word for it – but – then – no amount of words would explain it would they?

Maybe the first men on the moon felt like it – not when they stepped down from the ladder – but when they set the last bit of action before the spaceship feet touched the ground... Gramps said that everyone held their breath – wondering what was going to happen...

I guess that's as good a description as any... Stepping out of Cathy's place... (A day after the power went off, so's I pretty much had to finally get my arse in gear and move on...) What was going to happen? What planet was I on?

I didn't think "What's going to happen to me"... I – when I eventually did it – I – sort of watched myself do it... No idea at all what I expected, didn't expect – or what it felt like... I guess you would say that it was "traumatic"... That word gets a bit over-used...

[But it's a whole lot more polite than saying "fucking-diabolical!"]

I was seventeen. Wouldn't be eighteen until around end-of-exams time... Don't suppose it mattered how old anyone was... Stepping out into – no-one had any idea what... That was – beyond words.

Well – it was for me anyway...

When I finally couldn't put it off any more, it wasn't raining or windy, the food and heat were running out – so were my excuses... I'd only had to give up on my leggings. (You *really* want to know why???) I had the last food, some water, can opener, spoons – rolling pins and a couple of sharp knives...

I opened the front door on a lovely day – with a gorgeous winter-blue sky...

I just turned the other way from where I'd heard the big bang and started walking – carefully – trying to not be conspicuous... Just trying to get to wherever I was going – without wandering into bother... I didn't have a Bodger anywhere near to come and rescue me did I?

Okay, so maybe that sounds stupid – but I'd have given anything to have that great big dollop thumping along beside me on his massive paws...

And there was nothing...

No idea how far or how long I walked for. I had bits I'd put together in a "Bag for Life" – ironic huh?

I was still so weak that just carrying that little bit made my arms and shoulders ache in no time. I started by switching arms – but that got quicker and quicker until I took to hugging the damn thing in front of me and cursing it. I knew not to dump my supply of water though. That was about the one thing I did know for sure.

Had my head down for a long way – until I made myself look up – and then begin to look around... Which didn't tell me a thing – except what I already knew – that there was no traffic – and – no-one – not anyone – anywhere...

That was the worst. Far worse than having to watch out for plod, social workers – or trouble...

None of it was like any previous experience. Not the Estate, not school, not town; not – anywhere... All my references met with – nothing. I knew what to do – or learned damn fast – in all those places and situations. One and then two always helped with the next one... But this?

So I kept on walking...

I don't think I was terrified. Don't know anything that would begin to cover it... Stepping into – nothingness... A world that was nothing like anything I'd ever known. A silent, empty, no-people world that wasn't even like anything in any movie – ever... There simply isn't a word... Except... Maybe, "HOLLOW"... Like, I don't think I felt anything, not *one* thing... What *was* there to feel?

I'd mostly got good clothes. So I kept my core warm – managed to get a bit hot on one hill...

I kept walking – because – I had to go somewhere – didn't I?

Where?

There was – I suppose it was some kind of – fear... Once I got started... What was there going to be when – if – I stopped...? How – do you prepare for – nothing?

I – I guess that I didn't want to know the answer – though I did know it... Of course I knew it – really... I had to go somewhere though... Had to keep going...

No way I was going to the police...

An Ambulance garage had the shutter door part smashed open – weird – maybe the first real sign I had to be careful – cautious... First thing that sunk in – stopped the blur and got me thinking – sort of... Didn't know what to think though...

It was the first open door though. I don't think that anyone ever noticed just how many shut doors there were before. Now – there was nothing but shut-up-ness. Every place like a blank face.

At least with the Estate, for the tiny bit of raiding for food I did before I ran, there were names. I knew whose window or door I went in. I had some idea of what they were like... No-way was my brain around a guarantee that they'd be dead – but I could at least choose the ones I wouldn't be upset by... And the ones I figured wouldn't be so fast to react – before I legged it.

Totally off my patch I had nothing. The door being at least part open made some difference – plus, it wasn't anyone's home... It kind-of belonged to society...

I got myself together enough to look inside... Saw my first stiff – first after running away. No, it wasn't like that – that's not right... That one was the first that looked like it hadn't died of the sickness... With a dark stain on the floor all around the top end – which was away from me – which (without actually thinking it) I was glad of...

They never show you that in the movies do they? Only ever very quick glimpses, flickers in the action – often in hardly any light... It has a whole different feeling when the stiff is real 3D and cold on the floor in front of you... Worse if you're backing out and you fall backwards into one... ***Eugh!***

Yeah. So how do I know that? Guess.

I think I was amazed at how fast I could run – not that it was so far... (At least I kept hold of the bag).

Days still weren't long were they? Although – I'd got into an area where the street lights came on as that blue sky faded softly – beautifully – and I noticed that some houses had lights on...

That was kind of the first I made contact with planet earth again – maybe the lights meant people? Maybe – Could be there were others?

I wasn't alone!

There could be other people...

Run to the nearest door? Fall into welcoming arms? Greet and be greeted?

No way! My pre-Hermitage life taught me thoroughly to not to be idiotic like that. Bang on a strange door? More likely scare-the-crap out of whoever's inside – get the police called... Fat lot of good if it was them you wanted to get away from...

[Still thinking "old ways" wasn't I? Hadn't got as far as any risk of being shot at - or even poked with a bread knife...]

Even if I did work out a way round that... *Which* house should I go to? *Who* would be there? *What* would they be like? *What* state would they be in? *What* could I do – if they were...? (Never actually thought "sick" – not for – probably – weeks...) I didn't know what to do about me... What would I do? Could I do?

Okay – so – honest? There was no-way I was going to start to think about that... I'd seen Mum, Greg, the Spicers... Hadn't I? Was no-way on earth I wanted to see any more of that. I was hardly keeping myself going... No-way I wanted to face having to help anyone else. Wasn't selfish – I'm sure of that... It was being realistic – so much as I could be...

Never thought then that anyone might help me – that's not the way it was – not the way I was... There was no more Greg – Guess that had kind-of sunk in... No more Mum...

It left a kind of – numbness...

So – if no-one was coming out... By then I had got the idea that I had seen and heard no-one. I'd only heard one car and the bike – bike-crash. As I wandered I had seen maybe a few signs of three or four... *Possibly...*

Well, I didn't want to know why not... I wasn't wanting to go looking.

I have no idea how I didn't get frantic about anyone being hostile... Things were crap enough as they were... Probably I wasn't feeling that there was going to be anyone – at all...

Emptiness...

I kept walking... Then I kept walking...

It was what I could do...

Maybe there is a word for what I felt after all... "Inadequate"...

Everything, but everything was way, way out beyond all I could ever have imagined...

Like I've said... There were no tanks, helicopters or men jumping around firing off weapons for a start... This wasn't how any "apocalypse" was supposed to be...

This was just – empty – silent...

The clatter when I put up some birds shattered. It stunned me – left me shaking and gasping.

The day had hardly warmed up any, so it soon got colder as it started to get dark. (That must be how long I'd been walking). As I got more tired I got colder – my feet and legs first. So; when I came to a wonky-crossroads – staggered – the junction that is – I was also aching-hungry.

Once there I could see a pub – lights blazing – ridiculous! "The Winchester". I think I laughed out loud – maybe would have LMAOed – if

I'd had one left at that stage. (If you don't know only-too-well you *do not* want to).

Someone was taking the piss!

I've no idea why I thought a pub would be better or safer than any one of the hundreds of houses I'd wandered past.

But – I was shivering – beginning to freeze – below a coat and the jacket my jeans and trainers no way protected my legs and feet as much as they needed – despite all the work they were doing... (I'd had to give up on the leggings... Guess why... You *really* need it explained???)

So? Haven't I mentioned this before? I'd gone to Greg's place expecting him to be there, expecting him to know what to do... And then – well, I'd bolted hadn't I? I didn't stop and think "Right. Go home. Sort out a survival package. Get essentials... And at least all the right clothes". No – that was not what I did... I panicked and RAN.

From Cathy's I'd got a coat with a hood and some socks that didn't fit me. Apart from that all I'd found was aprons and a coverall thingy... I used the socks as mittens. In the Cabin I'd used the coverall to "hide my modesty" (aka skinny carcass) when I had to wash my few things... Or else I rolled it up and used it as a pillow – with the coat as a wrap-around blanket.

After the days sudden effort I was more than hungry. My mangled guts were twisting-painful... Add to that – my arse *burned.*

If there was anyone in the pub... Maybe – alive? It didn't look damaged – no smashed windows... Everything closed up nicely... Safe...

So I couldn't get in the blasted place could I?!

Not a chance!

Talked my way into all sorts of pubs, bars and clubs – even when I couldn't be arsed – but did it because we were a bunch going out – and the idiots on the door weren't going to turn me away just because I'm so small... Point of honour wasn't it?

Hurt my foot and my fists kicking and battering the Winchester's door didn't I?

If there had been anyone inside I'd probably have frightened them silly – or got me attacked...

Anyway – there was no-one there – or anywhere around close-by... Racket I made someone would have at least looked out...

Okay – so – what happened – someone did... Don't want to write about this... But – I will... (I must).

Couple of houses along a window opened... Didn't see it at first – was upstairs and I wasn't looking up at that stage – except at the pub... And she didn't have any lights on... Never did...

Don't know how long it took Shania to get my attention – maybe until I stopped kicking and started to nurse my foot...

===========

2 – 3

Shania looked gaunt – not as bad as I did – but – little more than skin stretched over her bones – like a refugee in a history book – which was another reason I never liked history... Wasn't one thing I could do about what had been done was there?

(Okay – so one thing... I should learn from it and not fuck-up the same way).

Wasn't anything I could do for Shania either was there?

===========

Except – maybe – be there – for her...

Truth? I haven't a clue why she didn't spook the crap out of me. Good aura maybe? It's likely I was too relieved, right then, that there was anyone – and they were wanting to get me inside – out of the cold – or I was simply too totally knackered.

Maybe she didn't look so bad at a bit of a distance – and kind of not fully in sight... You saw her full on... She was more like one of those things that jump out on you in the ghost train – 'xcept she was absolutely no joke at all...

Shania was hardly skin – and stretched tight over her bones so that her elbows and knees were raw. It was a good thing she didn't let me see her before she warned me. Even with my arse the way it was I'd have crapped myself – and running with your insides hanging out really, *really* hurts...

(That would be another story... I am <u>not</u> going there).

So, anyhow... She wanted me inside and safe – I could tell she was okay – like a decent person – though I could never tell you how I knew – she just was... Wanted me quiet, inside, getting some warmth and food – said I looked "utterly frozzed"... (Which was about right). And – after she had some soup inside me – she said that she was worried that there could be some "problems" around – she'd heard noises – a couple of nights before... Didn't say what though... I think that I nodded off while she was telling me.

I woke up with blankets wrapped all round me. Fleeces – Shania told me that space-blankets were too noisy and shiny... What? I had no idea what she was going on about... <u>Back then</u>...

I'd never thought of myself as too heavy for anyone to move... Says a load about how hammered Shania was.

Was pretty daunting waking up in the dark with no sight or sound of her – although at least that night there was a big moon. It was amazing that I didn't freak out at the lack of lights... I didn't figure out that the power had gone off while I was out-of-it.

Turned out she'd gone raiding for me. Sounds crazy – but I hadn't exactly thought of that then... She'd sussed that I'd got all sweaty with my long hike – I would need a change... Even with the blankets I would start to get chill. One thing I didn't need – no-one needed around then – was to get a cold.

Suddenly alone I thought about defending myself. I had no idea from what...

Before leaving Cathy's I had put that small rolling pin in one pocket – and one sharp, pointed knife in another; a little one – wrapped up so I wouldn't cut or jab myself with it... Old, practical, lessons learnt again.

An essential example – if you can't hit someone hard enough with a small thing you're not going to do much better with a big one. (Boys should note that!) More to the point – it takes more room to swing a big one and that gives whoever you're planning on whacking or poking more time to react. So – big or small aren't the issues – what you can do with it is what counts. <u>(Boys – take note!)</u>

In the situation – and finally figuring there were no police about – having a couple of things for "protection" was kind of natural – in the weirdness of it all.

I'd never have carried a blade before – too much chance of being seriously nicked. Regardless of the bullying and some worse, that had never been the way to go. Anyhow, long before Greg my Gran had taught me some basics of self defence – the most important one being – <u>*don't* put yourself where you need to use it.</u>

In a totally strange place with so much freaky-weirdness going on – "arming" myself, at least in a very minor way, seemed kind-of the thing to do... Probably with some added influences from watching those films with Greg... Like – *never* leave your weapon behind and *always* police up any laying around – ALWAYS!

[You wouldn't believe the things Greg and his mates yelled at the donuts that left weapons for the baddies to come after them with.... Was no good my laughing and telling them it was "only part of the plot"... They had <u>very</u> short answers for that!]

You're probably thinking *"Get a gun! <u>Why</u> haven't you <u>got</u> a gun!?"* That would be now (or some future time) though... That was really early, though.

Hardly anything was sinking in. Plus – this is England. Right? Well... It was – BACK THEN.

===========

So, by the time I'd arrived outside the pub, it *had* sunk in that there was no-one about... Maybe Shania suddenly being there should have shocked me? I think I was way too busy being relieved...

Didn't matter what state Shania was in. Her being there – someone – anyone... Well – that was a step back toward normal... A tiny step – but – a start... Way easier to accept than everything else going on.

The blankets were cosy and she'd put a cushion under my head... So – that was comfortable – comforting... The kind of thing Gran would do... I drifted, probably relaxed a bit...

I near went through the roof when Shania suddenly slipped silently in the room...

So, alright... This is one thing I did get right off... When someone else is finding you clothes and figuring your sizes – then you are in DEEP shit.

Mum hadn't got me any clothes for – I couldn't guess how long. Greg probably knew my sizes better than she did... And no – don't get any silly ideas from that. He simply got to sorting it. He travelled a lot. Right? Would pick me up nice things – smart, neat...

[Like I said – DO NOT get any stoopid ideas – keep remembering – he taught me where to kick idiots... And a whack on the funny-bone from a little rolling pin will make you go cross-eyed – not laughing].

Mind you – he found out the right sizes by trial and error. First thing was way too small – then he had me floating around like a hot-air-balloon... Was taking the piss of course... Had some great T shirts for nightshirts though.

Didn't help any that when I'd arrived with Shania I wasn't anywhere near the size or shape I had been. Of course, no one was. My bum had vanished – not that it was ever that big... DO NOT challenge that!

About then it wasn't "Does my bum look big in this?" but "If a puff of breeze catches me will this work like a sail and get me blown away?" I'm small, okay – but at that point there was nothing of me. Problem was – there was much less of her – when she was taller than me – should have been bigger all round...

I have no idea how she had any energy to go out, raiding, finding me clothes, getting us food...

But then – turned out she didn't... Mustn't get in front of myself...

I'd never been exactly bothered about fashion. Like, when hanging out with a bit of a crowd at college... I'd just made enough effort so as to fit in – at least – go un-noticed. (In a different way).

Once I'd confirmed that, short of roping and hog-tying them, the boys I might want to attract weren't ever going to notice me I went back to "practical". Plenty of pockets, easy to keep clean – and trainers or boots depending on the weather.

Keep changing to go hiking with Bodger was way-too-much bother – was never as though he was going to wait patiently was it? Tying your laces with eighty kilos yanking at you to get your arse moving is <u>*not*</u> easy.

Of course after all the Olympics, Commonwealth Games and all the fuss about obesity, riding a bike became cool – and Greg's bike for me was just flash enough to be alright – and not get stolen – well – not more than a couple of times...

I told you how he'd rigged it so he could get it back didn't I? Like; those thieves probably decided to go straight – fast... I would *not* have wanted to be around when Greg or his mates came by to collect my bike. Lovely guys. So *not* the sort you want to upset. Them more so than Greg.

Without doing a thing I suddenly gained a kind of additional, new "street cred" around college. Very different from my previous reputation. I was at least known to have friends that no-one with a brain would want to piss off.

Well before I first saw Anton any kind of trouble backed off from me. Ordinary trouble. One nasty creep failed to get the message – briefly. I was able to sort him for myself. My life settled down. I guess that I finally blended into the crowd in a different way. Maybe that's how come Anton figured he could mess me around... Sometimes you simply can't win... That is such a pain-in-the-butt!

Thing was – wandering off a bit here (for a change)... I'd always been a loner... Didn't think I actually wanted to be – it was – kind of easier – simpler... People – not only kids. (Although what are "adults" except older kids?) Kids big and small are too complicated. <u>Way</u> too complicated... Least they were...

One thing the sickness and survival has done for us all... (A bit more back on track...) Life has got to be simple – direct... There isn't time or energy for a whole load of playing games. You've got to be nice and you've got to be straight... You screw anyone over – chances are you're going to get shot at – at the least. Kind of makes life a whole lot easier.

So being a loner I guess that suddenly being on my own was maybe much less of an issue for me than for a whole load of people. I'd spent at least a couple of years mostly in the Hermitage garden (except when I absolutely had to show) – and I'd at least seen that the Hermit could make out on his own... So – being alone wasn't that much bother for me...

Like – letting my story wander further off...

Greg had changed a load of that. Nearly at once I stopped all the creeping around getting in the place unseen... Hadn't figured that would mean I couldn't easily skive off whenever I felt like it... Had to do school – pretty much properly for the last year – most of it.

His fixing the thing about my eyes and – probably – a load of other discreet "fixings" that I never recognized at the time helped a whole lot... Well – that last year was different. I was never going to like it – but I had reason to stick with it...

There definitely was a change in attitudes. I very much became far more than a statistic... Toward the end I was even getting what felt like real, genuine smiles from staff... The creep kids shied away from me... And that wasn't just because I still had fists and kicks...

Next I kind of drifted into college – but then – I'd effectively drifted out of going to school. No-one had seemed that bothered about that. This time my drifting got nudged in better direction. Greg *was* bothered. So was Bodger. If Greg frowned a bit at me – the way that reckoned I was getting up to something... Well – Bodger...

Shit! It makes me cry!

He'd slobber me – or get the arse of my jeans – or my leg... Never bit me... Just... I guess he thought I was some kind of naughty puppy that needed correcting...

Going to leave this for a bit...

===========

Shania was good though. Could be she saved my life. Got me thinking and maybe a bit "grounded" in the new way things were – a bit at least...

Despite the risk of condensation on the windows showing where we were, she got me boiling all water and sterilising all my eating things every time. She was right – we had no idea what the sickness was; or if it was in the water... The last thing we needed was to run any stupid risks. She had camping gas for a stove and checked what the water looked like every time she ran the kitchen tap. Might not have been necessary right at the start – but – like she said – "Did I want to go through all that again?"... Persuasive or what?

I guess I got used to how skinny she was – fast... Maybe it was because she made nothing of it – bothered more about me, about us having enough food (tins)... Kind of like Mum in a lot of ways – like Greg... Practical.

(We all survived because of tins didn't we?)

I don't think that it would have made any difference if I'd reacted differently... Don't think she'd have liked any fuss – she'd have hated it...

She helped me not freak out the first night of thick cloud that totally hid any moon. She'd seen that the power would fail and got candles and matches ready.

We didn't talk a whole lot. What was there to say? Bit like an old couple, like the Spicers – maybe...

Out of nowhere we suddenly had a whole load in common...

Naturally, we wanted to know "WTF happened"... *Really* wanted to know that... But no-way we wanted to talk about what *had* happened – what we'd experienced. No idea what she'd been through – reckon it had been a whole lot worse than I had... Horribly sure she'd been attacked, at least run into very bad trouble, in some way... She was shit-hot on keeping out of sight – more than I'd ever been when keeping my Hermitage hideaway secret... She'd had it bad – I figure...

Shania was cool though – good-style cool that is. Practical, sensible... She gave me ideas what to do... Didn't make the mistake of a load of telling me how-and-what-and-should... Lot like Greg in that... Pity more people can't be that way.

Weird thing – like I said we got on like the Spicers – real "old couple" style – but – she gave me space – respect you could say – both... Maybe old couples get on so well because they've learnt to do that? It's not "give and take" – nothing like that... It's some other thing – more than that... A whole load more...

Gran used to say that the "Me, Me, Me generations" lost out so much. You let her get going she'd get into blaming it on the socialists. She reckoned that it's no way society's job to wipe everyone's arses to provide the perfect society. Don't ever let her hear "From the cradle to the grave". That would set her off something chronic! She reckoned that it's <u>everyone's</u> job to make the best society they can – by making their own efforts as best they can. That's the *best* – not "good enough to get by".

Socialism? "Society knowing what's best and looking after everyone"? Don't worry about the "Nanny State"... Worry about who-the-fuck the Nannies are going to be! Some kind of "We-know-what's-good-for-you" bunch of super-beings? More like some gang of closet-fascists as crazy and convinced of their own rightness as the hierarchies in Stalin's Russia, Hitler's Germany and an endless list of places since then...

And that includes the people that kept sticking their "expert" beaks into education – wasting millions, changing the latest project into yet another initiative and never waiting to see if any of it worked. *Why* didn't anyone ever tell the "elected representatives", that were supposed to work for the country and the people, to *stop* sodding about?

[The Nazis were "National Socialists" and Stalin's mob were "Soviet Socialist Republic"... So what does that say?]

Don't ever get Gran going on "Brown noses" or "sucking up to managers"! "Apparatchiks"... She'd nail you to the floor and lecture you...

It didn't need Gran for me to see that everyone wanting everything their way – claiming their "rights" was total bullshit and never going to work. The only people that works for are the biggest shits and most selfish – those that work the system and grab all they can. It no-way matters what name they give their politics. I figured that out before I was three.

For a start there were always people, couples and families that were coming apart all round me. My Dad had buggered off and left us. Whatever anyone might say (risk saying) about Mum – that was selfish.

One thing the three people then close to me all said – that we all agree now here in the Valley – is that if anyone wants things to work – then they have to be willing to give – to put themselves into it... And to accept that some of it won't be exactly what they want or like... To accept that some of it will be crap. The thing is that we have to want the bigger thing to work more than we want our own little bit to be exactly the way it suits us.

A good thing that we have now. Is that we recognise (admit) that none of us have a clue about a whole load of the things we need to know. We hardly have any idea about where to go and what to do next. So we have to try to find out; we have to experiment – we have to see what works... Most of all – we have to be practical. There is no room for dogma – not even "pet-theories". We have to try different things and see what actually succeeds.

Beth says that dogma killed more people than bullets and arrows ever did.

===========

Meanwhile...

I make it sound like we (Shania and me) were together for ages don't I? We weren't together a week.

Fourth night – no, fifth, (when you count the evening I arrived) – I woke up from a nap. She was crouching inside the front bay-window – looking out... I knew why at once – there was a party racket. Cars revving and lights flashing – car light beams in the dark...

There was no-way she had to tell me to keep quiet and out-of-sight! That was *not* the sort of party I wanted to get into.

Fact was that I had got out of a few like that (before the sickness) – out of windows sometimes... You should be aware of when a fight is going to kick-off – especially if it's stupid women doing it. They are worse than men! Far worse!

I made only a tiny bit of a noise, so that I wouldn't make Shania jump, before crawling over to where she was.

Outside a pub window smashed... So, while whoever it was out there was looking at that, I carefully took a cautious look.

There were three cars all over the crossroads and lights from at least another shining from the side we couldn't see... People milling about – shouting – cheering – being crazy... Being smashed, stoned – off their tiny skulls...

Good thing – thinking about it – I didn't see any guns – and there was no shooting. Huh! Such "quiet times"!

We weren't remotely thinking of that then (probably). That was well before when I got shot at the first time. We both simply wanted to stay out of it – well out of it... It looked like the laughs could tip into fists at any moment...

I'd seen more than enough idiot behaviour well before I vanished into the Hermit's place. I had to learn back then.

Later, when out with the girls from college, I would get myself someplace else – fast. I didn't care what anyone mouthed off about it. By then, when some idiot wanted a fight, I didn't get involved. I didn't stand around gawping. People are that stupid – walk away... Then again – if they don't want to let you – that's going to be their problem... No-one has stopped me walking quietly away from stupidity for a very long time.

Seems to me that there had always been far too many arseholes who thought it smart to push it... To not back-off... I'd had to learn to fight first day at school – probably before that.

Greg taught me more effective ways – and better ways to not get seen...

Right then, in the house with Shania, neither of us had the strength to defend ourselves – much less to run away. So we slid silently down inside the window – smiled nervously at each other in the light from the cars and cuddled up for warmth...

Don't get any silly ideas – fact was, we had very little heat. With the power gone off we only had the camping stove. We knew that much heat could make condensation on the windows – well – Shania had got the idea – *really* got it... Although she wouldn't tell me how... I reckon it would have been that bad experience... She was adamant about it.

We were all learning a load of new essentials around then – some of them we learned the hard way...

Okay. Let's get this straight. (Settle your mind once and for all). We were not tribbing. Right? Got that? If we'd wanted to we probably wouldn't have had the energy – or the body fluids. Like I said – I don't know where she got the energy to go raiding for food.

Anyway. What if we had been? You have a problem? *Get a life!*

Right then we all needed all the comfort we could get. Yeah, it could be easier to be cold, made of rock or ice – just shut-down ... But anyone with any sense allowed themselves every bit of human comfort they could get – and could cope with. I know – I *do* know – sometimes merely being with other people was – difficult.

I mean – sometimes, especially when connected people had got through, together... Well... Is there anyone can honestly say that they didn't think "Why them?" and "Why should they have someone – from – before...?" Chokes me up writing it – even now.

Like I said – Shania was alright. We talked quietly until things outside settled down – and then we fell asleep.

It wasn't so bad waking up with a dead friend... I've always felt that she was glad to have someone with her – she didn't die alone... That is pretty good.

I think – I know – that dying alone was one thing we all dreaded – all of us that got through the sickness... Doing that was somehow more terrifying than the future... Probably kept a load of people alive...

I wouldn't say that I got used to bodies soon – certainly not by then – but – I was beginning to sort it – a *bit* better. At least Shania wasn't a mess. That helped. I think maybe her heart gave out. She looked very peaceful – and that was nice.

It sounds weird – but – I "made Shania comfortable" – closed her eyes and all that... And covered her with a couple of blankets.

I can't work out that it meant anything – or mattered – but it seemed respectful... At least – it was better than I'd done before... I was feeling lousy about that – still do if I tell the truth...

There'll never be any way I can go back though...

Maybe I looked after her for me? Maybe – I don't know – to at least do a bit better? I didn't run off again...

Anyway – I'd kept low and quiet all the time I was doing that – and the party had got louder and sounded like there were more people and more arguments.

I thought it was sodding-marvellous that the only large (largish) number of people I had yet seen should all be getting smashed and wanting to fight. *What-the-fuck was wrong with people?* Maybe they'd watched too many of those stupid programmes and thought that it was what they were supposed to do? Like kids "having" to dress like "celebrities" and thinking that it made them special?

Anyone can be special! But it takes what's inside them and things they do – NOT the trendy clothes and fake-tan that they put on. It takes actions – NOT the words and accents they copy from over-paid donuts on the TV.

One thing that was definitely wrong with this bunch at the Winchester though – there was never any leader. Not once. I looked and looked – never saw one – nor any sign of one.

School had (accidentally) taught me to always look out for who was running things – really running them – which any sensible kid can tell you is often not the person stood at the front who is supposed to be in charge – and/or thinks they are...

But in all that bother, there was never anyone with any clue what to do.

Somehow word had got out – or people heard the racket – so they turned up. It was mostly young people – no-one over thirty at least; I shouldn't think... They were kind of partying like it was the end of time... I reckoned that if they carried on like they were doing it probably would be the end for a lot of them. The end for their livers at least.

Don't get the idea I don't like to party as much as anyone. There've always been parties and "parties", though... And this was *so* clearly the kind any sane person stays as far away from as possible from the start... I guess that kind of asks why people kept turning up... But you could ask a whole load of questions about why a load of people did lots of crazy things in that time. Could be – probably was – they were simply mad keen to be with other people – get in the herd – feel secure.

Why did people get involved in riots – before...? Especially when there was so much CCTV around and the cops had cameras and helicopters? Why did people go to find the riots and get filmed smashing and stealing? I saw one thing on the TV – some kid that went from miles away to "get stuck in". He said that it was "brilliant" and "liberating" – like he was "really part of something". Something *stupid!* He got sent to prison for it. What a knobhead!

After the sickness though I reckon that some people figured that there was no come-back on what you did... So – some simply went crazy...

Problem was – that with no-one to end it or move it away the party went on for days – until the booze and substances ran out. Must have run out for some way around – anywhere close enough for them to go and raid for more. From time to time there were bursts of noise with cars leaving – but never all of them. So my hopes would be dashed – again.

While the weather warmed up a bit and dried out, the stupid party went on so long that I nearly ran out of food. I had to stop using the room Shania was in. I didn't have the strength (or the nerve) to move her.

With the impression she'd had given me I didn't want to risk being seen anywhere outside. Don't remember exactly what got me worried – probably all the yelling and screaming – on top of her original worries.

Shania had said she had a car – had sort-of suggested we might move on together... But I didn't know which car – so there was no way I could make a quick dash for it... And there was virtually always someone outside the pub – chucking up as often as arguing about the music... With no power they were using the players in the cars. They didn't all play the same junk at the same time. Would get into competing... Sounded diabolical!

For a time I thought that one of them had died in the road – gave me a hell of a fright when she suddenly got up. For a second she gazed straight at me. Nothing registered in her head though – she turned and staggered inside... Frights like that are NOT fun!

Eventually things died down and people started to drift away. Soon as the last of them left – in a howl of noise – I grabbed the car keys and some bags I'd got ready – and shot out to find the car. I'd figured that there were only two Fiats in sight by then... So that felt good...

Set the alarm off on the first one. If I'd had anything left in me it would have been scared out of me...

Tag thing didn't work on the other one and the lousy keys didn't begin to fit... I was freaking!

I was probably dancing on the spot... Before I noticed a big car I didn't recognise as a Fiat. (I thought they were all little cars). It flashed in response to the key.

So I didn't know? I'm a woman! Wasn't my natural job to know everything-about-everything was it? Leastways – not until I got to be a Mum...

Jumped in the car fast, got it started, no bother – and shot away quick as I could... At least I didn't forget the bags – although some of the water bottles leaked and made a mess... (Because I chucked them in the back seat too hard).

===========

2 – 4

So – WHEN I EVENTUALLY slowed down – same old question...

Where to go?

Plus a fresh one...

How to not run into any situation I didn't want to get involved in...? That "party" had not been exciting-and-fun... It had been way beyond control – and frightening... How many more people were going to be going nuts like that? What other madness might be on the loose?

===========

Oh right... Nearly forgot this. Talking of madness... This is nuts – crazy – whatever you want to call it...

While I was stuck waiting for them to bugger off – or at least give me a clear break out the front, to get away – in a car. I was not planning to do another day's hike...

[There was no back gate Richard! You suggesting I didn't look? And no-way I was fit to go over a single garden wall, no-way my guts would have taken that. Who's story is this? Sod off!]

So, while I was sitting around feeling pissed-off and hating their choice of music (noise) I got to thinking about how they got there – how they knew where to meet...

Maybe the phones round here were working? Maybe there was a phone or two in the house?

At least searching occupied me for a bit. Eventually found a mobile under some cushions – It had a little bit of charge left. (Don't know if it was Shania's – don't know if it was her house).

Greg had made me memorise his numbers – house and two mobiles. Did his nut (with a *bit* of a smile) and said that "a number in a phone memory is no use when that phone is dead... Is it?!" And Bodger had got hold of my leg... So I promised to learn them – and I did – 'Cos I keep my promises.

[Although Greg told me not to make them – ever. And much more to never rely on other people's promises... Unless I wanted to get dropped in deep shit... He'd go on about all that – especially when he was sad... And Bodger would always be there somehow... And Mum agreed with him about that too...]

Once I'd got the phone I thought for a bit – but then decided that if I waited too long the battery would die anyhow... So I decided to risk trying to call Greg...

See – well... Sometimes there was a crazy hope – half a hope... Crazy I know. *Totally* crazy... Blame it on the bloody awful noise from outside – white noise almost... Like one of those torture things... On-and-on.

Anyhow... I called... None of his mobiles or tablets worked so I wracked my brains for his landline number – and – miracle! That worked... Got the shock of my life when he picked up...

Fucking recorded answers!

No idea how I didn't smash that phone to a billion pieces – or more.

Maybe – because it had his voice in it...

Yeah – okay – so – it was insane... When I stopped crying (again) I called again – recorded his recorded voice... Well, it was something... Not much... Better than nothing... Wished I could have done the same with Mum... Was glad he had an enormous "WOOF" from Bodger at the end of the message... And that made me cry all over again as well.

I've still got that phone... Which is really stupid – because it doesn't work at all now... But it still has him, them, inside it... So? I'm nuts. Right? Live with it!

Going to go have a cry now...

Hey! So I cry a lot. Live with that too! Everyone has a whole lot to cry about. You look at any *real* soldiers in any *real* war – they *wept*. Real deaths cracked them up. Wasn't some poxey digital game. They couldn't pause the machine and go for a cold beer.

Genuine soldiers... Reality was – getting smashed out of their skulls – sometime later – did sod-all to help them. I know – I've seen it – scraped up the mess... Scraped up my own mess... We've all got more than enough to weep about... To get smashed about...

We go on though. We are starting over.

===========

Where was I? Right. Moving on from Shania's place. Buggering off quick in the Fiat...

One thing you do is get yourself in check – in control... You have to. The more so when it is hardest to do. Then, part of it, is that you slow down... Greg would say – "When something goes "bang" – make sure your arse isn't on fire – then pause – look around – get a clear picture of what exactly is going on..."

Yes, there was a time (early on) when I was silly enough to ask him what to do if my arse was on fire...

Greg just looked at me – and kept "just looking". (Like he would). Only nodding slightly when I got the answers right... And then kept looking... Until he was satisfied that I had stopped being a smart-arse donut, put my brain in gear and thought it through. He had a big thing about having your "brain in gear" – said that most people never do – "which is why so much crap happens".

Right from the start I knew better than to ask him what crap he had seen...

Anyhow – after I had scurried a few miles in the car I did slow down. I had absolutely no idea where to go or what to do next – except try to get a few days' supply of food and water stashed...

I stopped somewhere – outside a line of small shops. It wasn't like I learnt to do pretty quick...

I *did* learn...

If/when I was going to stop – do it either well out in the middle so I could see anyone coming... <u>And</u> *keep my eyes open* – or do it tucked right into the side to be discreet – after I'd thoroughly checked it out... (Usually better to do that). Best – find a way to get right out of sight.

So, that first time... I'd come to some kind of a stop at the side of the road by the shops – main road with a small road off each side a little further on... (I can picture it now – exactly... <u>Wish</u> I couldn't).

The weather had got better so I had the windows down. (Probably to let the smell of my guts out). It was very sunny, just a few of the earliest little flowers were coming out – Galanthus... Bet you didn't know that!

Suddenly a boy is each side of me – at each front door (all four were locked – got that right). The one my side reached in for the keys – so I knuckle-punched up hard under the chin – banged his head up into the roof before I twisted hard into his Adam's Apple.

The bullet went right through my door, across the front of me, through the other door and stopped his mate from reaching in to open that side. Probably stopped him permanently. He recoiled across the pavement with a yelp, followed by a squeal. His blood squirted out through his fingers – spraying right into the car. Must have been hit in the big artery in the thigh.

"Bitch! You shot Daz!" The one with the gun choked at me and yanked away.

I wasn't going to wait for him to bring the gun round again. I *floored* it.

Can't claim that I deliberately swung to hit him away from me – I more lost control. (Richard says "Traction"... Yeah, *whatever...*)

With the way I took off the car was all over the place – so more by luck than the least idea I smacked him out of the way – hard. By the time I ricocheted off into one of the side roads he was still flat on his back – I think I probably ran over his foot – at least.

Hadn't seen the gun until it went bang right next to me? I hadn't *seen* the stupid boys! Not exactly sure that I did see it – probably figured out what the hell had happened later – like when my right ear stopped ringing and when I had found some place to stop and hide – and could check out the line of holes from one side to the other. If I hadn't been so skinny I'd have had my belly ripped open... Kind of encouraged me to make damn certain I had a good look around me from then on.

It taught me five things:

1. *Wake-the-fuck-up!*
2. *Don't* be sloppy / *DO* pay attention.

3. *Always* have the safety on except when you mean to shoot. (When you have a gun – which I didn't at that time). Where the hell had they got it from? And so early?
4. *Any loaded gun can fire any time* – whether the idiot holding it means it to or not.
5. *Don't* think that hiding behind the thin bodywork of a car like an American film Cop is going to give you any protection at all... That bullet smashed through both windows as well as the metal skins and linings... Daz probably died of blood poisoning – if he didn't bleed out. Why'd you think soldiers use armoured cars not plain, ordinary ones?

Once I stopped shaking I had to change that car fast – couldn't shut the windows when it started to rain could I? And the blood stank... With the warmed-up weather there were some early flies around as well – they homed in on the smell didn't they? There was a frightening lot of blood – it was on the dash, windscreen and... Well – there was a lot. Right?

Wasn't my fault the boy got shot – died – I knew he was going to die – that much blood... I didn't get the idea that anyone was going to be listening to reason about gun safety. Idiots that totally-screw-up don't usually put their hands up and admit it do they?

Don't know what they wanted. Because at least one of them had a gun out – that doesn't actually mean much... Except that he was a total idiot for not handling it right.

===========

So – okay... I was shocked about that... More than that...

Guess I never thought it through before... Not much at the time for sure. There was so much going on... Like I said – a big-long-blur...

Don't know about "traumatised"... But it major distressed me. The idea that someone had got shot, was going to die... I wasn't so bothered about running over the other idiot's foot... Then again, it wasn't like I'd shot him myself was it? I didn't actually know for definite that Daz was dead – or going to be...

I – well – I think that I just reacted – got away – took in that the car was a bloody mess – didn't like the sticky, yeuky filth – or the flies and – well – did what had to be done...

In fact – I kind-of explained to myself that the idiot with the gun hadn't *really* shot at *me*... It had been an accident... It hadn't been for real... Loads of rationalising like that... Maybe that only came later? I don't think I was beginning to react... Except that I knew deep down that it had been ***way***-too-fucking-close...

===========

Next thing – changing cars... Wasn't that easy was it? Not like stopping off at a car-hire place – bit of paperwork and a credit card...

Well – you probably know for yourself – all those lifeless houses – and all those cars sitting around, for you to take your pick... Right...

Easy...

Like hell!

Not so bad when you were somewhere smart with a drive or a front garden to park the car in – except of course they were often more modern cars – with anti theft, tracking and immobilisers... Terrific – hundred metres down the road and the engine cut while a different alarm kicked off... Another, different alarm after the stupid thing bleeped and flashed when you opened it... Then started chirruping to tell you the door was open – before squealing that you'd not got your belt on... A fox among chickens makes less noise.

No problem... Everyone's dead... Yeah – except the ones that aren't – and they're as likely to be next door as on the moon – and they're as good as guaranteed to be hostile to you stealing their neighbour's car... Always assuming that you managed to break in to the get the keys or digital-thingy without anyone noticing in the first place.

Seeing as so many people snuffed it... <u>How come</u> such a lot of those that didn't – managed to be sitting on their arses – right next door to anywhere I wanted to break in? Seemed like a lot of times anyway...

One funny one – funny right then...

Looking for food I managed to sneak into a promising looking house. No car out front, nothing smashed, nothing out-of-place... Things beginning to look a bit dusty, neglected... (I was starting to pick up on that). So it looked like it could be okay...

I did get cautious when it was a doddle to get in. The place still felt alright... So I quickly checked out that there would be some still edible food in the kitchen, before I moved through to the hall; to begin seeing what else might be there... First place I looked (no idea why) – cupboard under the stairs...

Terrified the guy sitting there – it was a loo...

So funny! He was sitting there – desert cammo pants round his ankles – reading a book... Engrossed in it! I got myself together from the shock before he reacted... Must have been one hell of a good story!

He yelled. I slammed the door shut. There was a mighty great **"THUNK!"** followed by a groan and a thud.

I didn't hang around to ask any questions – instantly decided it must have been his home and made myself scarce – quickly.

Thing was – we're all "potty trained" right? So – once we got moving again – so long as we could find a bog that was clean (no stiff for a start)

– we did what we'd always done – including flushing... The noise of that being another sign that someone was – um – "doing things" in a place...

So that got me thinking a bit... Asked myself what Greg would have done – and started doing that – including burying any trace that I'd been around. I can't know if it made any difference – but... Well; you can't "prove a negative"...

Hmmm... Different kind of a "negative"...Never thought of myself as a burglar. That is – before all this I never dreamt I'd be breaking in places. But then I don't suppose I thought I'd ever need to – not so as to just stay alive...

That was more "potty training" wasn't it? We were absolutely conditioned against taking anything from anyone else... Except thieving little shits of course... What was with them? Was that genetic? Or did they learn?

In the new world we'd landed in, it took time to figure out that double glazing and insulation don't help. They meant that I couldn't hear activity and there could be no sign of heating being on... Although that all changed once the power went out and the systems shut down.

Heating and lights didn't actually tell me a thing I could trust. At first there was no way of knowing for sure what was going on if the lights *were* on – a TV flickering sometimes – and the hot gas coming out from a central heating only meant that the heat was running...

And then, of course (Yeah – "of course" – once you wake up to it...) – once the electric goes off – all the signs are reversed. Then no lights and no heat *does not* mean that nobody is in...

Although, condensation on windows can be a good marker – so long as it isn't from rotting plants – or stiffs... Cats, dogs – other pets...

The sound thing worked both ways. If I was in I also couldn't hear what was out. Vehicles could go by or pull up without my hearing them. For certain people could stomp around.

When I would decide to stay anywhere for a bit, I took to having a window open at least a little – even when it was freezing... That had the advantage of being fairly sure there was none of the dreaded condensation... I had to be careful there wasn't a flag of steam waving its way outside to grab attention.

Then again – I was soon using both indicators to suss out any activity for myself.

Another benefit of having a window a crack open... It meant I knew for sure at least one route that I could bail out through in a hurry... Except that, as people got savvy, that could be dangerous too...

About everything did that – got dangerous as people sussed what was going on. Being a bit safe meant keep thinking a step or so ahead. I got back to going out fast, ready to duck fast and/or whack-the-hell out of anyone that tried to grab me... Old (non-school) lessons proving useful.

There was no way of finding out whether a good looking car I wanted to (*quietly*) grab had much petrol in it either – not until I'd managed to get the keys.

How to get into the house (hopefully the right one) – well – if you don't know that by now...

No, you do *not* have to smash down doors or break windows... *Try* the doorknob for a start! Muppet! Take a quiet look around...

I'll tell you what... It doesn't need some idiot with a shotgun to chase you to get you looking damn hard before you go messing about... A kitchen knife on the end of a broomstick is more than enough.

I'd have to say that I amazed myself how fast I could get over not one garden fence, but a whole string of them – a couple of times... (A bit later on...)

I worked hard on revising some "extra curricula" skills...

So... Right back near the start, before I'd begun to sort myself out, at least one kid had probably got himself dead and another had taken a hell of a bash from my car...

Other idiots that had a go at me in the next days only got a good, hard whack at most... Just where could have been significant... You don't want me to hit you? *Don't* threaten me with violence! *It's simple!*

===========

Despite what was happening I still managed to conclude that one place to stop was going to be pretty well the same as any other – although close to somewhere I could get more food, warmth and clean water would probably be good...

Wrong!

On *both* counts.

You will know what I mean if you've made it this far. You should know that it isn't only being able to get in (discreetly) that matters... Being able to clear out – preferably completely unseen and unheard –matters one hell of a lot more.

Foot and car chases are so damn clever in the movies... No way they're fun when you're being chased! Being attacked...

And close to any larger sources of food – *anything* people will want – means that you're going to have people snooping around – and – the major problem – they will almost definitely have learnt to be jumpy around anywhere like that... So, once they are armed, they are going to be trigger happy – and probably a danger to everything around them – including themselves... And that's if they're "nice" people – not aggressive – not greedy... Not plain evil or insane..

Huh! Guns got to be a problem – as/when people began to get their shit together and get them – which meant finding them first of all. Before that I had to watch out that anyone I bumped into didn't pull a knife on me...

Or whack me with whatever came to hand. Even just grab me – although, like you've probably got the idea by now – grabbing me is not sensible... Not even just trying...

All my temper when I was a kid – I never guessed how much a tin of beans can hurt. My arm was bruised for days – right where the gash was still healing up.

I'd got myself a rolling pin like I said. After the first can hit me I used that as a bat... Could be spectacular. A burst of beans, peas, spaghetti, custard... Shocked me the first couple of times. Always made other people stop for a moment – and a moment is all you need when you're thinking right.

I got lucky with that. Some gorilla that charged at me skidded on the goop and knocked himself senseless on the shelves. It showed me that when I was going to do any charging of my own (if they were between me and my way out) I had to go round or jump over the mess.

When I charged I never tried to avoid them. Very, very few people expect someone (especially a small someone) to go straight at them.

You don't want to risk a broken wrist – *don't* point a blade at me! A good whack with a rolling pin will make you drop it. I am not going to mess about asking.

I was horrified how many times whacking the closest one fast didn't get me into more aggro with whoever was with him (or her) – but had the other(s) squealing and running away as fast as they could – usually well in front of the one I'd clobbered. It confirmed my thinking that I was better off on my own – no need to sweat about someone else.

"Safety of the herd" is all very clever – so long as you're not the sacrificial one for the rest's benefit – in that case – you are totally stuffed!

===========

So I got through trying a few different places as I majored in "Wrong Place Again 101". All sorts of stupid reasons – reasons you'd never think of – until they slap you in the face...

Like – it was disgusting – but it was always best to check out the whole house first. That would be –as soon as you were inside.

I guess that I did get lucky with that. I never found anyone still alive but dying when I got in... But a suicide that hanged itself weeks-and-some ago begins to fall apart... Told you it was gruesome... Totally freaks you if the thing comes apart and tumbles – first onto the top landing and then all the way down the stairs – in stages... *Aaargh!*

And then there was a whole new world of smells to contend with... Rotting goes through stages – evidently... And one thing sets off another... G-eurgh!

And it didn't help if you had left a bag at the bottom of the stair ready to grab if you need to get out quick...

It especially doesn't help when it all happens in the dark.

GRUESOME!

So – if you haven't learnt this already – when you get into a place – check it out right away... Okay?

One place is *not* as good as another – I got that *very* clear in my mind... Eventually...

But that didn't answer the questions of where I should go – or – probably more important – how to avoid hassle.

===========

I told you that Shania had sorted me out a bit... Well... We'd talked. It might sound kind-of stupid but it needed to be put into words for me to actually grasp what had happened. Start to anyhow. I needed someone else... What? To confirm that I wasn't dreaming? To tell me that, yes, this was for real? Tell me again... To shift me beyond – "It *can't* be... Just *can't...*"

It was all simply *too* much.

She'd also got me some clothes – dry jeans for a start – changes – even another pair of trainers – the right size, with two pair of socks to keep my tootsies warm. (Impressive or what?) She found me more Ts, jeans and a couple of hoodies. I've no idea where she got them from – or when – must have been while I was zonked. They weren't a good fit (wouldn't be would they) but they were better than the no-change-of-anything I'd succeeded in arriving with.

I'm waffling... "Displacing"... I was freaked out by what had happened with Daz and his mate... But at least none of the blood had actually got over me... Not on my skin... And I could wipe it off things I needed to touch as I drove... And I managed not to crash – just...

So... I had to dump that Fiat. I wasn't hanging about. So I went for an old car that I could hot-wire. (You don't need to know how come I could do that...)

Once I'd done that I got moving. Right then fast wasn't as frightening as what I couldn't stop thinking might be coming behind me... So it took a bit before I began to use my brain and slow down to look around... Ummm – well – I soon slowed down a whole lot when I ran out of petrol. (Yeah – *again...*)

I hadn't got my shit together yet had I? *Right?* **(Sod off!)**

I was having enough of a struggle driving the thing and not hitting other stuff. Six lessons and a near cataleptic drive for miles are not going to get me through any test are they? I was still crunching the gears and trying not to play kangaroo... I have no idea how I achieved that first journey – probably my brain wasn't thinking at all. *(Do not make any funny comments!)*

It took me a while – minutes – *not* hours *(watch-it!)* – to suss out why the damn car had stopped. I hadn't stalled it – this time. I got to looking at the gauges after about the 35th time it wouldn't start.

I guess I'm still shocked at the dents you can put in a car... Not by hitting things – but by hitting it... And the remaining bottles of water kind of exploded when the string bag they were in slammed the car... Hadn't learned that lesson had I? *Don't laugh!* You'd have been screwed up around then too. (*You* were. Weren't you!)

So I was stood there dripping and cursing – feeling an idiot – when I caught sight of someone taking a look at me – from a safe distance down the road.

Had my act together enough to think *"Oh shit!"* and wonder who they were, what they'd be like – okay or trouble... But before I could react they legged it... Probably decided I was a nutter and more dangerous than them.

I'd about got as far as figuring I had to get more petrol – or another car – or take another hike – or any mixture... And – where was I going to get either more petrol or another car...? How was I supposed to do all these things?

Seeing that person leg it, thinking a bit quick about the Winchester and what had maybe happened before that to Shania... And *not* thinking about what had only just happened... I did at least have the sense to get out-of-sight.

I shifted myself down a passage between houses.

Legging it wasn't easy with the bags and a small back-pack. Not with the "condition" I was in... As in – "lack-of"...

I pushed a fast walk on hard across a couple of streets. Maybe I didn't need to. I'd frightened whoever it was off hadn't I? That was not how I was thinking though...

I was thinking... About everything at once. About too much... About how my heart was banging so hard and loud...

I didn't run. Experience again – don't run unless you have to... You can't look around well when you run – not without risk of missing things you need to see – or hitting things like kids' bikes, stupid bollards – and potholes... Fucking-potholes can break your ankle – easy.

Anyway, I put some distance behind me – quick enough and safe. Then I stopped down a leafy passage between houses – semis... Had to – to chuck up.

That could have been frightening... But I'd done it before – a couple of times when I'd pushed myself too hard... Anyhow – it felt different from the sickness... There's nothing ever felt the way that did... You'll know that – or, if you're a young kid – you'll have heard it... Probably many times... From "us old farts". (All of going-on twenty something)... Yeah... I was there once myself... A couple of centuries ago.

That was a whole different world from anything you'll ever know...

Wasn't any choice about where I stopped. At least I didn't fall down – despite my legs gone to jelly and my heart banging in my ears.

Soon as I could get my head up I was looking around – checking.

Like I'd have done back in year seven when I scooted from some pusher I'd refused to mule for and kicked my way clear of.

That was the third load of that crap. I was skiving out of school to get away from one load of hassle – I no-way wanted to get into worse. First one I hadn't got near. She came after me – all smooth and "my good friend..." Creep stank of bad risk from the start. I didn't figure out how to get out of it quick enough.

I got away with that. The second one as well because I thought fast. Acted fast. Did the unexpected... I ditched the shitty A class soon as I was out of sight of the skank – well before I got stopped and searched... But did it so's I could go back and get it soon as I was in the clear... Took them back and shoved them down his trousers before he knew it – kicked out again – then legged it. No way was I letting the skank claim I "owed him" for any loss.

I was so *<u>not</u>* "tiny, so the Filth won't stop and search you"... I was already known – *too* well known. From all the bunking off for starters... Plus from an "incident" that they never managed to stick on me. From then on I was a target... They *<u>said</u>* I looked "at risk"... I was so not going to be left alone.

Not going to get stopped*?!* When I wasn't supposed to be in school the sodding CCTV around town would track me! "For my protection". Yeah... Right...

That was why I shifted out of the middle – into the "suburbs" (as much as they were) – and into a whole different load of hassle and crap...

Moving cash or leaf was one thing, even slate... No way I was touching tabs – of any kind... They were deep-shit every way round.

So... Well... All that was another set of reasons I needed to vanish into the Hermit's place...

It's not experience I'm proud of. Except that I did learn from it and I kept myself out of worse bother.

I did not want bother! School was hassle – so I wasn't going to be there was I? Both teachers and kids were problems.

Town, the streets – more trouble... Didn't plan on that did I? Not the way it would be... But – so long as I could keep in the clear – it was better than school... Better than being made to feel stupid and useless all the time... Better than being bullied – where I couldn't fight back – not without more hassle... Better even when it rained...

On the street I could at least make it cost any shithead. I couldn't always win (hardly ever)... But I built up some respect. I got a reputation... Which, naturally, got known by school – and the police...

And Mum... When the Social came knocking...

It's long since too late now to wish that I'd been some kind of "better" for her... At least in how I'd reacted...

Mum put up with so much from me...

Really, really wish I could do something about that...

Once things improved – well – I improved... That's a fact... But – it does nothing to change the crap times...

I hate to admit – Gran and Gramps couldn't sort me for a time...

I so <u>had to</u> get <u>myself</u> out of all the crap that was building up around me.

I'd got practice running okay? I knew to use my eyes when my ears wouldn't tell me... I knew my way around. I knew the way of things... Fast as I could I'd got the reputation as not being a sensible person to try and step out on sudden. Plain stupid to mix it with. I'd kick and punch as hard and nasty as I could before legging it.

I made sure I wasn't worth the bother. There was no street cred in doing over a shrimp like me. Not when any bruises would be an embarrassment... Which also meant that I hit them first where marks wouldn't show. Kind of a compromise. Same as not killing me for not doing what they wanted was a compromise... The bigger skanks didn't want a whole tonne of shit coming down on their patch...

A balance got itself achieved.

But... Now... Between the semis... Holding myself up, wheezing and gasping...

Now, I was in a whole new world... And in a totally strange town I knew nothing about.

I had no idea of the land, the street map, the territories, the people – anything...

No-one before had got shot so's they sprayed blood. I'd never run over anyone in a stolen car...

My situation was NOT "not great"... It was <u>***diabolical.***</u>

So? I was never going to have all my expectations, my "conditioning" out of my brain by then, so soon, was I? I was expecting a hoard of blue lights and stingers as much as Daz's mates wasn't I? It took time. Right?

But... Between the skanks and now was Greg and Bodger... A whole different thing. Now I could seriously put things together... Once I stopped – and checked that my arse wasn't on fire – or going to be – not imminently...

I settled myself quiet, out-of-sight – like I had in the hedge opposite the church gate when Bodger first showed up. I made myself get a grip... Made myself rationalise in the "Now"...

Some stupid cat freaked the crap out of me! Not difficult right then. Didn't hear it – naturally. Damn thing suddenly brushed against me. I only yelled at it quietly (managed to keep myself together – at least a tiny bit). I hissed real nasty. I hadn't got anything to chuck at it.

I don't mind cats – usually – but I am *not* put on the planet to feed them! I was Bodger's can-opener not every damn-cat-on-the-planet's. Mum always said that they'd got the cushiest-number-on-earth well figured out.

Cats now, more so right then, are a marker that someone's about... They scent a human a mile away and they home in on the food source... Like sharks. You have a can opener on you... It's like blood in the water to them.

That about did me in. I decided it was time to go to ground for the day.

I found myself a sunhouse place in a nice garden where I could clean up. It was between high fences on three sides, no sign of any activity in the house and – main thing – it wasn't locked. (I jammed the back gate shut soon as I was stopping).

So – I sorted myself. There were wet-wipes, sun factor and things there – made life easier for me... (Got me into the idea of grabbing as many packs of wipes as I could carry from then on in). I changed and my soiled clothes went into a bonfire-bin – did not light it.

Then I had about enough for a meal in the last of the light... I'd totally forgotten that I'd stopped to look at some shops to get food...

----

*[**Wipes...** So, hey, when did you discover – probably the scary way – that you can't simply jump in the shower or have a nice hot soak without a care in the world when the whole country has gone nuts and there could be crazy people close by? How long did you have to go without a nice clean-up? It was totally YEUK–DISGUSTING after what had happened. After a couple of cock-ups I got extra-careful about water in my ears – I want to hear everything going on around me! Yeah, I'm "reminiscing" about when the electric was still on in some places... But things only got worse when it went off – except you couldn't give away where you were so easy by accidentally forgetting and turning a light on... That was so dangerous].*

===========

Meanwhile – back at the sunhouse...

There was no sign or sound of life at the proper house at the top of the garden – or from what I could see of those each side. So, as it was late in the day and still wet from afternoon rain, I decided to stay in the sunhouse for the night. It was okay – until it was blowing hard and I was near freezing somewhere around three the next morning.

I'd seen no lights or sign of movement in any of the time I'd been awake so I decided to take a look at the house. This was my first real effort... I had never broken in anywhere totally strange before. You can't count when I explored the Hermit's garden – or taking a shortcut across the bottom of the vicarage garden – none of that... The Estate places were not strange – just weird... This was looking at breaking into some completely foreign-to-me place for real – and it wasn't the same as going into the cafe either...

Cathy's gave me an idea though... So – I tried the door... Was locked – solid by the feel of it... I was freaking as well as freezing – but

I tried a window – and got in – almost easy. (This was before the time I gashed myself).

Knocking things over in the dark makes a million times more noise than any other time – and you can multiply that some more, when you're terrified and creeping around with no clue what you're doing or what you might find...!

I froze – probably stopped shivering. No-one called out or moved though – so I felt around carefully before my next moves. (Should have known! And done it right!)

Well... I guess that going slow and feeling around at least saved me from falling over the body – what was left of it...

I guess, if you're one of the "First Generation" like me – the original survivors – not a "kid" – well – you'll know ***all*** about bodies... Guck, smells, stinks, nasty crud to skid over on – in... *And* all the rest... *Disgusting* – any time – any place... **YEUK!**

So... my foot prodded a big, soft object – like a roll of carpet – except it wasn't... I wouldn't say it was firm like that – more squashy...

How would you describe prodding anybody – usually warm and firm before all that happened? Like, if you were crashed out on the floor at someone's place after a night out and had to try to get to the loo without waking anyone up... Well – for 2nd generation kids and anyone else... Prodding a stiff in the dark – is *not* like that... Definitely NOT.

But at least stiffs don't swear at you, tell you to "fuck off", grab your leg – or all that sort of thing... You hope!

I'll tell you – when you're sneaking around some place that doesn't smell too bad – then – *the* thing in your head that you're working to not let freak you out – is the chance that someone will suddenly grab you. Don't care how many horror movies – zombies and all that bollocks – you've seen... The idea – the feeling that it could happen any second – is *way-too-much-terrifying*. It can have you climbing right out of any place – *fast*.

That first night... Still makes me shudder now... Well... I'm sure that it took some years off me. Maybe damaged my heart – it was banging so hard – and loud... I knew it meant I wouldn't hear anyone moving about – but they'd hear me even if I stood still – hear me thudding.

The stiff on the floor was long beyond hearing though...

Did I say there was a good, big moon? That night was so clear – and *cold!* Moon didn't light everything though. In fact it had hidden the body in shadow from a table... Kind of "detail" you had to learn as you went along... Children of the electric light – we had no idea about moonlight did we?

Big moon in a clear sky? Meant all what heat there had been in the day vanished fast. Not sure that my teeth weren't chattering louder than my heart. I probably made my own rhythm section...

Wasn't my first corpse by then was it? Still spine-chilling stepping over it though – stranger, in a strange house – probably their home... Eerie, sinister... If I'd been touched then – or heard a noise...

Couldn't have freaked any more than I was already doing – or done anything messy. That was, I suppose, something to thank the cat for...

You have to look for the positives!

Uhh!!! That night – that first time... Gives me the *shudders!!!*

Positives? Well – I did find two clean duvets (probably a guest room or the kids were away at college). Even with the stiff the kitchen was clean and I managed to slam the fridge shut before any green slime-monster in there got out.

There were tins of semolina – I could keep that inside me – and I loaded that with sugar and jam for the calories. The front room was clear and clean with a huge sofa faced away from the window. Curling up tight managed to stop me shivering. No sugar rush was ever going to keep me awake. I managed to get a reasonable sleep.

When it began to get light I started to look around with some sense and some purpose. I got more sloppy food inside me – keeping the table between me and what I didn't want to look at. I checked out upstairs for clothes – but everything I spotted was way too big – and there were what you might call "discouragements" to looking too close. But I did get car keys. Out of the hand of another stiff... I'd no-way got that used to it by then. I sat at the bottom of the stair and shook for a while.

Of course – I'd not discovered about things falling down stairs by then – If that had happened... Guess I wouldn't be here now... *Ugh!* If it *had* done...

Who am I kidding?! This was so <u>not</u> waking up at the bottom of the stairs after some night of partying... Okay – that could mean a few "OMGs!" – but this was big-time different. I never woke up from a frantic night knowing there was a stiff in the house – even if I did wake up with a worse hangover a couple of times – soon learned that stupid lesson. Always had some idea whose place it was and at least what county I was in.

One way or another I wasn't going to go leaping up this particular morning, though. Hangover or post-sickness jumping about is *not* a good choice – tends to lead to the floor smacking you in the face.

Well – I got going slowly and quietly, took a very discreet look around the outside from behind the lace curtains – got those car keys (Shaking all over and struggling not to gag). Must have achieved – I didn't forget to put some more bits of food (tins) in a couple of plastic bags.

I hadn't thought to look, though... That car out front was enormous. Well – in *my* experience up to then it was. Some four door saloon thingy. I had to yank the seat all the way forward – I thought about going looking for a cushion – but, after it had taken me an age to scrape the frost off, it had been difficult to start. (I *had* checked the gauge – and it <u>was</u> full). I didn't want to risk turning it off and I wasn't going to leave it running. I drove slowly away – frantic that I wasn't going to need to speed up until I'd got the hang of the thing. (Never thought about ice did I?)

Okay... Truth... I did NOT want to face those two stiffs again... I had a massive dread that they'd have somehow moved...

You could say that that was the start of a whole new part of my life...

===========

2 – 5

I GUESS YOU COULD SAY that I cruised around for a few days. That car gave me a (stupid) sense of security – false of course... But nice... comfortable.

IT WAS QUIET. TOO DAMN quiet. Smooth... I nodded off to sleep it was so – well – good.

It was so much more by luck that I'd nearly run it out before I managed my first real, big – no – huge – crash... It went up a bank and rolled over... That woke me up.

At least I didn't have a whole load of gear with me. Didn't waste much – other than the car. Wasn't too hard to get out of – despite the doors were jammed with the roof being squashed. No idea what speed I'd been going at – but it had totally flipped and mashed itself... Okay – so it was me that flipped it...

I was knackered – right? I'd been doing that "don't know where to stop" thing hadn't I?

Soon as I was out into the middle of the field and on my feet I was so mad at myself!

I was miles from anywhere. Right then I couldn't see a house – no building of any kind. Didn't kick the car though... I kind of felt sorry for it... Until it suddenly caught fire.

I thought they were only supposed to do that in the movies? Damn thing didn't give me time to grab one thing out of it – not even a duvet ... So I was knackered.. "Retribution" I suppose you could call it.

As it worked out I hadn't been rubbing my fresh bruises and cursing for long when another car showed up – attracted by the great big cloud of filthy black smoke. Only enough of a fire to blow out a couple of the tyres, though... Which taught me what I *should* have known – to get away and not stand there with my gob open... I was lucky nothing hit me.

Tamsin and Ozzie were well impressed with my "achievement". (Hell of a sight more than I was!) Actually called it that. "WOW! Some achievement!" Only reason I didn't kick him was that I needed a ride out of there. Didn't help that he stood there grinning at what was left of it – still smouldering...

They weren't bad people – just village posh types. Pain-in-the-arse to me (like you'd expect). I wasn't fair on them. I know that. Wasn't either fair on me or sensible. Quite likely I should have stayed with them longer. At least they weren't slobbery into each other – not "student style" – not nauseating.

Alright – truth is I totally felt an enormous dork having to be rescued from trashing a nice car... At least they were in a good car they'd stolen themselves – made no pretence about it.

In fact they were dead chuffed with themselves. They were getting their shit together. They were having fun – having a *real* adventure... So much better than their gap years had been. So much better than boring Uni...

Bugger Off!

Yeah? So? I was going to react that way wasn't I? Just because they weren't constantly displaying being Madly-In-Luv and all over each other, didn't mean that they didn't have me wanting to slap them after a day. (Had lost that rolling pin in the fire hadn't I?)

I was NOT having fun. I was NOT having an adventure. I was NOT jumping out of helicopters or any of that bullshit.

I *was* hurting for the people I'd lost... Mum, Gran, Greg, Bodger... I was missing going for loony walks and dodging being slobbered... There... I'm saying it. I was grieving – *fucking grieving*... Didn't know it then of course – couldn't... Still hadn't got my brain around what had happened had I?

Probably they hadn't either... If I'm fair to them... Could be they were in some kind of denial... (That's the explanation everyone uses). Probably they were finding their own way to cope... Never know...

Thing that broke it up for me – not the yak... They started doing drugs – probably had been all the time – but – they stopped hiding it... Laughed at me when I didn't like it... Pushed me to join them. They said (don't all the idiots?) "How could I know if I never tried"? All the usual bullshit.

They had no-fucking-idea did they?

Probably "city-suburban" (posh) and "Blairite University". (*Do not* get Gran started!). Tamsin's Mummy bought her a car for getting A-stars...

Concrete-car-park pushers and stinking stair wells weren't in their "widened horizons" were they? Not wanting to "go-kiss-a-train" didn't mean a thing to them did it? But I was pissed-off by then... "Legal highs?" You mean "No-idea-what-the-fuck-is-in-it highs"?

Bugger off!

I was out of there.

Few days later, I'm in a fresh car (more my size and loaded up with practical stuff), I see their car stopped outside a shop some way up front. No idea why but even at a distance it didn't seem right... In fact something felt *really* wrong.

I was fairly sure that I could see them both sitting there. That didn't make sense for a start. Early on like that not everyone had got into going in, grabbing and dashing. Not everyone had figured that it wasn't wise to park out front...

But... Just sitting there wasn't right...

I knew that they were loved-up and not the most sensible – quite likely stoned – but they hadn't been completely daft... So, well back from them, I carefully reversed into a front garden between other cars (without hitting a thing – Yay!)... Then I started hedge-hopping and wriggling my way along the opposite side of the road to where they were.

Icy, slippery ground made for quite an effort – especially when, the nearer I got, the better I could see that they were still sitting there – completely still – clearly not talking to each other... I stopped for a think. (Greg influence kicking in).

Okay, I did think that what I was doing could be real-extra-stupid... But – I was more than half way to them...

Could be they'd had a row? They weren't sleeping – wrong positions for that. Could be they were off their skulls?

Then I saw that the windows weren't misted up – although any frost had been warmed off... Meant they certainly weren't sleeping...

Could be they were dead? Dead sat up? Committed suicide? Poisoned themselves? How did you knock yourself off sitting up straight in a car...? Okay – some shit tabs were massively dangerous – but...?

I was getting convinced that they *had* snuffed it – somehow... But – how? Could they have and not moved, not fallen some way?

I didn't want to walk into – I had no idea what

I settled down on my heals to watch – and study... Checked all around me for a start. Like I would if Bodger suddenly froze – and more when his hackles went up... (This being different from pushing on ready to smack anyone and everyone as hard as I could).

I got myself as out-of-sight as possible and comfortable. Wasn't watching them by then. They were lolled back against the head rests – heads not right... It was looking definite. I totally wanted to know who else might be about before I went look-see. <u>Before</u> I headed back to my car.

I knew how to be still, silent and watch for ages – well – fifteen to twenty minutes – more if pushed. Bodger wouldn't last that long... But he'd never had to wait for blasted ponies to be loaded before he could slip out of the Hermitage garden without being noticed.

Nothing looked wrong with the car – same dent in it that I'd last seen (I wasn't the only crap driver around)... Only thing was – both of them frozen still... Anton having a sulk couldn't outlast me. (Not that I'd *ever* have a moody – <u>of course</u>).

The shop door beyond them was slightly open but not kicked in. No other sign of damage. That was good – and odd at the same time. If something was wrong...? Some shops were getting the front smashed in, in one way or another, by then. But – if this one was okay... Why...? Only thing different was some fresh spray paint on the door. Graffiti? *What...?*

No sign of anything at all in the whole of the rest of the street. I could see all the way back to where I'd hidden my car and more the other way. There was a crossroads further up but that was well away – I figured a safe distance. (Now I'd ask "safe for what?").

Still they hadn't moved. So I worked my way closer – keeping real low and in against everything that would hide me – not going in a straight line – *and* checking my back *all* the time. I sniffed the air for the least sign, listened in case I could hear gas escaping or anything... Trying to recognise what could be dangerous for me... 'Cos by then I had little doubt about them.

If they were only stoned out-of-their-skulls... That was some shit I did <u>*not*</u> want even a sight of!

I simply couldn't see any problem. Nothing to explain them being frozen still. Couldn't hear a thing either – nor smell... Not a thing that I shouldn't detect – nothing that would have me going to earth or getting-the-hell-outa-there...

I had to focus a lot on the ground around me until I got level with them – right across the street but still in a garden – which had a nice helpful hedge at the front... I was going to chuck some pebbles. Wake them up – get them out of their trance... Saw I'd need a boulder or two to get them sitting up...

Dead? Stone cold... Ummm... Still warm actually... And – dripping – more oozing – from holes in their chests... Not big holes. Shotgun though – close range – very. Not the same as a bullet... I know about that kind of detail now... Could make a good guess then.

I have no idea what happened – other than they got on the wrong end of a shotgun – maybe two. At least it had been quick for them. Straight in the heart. I could see that from the next garden (between parked cars). I stayed still and watched – not them – I knew they weren't going to be anyone's problem – ever... I definitely <u>wasn't</u> going to go leaping around if there was some nutter killing people – and I had no idea where the nutter was.

I didn't look to see if there was any food left in their car. Didn't go near. Didn't break cover at all. While I was thinking about if I should go closer the shop door suddenly moved... Not a lot – but – no doubt enough for someone to peek out... Not quite straight at me – but I couldn't see straight in either...

My arse got back into the concept of pinching tight shut right about then... Heck! That was a *real* improvement!

Then the sudden wind swept across me too...

It can only have taken a moment – seemed like an age... And then the door shifted more – no-one there. No-one I could see anyhow.

So as to play safe I took a whole load longer working my way back to my car... Then I made sure I got away from that place *real* quick.

It angered and saddened me. (Began to get some idea how Greg felt). Main thing it did though was make me look around – *extra* careful. If whoever did it was anywhere near I wanted to see them before they saw me... I got away. Scooted. Real fast... Which was hairy with my driving skills. (None).

Strange thing... I think – maybe...

I kind of felt – indignant – about them being dead... All those people – billions of them... All the people I knew – all gone... And I got major-pissed-off about what had happened to Tamsin and Ozzie... They might have deserved a slap – from a grump like me... They didn't deserve that.

It didn't make me consider looking for a gun of my own though. Not right then. Still didn't sensibly think about me and any weapon – other than what I'd already had. It wasn't deep enough into my brain by then. Despite what I'd seen making me <u>determined</u> to not have that happen to me.

I didn't wonder much about the graffiti... Until – it clicked... It was a tag – a territory mark... I understood that.

That freaking *terrified* me!

People were marking territory? Already? Killing for it?

That near had me wetting myself. Had the eyes popping out of my head for any more marks...

I had to make myself stop. I should know better than to run from one patch straight into another – maybe worse. I knew about moronic trouble though. I knew about fights – even stabbings... Although – no-one I knew of got killed... Shot? Fuck's sake! That was way more than a whole different league!

I had known all sorts of crap... But – small town. The biggest fish would have fit in a goldfish bowl. No shark ever bothered to look our way. (Not that I knew of then).

So, now I did vaguely begin to ask myself... Should I get a gun?

Of course I "<u>should</u>"... Obvious... For real? In England?

Okay... So – where from? Exactly?

Next stop to raid a couple of houses for food I got myself a couple more nasty kitchen knives that I could keep on me without injuring myself.

More than anything I got my eyes open...

So – naturally – I didn't run across anything more like that for days... Which was an almighty relief.

I trashed that car. That was the fault of the ice – not me!

Anyhow – after the Tamsin and Ozzie fright I'd got into snatching essentials and clearing out FAST...

Another car – I couldn't believe the noise smashing through a house porch backwards made... The pedal jumped out from under my (wet) boot – right? Fortunately when I was leaving...

Yeah? So you're supposed to drive out front-first in a forward gear? *Now* you tell me?!

After that I got a real, hard grip on myself and made me take sensible time to get crucial supplies. Take a good look round first. Know the way out. Be set-up for a clear get-away.

What do you absolutely have to have? Then? Can you find it? Find it nice and quick? While your arse is clenching so hard it hurts for the next few days? (Different hurt. I suppose that was some kind of good sign... Didn't feel like it then).

Anyway I stuck with houses – farms and farm buildings were so <u>not</u> good places to go looking around... Those that had, had animals – now had <u>dead</u> animals... No-one to feed and water them. Not everywhere let them out – a lot, probably plain didn't manage to. Once the sickness struck... At the best, you could reckon that they'd only have had a couple of dogs. I did *not* want to see that. That turned me over every time.

It wasn't until later that the business of reliably finding where shotguns were kept safe and opening locks really became important in my thinking... But that is way, way ahead of my story...

Indignant – yeah – that was what I was – still am... All those dead (could be the first time I specifically thought that) and some moron was going around killing healthy people... Well – not entirely healthy – but – they'd got through... That kind of made them special... Sort of... No-one should have just gone and killed them. Not sitting in their car – not doing a thing – other than being there... Makes me mad-angry still...

Doesn't help that I'll never know who did it or why... Those two were never *that* annoying! Okay, probably over a bit of food, probably staking a claim – marking their patch... *Stupid!* *Outrageous!*

How do I know it was shotgun? I know. Right? You still don't know what that looks like? You're damn lucky!

I could have got dead too – if I'd stayed with them.

===========

Box 1
File 3

◆ ◆ ◆

3 – 1

Er... Where was I? I wandered off a bit... (For a change). Was going to say – oh yeah – about a whole new part of my life... I guess that was one part of it...

I know that I was lucky. I did have the advantage of understanding tag signs didn't I? I spotted them easy. Once I woke up and got looking for them...

Yeah, okay, so I got shot at a couple of times... And (helped by what I'd seen) decided to slam into reverse and get-the-fuck-out-of-it a couple of times more...

When I got to see anyone else first – or at least at the same moment – I figured that waiting to see if they were going to shoot was *not* a good idea.

Anyway – I knew from some of my College experience, that even in an extra fast car you don't just run away... It didn't happen to me ('cos I'm not that stupid) but I did know (from people that were) that if you run fast you *might* get away from who's behind you – but you can run slap into worse crap in front... . (*Totalling* a police car never gets you in-good with the law).

So – sometimes – you get out of sight of those chasing you, stop, get out of the way (go sideways if you can) and get your head, arse and everything else down, out of sight – tucked up like a tortoise – with a bit of luck they will go roaring straight by you – intent on catching up.

I do *not* mean skid sideways with the car... Although – that can work – sometimes... Suddenly spinning right round and zooming back the way you came confuses the hell out of people... But that was entirely luck – I hadn't thought of risking it. It *confused* me!

If there actually is trouble up front and you duck-out okay, it'll be them that runs slap into it – sometimes it'll be their own people...

Yeah, yeah – so I'm "unkind"... But when they've been trying to catch you (or whoever) in a trap, it's a whole load better if they take a crack at each other – than you get to be sandwich filling...

Don't get all pleased with yourself, though. If they've not caught you first time there'll be a big chance they'll be pissed-off and put in more effort going for round two... They can easy come around again looking for you.

So – I already knew some principles. Wasn't anything that school had taught me. Nor college... Well – none of it on the official curriculum anyway...

I got into developing fast some better ways to put it into practice... When there was hassle – maybe only potential hassle – I was not now dealing with "nice police officers" that had to make some effort to work by a set of rules...

There had never been that many skanks... And even when I kicked them they weren't in a rush to shoot at me – or get out a blade once I started to get a reputation... I wriggled like a cat that's seen a thermometer – and could scratch and bite at least as much... I could stick a blade in its owner...

I still didn't get round to finding a weapon for me – other than a replacement pin to go with the blades... There was <u>no-way</u> that I wanted to be close enough to <u>any</u> need to use them.

It did make me think that I should have broken into Greg's place and had a look to see what he had – because I'm sure he would have had useful gear tucked away ... He was always organised like that...

But there was no way I could set myself to go back... Whatever I might be running into here, now – I *knew* what was back there... And I simply could not deal with that... Merely hearing his voice on the phone had done me over – and more when I stopped gabbling to him and caught on that it was just the lousy machine...

===========

Well then...

Driving and keep moving on was all very good – but – I had to think about fuel for the car, fuel for me – food and water – keeping clean – not getting injured (no stupid cuts) – probably shelter... Although being in a car – any vehicle – gave me some sort of shelter – if only from the weather – so long as it wasn't too cold. No-way you sat with your engine running for the heat – and much less did you go to sleep like that. Some places that seemed dodgy I didn't risk sleep in the car.

Somewhere, sometime in those first weeks, I did actually hear my first sounds of shooting. Not at me – before that happened – and it was away in the distance. Seems crazy now but I didn't realise what it was at first. It kind-of sounded more like someone popping big bubble wrap... Pop-pop-pop-pop... You know the thing.

The first time, I looked round to see who was messing about. I simply didn't connect the sound with what it was. Gunfire? No way! Not here! Not in my place... *No way in my England.*

It's not the same when it's real. Not the same as the TV or stupid games. Anyhow – it doesn't "belong" in England. At least – it didn't belong in our England – that England... It totally wasn't in your thinking... You'd probably have recognised a call to prayer quicker. Most there ever was, on the Estate and even in the shittier neighbourhoods of town, was air guns... And the law would come screaming out in a mad rush – with a chopper above – if anyone called in that they'd seen one of those. There was no way to connect a sound like a firefight with England – not the England I grew up in anyway...

Yeah, so I'd heard a bit of hunting and a pheasant shoot or two. Nothing like a gun-battle though – and definitely not woken up by it in the middle of a pitch-black night. I knew it wasn't thunder had woken me – and it damn sure wasn't fireworks. Who'd be doing that anyhow?

At least those first times it wasn't near me. That was good. Even better when I finally figured what it was...

Gunfire is different between shotguns and rifles. A firefight and a hunt don't begin to sound the same. We all know that now. And how! Wish I'd known it then... I would have got into going to some farms and finding some weapon – something more useful – a shotgun is way better than nothing...

I did get round to thinking a bit about guns – and – where to get them... Like – *where???* Farmhouses? Maybe... Beyond the dead animal thing though – did you ever wonder which houses in the countryside were actually real farmhouses anymore? Not all the ones with a farmyard were... Could be a better bet to go look in some close by office building.

Some kind of army place? Yeah... I thought of that. Good idea... How exactly was I going to break into one? And get into their stores? Always assuming I found a place... A police station? I spent any time around one of them getting myself *out*. If they had guns I had no idea where they would be... Figured they'd be locked-up extra tight. And Nicks were not the kind of place I was keen to break into... I'd seen what happened to animals that got trapped in barns and couldn't get out... I near had nightmares about the risk of getting trapped inside...

===========

It seems funny to think about it now – ("funny odd" not "funny ha-ha"). Back before, back in the Estate and the village, what was in fact, truly such a quiet life was all so – *usual* – I wouldn't even call it "normal" – nothing so definite... Back then everyone wandered round without a care in the world (mostly with a load of fog in our heads) without imagining anyone else, certainly not them/us/me, carrying any sort of an army gun... We never "took it for granted". It simply never really came into our lives...

Didn't even manage to come into my life knowing Greg and his mates. If I saw anything like that it was on TV or a film – it was always "somewhere else"... Just like the sickness got to be...

Okay, some of the Estate boys – the more stupid ones – carried knives... (Like I was doing now). Some donuts (in town more) talked about other weapons – "shooters" or "tools"... You could tell – the main "tool"/weapon they had was near certainly between their legs – where they did any thinking they did (if any) – and their "ammunition" was probably more of the germ warfare kind... Total arseholes like Sheridan and Carlton.

Yeah, so the skanks sometimes carried blades – except that the law were red hot about that. They'd more often try to have a blade tucked out-of-sight near their stash... But – for those of us that it was any part of our lives – we just knew about it. We knew the signs. We knew where to be careful, where not to go... Or – when we had to go we had our wits about us... Most people never began to guess at any of that... The reality was – they enjoyed being spooked by the cop-shows on the TV.

Thing was – those days – anyone who would seriously have a weapon and, more important, know how to use it – (have got their thinking straight) – was someone like Greg... And; even when he was playing Robot, coolly stepping out of his big, black 4 by 4, you'd never really dream that he would be a soldier...

We had *no idea at all* what a safe, easy and comfortable life we had... *No idea* how much we had to be thankful for... People with guns, especially people actually shooting them, were on the TV. Most of it somewhere-else-on-the-planet.

A few shots some place – some place not "abroad" – was big-headline news – probably an hour long "special programme" with whatever "experts" they could drag in or call up on the internet.

Okay – Greg... To look at him; he'd be maybe some kind of "security", just possibly one of those quiet, never-saying-much (scary-as-all-hell) doormen that did any real sorting of bullshit that needed doing – quietly – and out of sight – when the Fuzz weren't paying attention... (Just happened to be looking the other way).

So... Okay – there was (sometimes) something about Greg... I loved him to bits – love him now... (Never said that before...)

Anyhow... There was so much about him – that was – I don't know? "Playful" maybe? When he rode up to the chippy on one of his bikes... He kind of made a joke of it – play-acted... Except – there was no way you'd ever have thought to try it on... Unless you were stupid like Sheridan... Which (now I think of it...) was seriously odd... He wasn't *that* stupid... Must have been on – cocaine – probably... Firing him up and making him feel invincible – along with a can or three of caffeine and some booze... *Idiot!*

Like I said – no-one ever saw Greg even touch him – and *that* was for real...

Greg had this lovely smile – and his eyes... OH FUCK!

===========

Here again – wiped all the snot and tears away...

So – where was I...? Yeah – back then...

In that world (our world) you simply didn't see weapons. Okay, farmers and a few people had shotguns. Some police had guns – but you didn't often see those unless you were at the airport, some big rail station – or watching the News on TV... Or some drama... There were probably ten times as many guns-with-cops on dramatic TV as you'd ever see in real life...

Even on a Friday or Saturday night you'd most times only see a Tazer – more often a can of spray – or a dog. (You wanted to keep well away from those – if you had a functioning brain cell).

The only place you'd be likely to see any soldier with a gun was up in London at the Palace or anywhere like that – all ceremonial. You'd usually have to look hard around the gates of army bases to see anything as you drove past.

That's all changed.

Now everyone regularly has at least two guns – and any shotguns are usually extra to that – for going hunting – real hunting – to get food to keep you alive... Or to get rid of any wild boar that are making a nuisance of themselves – that need to go into a pie. (Don't ever dream of trying anything less than a 12 gauge).

You see a dog – you *want* the biggest, longest-range rifle you can imagine – KILL the thing before it can get a scent of you.

Then again – you'll probably know that...

Me? Guns? Well – it's like the mall-ninja "SAS" wannabes used to say... "If I told you – I'd have to kill you"... Innit?

There is *totally* NO WAY any future reader is ever going to have any idea at all about the gun laws we used to have... Certification? *For real?* WTF*!?!*

It's "back then" that would be a mystery to any kids that ever get to read this... I wonder? Will that ever happen? Huh! They'll probably think "history lessons" are a pain... Like I did... If they ever get *any* kind of lessons...

Well... I wear armour now, as you know... Trauma plates when I'm "busy" – the whole works. That's simply routine. Even though we aren't at massive risk of anyone attacking us all the time... There's always enough risk – *any* time... And – things I do – I like to keep used to it... Did I mention that before?

We all keep a gun very close to hand...

Guns and everything else... Anyone with any sense keeps it simple and practical. None of that dramatic nonsense! What you load yourself up with at the start of the day is going to be what you carry for the rest of the day.

<u>Keep that in mind!!!</u> Any item that you get so pissed-off with that you dump it – that leaves a marker telling anyone you've been there... Anyway – you don't want to give equipment away for absolutely anyone that happens to find it to use.

So – GET PRACTICAL! GET REAL!

Practical...

First thing – this is England – right? So – <u>***waterproofs!***</u> At <u>least</u> a poncho... England? Yes? So take a sub-aqua kit and it will <u>*not*</u> rain. No way! You'll get a chuffing drought! Go out in a heat-wave with nothing – could hardly do a better rain-dance could you? You'll get snowed on! *Guaranteed!* (No cricket or tennis seasons now though, are there...?)

Wear a gas-mask? You gotta be kidding! Disgusting! Who's going to gas you? It stinks in there! It's hot, sweaty and – wears you out – fast. Anyhow – two things...

1. If it's in the air it's probably got you long before you ever know it – like radiation... And where would you go from that? You'd need to be 100% suited up anyhow.
2. Who's going to bother to try gas on you? What? And piss you off? If they're going to have a go it'll be with the biggest bullet they can send your way. Do the job once and for all – get it done. No arguments.

So – use for a gasmask? Clearing houses is about all... Although most stiffs and their mess, are way-past smelly by now.

Oh yeah – some people's farts... Yeah. You could need a mask for that... While you kick them out the room!

===========

So... Where was I? Oh yeah – then and now... Must have been millions of guns around back then. (The ones we have now didn't suddenly appear by magic did they?) Thing was that, here and in the "civilised" world, they were mostly kept locked away out of sight. We never imagined a world seriously crawling with them. We didn't consciously see them on the news or with all the films and games – they weren't solid in our lives... Incredible now – looking back. The screens put a safe barrier between us and guns. Between us and violence.

Someone told me that there were a hundred million Kalashnikovs... That the Russians alone made more than a million a year. Insane! Think of what else they could have done with all that effort... Then again... I wonder if they had made a similar number of condoms every year... They both did the same job didn't they? Population control.

Surely condoms would have been a lot less hassle?

Gran said that "anti-birth-control" was a military strategy. Make sure you had more cannon-fodder than the opposition... That was why the church and the politicians were so keen on it...

===========

What next...?

Time lost meaning... I know that I got shot at and heard the firefights around then... They probably helped it all get to be a blur... Times I'd rather not remember... Doesn't matter how many times you see the results of a firefight... The first one is (ones are) always a hell of a shock... They stick with you – however much you don't want them to...

After I suppose a total of several weeks of wandering I got together with two couples that seemed okay...

For a start the first meeting began with a "Hello. Who are you?" They sounded horrifically toffee-and-TV-presenter but it beat the hell out of the whiz/snap of a bullet going by.

I was getting the hang of that – fast... Hear it, duck, locate it, where'd it come from? – <u>*BUGGER OFF*</u>... **FAST**.

When I heard it – well, even once I had my first gun, there was no way I was going to play cowboys unless I had to. Logic and arithmetic told me – when I was hearing a load of crap whizzing by – they probably had a whole load more than I did.

I soon began to reckon how far and where shots not directly on me were. Wasn't expert at it – not enough practice – and I did <u>not</u> want *any* practice. <u>*None at all.*</u>

I *so* didn't want any of that crap going on – anywhere. <u>Specially</u> not close enough for me to hear it – not faintly, not even way-upwind on a real quiet night... And everything was so, so quiet all the time then – peculiar quiet.

(Still is insanely quiet – but we've got used to it – more used to it anyhow...)

Anyhow...

Much as I said... These four *seemed* okay. *Duh!* How stupid can I be? Beginning and end of our "association" they were selecting bottles of wine... That's right – "selecting" it. Muppets! Discussing bouquets and what the textures did on their pallets – Donuts! Haydn managed to hold a bottle "just so".

Laughing gave me away. Could have been dangerous of course. (It kind of burst out of me – never made that mistake again...) These two looked about as dangerous as the pair of Thespian Luvvies that "dwelled" in the village though. I didn't expect these two to have partners – female that is. They certainly weren't carrying any kind of weapon – and no-way they'd have wasted a good wine by throwing the bottle at me...

Right, what happened...

I'd sneaked into a big store by my usual kind of discreet way – usual by then – and had no idea there was anyone else about. I *had* made a check.

About the one thing they'd got right was their parking – that at least was out-of-sight. (Big Merc of course).

Once anyone with any sense was in a place, they found what they wanted and got out. That would be – so long as they were sensible... You so did *not* stand around – full view of the front windows – discussing vintages in dulcet murmurs.

Those two Muppets were all "Casual Friday", impeccably shaved – "styled"... Looking back – it's maybe more surprising I didn't find them looking at skin-care products...

Uh! No... We all needed those – certain creams at least...

I'm little. That's *no* reason to begin to imagine that I can't ever be carrying a gun, a blade or any other means of killing or at least injuring you... Was lucky for them that I'd settled in with them before they laughed about my sudden appearance and the fact that they had reckoned I was "only a kid"... GRRR!

When we met I had already picked up some cans (soup probably)...

And I can do a lot of damage hurling one of those... Can't I Richard? (Was how people here got the idea that I'd be a good shot... Another story...)

When we met I held off though. They were no threat... Barely annoying – just – "ludicrous"...

Yeah – and there's a whole load of words in quote marks through this bit... They always did the "thing" with their fingers...

Why did I stop with the couples? (Those two Muppets and their "ladies"). Good question... It probably was crazy – if not stupid...

As if you wouldn't guess that they'd wind me up... It was not so that I could prove to anyone that I could "be good". (Damn! Now I'm doing it!)... Wasn't that – although I did behave exceptionally nicely while I was with them (most of the time).

Thing was, around then, I was knackered. Being on my tod was okay – but I was fed up with moving around and pissed-off with having to look for somewhere every night. Added to that I'd taken to little safety measures – like trip wires and that kind of thing... And that all meant extra effort.

I needed a bit of a break – and figured that being around some people should give me one – maybe... They at least looked more harmless than most. All of them were so into each other, *and* themselves, that they seemed very unlikely to be a risk to me.

The men did have a couple of shotguns. People were starting to find weapons for protection if not hunting by then. The men had them of course... It should have woken me up...

With the gunfire I'd been hearing it was kind-of reassuring. Also I could figure that the break action guns I had caught a sight of were nowhere up to the pump-guns these "dudes" had. Didn't figure that a damn great long thing wasn't exactly the most practical – not for everyday wandering around with... "Absolutely inconvenient in the motor"...

Good grief! The little I knew then!

Those guns were UK Legal. They were probably their own – for "weekend sport"... (Damn! Doing it again! Their fingers were "infectious"...)

I should have seen that practical wasn't exactly a priority in their thinking. Conventional social behaviour was... As with "the way it had been"... Plus – they were *totally* into each other – and their egos. As in "Up their own..." – in *my* "vernacular"...

The four of them had settled in a house ("detached with grounds" naturally) a little way outside some small town. It was a nice place to stop for a bit... A bit like a hotel for me.

They sort-of approved that I would stay. They were kind-of alright with me tagging along when they went out scavenging food and other supplies. They also liked the way I got things done – mainly cleaning and washing up...

In fact I could probably have been their servant for life if I'd wanted. They weren't exactly good at picking up on subtle hints – like putting their food on dirty plates. (Mum's trick).

I guess that "they" keeps describing them – some kind of blob – not individuals... Everything was a group decision, a group activity... Some kind of little orbit of convention and mutual admiration... With me allowed to tag along – but – essentially ignored...

I had no idea how witless they were. Okay – so I have to admit – I was thinking "old world" as well – sort of got sucked into it – a bit at least. They had had good jobs, dressed well ("impeccably"); had all been to university... Had all taken gap years – plus a "Masters" topped by a "Doctorate".

They somehow found tiny ways of letting me know all their "significant" details. They did sound like they had their shit together though. Like they had plans and knew what they were doing... Issue was – a lot of their plans turned out to be for things like finding ways into good fashion shops – for Sophie and Annette...

So... Knowing from the start that they were all pains-in-the-arse Old-Guard style was one thing... Completely witless was a whole matter...

The "ladies" did manage to get the idea and give up on trying to discuss crap like foundation and blusher with me...

Of course – it would have been "so much more helpful" if I'd at least been training in cosmetics or similar useful subject at college... "I absolutely *should* have thought of that"... *Bollocks!* I was catching up!

Once they'd accepted defeat on that bullshit things weren't so bad.

For a time the big persuader for me was that Julian could make some *extra* nice meals... (I was getting back to keeping ordinary food inside me by then...) But, once settled in, the real hook was a nice comfortable bed. Almost the best I've ever slept in.

None of them were stupid enough to suggest that I (probably "the maid" if they'd dared) should eat anywhere except with them.

For a while stopping with them wasn't so bad... Freaky. Entertaining in a way... A glimpse of a whole other world. Half the time I might have looked around for a Reality TV crew... Plus, not having to work out trip wires (fishing line and cans) every night before I bedded down made a good change...

For a time...

Right up until we were in a store collecting up what food there was left – when some other group turned up...

Tell you what I did first... I got right into the *now*, got my skinny arse out of sight and confirmed where there was a back way out.

What did they do? All of them? Stood up straight and said "Hi!"

Me? First shots – a whole roaring load of them – I was gone – keeping low. Sorry – but I was *not* hanging around to find out whether that was a warning or what. I "got out of Dodge" – FAST. (AKA "Buggered off").

You could say that it kind of made my mind up... I'd been on the edge of leaving for a week or more – just not actually deciding to shift my butt.

Truth is – I have no idea what happened to them – whether they got shot or not. I plain got out of there as quick as I could. *Maybe* they were only warning shots?

Wasn't so far from where we were staying so I got there *sharp*, grabbed my belongings and got on my way. I'd seen enough. I was not risking my neck with idiots who were that stupid.

This life isn't about interior design, successful careers and achieving promotions – it's about *not* getting *dead*.

I didn't have a gun then and there wasn't a thing I could do – I just knew that I was absolutely *not* into any chance of anyone shooting at me.

===========

If they were so clued-up and so clever – how come only two of them had any kind of weapon? How come, when they were so "intelligent" they'd left one at home and one in the car? (Never let on to them I had my rolling-pin and the knives and was thinking about a gun – I can't imagine what kind of "frightful shock" that would have been to them). *[As in "can't be arsed to imagine"]*

Things could be like that though... In reality all that they were doing was carrying on as before... Sticking with what they knew. In a way the fact that they did have guns with them was the unusual thing. By that stage hardly anyone had got round to the idea of carrying all the time.

Except that a few of the nastier survivors had got into it all too quick...

I wouldn't dream of stereotyping of course... But – the nastier ones tended to be those that grabbed all they possibly could (or more) and got into marking their turf right from the start...

Nice people took longer to wake up to reality...

So – that means I must be nice – doesn't it?

===========

3 – 2

The fact is that I was like most people – only beginning to slowly wake up to what was going on... I still had a whole ton of learning to do of course.

I'd begun to get some ideas so the next house I "lodged" in was okay – no smells – no flies – no stiffs – no car outside. *So* – no reason for anyone else to break in to get keys to take it away...

Which someone did to the house next door... Infuriating! I liked the look of that car and was thinking of taking it myself... Except that it reached the end of the road and ran out of fuel... So they came back – not looking very happy... But, like I said, my place had no car – so they tried next door the other side.

Must have thought to look at the gauge (at least I already knew to always do that by then) so they kicked that car and moved on. About four houses down they found one they liked and tore off into the distance.

Yeah, yeah... So the car I arrived in, that I'd parked along the road a bit, died... Wouldn't start... I'd killed the battery with keep starting it up after I ran out of petrol... That's something *else* you tell me about now!

That house had a good pile of sensible food – canned – dried – preserved – and rice. Looked like someone had appreciated things were going wrong a bit quicker than most people and put away a bit of a reserve – including salt... I'd not thought about that before. It wasn't a big "survivalist" cache but at least a good stack of basics... And then – for some reason – they'd not been there to use it. Wasn't a sign of a soul anywhere.

Turns out that all that "Survivalist" preparation depends on a whole bunch more than your being right with your kit or able to get to it fast when the shit hits the fan... To do that you've got to survive the first impact... Then you've got to want to keep going... All that and if you've achieved a large cache, you need to stay and be able-to-stay where it is... That might not be practical – it might not be safe. All real technical matters...

The place was good for me though. So I kept quiet, low and very discreet – and tried to figure out where people got guns from...

All those games had whole army loads of everything you could think of – which I <u>always</u> thought was absurd... I sure did then when I couldn't figure out what I could get; or from where. I had at least worked it out that none of the big stores would be open for a while – and I <u>knew</u> I had never seen "AKs" or "M16s" (whatever they were) on their shelves.

Somehow I'd lost interest in the fashion section and the cosmetics...

Oh yeah – I slipped over a few times outside – I forgot to say – it snowed again quite a bit about then... One of those late flips of the weather. Of course that made it even quieter... Like so you didn't hear anything – if there was anything – moving about.

It meant that someone suddenly appeared one morning, looking at all the house fronts, when I was stood right in the window where he couldn't do a thing but see me if he turned around my way... Stunning – but – I didn't hit myself diving out of sight...

Then I thought – "footprints" and "*Oh shit!*"

Turned out it had snowed again in the night – so he kept going – barely began to glance behind him at my place...

I don't think I heard a shot any time that morning – or that day... But when I went the way he'd gone some days later he'd blown his brains out – right in the middle of the street.

So I got my first gun – and two whole bullets...

I've sometimes wondered – what if I'd let him know I was there? Of course – he might as likely have shot me... You can never know.

Anyway. A gun (a revolver) and a couple of bullets, was better than nothing... So long as I ignored that the whole idea *totally* freaked me out... *What-the-hell* was I doing with a gun? What would – what *could* I do with it?

Yeah, yeah. "Shoot people"... Like that's *so* easy – sat in your nice warm house, on a soft couch with your mates, a few beers – and a screen in front of you...

Different matter when it's for real...

Different matter when it's hard metal weighing in your hand.

Then I thought of Greg again... I had a bit of another cry...

I was "stressed". *Okay?*

College did not have a 101 in "Emotional Response to a Suicide".

Anyhow – I got serious and thought about things Greg had told me – ideas he'd – planted... I decided it was time to get serious...

Which I did. Right on the doorstep in front of the wide open door – when I came round – on the ice – the gutter had peed all over the step...

I was <u>not</u> a happy bunny!

===========

Once I'd got myself inside, the thing I did – fast – was take an extra careful look at how the gun worked – and "made it safe".

There was no way I wanted to turn up at any Heavenly Gates to find Greg there waiting to give me an almighty bollocking for stupidly shooting myself.

Two bullets? Six holes (chambers?) I made damn sure that the bullets were down the bottom as far away from the barrel and the hammer as I could. (Including maintaining the discipline, after I'd figured out the safety).

Cleaning caked blood off wasn't easy. (You want to know how someone shoots themselves and gets blood all over the gun? Ask someone else!) Kitchen gloves made prising the bullets and the used empty out difficult, on top of disgusting... But I sorted it – and found some sewing machine oil and a bit of cloth to clean it all up thoroughly.

I felt pretty pleased with myself. I reckoned that Greg would have approved. So I cried my eyes out some more and didn't touch the gun again for a day or two.

Hey! Don't even think of getting smart at me! I got my head round it. First off I cleaned it, then I made it safe and right from then on I kept it safe... That was a whole load better than anything I'd seen up to then.

Okay, so I'm not going to jump way ahead of myself – but I'll tell you this... Not firing a gun – except when you really have to – is a far greater "skill" than letting rip any-old-how. Totally better than a moronic "accidental discharge" – even one that misses.

I didn't think to go to the body again to see if there were any more bullets. I hadn't taken a look at his backpack – which (to be fair to me) was all splattered with yeuky goop. (Probably brain). I'd only got the gun by prising it away with a stick and lifting it with a bit of bent wire... That was more than disgusting enough. Truth was, also – I didn't want to find a name – or do anything that made it (him) more real to me... I was massively shaken-up... *How* could anyone do that?

Didn't want to think about it... Still don't.

I would "police up" every single thing now though – regardless... It's become habit – necessary – routine... When working we carry loads of disposable nitrile gloves and face masks – just routine... Hopefully the main need will run out before the supply does...

So – I didn't have any protective stuff with me at the body... The pack was totally gucked anyhow... My street-cred tough-bullshit taught me to just not take risks – not get myself messed...

All this sort of thing changes your life. Changes how you think – and how you act...

I'm different now.

===========

3 – 3

Moving on from that first place was *everything* but easy. Wasn't better or worse than leaving Cathy's – just different. Thing was – there were never any clear answers.

Now I was being serious, the question was – what to do next – what to do first...

So... Do what Greg always told me... Don't try and keep it all whizzing round in my head – write it down. Don't bother about order, don't try to get it "right" – just get it written. Give my brain a rest – and then sort it. Make it stay still and then shuffle it into order...

Why don't they teach that in schools – or at least colleges? Why so much theoretical, "academic" waffle and not more useful, practical and everyday stuff? What's the use of a whole load of complicated maths when what you really need to know is how to get a bank account – and how to manage your money? At least – that was what you really needed – back then. Like I've said – what you need to count now – is how many bullets...

Time for a rant!

Just because the teachers have it all laid out in their heads – probably using only a book someone else did hours or days of work on – why'd they assume that spouting it all at the kids will make it obvious and easy for them to pick up in minutes? They don't even try to connect it to any real, useful purpose.

Why did *I* need "trigonometry"?

Okay... So it is pretty useful now – for some of us – to get the range of bigger guns right. To not shoot our own people in a battle...

Think about it... That's why "universal education" suddenly got to be so important, why learning went from being the private privilege of the elite to "free" (paid for by taxing everyone) to compulsory – to constant pressure to do better... To endlessly testing kids...

Kids aren't computers – regardless of how much you want them to tick boxes with digital-correct answers for your statistics. Humans are different – every single one wired differently, uniquely, inside. If they ever started out programmed the same that all got jumbled up... They don't have the same settings for survival – and half (at least) of what modern "Western" kids had, or might have had, got lost under a whole stack of other trash – probably generation loads of it...

Kids are NOT robots! Governments and the military would like them to be – but the Education Ministers would spend billions on their latest fad – aka "initiative" – go way, way over budget and then have to abandon the whole thing – because they'd loused up the original idea... Which anyone with a gram of sense could have told them from the start. Or the know-it-all "experts" would quickly switch to a better "concept" before the last one had got off the ground anyway...

Silly question of course. School and college didn't want us to actually understand anything – only get the right answers – in the right order – quick as possible. Pretty much like old style drilling conscripts to all jump the same way at the same time... Just memorise the lists – do it – tick the boxes – get the grades – meet their targets – and bugger off... Bleep, Whirr. Bleep, Whirr. Bleep, Whirr. Bleep, Whirr.

Wasn't all like that... I'm told. But I know for sure that I wasn't the only one who "slipped through the net" – and it wasn't only my fault – maybe they should have designed things a bit differently?

They said they wanted "innovation" and all that Dragon Entrepreneurship to make the country rich – but you're not going to get that out of squishing everyone with the same jelly-mould are you?

You take a whole load of super-successful people – such as Mr Churchill... No-one rated what they "achieved" in school did they? They said that no-one trusted him, he was "an adventurer"... I wonder if any government/ political test would have won us the war?

Stupid government departments rejected things like the jet engine. If they kept having to improve the education system because it "wasn't fit for purpose"... Why didn't they change the clowns that had come up with the last scheme? If they kept screwing up how did anyone *ever* expect them to get it right with the next "initiative"? Why didn't anyone tell them to "Sod off!"?

"If it ain't broke – don't poke"... But if the poking person isn't fixing it... Get a new mechanic... Or go back to the way that did work before.

So there we have today's rant – inspired by Greg...

And his ideas got me through... Don't know what school or college ones did – but then – they taught us to pass their exams in their system not how to survive didn't they? Didn't manage to teach us how to fit in and get along in the practical workplace did they? All their "prepositions" and "calculus" waffle was sod-all use for picking from warehouse shelves or working an assembly line... They did sod-all for "customer care".

I keep on saying – we need practical skills. Like patience and persistence.

Alright – so I'll admit... Not shooting ourselves is an extremely useful, practical skill...

===========

The thing to do first then (after listing everything) was get enough petrol for one car. At least I knew that some run on diesel.

They don't teach you helpful little things like that either do they? Nor what happens when you get it wrong – like the woman who lived opposite on the Estate found out – her husband (rotten git) went frenzied at her...

Anyhow – I worked out how to get the fuel out of each car along the road into a can and get it into the one I'd decided I'd take... None of which is as easy as it sounds – and diesel tastes different from petrol – different *disgusting* that is. You do *not* want it up your nose! It's best washed off quick as well. *Do not* leave it on your clothes! Some people have horrible scars – that's the ones that didn't get themselves totally fried the next time they lit a fag, a stove or a fire...

Filling up the car took me days – creeping around, staying as out-of-sight as I could... Because I did figure that no-one would want me grabbing petrol but anyone probably wouldn't mind taking any I'd put together... Didn't want to put it all in the one car at first (was getting a bit wise by then) – but had nowhere to store and hide it – not safely – and I'd seen a car go up in flames a couple of times before – before "it".

In between swilling doses of petrol out my nose I worked out some safer ways into houses to collect up any food that would keep – mostly canned and dried supplies. When my guts improved and I experimented, it amazed me how enormously the departure of a single cabbage stood out – even in the middle of a patch. Pulling up a few carrots seemed to make a minor volcano rather than a molehill.

Difficulty was (as you probably learned) you can't know what food you'll find in any house from the outside any more than you can make a wild guess at how much fuel a car's got in it. Or what the fuel is...

So many cars, there's no way of knowing what they use – unless you take the lid off and check the tank... I tried looking under a couple of bonnets... Fat lot of good that was! All that junk wedged in there... Might as well have been an alien spaceship.

Do NOT say "that's because I'm a girl"... I'd challenge any man to know what the hell any engine is from a fast look – because you aren't going to be hanging around to ask the neighbours... Not unless you're *mega*-stupid!

Having a few doses of "hydro-carbons" up your (already knackered from puking your guts up) nose doesn't make identifying fuel any easier either.

One good thing about the petrol, though, was that it did help to stop me smelling the stiffs and mess in the houses so much – except that could mean I would walk into a room and find one... So I tried as much as I could to only go into kitchens. They weren't usually too bad...

Except that was where the dogs had often lived – and died... Somehow that got to me worse than people – dead ones... The smell was often worse for a start.

The vile thing... That confirmed to me why I'd not seen anything of Bodger.

And that made me weep – for ages. Stoopid – but...

Gramps said one time that we'd all become used to dead people – immune to seeing them. They were always on the TV, always in the news – but – for some reason animals had got to being different in our thinking – or our emotions... Someone invented a word – "furbabies"... He said (he was right of course) that it was insane when you thought how many animals we bred in order to kill them and eat them – or plain ripped out of the sea... Yet he wasn't a veggie – and couldn't figure out how anyone ever managed to be a vegan...

I worked out that I should get camping gear – a couple of fresh sleeping bags, a cooking stove (and gas), bed roll and more clothes – and weatherproofs.

Finding any clothes that fit me wasn't merely a problem – it was horrible... Meant going – well – you figure it...

It was bad enough being small before but I'd kind of shrunk... I was almost looking for kid's sizes... Did a lot more of having to control my retch-reflex – trying to at least – and crying...

I figured out fast that, soon as I found anywhere with the right sizes, I grabbed a whole load at once. For one thing – washing and drying got to be a bigger pain-in-the-butt than ever.

You weren't going to hang out a load of washing on a line like a set of signal flags or bunting were you... Were you? You're that...

I did see stupid things like that though – I guess it took some people longer to wise up than others... Different kind of education wasn't it?.

But at least any gagging and chucking up I did do then was the proper kind – not the sickness again... In the end I suppose I got hardened to it. I got good at keeping it quiet at least. Wasn't nice – but you can't spend all day...

So I toughened up. Everyone did I reckon – else they topped themselves... That could give you some nasty surprises...

Oh yeah – when I was organising moving on from that house I made sure I got the keys for the car I wanted before I filled it up. Learnt that from Git Opposite as well... Because he was always losing his keys – and blaming her of course... Was also "her fault" when the battery went flat – when *he* left the lights on all night (saw him do it – wasn't going to go anywhere near to tell them. What? And get yelled at for "thanks"?)

Anyway... I had my own recent "experience" with a battery didn't I? It meant I checked that the car I was filling up would start and ran it a bit every other day when things looked and sounded not too quiet – preferably blowing half a gale or tipping with rain – to cover the engine noise – and get rid of the exhaust.

I did wonder if I should get a spare battery out of another car... But I didn't have a clue how to tell if it would be any good... And then I recalled – just in time – that disconnecting a battery could set an alarm off... I no-way wanted to announce my presence like that!

On the other hand... The quiet was driving me nuts... So in the house I'd play music – quietly. I always loved dancing – so I raided an ordinary battery player and I boogied and bopped a bit more each day to start to build a little bit of fitness again... Because the sickness thoroughly beat me up. (As if you wouldn't know). I wasn't as bad as a load of people – but it was more than bad enough for me.

Then I was practically ready to go...

===========

"Practically ready" was one thing... Ready-in-my-head...? A whole different thing.

Question was... Same again... *Where* to go?

So I spent a few days double checking everything, making sure – putting off moving... "Reasoning" that I shouldn't "just run"... Brilliant bit of logic that was! Wasn't it?!

I couldn't go back. I *did* know which way to head. I'm not *that* stupid! I could read a proper map a bit once I'd found one (guess who'd shown me). At least I could get one the right way up... Working out where I was on it (when it didn't have street names) was – um – a bit more of a problem...

I could figure out where towns were though. That was a start... And I knew what town I was in by the council labels on the wheelie bins.

Neat huh? I'm not so "thick" am I?

There have just been so many towns since then that I've no idea now, which one that was...

One stunning thing, though... Later, on my wanderings, I saw the Spicer's car at the traffic lights – and I'd not put any dents in it – hadn't even knocked a mirror off... I'd gone all that way and not bashed a thing... Pity I didn't keep that up... Some ratbag had robbed my gloves!

But – going back to the village... The Estate – Home... What to? I already *knew* what was back there... And in my head I was stuck – due to how, by then, I could easily guess what would be – absolutely anywhere else...

You can't imagine something like that... Well – I suppose people could now... Couldn't have done back – before...

===========

One thing no-one had ever seemed to say – leastways not that I can recall – nor anyone else can... You don't only get stuck with just one all-out-enormous apocalypse thingy, disaster...

The sodding things keep coming...

It's not like a movie. It's not an exciting ride to a climax – all done and dusted in ninety minutes – a couple of hours at most...

Get to a happy ending with uplifting music running with the credits...? Me? I'll settle for a good sleep any time.

Look for a sequel? Find a new (thrilling) angle? Like buggery!

The thing you get to hope for is that you'll work out fast how to spot "excitement" coming... So's you can get some place else – *ASAP!*

So, alright, I could figure the regular electric would go off – made easy by the cuts we used to get. Greg had taught me about safe water. (I got water purifying tabs and clean containers with the camping gear). But – there was never a clue about how you'll keep on finding bodies – then more bodies – least of all how they rot – and the flies – worse – the maggots... YEUCH! And a whole corpse full of them!!! Even the empty husks... NAUSEATING!

Then there's the weather – and no weather forecast... Didn't mind no "News" – same "items" sixteen times a day – or more... But weather *does* matter – 'specially if you ride a bike...

You do *not* ever want a wet arse! Not now – not "back then". When I got to college and had a whole day ahead to sit on it. Neither did I need some smart-arse pillock in the canteen make comments... (Was where I got some of my "added" reputation from – I "imagine"). So? A cold wet bum is bad enough... Okay – probably not worse than near scalding bollocks... And that cost me another coffee from the machine... I still say he should have paid for it! You want to dry my backside – give me a towel!

These days? Wet clothes chafe... You probably know that.

The power failed – not always so long after the net and phones crashed... We had plenty of cuts before we all got sick... The power fails... You can see that coming... Well – we (aka "I") *should* have done... Wasn't exactly at my best at the time was I?

Then, when you've sorted the water – you have to deal with food – and rotting food that's contaminated what you might otherwise have used... And medicines to find – any kind of medicines – anti-hay-fever – or for a horrible cough...

Worst? Most bother of all? You'd probably guess this one – *people*... Unreasonable people, stupid people, selfish people – and people that mean to be helpful... Even nice people...

But no – they're not the *worst* thing – and it's *not* zombies. (What a joke!)...

Worst thing... ***It goes on***... Day after day after day...

It's totally nuts – but – you plain don't see that coming...

Like your first day at school or in a new job... You don't begin to think that this is how it's going to be – for days – weeks – months – years... This, or days very like it – is going to be how it is – unless you can come up with a way, make an effort – and take steps to break out – to make it different... *That* is the tough part – simply realising the idea in the first place...

Then all you've got to do is – start to do it...

You wake up day-after-day-after-day and each day you just know where you are and what's going on – what has happened... Probably what's going to happen – today – and tomorrow...

Beyond the great big event it's worse than the early days when you woke up and couldn't figure out "WTF?"

Even when you've worked out "TF" you can have some hope... Probably that someone – like the army or whoever official – will come and sort it all out. Someone at least will come and tell you that it's all going to be alright and what to do...

That is so not what happened...

Where anyone did start giving out orders, that frequently created a whole different heap of troubles... Like jumping from one school or job to another – there was never any guarantee that the next place wasn't going to be worse – or just more of the same old crap.

In the end... It comes down to – you have to win some sort of mental battle for yourself... You have to decide "So – okay – this is *total crap* – but I've got to simply get on with it..." Now – today – and – tomorrow... Ultimately, we have to make our own decisions, act on them – and follow up by living with it... Just keep on going.

===========

Crap you'd never guess at... (Never saw it in the movies even)... Rats, mice – and cats – got hungry – got *very* hungry – got aggressive. Sudden massive drop in human activity? Equals sudden fall in easy food supply – for all of them. Yeah – even the lubbely-pussy-catty-cats. (Buggers!)

That made us all change our perspectives didn't it?! And some!!

Some reason it took ages to wake up to the evidence that there were no foxes... Was all-too-much proof of what had happened to pet dogs – lying around the kitchens – rotting...

So rats especially had been getting bigger and more confident for a long time... They wouldn't usually stand their ground aggressively though – and I don't think I ever heard of one attacking...

Right – so it could be true that they (some of them) got a taste for human flesh... I am *so <u>not</u>* going there! The stiffs lying around were bad enough to step over – I was <u>not</u> stopping to study them!

[Anyone wants to make a smart crack about now – I <u>will</u> whack them!]

That wasn't bad enough? Seagulls. E-normous BIG bastards. You were outside with any open food – **BAM!** Out of nowhere you'd get hit. Anywhere, anytime – except it was *really* dark. (One good thing about the street lights going off...)

They'd grab everything – including other birds. Even a rat. Some people say rabbits. Anything mouse size didn't stand a chance – was hardly a beak full was it? Never saw a cat taken – but I heard one hellish yowl one time... I kept out of sight.

The gulls would attack a person. Serious. There are a few people with a rip out of their head or arm. (You have to most-carefully watch-out for infection if that happens... The damn bird's been eating rat... Go figure...)

We'd happily ignored them spreading over every rubbish tip and seaside resort for years and years. Multiplying. Raiding. Way more than pigeons – and more than the crows, magpies and the rest that farmers weren't shooting any more. ("Mustn't be nasty to nature").

The "end of the world" stopped the dump supply didn't it? Ended the road kill. (Mostly). Stopped the chips and burgers too. <u>Didn't</u> stop the rotten gulls being hungry.

Freaked the life out of me the first times I got "Stuka'd". **WHAM!** Didn't know what it was. I learnt fast to <u>carefully</u> cover every bit of food when coming out of any place. They'd knock a placcy bag right out of your arms – and then have a go at you to force you to back off. Aggressive? *Fucking evil!*

Other birds – crows mainly – could be bad – but nothing was like the gulls. Soon as anyone had a shotgun, plenty of shells and a safe(ish) territory we blasted away at the bastards like there was no tomorrow. We still do!

Just hear the cry "Gull!" and there'll be more lead flying skyward than you ever saw in some Middle East victory celebration on the TV News. We go nuts!

(*Watch out!* What goes up – comes down!)

The bastards even learned the different look between someone with a shotgun and a rifle – learned fast. At least – the ones that saw their mates blown-to-bits did. Humans the only "intelligent" species? Yeah... Right...

Me? I've gotten to be a good shot – I can get them with near any gun – that has the range – including when they're dive bombing. Disintegrating gull is a wonderful sight! **BOOM!**

===========

Meanwhile, way back then; farting around getting up courage to move on from the house... What got me off my (warm-dry) arse?

I was returning from another exploration (aka "excuse") when a Big 4x4 with gun-toting men in the back came cruising down the street. They came quiet – I almost didn't hear them... Except one of them laughed – and it didn't sound like a good joke...

I got down flat just in time – and under a car (which is a lot harder than a van – good job I was so thin)... Watched their wheels go by – never saw wheels turn so slow – thought they were stopping – that they must have heard my heart.

There was one thing school had taught me though – don't just stand up and show up as soon as the bullies/teachers have gone away. I was *very* careful about how I came out and took a look after them.

I only clearly saw two – in the back of the pickup. I reckon (now) that they had shotguns – and I know that they didn't have a clue what they were doing with them – so much they were dangerous – to everyone – themselves included. (That was far too much the way people were... Still can be...)

Soon as I felt sure it was okay I did a quick, *quiet* retreat into my house... That involved not kicking around some convenient litter I had outside so that anyone creeping up would make a good clatter unless they were extra careful.

Once inside I quickly checked where all my prepared bags were put ready.

Those men had me freaking. I *mega* didn't like the sound of them – more than the glimpse I'd had. Meant I was very glad I was inside again when they came rolling slowly back down the street – stopping and looking around. I figured that they'd got some sense or information that someone was around. Could be that my activity was attracting cat or bird action and they'd spotted that. I was *not* putting the bins out! Anyhow, as far as I knew any sign of life they might be looking for would only be me... So it was time to move on.

When I was sure they'd definitely left after their third pass I quickly and quietly got my bags into the car...

And...

Bugger me! It didn't want to start!

I bricked myself! Imagined for a second they were coming around again... Then it started... I didn't know whether to cry or get out and kick it...

I cried anyway – 'cos kicking a car hurts your foot.

And falling over into a rose bush doesn't help. (Thought they'd invented ones without spikes. Was *so* wrong. Evidently).

So – after a bit of chaos and yelling curses (quietly)... Where to go? Not after them – wouldn't want to catch up – plus, they might come back.

The opposite way? Was where they'd come from – so – maybe they lived that way – maybe with others?

I didn't know!

Very logically – I went the other way – as far as the first road and turned right.

Then, after I got myself out of the dead end...

When you're a little kid and they say your brain sucks up lots of new ideas – like languages – why don't they teach you the language of road signs then?

They don't usually teach you that numbers and arithmetic and all that are simply languages – for – er – numbers and what numbers do... They just expect you to "get it"... I suppose that's because they've "got it"... Which doesn't actually mean that <u>they</u> understand any of it... That was (possibly) my trouble... I wanted to be able to see what was going on... Got my head round the arithmetic at least when Greg showed me... If I was so rubbish at it before – why didn't...?

Oops! Kicking off again...

Whatever...

I suppose – well – I could have not just accepted that I was "thick"... But – no-one told me that that wasn't what was real either – until Greg...

Yeah-so I was ashamed of being so dense. Who isn't? Was I ever going to go and ask anyone about it? What kid – what adult even – is ever anything but defensive about it?

My family did care... Truth was that I'd explode at them – not just at teachers and anyone else – everyone else...

How was Greg different? He kicked off about school, people, "the system" and all sorts. He never let me call myself anything negative. Wouldn't let me say I couldn't do anything unless I showed him that I really couldn't do it – and still couldn't do it when he'd shown me some other ways of looking at it... He could be a TOTAL pain-in-the-arse! Wouldn't even let me slip around something and pretend it didn't exist. He drove me NUTS! Sometimes... But – he always "bothered".

Plus – he'd come back on a subject and check how I was getting on... I have a suspicion that he somehow had Bodger reporting back on me...

Greg said this thing about "poxey schools – teach kids to fail"... Get him on a bad day (or maybe that should be called a "good day") – and he'd really kick off about it.

He had me read the famous "All Quiet" about the First War – well, he showed me the bit at the start where they're all still at school and brain-washed into being mad keen to be soldiers... I kind of got into it from there... Scary book – when you thought about all it said. Good author though – not stories you usually see – and they don't teach in schools... (Like bordellos and concentration camps – from the inside – and political not only Jewish).

So – all the Nazi thing was bad – diabolical – but – how'd you get that way? You terrorise the whole population first. That's how. You tell them how right you are, and <u>only</u> you are, and about all the dreadful threats around them. Tell them that only "their" strong government can protect them. (The one that got a mandate through less than fifty percent of the votes cast...) *That's* how. You get everybody too fearful to object to anything... You start small – fining parents if their kids are out of school, constantly testing kids and finding their schools "failing" (instead of ever mentioning any achievements). You have the media constantly droning on about problems and – better still – crises... All that before you build things up. You get them ticking all the right boxes and not asking questions... Just like... Guess...

To be honest – what truly got me started reading "All Quiet" was the real beginning – the bit they'd have skipped over in school... It starts with the guys sitting around in the sunshine playing cards – and taking a dump

– enjoying being safe out of the trenches... I thought – well – I thought it was a bit disgusting (potty trained aren't I)... But – well – it painted a picture – it made sense... And it was kind-of crazy...

Was like Gran playing me Dean Martin "Little Old Wine Drinker" and Gramps with Thorogood's music... We got chased by the police for playing that so LOUD! That's a real GOOD memory... The van was *rocking!* CRAZY!!! Couldn't hear their siren could we? ZZ Top too... GOOD TIMES! YEAH!!

Gramps taught me about drinking... When I was eight or nine... Before I took myself into dangerous places. He and Gran reckoned that all kids needed to learn a whole load of "off the curriculum" matters – well before the hormones started kicking in.

Never got a government/political test on any of that practical stuff did I?

Gramps reckoned we should get our heads straight about booze like the Europeans do – mostly... Wine is supposed to be enjoyed – not make you sick with a blinding headache... Anything you can't recall is a waste!

Wish I'd talked to him about how crap I felt about school and being useless... But I was so humiliated by it. Lousy school did that to me! *Fuck it!*

Greg put some sense into how I felt about things – showed me that it wasn't just me and I wasn't bad, different or stoopid. Greg started me looking at the world differently...

I'm pretty much a success now.

Sounds wrong – but – I survived didn't I? All their "knowledge" and "right answers" – what did that do for them? All their status – and all their qualifications – proved no use to them did it? Including some of those that survived the sickness... When they couldn't get a grasp of things – the way things are now – they fell apart. Many of them didn't make it through the next bit...

Some ways that "next bit" was worse than the sickness...

===========

Then again – once you do know what the road signs mean – it seriously helps if you read them... I did get good at quick three-point-turns though. I got into working out how to shift into "reverse" as soon as I switched to a new car any time... It's almost as important as learning the feel of the clutch and the brakes... See! I do know what all the things are called!

Before this all started I'd hardly completed my very first lessons had I? I was concentrating on not hitting things – and, when it's all new, the road seems to come at the tip of the bonnet really, really fast. (On those cars you can even see the front). It's not fun! But it got easier – especially when I got out into the country a bit. Thank God (or whatever) Mum refused to pay for lessons on an automatic! I'd have been screwed!

Few times I got a lift from one of the college boys – usually showing off when they said they'd passed their test – which you couldn't always believe – I spent most of my time with my eyes shut. Why do boys think that they're all racing car or rally drivers?

I suppose it's the same that more than three quarters of them think they're the world's greatest lovers...

Okay – I've got to laugh; because I know what Greg's answer would be. He'd say it was because they believed the DVD's and the games. Believed that if they acted the same way they could all be heroes...

So I was supposed to "Ooh and Aaah" like some actor in a film? Might have done if the boys had been so well toned – and had such big dicks... Probably a bigger chance if they'd known what to do with them – better – a *whole* lot better!

I knew better than they did! Pity they had no idea what to do with me... There are two people in a shag boys! Not just you and your dick!

And... And... *Oh! What's the point!?*

Mum said that she blamed the Mothers... Not sure that I've figured that... But – I did used to see that the Mum's definitely discriminated – girls were still supposed to be "good" while the boys could get away with all sorts... And they *still* got told not to be a "girl" if they got upset and cried – although that was well into being the fashion...

So – anyway – I was driving – missing things (mostly). Wasn't hitting enough to leave a trail that could be followed anyway... And I never crashed into so much... Rolling it – *doesn't* count. Hitting a cow (that shouldn't be in the middle of the road anyway) is 50/50. Did learn that potholes meant that I did always have to keep my hands on the wheel...

So – after I had moved on a bit from the house and bashed-up that car, I decided to get a bigger one. So that I would see the front of the bonnet – and that would come out of a crash a bit better – at least if I only hit small things...

I knew not to go for something too big. (Car! Not "target"!) Nothing that would use too much petrol. I *hate* the taste of diesel far more – so I wasn't going for one of those...

Got some sort of sporty SUV thing... I actually thought it looked good... (Amazing!) And it was powerful...

I shit myself! *Wasn't funny!* It went off like a rocket... Managed to miss everything though... And I didn't want to shift my load again – as it had a full tank... So I cleaned up – chucked the seat cover out. That was a bit of luck. I switched the one from the passenger seat to the driver's – just in case...

That car was dark green. I reckoned it wouldn't show up as much in the countryside... Figured I was being a bit smart...

So then I drove into fields with loads of lovely yellow crops... Genius!

I thought that I'd gone quite a way from the house by then – maybe I'd looped around a bit... Not sure. I wasn't aiming anywhere – just wandering. I'd got a map book – but I wasn't looking at it. I didn't see any point. (Being a bit "male" there wasn't I???)

Anyhow – bends, hedges, parked cars – all sorts of obstacles – sneak up on you if you look at a map – even for a moment...

Wherever I'd got to... I got a real, nasty, shock when I thought that I saw the front of some kind of big pickup way down a road to one side. Thing was – it was the same colour as the one before. Yeah, yeah... I noticed the colour – not the make or the engine size... Anyway – I'd seen it... I wasn't interested in details or what stupid things three-little-boys on repeat-repeat-repeat-TV could say about it.

Told myself that there were probably loads and loads of them made – and painted that colour... Like the one I saw closer a bit later – on a parallel road... Moving – men in the back... Uh – right...

No idea if it was because I was there anyway or if my car did stand out – but in no time I had some bunch of crazy nutters chasing after me. They suddenly seemed to come out of nowhere – hooting and flashing lights as they raced up behind me.

Maybe they were trying to catch up to see who I was? Maybe they wanted to help me?

Who knows? Thing was – they had guns – I'm sure of that – even if they were only shotguns... They were all big, noisy men... I don't think they shot at me... I wasn't hanging around to find out was I? It was so not a fresh bit of excitement fun. *It was sodding frightening!*

I wasn't hanging around to see if they wanted to tell me a brake light wasn't working. I got-the-fuck-out-of-there – QUICK!

I'll tell all the "grand theft" geeks one thing... You can learn to drive fast and hard for real a whole lot quicker when someone is chasing you for real – and you know there's no start again if you "game over".

They "game-overed". No idea if it was the pick-up I'd seen before – but it had much the same two men sticking up behind the cab with what looked far too much like large guns. That was more than I needed to make a damn quick decision...

And *no* I *didn't* notice the reg plates to know if it was the exact same one... But it was bigger than me – coming fast and looking terrifying. Only sensible thing to do was to flee – *fast.* Fast as I could – dangerously *fast...*

I hardly managed to stay on the road – and whoever the driver was – he didn't make it round the sudden bend... Don't know what happened – I was too busy wrenching mine round the next one... But there was another *massive* bang – sounded awful – and when the road straightened out again there was no sign of them at all...

So I slung out that seat cover and went to find some nice green woods to hide in for the rest of the day. Was a bit difficult checking I wasn't being followed with no mirrors on the outside – but I'd thoroughly learnt the importance of using any mirrors I (still) had – way more than my previous trip into the ditch had taught me that it's so much better to stay down the middle.

===========

3 – 4

Had the life scared out of me by a squirrel next. (Wasn't anything else left in me to scare out). I was taking a break, pushing some food into me – when a squirrel landed on the roof. THUNK! Spilled my gloop, about went crazy – leapt out – and there the bugger was – I'm still convinced it was laughing at me.

That decided me to find some sort of nice house – a remote place – that would have a good stock of food in it. Maybe a generator – because I'd started to think that, if there was no-one around and so long as I was extra careful to not give myself away it would be a whole lot easier to have a bit of light – and maybe a fridge so's I didn't have to be so careful all of the time about food – plus – I was well fed-up with eating out of cans.

That and living out of a car... A car is usefully mobile – but cramped (even for a small person) and distinctly lacks a load of useful facilities – like a toilet for a start. Better still – if I found a good place – maybe I could use a washing machine sometimes...? Maybe?? What sort of generator would I need to be able to do that? At least a biggish place should mean I could dry my clothes inside – out-of-sight...

Thing was, with all the automatic appliances (that we assumed would always be there when we wanted them) gone dead – like the computers and all that – it was only going to be a matter of time before everything else packed up absolutely everywhere. It was getting far less common to find water systems working "like they should".

As I said – there was no way I was hanging washing out on a line. Waiting around for clothes to dry was more than bad enough. Putting things in front of a heater? What heater? *No* electric? Yeah? (Not that a bar fire is remotely safe without being watched for the first sign of scorching). Gas doesn't work without electric... Okay – bottle gas, yeah... You can use that. Makes a load of condensation on the windows if you're not careful, though. Anyhow – modern fabrics tend to suddenly go "whoomf" if you get them near any serious heat for long...

Then again... When you can get a solid fire going – and early on it was still cold enough most nights to need to keep warmed – then you have to be extra careful that even a breeze doesn't shift or flare the flames and burn your clothes – and – the light/heat/smoke/smell can show anyone where you are.

How did the human race ever survive for centuries without tumble driers???

There is no way that you want to have to leg it away too fast to grab all your clobber, after you've finally managed to get some washing done! That is a <u>total</u> pain-in-the-arse!

"Cool wash cycle" be buggered! I had to simply do what I could with cold most times. Washing me with cold just had to be got on with – when the water had bits of ice in it as well.

Plenty of clothes laying around in the houses? Oh, right... You mean go look for it in the stiffs' bedrooms? Take no notice of the bodies and the mess around them? Yeah right... Then find the right sizes... Make a fashion choice or two? *Sod off!*

One thing I was going to do though – was keep myself <u>clean</u>. After what had happened. After the state I'd been in... With the mess in most houses.

You're a survivor... You KNOW that!

It's achieved making all the boys keep themselves <u>*real*</u> clean. Not the hair-gel, body-spray and aftershave TV-celebrity-boy clean of the last years but –plain <u>scrubbed</u>.

There's no way anyone is going round in mucky, falling-apart clothes like in the movies and games. Post-Apocalyptic "mucky/scruffy" is NOT a fashion trend. Doesn't matter what clothing it is – it's got to be in one good piece, the right size (as near as possible) and be *clean*. This has been right from the first crawling out, looking around – starting over.

Not everyone was crazy/mean/stupid... You had to always be careful though. Especially when you were a stranger wandering around – or trying to get some place.

I reckon about half of all the survivors went wandering for one reason or another. Maybe going to find family – looking around – or running away from the horror...

Like me – once you got started – where did anyone head for? Where did you stop?

Moving was a whole load better than sitting on your arse... Well; for some (many) of us at least... Yeah, it meant risk – but – you felt you were doing something – not just waiting for something to do you.

Only the truly stupid went looking for thrills. Wasn't the energy at the beginning – and by the time there was it fast got too risky – plain dangerous in some places. There was some stuff like the Winchester – but not much really. You hear anecdotes, things people say that someone they met had seen... But most people got on with sorting themselves out – sensibly... That's kept us all more than busy enough.

I don't know, I'm not criticising or anything... But, I reckon that any group insanity was more likely clusters of established smack-heads and piss artists – that "the End" simple gave free reign to go crazy and wipe themselves out. Most people, that I'm aware of, that topped themselves in one way or another, did so on their own... Some were probably just unable to cope before they could have met up with others... A few took themselves off – did themselves in privately...

Anyhow – when you did find a good place with a heap of food – there wasn't any point in grabbing a big pile when you were on your own and travelling – you got to hating the same tins so much that you ended up chucking them out the car. Wherever you were, you needed to have a car – not only when you were on the move – but (like before with the big edge-of-town stores) – to shift your "shopping" without a whole load of effort – that you haven't got spare energy to do.

There were no buses running were there? You couldn't have called for a taxi – *if* there'd been any phones...

Another thing – you load up with a load of tins (boxes of tins) – what's all that pile going to do when you have to slam on the brakes and back up fast? And, again, weight slows you down, burns up more fuel. Worst – a heap of junk changes your vehicle's centre of gravity – which can be disastrous around tight, bendy lanes when you want to run for it...

No. That wasn't one of my mistakes... But it had made a mess of one man I saw... And I did know about centres-of-gravity before all this... Part of my reading... I just had no idea what effect it could have...

So "Little and often" is great...

NOT! Every raid you need to make you have to start with a look around, check out at least the immediate area. See if you can see any "property tags", any "**KEEP OUTs**" or any other signs...

Someone stabbed in the chest makes a clear warning... A trail of blood can be a good guide... But – is it going in or out? Cut yourself when you smash a shop door in – you're going to go hunting clean bandages to cover it with... (Keeping all wounds safe is essential!)

Meet the wrong person inside – the tracks you leave behind will probably lead to where you were parked – or your corpse...

One woman I bumped into inside a store screamed, ran for it – and tried to dive out the wrong door – not the smashed glass one... I heard her friends coming so I vanished quietly out the side door – the out-of-sight way I'd got in by. I have no idea how much damage she'd done herself – but I wasn't figuring that her friends could be relied on to see the funny side of it. (So many people lost all sense of humour around then...)

Little-and-often has so many problems – but isn't so bad as piles too much of the wrong assortment...

===========

Where was I?

After the pesky squirrel I paused to think...

If I could find somewhere decent to stop for a bit, somewhere a bit out-of-the-way, I should stock up properly instead of going a couple of days at a time. Do a bigger raid from a large store, maybe a warehouse. Better somewhere without a load of nutters in a 4x4... And probably get some cans for petrol – fill them up...

How the hell would I get a good supply of petrol?

By then it was nearing dark so I decided to stop for the night and try to get a sleep. I had soon seen that if I drove at night, or just late in the day, any lights on the car would tell people for miles around where I was. I was definitely wanting to take a look at anyone else before they looked at me...

Although – I was long since asking why-on-earth, after so many people had died, everyone seemed to want to start with a fight...

Was it only around here or was it everywhere?

By then, to try to be safe, when sleeping in the car, I would sandwich myself between the sleeping bags and put the gun (with its whole two bullets) down tight between the seats.

===========

Next morning I banged myself on the roof I leapt up so hard – again... Don't know if it was the same nut-muncher had followed me... Or come along for the ride. It got lucky – if I'd had a third bullet...

I still shoot squirrels! (Grey). Once you get used to the idea they taste quite good anyway...

I had slept well though – which I hadn't done in days.

The metal flask I'd brought along was superb, so I was able to start with a hot coffee – lots of sugar. Then I got moving – deciding to see if I could get somewhere high up to look around for a big store type place – and maybe see if there was any sign of movement – so I could plan on avoiding any more "difficulties" – at least until I could get another seat cover...

Away from the furry pest I stopped and worked on swallowing some cereal, well-softened overnight with re-made milk powder into a sludge... A good dollop of honey in it... Food that I could get in and keep down at that stage wasn't all nice ready-made-meal and microwave snacks. The complete lack of fresh milk was devastating...

Don't even start to think about what the sickness had done to the cows... Despite the fact that it never directly infected them – as far as we can tell...

Anyhow, I sat and slurped – and thought evil things about squirrels – and caught on that the latest one probably got attracted by the smell of my breakfast. So I was near ecstatic that I'd hardly left the window open at all – only enough to make sure I didn't steam up the car and make it obvious to anyone passing that there was anyone alive and breathing present.

Back when I was cycling home from college a steamed-up car in a gateway could be a laugh – provided it was faced uphill and I was riding down – fast getaways were important then too...

So I'd learnt that little bit of discretion...

Then again (looked at the other way round) if you work it out right the cold air doesn't get to freeze your bum... However – apart from that...

Two bits of fun to remember from "The Old Days"...

Finishing my breakfast I started to think around what I should do next...

Guess what? Other people had the idea of finding high ground too... I'd not anticipated that one...

I missed them... Wasn't my fault they hit a tree...

They didn't shoot at me though...

Okay – so I had stopped – after we missed each other (by fractions). Wouldn't have stopped to look at them. I expected them to be mad at me. I'd got stuck in the hedge on my side though. After a couple of spins my car shot in backwards and crunched. I had my belt on – always did – wouldn't dare not to... (Mum's training this time). So once I'd fought the stupid airbag out of my face the first thing I saw was them running at me...

How was I to know that they were worried about me!? That they weren't going to attack me...

I – um – petrified them when I waved the gun around... Amazing how fast people can stop... And change colour – to very, *very* white... Funny thing – people seem to see a gun barrel before they look at who's behind it... Which is always wonderful – makes sure they take me seriously.

Once he'd stopped – and stopped shaking – he didn't help his case by practically yelling "Good God! It's a child! It shouldn't be driving!"

"It"??? Way to go! He was lucky I didn't shoot him there and then. (Didn't want to waste one of those two whole bullets, did I?)

Seems like I was the first person that actually pointed a gun their way.

So – introductions sorted out nicely – they pulled me out of the hedge – and – seeing as their van was a rear-engined VW it didn't matter so much that they'd scrunched the front a bit. At least the windscreen had only cracked a little bit – and he said that they were thinking of changing it anyway... To me it looked more like it should have been scrapped years before it met the tree... But it was their own van – they actually had a name for it. (Yeah, okay, I had an "adjective" for it...)

Truth is – still – I reckon the gun went a whole long way to making them "okay" about what happened...

You wouldn't credit it – she was some sort of vicar – and he was a school teacher...

Aaargh! Just what I needed. *NOT!*

I'm small. That *doesn't* mean I'm still in *first* school! I was not "Far too young to be driving". I didn't need them telling me I'd *have* to go with them – "For my own good"... They reckoned I'd be safe with them...

Okay – so I'd got a lot of practice pissing off teachers... These two were real easy... Got proper huffy when I reminded them they'd hit a tree while I'd only landed in a soft bush... Neither of them had the marbles to remind me I'd needed them to pull me out...

Did they get the idea? Did they fuck! He was stupid enough to try to get my keys – got a bloody nose instead – from the top of my gun barrel... (Nasty).

I made him shut his eyes and hurl their keys well out over the hedge to give me good time to get away from them. Didn't want to shoot them – but they didn't know that... I did *not* want Donuts telling me what to do... So I cleared off – not so fast that I lost any mirrors – that I didn't have...

He'd actually pointed that out – said it "clearly showed" I was too young to drive... And on and on... Like any teacher – he didn't ask – didn't think to ask – how come they had got knocked off...

I reckon that showering that pickup with smashed glass and plastic when they were going to ram me was a good move... Even if it was sheer fluke.

===========

Once I'd moved on some way I decided that the car was sounding a bit unhealthy and that I would be better off with another. For a start, driving with what was left of the airbag was damn difficult.

The idea of using some sort of camper appealed... Wouldn't be as quick as a car – but I'd definitely confirmed for myself what fast could do. I was beginning to think that "empty roads" weren't such a safe place as they might seem...

With the different cars I'd been driving, I was getting more confident – at least that I could usually miss things. Reckoned that I could at least give a camper a try. For a start I would be able to put more food in one while I looked for a big house – and sleeping in it should be a whole lot better than a car seat... Would be room enough to not bash my head...

It didn't take me long to find a van like theirs – another VW – but a whole lot younger – and it had a bit of a bonnet on the front that I could see (mostly)... And three quarters of a tank of fuel.

The new van was a lot quieter than Lindsey and Andrea's had been – and it had a couple of big metal fuel cans outside in a rack – and a gas cooker, water – a tiny toilet under a seat. I was impressed. It was also two shades of yellow – would have been well hidden in a corn field!

Oh – and the roof could go up – but I didn't bother with that. Didn't need to did I? It would have been a stretch for me – and made the van show up a lot more anywhere I parked up... Wouldn't have been much of a good idea if I had had to get away from anywhere in a hurry either. Although – if I could have found a low bridge...

Didn't bother with whether it had any water in the cooling system...

How was I to know!? Lindsey had said the weird noise their van made was because it was air cooled. He said "I *should* know that – if I wasn't so young..." GRRR!!

At least I didn't discover the difference until I'd located myself in a big house and raided some stores.

I just had a thought... Maybe those men riding around waving guns had met Lindsey and Andrea before me? That would explain their aggression... (Well – it would to me – you didn't meet them...)

===========

3– 5

What I've been saying makes it sound like everything was hassle, bother and bullshit – always trouble around the village before the sickness and then always dangerous after... Wasn't like that though – not exactly...

Explaining good times – with Mum and Gran and Gramps... Before...

So – it was devastating losing Gramps – when he died... No messing about with "passed-away" and waffle like that for me... Not in my world. At nine I knew what dead was – knew that he wasn't ever coming back... I did *not* need counselling!

Gramps had explained to me – practical and sensible. I trusted him. Trusted him a whole load more than any stranger.

There were good times. Really good... Although – there was often a taint of the nastiness around us – the hostility of the estate and the enmity of school. We could separate ourselves from that though. Whenever Gramps' old van was parked out front the trouble vanished...

Should never have been that way. Like I said – I've never known what caused any of it...

But – against any expectation – all that set me up for now... It's so much easier to explain that, than to try to describe even the simple things – like watching TV together... And that is way, way, *way*-too-close... And painful.

Thing is – I've always been independent... Okay – a bit of a loner most of my life... Stroppy. I could never see why I should just do what the crowd is doing – and certainly not put up with any crap "to fit in". Yeah – I do know that things could have been a whole lot easier in a lot of ways – so long as I didn't mind taking a whole load of shitty attitude and being told what to do and what to think all the time...

I had nothing to do with us landing on the Estate and the "them and us" attitudes that were already there. It wasn't me that invented "modern education" and set up all the things that decided that I "wasn't bright"... According to *their* version of it.

I had to get on with my life as best I could. So, I could have done it some other way... Everybody could do everything "some other way"... Like not stitch people up and not discriminate on sight... Like take action to thoroughly stop bullying... Wasn't just in school... More than one supervisor at jobs I did thought that the way to do things was to treat people like shit... That was totally ignorant!

I am not bitching and complaining though. I'm not!

I chose my way. I refused to go-down-the-tubes. I got myself off the street and away from disaster. I didn't actually plan it – but – I was educating myself... All that reading.

Truth is my "independence" probably helped me a whole lot... Once the sickness struck a load of "in crowd" people couldn't cope – never really got started... Or got themselves into a real mess.

Might have been, if things had been different, that with Greg's help, I could have become one of those super-rich entrepreneurs... We'll never know now will we?

After the sickness – thing was, one of the things was – once you'd survived – you never had any idea what was going to come up next... At least – I didn't. I think it was the same for anyone else – at least, anyone else that wasn't simply going to go for the first (hopefully soft) easy option.

Wasn't only that it kept happening... Day after day there was always something new, another unpredictable cropping up... Often silly, little "basic" things... You wound up tight all the time trying to figure what was going to hit you next... It ground you down. You got so you worried about anything good that might happen...

I did know from way, way back (long before Greg) that "easy options" are usually the fastest way possible into deep shit... Even if you pretend that you always meant to go swimming in that brown stuff.

One thing with Mum – she never moaned about how things were for us. I kind of asked her about it one day – indirectly at first... She only said "I made my choices... Didn't mean to lumber you... So now I'm just trying to get things as good as I can". She didn't add "for you". I wish I'd been able to tell her that I woke up to that – eventually...

===========

But driving around you could spot some potential aggravation...

Like the woman I ran into – nearly ran over – but missed – who said "What are you going to do?"

I'd so been there before – Carrie at the start of College. Both of them clearly meant "What are you going to do *for me*?" No way was it "What are we going to do?" So I told Carrie to get lost... I told the woman the same – somehow she didn't understand – so I told her "You're going ***that*** way..." The other way from the one I was going. She started to moan about that... Until I pointed my gun at her and made up her mind for her – then got out of there fast.

===========

That gun I'd picked up was most useful – without ever firing it.

I didn't want to use up what little real "power" I had – plus, anyhow, I had never, ever, begun to imagine firing a gun actually *at* anyone... You don't ever do that. Well. I hadn't... And it looks for certain that a whole load of boys (and men if that's what they are) hadn't either.

Whatever shoot-em-up games they had played I reckon nearly all of them found it was a whole different thing when they had real metal in their hands and a real, squishy, warm human body in front of them; that they needed to at least shoot *at* to stay alive... Or even just a chicken, a rabbit or pig that they desperately needed to kill to eat...

Not sure if it was Greg or Mum that told me that a whole load of cops and soldiers got killed or wounded without ever drawing their gun and having it ready to fire.

At least I would have turned the cylinder round (with my thumb – got good at that) and had a bullet lined up where I could actually use it if I had to – when I needed to... I got myself into the discipline of shifting it away again when things calmed down – like my breathing and nerves.

The fact was; that I kept it out of sight way more times than I showed it. I think that having it gave me some kind of confidence though. Maybe?

I think that clearly being firm, looking like I knew what I was about, made a big difference a lot of times when I met anyone.

Wasn't only the gun that gave me coolness. Turned out that my experiences had taught me to at least look solid with confidence – even when it was nothing but bullshit and I was terrified silly. Thing was – most people hadn't got clue-one what to do or where to start... So – looking self-assured gave me a serious advantage...

Also; I had a shrewd idea when anyone else was trying it on. I couldn't explain it... Not properly. Quite often people do that bit too much or talk that bit too loud.

Anyhow... The gun was a nasty piece of metal to whack someone with – when necessary.

Managed to never let anyone who was waving a gun around get close enough to make a stand-off – at that time.

And...

Then...

That was except the one time it mattered beyond words of course...

FUCK!

Don't go there. Not yet. – Not until...

===========

None of those Game Designer Geeks ever came up with the pain-in-the-arse it is finding enough safe food though did they? All that leaping out of helicopters and blowing things up would have needed one hell of a lot of calories – even if the game weather never pissed with rain or froze solid all over you on your sofa in your comfy warm home.

So – point your digital gun – "Bang" – baddy dead (or alien, monster or goblin)... Or it was you that got squished. No problem – next game...

Okay, I'll skip the details about where to shoot a human...

Then, if you're near starving, you need fresh meat – *urgently* . (Totally fed up of tinned hotdogs... What's in those things anyhow?)

Exactly where do you shoot any animal to outright kill it? Apart from the problems of all the noise of a shot, it's an absolute bitch if your next meal staggers off to die somewhere else.

For one thing you have to ask yourself if it's going to be safe to trail around following it? Will it turn on you? Will you have attracted other people? People who might want it and/or object to you "poaching" in *their* territory.

If you could've attracted attention is it safe to leave your vehicle unguarded?

Calories. Right. So none of us were going on any "Magic Slimming Diet" – leastways, not for a year or two. Problem was getting enough – of anything. Enough that you could keep inside.

There must have been thousands of tons of food sitting around. Millions of homes, all the shops and stores, enormous great warehouses – all the delivery trucks... A whole system – a whole system had been there... This is the thing. It "had been".

Then it stopped. **Clunk!**

You could say that it "stopped dead"...

What did we do? We raided... Aaah! That sounds so simple!

It's obvious to anyone who was there – obviously. We just did it, had to, to get through... But – anyone reading this as history... You're going to live in <u>such</u> a different world. You'll more than likely be doing a version of what we've started to do now – growing your own.

I hope that you'll have a load better idea how to do it than we have!

So maybe one of the "good old-world things" I should write about for Ben is the hassle we used to moan and grumble about of having to pop to the shop for a packet of crisps? It was *such-a-drag* having to drive to one of those big stores and stock up for a couple of days. Such a business choosing which variety...

If, on your post-sickness travels, you did manage to find a really good house to squat in for a bit, then most times any safe food there would only last a few days.

So – <u>*where*</u> did all the survivalist types that were supposed to hoard for a year or three of Nuclear Winter hide their stashes? I never found any of it!

===========

So, anyhow...

After I took the camper I did meet up with a couple of lads who seemed okay. They were in a car I didn't crash into – and they were really impressed with my van – so we teamed up and found them another one like it.

Phil and Barry hadn't clue-one how to do things though – no idea of even basics they should do. They were what Gran called "the blind leading the blind".

I spent a few days sorting them out... Getting them thinking about carrying clean water and at least a bit of a stock of food (solid grub – not just beer) in their new van. Why I bothered is beyond me now...

After a few days we parked up for a meal well out of town, somewhere discreet and a bit safe. Once we'd had a meal I took myself off some way into the trees for a pee – after a subtle hint that they might police up the debris – and clean up the back of their van – already... (Yeah, right – some hope...) Not sure why but I decided to slip back quietly to see what they were doing and maybe watch for how long it took them to shift their arses...

You know how boys act big and have an argument? All faced off and flapping their arms about? At least they had the tiny bit of sense to not be yelling at each other – but I could still hear them no trouble... Going on about which one was going to "take her" first.

That was *so not* a good idea.

It was no great effort for me to work around them while they were distracted and then wait out of sight until they woke up to the fact that I'd been gone some time.

I let them wander the way I'd gone before they "discreetly" yelled for me... Like they had such a good idea of keeping themselves out of the shit...

And that gave me easy time to grab their van keys out of the ignition and chuck them back deep in their mess of stuff – before I got myself out of there sharpish. Last I saw of them (in my mirrors) they'd managed to dash back to the road. Where they were just standing (wheezing) trying to figure out what was happening...

Me – I was moving on!

I didn't think they were necessarily bad. Could be it was all nothing more than bullshit – but I was *not* risking finding out... One of them wasn't too bad looking – but there was no way I was going to become their "property" or be handed around... Doesn't matter how hunky and wonderful you look – if you've got the wrong brain you're useless at the least – if not plain dangerous.

What sort of way is that to talk about anyone?! I'm not going there now though... I'd get raging...

While I'm on about people I met... Or saw... There weren't a lot – before or after what I want to write about – but a whole load of them reckoned I had to join them because I "was only a little kid". That was always going <u>nowhere</u>.

===========

After Barry and Phil...

I was seriously pissed-off! Okay – they might have been talking "lads' talk" – aka TOTAL BOLLOCKS. I'd seen enough bodies though. Not so many but <u>too</u> many. I didn't want to be having to make a couple more – not for any reason.

I guess that it was probably like college and Anton – and like the fuss that had ended things with me and Jerry... (Different story).

Thing is – that whenever it happens – bullshit like that doesn't exactly make you feel like involving yourself with anyone again does it?

I don't care how sociable you are there's no sense in putting up with a crappy relationship. Not ever. Not even if you're one of those poor, desperate people that has to take on whatever relationship you can – regardless of what crap goes with it...

I am NOT going to say I "feel sorry" for you if that's what you have – because I hate people "feeling sorry" for me – no matter what bad things have happened... But – well – I so hope that there will be some way that things can get a whole load better for you...

Plus – with what's happened now with the sickness – and there can't be much worse than that – not and stay alive... Well – despite all that – we've got this far haven't we? Things are improving. When we were lying on floors screaming and wanting to be dead – we never imagined this did we? This isn't what we expected – but it can be good.

Thing is – true, for sure – we have to be careful – sensible...

===========

So then what happened?

Okay – so, this didn't all happen in one go – but it kind-of makes more sense if I put it together...

The squirrels were – pests – would really make me jump. We all got jumpy at one stage or another – probably for most of the time. Anything happening that we weren't expecting – like a bunny hopping out from somewhere...

I think that this was because there was a while when rats got *way* too confident about people – especially in the towns.

Big difference between a rat and a bunny you say? Not around dusk or dawn – or any other time the light's not so good. When you've guessed what it is the wrong way a time or two... Or had a rat jump out on you...

Well, I took to carrying a half brick around. If nothing else it's enough to chase the buggers off – and they weren't so little a lot of the time.

Meanwhile...

What I keep meaning to tell "history" about is the dogs... Took us a long time to see and then get our heads round this – much longer than realising most of them had died...

Any time in the next ten, maybe fifty years you'll probably know ALL about them anyway... But we didn't. Right?

You remember what I said about when I first met Bodger – correct that – when Bodger first appeared... Well, one thing Mum had taught me right from I was a toddler – was to be cautious about any dog. Have respect for the wolf *still* in *every* dog – especially the "darling little ones". (Yeah right!)

So, as you'd expect, some of the idiots on the Estate had Japanese Tosas, Akitas and what were really Pit Bulls... Mind you, some of the snooties had some big and aggressive pure-breeds – and some nasty little ratters as well...

So – one way and another I was well used to being careful around any canine. That was even though I knew well that there were very few actually bad dogs... Ninety nine percent of the time the problem was the idiot on the other end of the lead.

Anyhow...

I was clued up about dogs... And I was missing more than just Bodger. All of them vanishing (except the dead and rotting ones) put a big hole in the world as I knew it. It seemed so weird to never see one from one month to the next...

I still wasn't going to go all gooey when I did see one though was I? I am <u>not</u> stupid!

Lips curled back and snarling is *not* behaviour you change by going down on your knees and talking soppy... Not if you don't want your face ripped it isn't....

The first one was a toy poodle...

No-one has any idea what's happened to them – and it's all of them so far as anyone's seen. There are very few – but we shoot on sight now. You're safer off with a sow and her piglets gone feral. The dogs are crazy; insane. Might be worse than some of the humans – so that tells you how bad they are now.

Why a half brick? Because I only had two bullets. Yeah? Because a brick doesn't make much noise – not for anyone to hear – but enough for a rat up close. Anyway, even if you're a good shot they're damn hard to hit.

Most people are lousy shots at the best of times. Helps if you keep your eyes open and don't jump when the gun goes "Bang"... So guns are useless when you're all jittery with adrenalin and freaked, plain terrified, by a rodent.

So a rat's hard to react to fast enough and get a good shot at – especially in bad light. This means that shooting – at – them is usually a waste of ammo. In town there's also a hellish danger of any bullet powerful enough to kill a rat ricocheting... That happens, you have no idea at all where it will go.

Anyway, you start shooting, it tells the whole neighbourhood that you're around – and that is not a good idea in most towns. No-one, anywhere, likes anyone to announce their arrival with a shot – or three...

Then again – a dog... Massive all the way to tiny... Keep firing until you hit it – or it gets you... It's going to be one way or the other. They don't suddenly recognise you like some lion you took a thorn out of the paw of. They don't suddenly go back to waiting patiently (drooling) for you to open a tin... I hate to say it – but I would even think twice if I ran into Bodger again... Way they are now though – that second of thought could be fatal.

All that is another thing they never talked about in their "post apocalyptic scenarios". Zombies – unrealistic as super-heroes – by the score. Mad, demented dogs? Never.

Ben says Sherlock had some... Well, he would – wouldn't he?

Umm? Maybe werewolves? Fantasy again... Nothing like as crazed as the real things we're stuck with. Maybe the legends had some previous basis in reality?

Anyway...

First dog attack (that poodle) I saw... Stunned me – freaked the crap out of me... Was my good luck that it was ripping chunks out of some woman called Anita that I'd just met. ('Cos it might have been me otherwise). I did yell at her to stop and shift her arse away. Wasn't my fault the stupid woman ignored me.

Wasn't down to me that she jumped into the path of one of the bullets I fired either... Only gave her a flesh wound anyway... Got the damn dog. Had to get it twice more – it was like some insane monster – despite it was only small sized.

It looked insane when it was laying there dead – all foam and blood round its snout.

Anita? She went mad at *me* for being "wickedly cruel"! Said the dog "didn't mean it". If that's what it was like when it didn't mean it – I do *not* want to see one when it gets serious!

I met the people she was with again sometime after... She died of blood poisoning...

Yet another "post apocalyptic" thing they hardly mentioned... Infected wounds.

At least those guys thought she was as stupid as I did for saying it was a "severe wound" from a bullet that poisoned her... Yeah, right – it was a clean scratch (that I <u>did</u> clean up with surgical spirit – despite her squealing). Couldn't have been the bites of the lovely, slavering and snarling likkle-doggy could it?

Yeah well... Remember the days when Britain was full of "animal lovers"?

Then again... If anyone had harmed Bodger... I'd probably have gone crazy at them – or any bits of them that Bodger and then Greg had left behind...

That was a different world – back then – before...

[This incident, you might work out, was a bit later when I'd got more ammo, a better gun and a bit of target practice. It's so difficult trying to write everything in proper order...]

I guess that I'm glad that I've not had to face the question about what I would do if Bodger was around...

It's so much easier with people – mostly... They are so much easier to kill when you need to – which is totally crazy... (That too is "another story").

Weird. I haven't changed what I feel about Bodger from before. Those were good times. He was a good friend. This is another of the things that have completely changed in our world...

Never, ever imagined that I'd get to figuring that it made sense to kill people... Not even in my most enraged moments. "We" never thought that way... In our world it wasn't "civilised"... Unless, of course, we were bombing the hell out of the "bad guys" in some far-off country...

Huh! There's an "Old World" expression if ever there was one! "Our World". Yeah. Right... We thought we were so great. For the real World, the planet, we weren't anything more than annoying little fleas – probably more like mites...

Talking of mites... I HATE bed bugs! They didn't mention them either did they?

Ben said "Bring back DDT". Beth looked horrified the first time. I've never heard of it or what it is – but, since I've seen her scratching a few times I think she's agreeing with him. If it kills bugs – and fleas – BRING IT ON!

===========

So – um – I was supposed to write about good memories... Well... I got through all that didn't I? I learned how to do things... Masses of things... I kept myself out of trouble – danger... Well – mostly...

I helped a few people – as much as they could be helped... I've definitely achieved! Got to be good.

I had even got myself out of trouble and was achieving before everything fell apart... Okay – I had a load of help toward the end – but – even that was something I had to accept and take hold of... There were more than a few that let themselves sink and just wallowed waiting for someone else to do all the work to rescue them...

If the sickness was some sort of apocalypse thingy then it could be argued that our world before it was at the least *becoming* dystopian... All the pollution, over-population, global warming, extinction of species, wars and famine – terrorism – "Globalisation" even... After all – that last one – that was said to be so good – could mean that anyone, anywhere on the planet could be suddenly chucked out-of-work with sod-all warning because of some "financial decision" taken the other side of the planet – or – in the office next door...

You didn't have to look far on the internet to find whole heaps of people in the richest nation in the world going on about collapse of society and/or excessive government doing everything wrong... You read for very long, you began to wonder why the whole thing hadn't collapsed decades ago...

For me of course there was the "dystopia" of the education system that the government persisted in sodding about. Mum had years of shitty low-paid jobs... What sort of world had Greg had? Yeah, he was a massive success – at taking bombs and IEDs apart...

I'm suspecting that, now we're beginning to get our acts together, there's more than just a few of us thinking that things could be a whole lot better from now on...

Except – we <u>really</u> could use some decent hospitals, people to mend the roads, a proper police force to stop the outbreaks of trouble before they even started... Someone else to be soldiers – like their <u>used</u> to be...

There's no worries about not having a job (or five hundred) to do now, though...

Plus... We utterly miss all those people we lost...

===========

Box 1
File 4

4 – 1

So – I was saying – about how I got the camper – dumped the boys – and was looking for somewhere to settle... I was figuring that when I had a place I would be best sorting myself out first and then taking time, plenty of time, to see who (if anyone) would be at least reasonable to get along with.

Following those experiences (Ben calls them "fiascos") with the graduates and the boys I decided for definite to go it alone for a while. Let things settle down. Get somewhere and some time to see what developed... Like I reckoned Greg would have done – wanted me to do... He was like my reference point in a whole load of things. (As if you wouldn't notice).

Thing was, seeing as I wasn't in my own place and never going to go there ever again, it was nowhere near clear what to do. If I settled in any one place – of any ordinary kind – it had all sorts of problems. I could joke about it and say that the shops weren't open and the buses weren't running – the taxis were worse than ever... Take-away delivery was pathetic! Yeah, right...

If I had found a good neighbourhood and another reasonable house that started off with a good stock of food – and hopefully no stiffs – it would have soon run out. Everywhere usually did. What then? It was soon clear that raiding all the houses around any one place started to show up much too quick. I could be careful about how I got in and out – but anyone else looking around would soon notice that there was a lot of activity – that it was a cluster – and probably draw an easy conclusion. I had no way of knowing if that would mean they would run away or start looking for me... And if they looked – what would they do then?

So I could spread my raiding more thin around a house. Fine – except – that meant extra time wandering about. Which is exactly what I was peacefully doing the first time I got shot at. (Remember that?)

Okay... I'd let my guard down – it was a lovely day. I was feeling good for a change... I was actually feeling maybe the best I had up till then – until that prat shot at me...

Anyway – was no way I was going to stay around that area – not with what I'd heard next.

I already had a car. I'd been beginning to think that it was a conspicuous way of moving around. I mean – if I could hear other cars – then anyone else could hear me. The noise was most times the first warning... It stood out so much in all the quiet.

Lights (so many cars had automatic lights by then) really got your attention – like they were supposed to... Had been supposed to... Blasted "unlocking" lights were a real risk. Brake lights... You can easily tell a lot of cars that got used in the early days – the lights are all hammered-in.

I'd also thought that it made sense to save on fuel... Plus, when my nose began to work better (when I stopped getting puke or petrol up it) I discovered that the world smelled different. The sudden nearly complete stop to emissions let nature come back... The world began cleaning itself up – and smelling all earthy and fresh.

The environmentalist's dream! Um... Yeah – if you like mud and trees... Oh – and rotting cows or sheep some places... Rotting just about everything. Some places were appalling! I'd guess where the drainage system had needed some pumping... Inside houses, anywhere someone had died, got to be totally vile for quite a while.

One thing we are still not running out of is – stiffs...

All those things wore off – or we simply got used to them... But nature returning meant that any vehicle spewing out exhaust left a very clear trace that it had been around... There was nothing anyone could do to disguise that... The only effective thing was a good windy day – except sometimes that spread the pong further – or took the sound away from you...

Yeah, I know "selfish"... I always wanted the weather to hide me but tell me who else was around at the same time... Typically human...

Whatever – saving fuel and being low profile seemed nowhere near as important as being able to get-the-hell-out-of-there *fast* if I got shot at. Thing with a car is – in a minute you can be a mile away. Okay, so a bullet could be more than that – a lot more if it's one of those that goes "snap" as it goes by you – speed of sound and all that... (The boys tell me). But – so long as it misses you and you don't wreck the car – then you're out of there – fast... And that, Ben, is not merely good – it's *excellent.*

I'd sorted out stealing (aka "obtaining") fuel by then anyhow. I'd got a few good cans – with spouts – spouts are *so* important.

I was not thinking "If I get shot at again" as if it were a question...

Wasn't long before I'd been shot at more than once – once was more than enough – even if they might have said that they were "only warning shots"... Yeah, right – one of those *can* still *kill* you.

Yeah, I'd got the gun by then – by the time I was looking for a place to settle as permanently as possible. I had waved it around a time or two as well – but I knew from Greg that a pop-gun doesn't shoot as far as a rifle – and it's only the goodies in films that hit their target first time every time at two miles range with a little handgun – and never once get hit when they're stood right in front of an attack helicopter firing mini-guns...

Okay. So I did sit down and watch some movies with Greg... And his mates a few times... They watched them as comedies – used to cheer and shout like football hooligans. It was more fun watching them than the stupid films... So long as they didn't go all sad and closed up later... You had to watch for that with some of them – Greg sometimes...

I learnt about his screaming in his sleep from that.

(I did not ever sleep with him).

[Sometimes I think that's a pity – but – there will never be a thing I can do about it].

So, anyway... If staying in one place and not driving much was going to be difficult...

Everything was sodding difficult!

Wasn't so much "things" of course.

A flat tyre is more of a pain-in-the-arse than ever and no electric is a monster-pain-in-the-arse... Car batteries gone flat – knackered... The damn racket an engine makes turning over – no guarantee it will start... We've all played those games now.

Potholes in the road were bad enough before – but – whole chunks of road are breaking up. There are wash-outs and landslides. Used-to-be that the Council would clear fallen trees... Yes kids – that actually happened... Might have taken a few hours – but it was very rare for anything, even a real big tree, to be there long. Nearly nothing gets moved now... Plus – when we do shift stuff we can need to decide whether we should disguise the work we've done.

Just keeping the most energetic bushes from taking over the roads leaves clear sign that we're around. Who doesn't know that we can have all sorts of problems shoving through? How come so many solid things manage to hide? Not to mention booby traps – at least alarm signals – that people set up?

Yeah? So? Of course we do that too!

You kids will yawn if I say that "the weather never used to be like this". But – it didn't! At least it seems to be settling down some now... Definite improvement. Whether it was the over-run of us warming the planet or a result of suddenly stopping... Who knows?

Think the recent storms are scary? We had months of craziness. In our "Old World" (yeah, that's right, that one us "Old Gits" go on about) we had a few twisters – little ones that were so unusual they made news headlines. So – nothing like the ones we get now – back then... But the first new ones were worse than this year's. Believe it!

Anyhow – we used to get weather warnings. We had some idea when to tie things down – plus – there were people to tie things down... Driving through any town in the last couple of years... Even past just a few storm damaged houses – with nothing made safe – could suddenly get hellish. A roof slate coming straight at you like a Frisbee is hardly visible. (I am not going to explain what a Frisbee is! – Was...) *[Go ask Stuart].* I was lucky my encounter only smashed into the roof and didn't come through the windscreen. Smashed windows – they were another problem... Looking at an abandoned vehicle I can't always tell if it was done by the weather or people... Nor how recent it was. We all know how many places and how much stuff have got wasted by rain soaking in.

But the truly-serious problems – far more than roads, plants, weather and traps – all came directly from people – in one way or another. Frequently they were much smaller, really ridiculous things.

I go-on about this? Yeah? So we were all stressed-to-hell – traumatised. The trauma had got stressed... Who wasn't going to be freaked out? It's ***no** excuse* for being an arsehole! Seemed like there were more ways than ever for people to be that. People were getting together and breaking up in no time at all for the stupidest reasons.

I stayed out of it as much as I could – my "old habits" – they worked well for me. Whenever I stumbled on anyone and hadn't been seen by them I took time for a look before I got involved – or before I vanished quick.

How-the-hell did people have any energy to get into rows about who'd had the most corned beef? Why would anyone grab a wrong-flavour-of-jam on purpose?

Some people looked okay – but that was no better guide than it had ever been... We thought some people at college would be fine – but got proved wrong. There were pointless arguments about whose turn it was to get coffee from the machines... Should I recall the Christmas shopping? Maybe we only continued in our old habits?

That "fit" copper I saw when Bodger showed up – ran into him a year or so later. Total Shitbag:. He tried to plant some powder on my mate... 'Cept I'd got my phone filming him... Least – he thought that I had – and that I'd sent it to Greg and Mum before he got wise to it... Prick!

Other people (since) – well – they looked a disaster from the first you saw them. Just had to hope you saw them before they saw you – and they didn't spot you sloping off as discreetly as you could.

It was all such a pain-in-the-butt! You simply couldn't keep on the alert 24/7... You had to rest – you had to eat – and you definitely had to sleep... More than that – there's no-one that doesn't have to take a dump from time to time – and you're seriously vulnerable then... Someone tell me how you can avoid that!

So... I'd given up on sitting around. I did figure that taking a bit of a wander around might run me into some difficulties – but – against that, stopping on my arse would depend on anyone nice stumbling on me. Seeing as I was keeping out of sight and scuttling off from the least sign of trouble – that would take some kind of miracle.

The best thing to do seemed to be to only drive around when it was sunny and I could have the windows open – so I could hear all there was to be heard. So that I could hope to smell at least recent exhaust... Either that or move about when it was absolutely chucking it down – which would cover my noise – and most people would be inside sheltering – hopefully... Of course – anything that covered the noises I made – did the same for everyone else... But you could hope...

Yeah, yeah – some hope!

On the other hand – I got lucky... Taught some kind of road block people that a bit of chain across the road doesn't do much against a camper van. That was fun!

Uh! Only for a moment...

A pair of big oil drums taking off down the road behind you at speed scares the crap out of you. I guess that at least they hadn't got round to filling them up with mud or rocks. The noise alone would freak anyone out.

Well – I was in front of them and they ***terrified*** me...

So what it did to them – standing around one moment and flinging themselves all ways the next... Well – they didn't do any shooting at me – so that was okay.

What-the-hell did they think they were doing anyhow?

Another lesson there – putting your road block immediately round a sharp corner when no-one is taking any notice of speed limits is *not* a good idea. I would probably have stopped and decided what to do if I'd been able to see the stupid set-up from a bit of a distance. A raised gun would more probably have had me shifting out of there fast – backwards if needed.

Oh – one thing (I meant to say) that helped with that... Don't put your road block where there'll be an enormous puddle or two... Or three.

Definitely stopped them seeing what was going on – and drenched them too. Yeah – so I'm horrible... Near wet myself laughing at that – right before I saw I was being chased by those lousy drums... Did more than wet myself then...

===========

All that wild excitement (changes of knickers) happened different places over a few weeks or so. I took to riding on bin-bags... It was a long time before the state of my guts improved enough to be helpful... You want details? Changing black-plastic was <u>way</u> easier than changing cars... Looking back, I've no idea now, of how long, when or where... I wasn't exactly keeping up a journal or writing a Blog.

Winter ended and then we got into and through spring. There were no nice, convenient markers – like half terms or weekends. Nobody was going to church and ringing bells on Sundays. There weren't bigger-than-other-nights piss-ups on Fridays and the weekend... It all just happened – kept happening – one thing after another...

The beginning-to-be-mad weather was no help for telling where we'd got to. The TV used to talk about "unseasonal spells"... Yeah right. So once we were on our own there was no way of telling if a few warm days were going to be the start of Spring or whether the daffodils coming out meant we were in Spring and there wouldn't be any more frosts. I have no idea how gardeners and farmers ever had a clue what to do before proper weather forecasts... I do know for sure that we haven't got a clue.

Sometimes in those first months I absolutely had to hide best as I could and sleep... Wasn't always sure how long I did that for.

"Excitement" is disgustingly knackering.

===========

So – although I'd sorted out the camper by then (and wasn't putting any dents in it) – I decided to definitely find some out-of-the-way place that I could hole up in. Some sort of place that... I had no idea...

Making lists of what I would want didn't help. A kind of survival bunker seemed like an idea – except I knew exactly what sort of conclusions I would jump to if I found someone coming out of one of those – especially if they seemed a little bit healthy – "un-battered". I did <u>not</u> want to put myself in that role...

I did succeed in thinking about the Hermitage without weeping long enough to recall that one reason Greg had chosen it was that it had a bore-hole for fresh water. That was in one of the outhouses. He got me passing him spanners and showed me how he fixed things as he got the old single-cylinder pump working again. We cleaned it up, painted it nice and shiny green with the cast letters picked out in red... That was so satisfying – I did the red details...

When he sorted the house all the wiring and plumbing were done. Cost a fortune. He used copper pipe rather than plastic – reckoned that it would last longer...

Oh shit! That makes me think... How long is all that plumbing going to last here, now, around the Valley? I'll have to piss everyone off by raising that...

Not to mention the plastic window frames...

I'm going to be *<u>so</u>* popular...

Maybe I'll forget the windows for now...

Another thing Greg had done pushed my thinking on... He got a generator. It seemed massive to me. The diesel tank for it only just fitted in the outhouse door – and he was planning more (discreetly – because of laws...) He did have two tanks for water with no bother – filled those before you switched the pump to lifting the water into the attic. He wanted more power though – so's he could fit an electric pump on a second bore-hole he wanted.

I have to ask myself... Did he see all this coming? Had he a premonition? Or – was it only his response to the way things were – the way he thought the world was going?

Greg wasn't ever an "End of the Civilisation" kind of person... Okay – so it's a total bummer that he got caught by "The End of The World"... (I am NOT going to cry!) He was no survivalist – although he totally knew how to...

Definitely wasn't any freaky supremacist... In fact – he'd go off about that kind of thing way worse than Gran and Mum put together... He'd been in bad places, seen some vile behaviour – and the results of it...

Greg reckoned that all the extreme groups, whatever they called themselves, were "Follow-my-leader fascists looking for a messiah – looking for a superman, a supreme-leader who would put the whole world right – *exclusively* for them..." He reckoned that it wasn't only "them-out-there" but a whole load of church people at home were that way – for all their talk about "love". If only the people that saw things your way were going to be "saved" – then that meant a whole load of people were totally-fucked... Probably more than the number that the sickness killed... Although, of course, he didn't see that...

Some of what I was seeing had me worried about that kind of crap. Especially what had happened to Tamsin and Ozzie.

People all-too-clearly needed some kind of leadership. Loads of them were clucking round with no sensible direction at all... But – exasperating as that always was – it was nowhere near as terrifying as the idea of some kind of loopy dictator – or – some load of crazy barons running the show...

With the people I knew (before) "expressing" themselves I didn't need a few TV shows with Tony Wots-His-Name to show me that all the historical fantasy about being Lord-of-the-Manor was great – for the tiny number of people that got to do the Lording it over the vast majority... (Great so as you didn't get stabbed, poisoned, your eyes gouged out...) You got to be anywhere lower down the heap and life could easily be crap... (Plus you could easily get smacked on the head by a henchman).

Remembering that had me wondering about eighteen hour working days... What was the "new life" we were headed for going to be like? Maybe it was going to put "Zero Hour Contracts" in the shade...?

However; before I could do any lording-it over the serfs or eighteen hour days – I not only had to figure out what sort of place I wanted... I would have to find it... Or – at least an approximation...

Which was just great... I didn't have clue-one what it would look like...

I didn't pick a monster mansion place – I stumbled on it.

I'd had a nasty night. Bad location after a nervy day. What sleep I did get was full of bad dreams and nasty wake-ups...

Despite the birdies waking me nice and early I didn't get going for a long time. There could be mornings that I felt just empty. Better than any "black-downs" or even "grey fogs" – but – still... Well... I guess most people have had at least some of those. You're damn-lucky if you haven't! There is no need whatsoever to feel that you've missed out!

Making myself eat was hard work. Hugging a coffee – black – a tonne of sugar – I tried to figure the best next move.

High ground to look around seemed good – again... No dickheads this time though! Go steady.

Problem... I was way out in some low and mostly flat land. A long way to any good rise... With quite a lot of expanded villages between me and the nearest hills. A decision between pushing through them or wiggling between had to be made...

Who says I never compromise? I wiggled *and* I pushed... Depending on what each place felt like... Ummm... Not entirely clear that it didn't mean going round in a couple of circles... Loops really – definitely...

So... By the time I'd climbed up onto a ridge I needed a break. Decant, rehydrate, refuel and rest – at the least...

I reckoned I was near the top level when I trundled along beside a high wood-panel fence. It was on my right side toward the hilltop ridgeline, from where I figured I should be able to see a lot of the low land beyond.

Out there in the country the solid barrier spooked me – seemed like it would be some sort of government place or animal experiment factory... The kind of place no-one was supposed to go – to even recognise was there...

Yawning and struggling to concentrate, I reached ordinary hedges and fields again. Grumbling guts spoke louder than concerns about what might be lurking behind the fence. Could it be some kind of bunker? I definitely needed... It *did* look like somewhere secret – industrial – mysterious – at least... Must stop for a pee... Right on the edge of discreet-but-mean security guards. Whatever – needs must... The kind that started with a sharp "You don't want to look here" attitude... Chances of even a single surviving guard? Maybe guns – and real knowledge how to use them...

Enough of possible problems... I needed a break... I didn't need to look... More important – my guts were grizzly.. Demanding....

So, at the end of the fence. I backed into an overgrown trackway on my right.

Should have been more careful.

I *did* check what sort of overgrown track I was going to have to shove the van back into... Broken windows were not going to be a good result. No issues though... So I got well hidden and quickly covered my tracks – and went for that pee – a vital one.

Squatting, I found myself looking through the bottom stems of a tall yew hedge across the most massive, perfect lawn. It was bizarre... But – there were no vents – nothing to suggest the top of a reservoir... No sign of some underground facility.

All there was, was this vast expanse of smooth grass stretching away to a solid wall of screening trees... Not Leylandii. I might have found those reassuring.

Soon as I could, I paused to examine every detail... Inside the hedge an extra-strong chain-link fence. Four metres high – but no razor wire on top like I was expecting... And no threatening signs... Away to my far left the grass rose absolutely evenly to what turned out to be the top floor of a modern mansion.

No way you'd call it a "house".

While it was clearly a home it was obviously the sort of place you'd expect to get chased away from. More than ordinary security – probably dogs as well – nasty ones... So – I froze... Which isn't easy when you've got your jeans round your ankles and you're trying to manage a bog roll in one hand and a revolver in the other...

You're so clever – *you* tell us how it's done – easily.

At least there weren't any nettles!!!

Anyway – no-one showed up for ten minutes or more – after I re-positioned to observe.... There wasn't the least sign of life – and the lawn was growing tatty – which you'd never see in a place like that.

(I was right – they had ride-on mowers – not merely one – but three... All big enough for me to have gone to college on).

I snuck back to my van like a cat creeping up on a bird. Had to have a think next. It would inevitably be a racket pulling upward out of the trackway... A lot more than pretty-much rolling back in... I'd forgotten to check what the ground was like – which was wet woodland-type grass... *Lousy* for tyres to get a grip on. A fast exit looked distinctly unlikely...

There'd been absolutely no sign of life though. I knew that I was very near the highest point and still wanted to take a look out across the land below – see what was going on. So I decided to stay a while.

I crept around setting some trip-wires with pebble-loaded cans before, keeping my ears working overtime for the least movement, I made myself eat – and figured...

Nothing of the place had shown from down below before I'd started up the hill. It must be set-back enough to be hidden. Despite the fence it certainly wasn't obvious from the road – but looked pretty secure. The place clearly wasn't a bunker... If I could get in, maybe it would be the unknown kind of thing I needed? So long as it was unoccupied. It didn't look like it would be into sharing or doing B&B with a scruffy kid like me.

If the last few weeks, months, hadn't taught me, then my whole life before the sickness had – loads. It was not just the OG with their expensive houses in the village... Far more than enough people on the Estate could get nasty at the least excuse – if they thought you might put a scratch on their car – or a footprint on their smart new block-paving... Even in our tiny world people were red-hot to protect their little heap of possessions. People were ready to yell at you – try to give you a slap if they thought they could get away with it... Town was a "whole other thing"...

So, now, since the sickness, I could at least half-expect that any idiot with a gun might take a potshot at me – without the least warning. The place looked exactly like anyone still in it would be very keen to keep away any intruder.

In fact, what I had seen of the place so far, looked like the "gentleman owner" wouldn't bother to go clay shooting but would fly off to game hunt – or be into competition shooting – like in the Olympics.

I was totally *not* into providing anyone with a bit of target practice.

With that very much in mind I went out the van's window, slid cautious-and-low to deeper along the trackway and burrowed under a thicker part of the hedge. The wire was recent, tight and strong. Cutting would mean returning with tools and would certainly show. The work might well be noisy. The place was definitely meant to be secure.

Another crawl found me a position that gave me a better look at the windows... They were smeared – rain and dust tarnish that hadn't been meticulously erased. Did that mean (as it did in most places) that there was no-one alive? I had niggling doubts.

Cleaned windows, like clean cars, could be a sure give-away of recent activity... As could smashed glass, especially doors – or wrecked cars. I resolved the doubt – this place was too big for anyone (anyone without over-powering OCD) to keep smart and shiny... The windows were not going to help me.

Still, no-one had shown... So I decided to sit out the rest of the afternoon and well into the evening before looking around some more. Then I would decide whether to stay around a bit, scoot immediately or at first light. I might at least be able to see any lights – even just candles. Better than that, most people relaxed at the end of the day – which was stupid – but it always helped me.

Hanging around was a pain and I got jumpy knowing what might be right next to me – not-knowing whether it was going to be good or could be seriously dangerous – so I couldn't begin to relax – much less get some much needed sleep.

Not knowing – anticipating – with imagination... No real knowledge and too many ideas... That was always the worst.

Greg had told me that – well – had agreed with me about it...

Probably when I'd moaned about my exam results not having arrived. He was good like that – wouldn't tell me something stupid like "You'll have to be patient". (Yeah. Right. Like I couldn't know that!)

He went on to tell me something that I thought was strange at the start. I expected him to talk about Afghanistan or wherever; about one of the places he'd been in combat... But he said that the most-God-awful tension was having to be inactive while the medics checked out what was wrong with his baby daughter... Told me that he was near climbing the walls – his wife and his best mate had to shove him outside...

Any time waiting, sitting around unable to sleep – like that afternoon – was a bitch for keep getting memories. Good ones could be much worse than bad... I had to be very careful to not let myself get wound up – or depressed. The disgusting thing was – that there was no way I was ever going to be able to do the least thing about so many things – not even take Greg's hand and just sit there with him – not once more – ever...

I "go on about" Greg a bit I suppose... And Mum... And Gran... Well? I'm hardly more than a kid. I know that *now*...

Like, when I was an "ordinary teen" I figured that I knew it all... Maybe it takes getting completely out beyond everything you've ever known to start to appreciate how little you do ever know – and – will ever know. I needed – still need Mum and Greg – and Gran and Gramps – and Bodger – as my reference points... They couldn't be there for me after... But – what they'd done before gave me a foundation to work on... I *owe* them.

===========

Reading to keep my brain from exploding, I sweated out the afternoon. (I always grabbed books to read on my travels. In the long evenings when no-lights meant driving was insane I always stopped early. Sod's Law meant that almost however knackered I was I wouldn't go straight to sleep. At least – not without some sort of wind-down time).

In some Oz novel I found a quote that I memorised... *"In this one small thing at least it seems that I am wiser – that I do not think I know what I do not know"*... Socrates... I didn't memorise the name... Ben stumped me when I tried to bullshit him with it. Then came back at me with "Wisdom commences when one realises how little one knows and how much more there is to know..." Socrates again? No... Ben's Granddad... Maybe, Ben says, misquoting – whoever...

Thing is... Times like that, when you have no idea what you're getting yourself into... The importance of not thinking that you do know is critical...

Back before, when I was fretting about upcoming exams, Greg told me not to bother... If I didn't know it by then I wasn't going to – it's a simple fact that you cannot know what you don't know. With exams the problem isn't going to be getting the answers you have sorted and written down right... The serious problem is going to be the things you don't know – and, until someone asks you about them... You aren't ever going to know you don't know them...

So Greg succeeded in stopping me worrying about what I knew... Then I freaked about all the rest!

I saw right off that there was, there could be, there would be – one hell of a lot of that "other stuff"... That I had no clue about.

He did get himself yelled at for that.

It really pleased him. Ratbag!

There was a lesson of course... In his terms – "Don't *know* where you are going or what you will be doing when you go out on patrol". Huh? His point of course (yeah "of course") was to have a plan, have an intention and some expectation (of what you might find) – BUT to go with your eyes open. "Knowing" shuts your eyes. "Knowing" is dangerous. "Knowing" can drop you right in the shit – easily.

Okay – so I won't go off on one about the lousy government/political tests doing no more than asking if you know (can regurgitate) just what has been pumped into you – to answer the lousy tests... Pavlov's dogs can prove learning skills better than that! What you've learnt is a fat lot of good – if you've not learnt how to learn... And how to adapt and apply it...

The moronic government tested the wrong data! The statistics weren't relevant to what was actually needed. (They were just easy to collect and make a picture – the picture that was wanted...).

Ummm... Like I said – I won't go off on one... Much...

Anyhow, that day reading and memorising kept me occupied until I was stewed enough and the sun began to set. I negotiated my trip-wires and began to work my way cautiously around the outside of the place in the early dusk.

Near where I started at the front there was the high wire fence inside the hedge but they soon swapped position once the wire wouldn't be seen from the road. The public side was a sort of "nothing special to look at here" kind of thing. The security didn't draw attention and get people wondering. (Sort of the opposite of what we do in the Valley now – our "We're ready to take you on" approach).

Knowing what I know now I'd guess that the trackway was an old field access; probably the house had just been stuck into a field – maybe two. A lot of the hedges and trees in the surrounding fields must have been there for ages – long before the place had been built. It was nice – and *very* discreet. While I faced the house I had nothing behind me but nice quiet fields of grass and old hedge lines.

I took my gun with me. I wasn't planning to use it. It gave me some reassurance that if anyone did leap out on me I had some chance of putting up a fight. I might at least make enough noise to get them to keep themselves down for a bit – get them to stop, think and *hopefully* not follow me . If someone started blazing away at me from inside – then I would prefer to quietly melt away – as quick as possible.

The track rose steadily and almost straight to the crest of the ridge where it suddenly stopped at a thin wire fence with an old wooden gate on each side.

Terrific security! All that wire mesh fencing – and it was the same on the far, fourth side – but the third side, now on my right, was only a post-and-rail fence. There wasn't even rabbit wire above the bottom rail. Not that I was going to complain – it solved the question of how I was going to get inside for a look...

It wasn't surprising that the security there looked thin. The trackway stopped because it ran out of hill. The land in front had been quarried away at some time. The track had become near pointless – so both gates were knackered. The ground crumbled away right under the loose end of the left hand one.

I stopped for breath. When I looked out into the distance the startling thing was the number of lights that I could see. Nothing at all like the bright snakes of light and massive glow of before – but – against what I would have expected – still surprising. It suggested far more life than I had seen – except that I had hardly any indication of distance. In the gathering dusk it wasn't clear how spread out everything was down there.

It set me trying to figure how many people in how much of the country... Which I couldn't get at all... If there were loads, how come I'd not seen many? Even with my keeping my head down I began to think I should have seen more... Maybe, just possibly, more of some that weren't as bad as the Donuts I'd run into so far?

Going real careful over the right hand gate put me on a path with the deep drop on my left and an expanse of grass on my right. Nearly right away I was surprised to be on a flat concrete path about two metres wide. Lightly covered in dust and stopping short of the gate it didn't make sense... Until I realised that I was on top of a massive wall along the quarry's lip.

So I had a couple of metres of good, flat concrete to walk on between the rail fence and a precipitous drop. Over the fence more high quality lawn needed a haircut. As I kept low and moved on, the fence stayed level at the back of the wall but the grass swept up to a near vertical, clearly man-made bank, up to nose level. I straightened up. My view of the house was reduced but I reckoned that it also kept me out of sight. Being careful I could see enough without leaping up and down or being silly.

I could see a balcony and the top two floors easily. Under the lip of the balcony there were massive windows, with apparently nothing beyond. I'd got used to looking for lamp light glowing on ceilings by then – people tended to forget about reflections like those. Nothing showed to concern me...

Despite a cold wind coming up from the miles of land below I slowly carried on, intending to check all round – to make absolutely sure. The strange bank only lasted about ten metres before sloping down again with more ordinary lawn and loads of ornamental trees all carefully spaced. It looked – exotic... And expensive – very!

The next corner was more difficult. Well, it would have been for anyone with less wriggling-through practice.

The edge at the end of the wall had crumbled right back under the end of the chain-link fence and taken the last post with it. I was not going over that! In the gathering gloom I could see the tops of trees below but no definite bottom...

Easing forward between the wire and the hedge to where I could carefully squeeze under I circled all the way forward to the road.

Carrying on round to my van would have been the short way back. But it would have been very difficult to get out of sight off of the road, if someone did suddenly come along. Sound and lights should warn me, but that side was barren – with no obvious way out through the thick hedges opposite the fence. Knowing what was there I turned back.

Getting back to the edge again confirmed that you couldn't see the house at all through the hedges. I carefully removed the signs of my way under the wire and disguised the weakness... If I was staying I would be happy to have a possible escape route – but I didn't want anyone else using it to sneak in.

From the collapsing end of the wire I looked out into space. A bank of low cloud had made it a whole lot darker out there while I was sneaking around. The view made me stop. What was shocking, when it sunk in, was that the lights stood out extra sharply...

It was kind-of confusing... Experience made me aware that each little dot could mean nothing... Or it could be a spark of life...

Also – that could be good – or a threat.

It made me desperately want to get somewhere inside and safe.

Anyhow – I'd seen enough. Except that I hadn't seen inside the perimeter for – however long...

I controlled my reaction. I was sure as I could be that there was no-one around the place.

Wanting a final check I cautiously made my way to the near end of the high bank, eased up onto the first rail of the fence and checked out the house with minimum chance of anyone seeing me. A break in the clouds let me carefully study every detail of the back of the house.

I wasn't expecting to see everything well swept and wine glasses set out on the patio furniture... But in the now cloud-and-moon dark the kind-of-obvious details were there. Things like sun-shades that had fallen over, windblown bits and not the least sign of recent activity.

Okay, so I hadn't been out at night except when I absolutely had to be for ages – seemed like forever. I still knew how to use my night-vision. We used to say about some people – the lights could be on but it didn't mean anyone was home... Now the opposite was all-too-true. Making sure to let my focus slip from anything specific I scanned across the whole face of the building – helpfully white except for the enormous windows across the mid two-thirds. With care I could at least get some sense of what was inside them... A vast space – but no sign of life at all.

There was definitely no sign of any light or movement.

Something clattered. Like it meant to shatter my growing confidence... I near went airborne. It was up near the house...

I froze. Barely breathed... Another clatter, and another... Then... A snuffle...

Not human! I *knew* those sounds...

Hedgehog!

I could breathe again – and unfreeze.

A moment to clarify strategy... Actually, more like several moments while I got my breath back and slowed my pulse... I reckoned that popping up at the middle of the high bank would be least expected. It also gave me the shortest sprint to the house. Keep low in the darkness, move fast and get tight to solid walls. Work out what to do when there... But, get there fast – watching hard for lights or movement... Not, *definitely* not – close to the edge of the pool...

What pool?

I am *not* clumsy!

No-one can fall in sudden deep water quietly. *No-one!*

Hopping over the fence I went *very* carefully, *slowly* up the bank's face – watching for the least movement in the back of the house... Steadied on the grass at the top ready to dash the open ground – there were no lights on. No automatic security lights ... So – time for a quick dash – and *nothing* to show me...

There was a *fucking BIG pool.*

And it was *COLD! Freezing!*

The yell I gave out would have raised the dead – which there weren't any...

Or anyone alive.

At least I chucked the gun clear onto the grass as soon as I started to hit the water.

I could swim in my clothes – reason how comes later... I knew that cold was lethal – so I dumped stealth and struck out hard for a side – and then a corner and steps to get me out of there.

My teeth chattered like a road drill – made more noise in my head than all my splashing.

Soon as I was out I was so cold I frantically found the gun (by stubbing my toe on it) and headed inside as fast as I could. If there was anyone in there they hadn't reacted to the racket... Could be I'd scared them... (Probably terrified them with my banshee howl). I risked it that I had some advantage at least...

I was FREEZING! I had to get out of the wind.

Anyhow – the house was far closer than my van and I didn't want to mess with the overgrown trackway again – nor fall into anything else.

Someone had been sloppy. The window I hit with a metal chair leg didn't break but bounced open – so I was in – and no alarm. My teeth were still hammering so hard I wasn't going to be pleased by that. I got careless. I got crazy in fact.

I found a light switch. Sticking lights on without having covered the windows would have been like shining a searchlight from where the house was up on its ridge. So it was as well that the ordinary electric was off.

Important – very significant... Not only because it meant I fell in the *freezing* water – but – because no security kicked off and I didn't manage to put any lights on while I wasn't thinking straight... I didn't display my presence.

Okay, so my excuse is that I was stunned by the sudden soaking. I was desperate to get dry and warm again. Being nothing but skin and bone does not make for keeping warm – or warming up again.

Any other time, I don't reckon that I would have wandered around any house shining a torch around as freely as I did...

It was as well that I had nearly worn that set of batteries out and that I soon found candles – with matches in a decorated box put ready beside them. For one thing – that cheered me up a whole lot.

(Candles are *really* good). (So are fire extinguishers...)

I reckoned that if my yell hadn't startled any response from anyone then there could be no-one close enough to see a couple of candles – and, anyhow, I did *not* want to smash any more toes, knees or hips against furniture. (American White Oak furniture is very nice – and sodding hard).

Where to look for dry clothes in a mansion? Upstairs – you'd think it kind-of obvious... With a bit of experience the idea is extra creepy – when you know that most places you've been in so far the people died upstairs in their beds or in the bathroom. I wasn't going to be able to use my nose to avoid horrible guck – it had gone all snuffly and messed up with the freezing chill of the water.

I sort of got the brain working a bit... I thought "Big – no – ***enormous*** place? Maybe a laundry room?"

Bingo! I found a whole line of neatly piled, ironed clothes – all way-too-big for me of course. There were towels and bathrobes though. So I dried myself off and wrapped up all snug in the smartest stuff I'd ever seen or felt in my whole life.

Next question (as there was definitely no sign at all of anyone) was food. Calories to warm me from the inside.

Finding the kitchen wasn't too difficult. One glance told me that no-one had been there when the sickness struck. Everything in the warehouse of a place was precisely how it should be for a photo-shoot. Perfect. Straight out of a magazine.

Even on the (immaculate) kitchen tiles I felt good that I had not put my boots back on – which was most unusual for me by that point. *[Future reader NOTE! Boots on **all** the time is mega important for running away].*

Then again... Now that I think about it – I have no memory of when I took them off... Not squelching around in that place was just kind-of natural.

The lights didn't work – hadn't worked – that meant no electric – I got that into my brain – at last... (I'd known it outside after all hadn't I?) So how come the immense fridges were humming and all the little lights on? I risked taking a look. (That is, I risked the awful goop and smell that anyone that has opened a long-dead fridge will know only-too-well).

Terrific! The things were working perfectly and there were wonderful goodies all properly chilled inside – and way beyond use-by date.

I figured that cheese is kind of preserved milk and I'd long since reckoned that pickled food was supposed to last forever... So my meal was a weird mixture but quicker and better than anything I'd had for days. <u>It made such a change to not have to use a tin opener.</u>

The anchovies were monster salty... SO? I'd never had them before... They were fish right? Anyhow – the salt boost was maybe good for my system around then...

It meant I had to grab a drink quick. Maybe it was the bottle of wine that made me so sleepy? *Whatever.* I was so happily gorged that I hardly bothered about all the precautions I had got used to taking before I settled down to a sleep.

I found a comfortable bit of a sort-of staff room, hauled a duvet from the laundry and curled up cuddling my gun. (Made safe – you *make* some activities <u>habitual</u>...)

===========

4 – 2

WAKING UP IN THAT PLACE was freaky.

It was the first time I had slept inside for a lot of days and the room was nothing like I had ever seen – sort of a mix between the staff room of a shop and anyone's ordinary home. An extremely posh shop.

That house was everything other than ordinary. You could have fitted most of our house on the Estate into the kitchen. Our home felt so much nicer though.

The feeling wasn't because of all that had happened. I think that place would have felt bizarre at the best of times. It was *way* too self-conscious. Everything looked like someone had picked it from the perfect catalogue – and then kept it all flawlessly shiny. It was like no-one should breathe and disturb the perfection.

When I explored from the kitchen I was expecting the chairs to still have their wrappings on them. (We had an old couple on the Estate that never took the plastic sheet off the back seat of their car – it was still there when the car got so old it had to be carried away for scrap).

Now that I was dry, topped up with another quick meal and warm again, I was much more careful about looking around. I did a fast tour of the place before I did any more. I had taken a load of risks in the night. Truth was that, with the cold soaking, I'd lost it. My caution got blown away.

In the dark outside I had crawled dripping out of the water, staggered around finding my gun – frantic I'd fall in again – and crashed and banged around like a drunk coming home from a party... But – I had needed to get inside – out of the wind.

I should never have assumed that no response meant no-one there... They could have been a heavy sleeper – the place was triple-glazed – they could have been plain stoned and out of it... All sorts of shitty possibilities...

In the morning, waking up to all this as I fed my face slowly – more carefully. I started to tip-toe round more thoroughly – still wrapped up in a vast, white, hooded dressing gown.

Food in one hand and gun in the other – I wasn't certain if I should storm each room like some TV cop and yell "clear!" each time or make like a mouse... I reckon I'm more mouse-sized – so I went with that option.

With the hood flopping over my eyes and the robe trailing on the floor anyone I had run into would probably have thought I was a ghost... Maybe except for the munching... I could always have chucked the bowl at them...

Or I might have erupted and driven them away... I was pretty concerned about what my guts would do after their mistreatment the night before... I made sure I knew where all the loos were... And there were many of them... Incredible places – probably costing half our house – at least...

The search took me ages... Good thing though, was that despite the extent of the place, I didn't get any of those creepy feelings that maybe someone had moved in behind me or was playing games...

So vast, with so many rooms and countless doors, you could have staged a cartoon story in it... But – I did find the wine cellar... And no actual ghosties or beasties. Better still – for a change – no stiffs.

Naturally a place that big would have a wine cellar wouldn't it? Bloody great *enormous* room.

Could I find a corkscrew?

So I had to settle for champagne.

Later I totally freaked when I learnt the price...
(I'm not telling anyone here what happened to a load of it – especially not Ben).

So – anyway – the place was empty. Clearly no-one had been in for months – probably since the sickness – or a while before...

The place *felt* more than empty. Like – desolate. The Village's burnt-out, Victorian vicarage felt more lived in...

There was close to no sign of life ever having been around the place... Only a postcard from the Seychelles on the first fridge (one of those huge triple American ones). It reminded ***"Küllike"*** that "WE! [*the owners*] will be flying in on **February 5th**" – and the flight number for Üllar to check the ETA before he left. He "must on ***no*** account waste *any* time hanging around at the airport" – but he "must take ***no*** risk ***whatsoever*** to arrive late! ***Timothy*** has **important** clients to meet and **must** have a *good night's sleep* after the flight...."

Tacked on the end in tiny, tiny writing there was a note to remind Küllike to be extra careful dusting some particular cabinet's treasures.

It said a whole lot to me that, whoever the "Mistress-of-the-house" was she felt the need to say all this – with so much stress – and not a single please or thankyou.

I also wondered – why a postcard? Who the hell has time for snail-mail? Answer – the snobby-disgustingly-rich that didn't post it but sent it (all double-sealed-up) by security courier – and too paranoid to e-mail... Got those answers later...

Well – all that clearly hadn't happened. If they were still alive – they'd have to walk home.

It looked likely that Küllike and Üllar, whoever they were (apart from being put-upon minions) weren't happening any more either.

It hit me then that I'd probably never get to go see the Seychelles or the Grand Canyon – or even the Alps... All that sort of thing is probably gone...

It's ultra-bizarre the things that you never, ever thought you wanted to do – that you suddenly feel angry, robbed – you forever won't be able to...

And it's funny the odd details you recall from those days... So much happening – and I *know* those strange, foreign names like I'd actually met the people – alive...

It wasn't so hilarious when my brain jolted into gear and asked "So where are Küllike and Üllar then?!?!"

That woke me out of a food-and-comfort snooze... Alright! A "food, comfort, fluffy bathrobe... And two bottles of champagne... TOTALLY-out-of-it flake-out".

I needed a rest! ***Okay?!?***

Fortunately for my plans they were in a staff house, hidden away well out of sight of the long front drive near the front gate – and it wasn't me that went exploring and found them. Danny said that they didn't look a bit like their pictures – just before I smacked him one for being an idiot.

Which could leap-frog me forward to Danny...

But I'd better say a little about the house first. (So I don't crack up). Edge my way towards things...

Ginormous would be the only word to begin to describe it. Sort of like it had been air-lifted from Texas. Everything about the place looked like they could have afforded to do that... Maybe it's enough to say that they didn't just have three massive double or triple fridges – they had a walk-in freezer... *Crazy!*

Insane – but it was an exceptional bit of good fortune for me. It made life a whole lot easier for a time.

The place was like a huge spaceship had settled down on the edge of the hill and dug in a bit – shuffling its bum to make space for cars to get round the back – which kind of meant that the front door was in the back – or that the front had got all confused with the back... I don't think I can explain... It had me in a muddle while I was living there.

Anyway – from the huge, solid oak, front door (in the back) you came through an entrance hall. A "cloakroom" on one side and two, yes *two*, big loos on the other... Each three times the size of our bathroom. Okay "washrooms"... (I do not mean "laundries"... That was beyond the kitchen).

You... That would be "One" *emerged* into a vast open living room – correction –"Reception Zone". (Bullshit!) It was a sodding-big-space. The "emptiness" that I'd seen (or not seen) beyond the vast windows. Okay? With elegant furniture discreetly spaced on rugs bigger than our front yard – with two balconies above the left side... The lower one curved right round the opposite side to the entrance as well, with a spiral stair in the right hand corner. Both floors were mostly "bedroom suites"... Floor space of the lower balcony alone was way more than our back garden. I reckon you could have got aggrophobia in that place.

[Yeah, okay Ben – wrong spelling – I'm afraid of aggro as well – okay?]

Meanwhile – back in Texas... I reckoned that Küllike should have had a ride-on vacuum cleaner for all the miles of carpet. How anyone ever kept all the hardwood floors polished shiny I don't want to think. Maybe everyone kind of hovered around the place? (I felt I *had* to leave my boots off – even when I did that first search). (And again when I frightened myself silly freaking-out about whether Üllar and Küllike were around).

At least the walls were pastel shades – you'd have gone snow blind if all that expanse had been white...

Astounding thing turned out to be – the furniture was remarkably comfortable. It didn't look it – but it was... No ancient battered sofas and chairs like Greg's place – and, naturally, nothing clapped out like we had at home...

[How d'you ever achieve battered and comfortable without knackering it? Mind you – that was a bit like Greg himself in a lot of ways... He didn't so much sit in any chair as become part of it... You'd probably think – from all I've said – that he was up-tight and strung-out the whole time... But that was so not the way he was... Could be he was somewhere <u>way</u> beyond that? "Transcended"? Maybe the way he kind of flowed in a chair explains it... He didn't even do it "effortlessly"... "Effortlessly" was how he did effort... Unless he wanted it to look like people would expect].

So – off to the left under the balconies and the bedrooms was the dining room... The "formal" one. Size again? Well – you couldn't have got the table in our living room and kitchen – right? Then there were studies, TV, games and other rooms. Every single one of them spotless and <u>lifeless</u>... Not just – well – I guess you've got the idea by now.

All the kitchen, utility and rooms like that were beyond that – because of course in our "modern world" not all the rooms had to have windows did they?

Maybe to make up for that the two other sides of the living room weren't walls – there was a vast expanse of glass. The one opposite the entry, that I'd seen first (from the quarry-wall) could slide open nearly all the way – which in England seemed crazy – crazy even with the balcony curving round outside as well as inside and sheltering like the peak of a cap... Same sliding glass up there too... On both levels outside the floor was all smooth stone. (I don't think the blocks would have dared to be out of level).

Beyond the stone was the famous pool – big... Well – eight metres across the face of the house and twenty five to the far side... Yeah. That's where I fell in. It's a bit of luck Mum found a brilliant swimming club for me when I was little.

Beyond the water was the drop down to the fence, the top of the protecting wall and then down the quarry face. The view was incredible... Magnificent.

The right hand side was also glass... Fixed top quarter and slidy sections that could be shuffled around below. Only a small bit of stone outside and then the perfect lawn – stretching away through gorgeous Japanese trees... Spaced out "precisely so"... A year-round flow of colours and shapes... Better than the sterile, designed, inside by far...

All that meant that anyone could have seen in far more easily than I had realised. Except that unless they had crept close like I had, they would have needed to be flying – the place was so high up.

Quite soon after my first search I found some binoculars and did a bit of watching – but soon gave up – because there was nothing to watch. All that looking did was tell me what I already knew – there wasn't a thing happening. No-one moved around much. When there was any activity I would spot it instantly without any help. Most of what I did notice was well off in the distance beyond acres of bare fields that were going back to nature.

Distance meant that, even with the binos, I couldn't clearly identify anything for certain. Often not the number of people for certain. I did get to figuring that I needed one of the spy drones they used in Iraq and all the wars after.

===========

So – on the Grand Tour... It would take all day to describe the bedrooms – the Master Bedroom alone was – *impossible*... Maybe I'll get to that – when I can – later – maybe...

That room also opened outside onto one end of the balcony. So you could turn right and go above the main room windows on the peak and down some long, wide stairs... Or you could go left past the "en-suite" windows and get into the gym from the outside. (More huge sliding-glass). The balcony reached out above the end of the pool – which is relevant – or will be – when I get round to it... If I do...

Like you'd expect it was a state-of-the-art gym. It looked like it was actually used. Not one single item, though, that looked sweaty, scuffed or out of position by a millimetre. I think you probably had to get permission to perspire in there – and you'd be told to not drip... (Guess who took no notice of that...) Most of the walls were full height mirrors – so I figured that someone liked to admire their physique.

[See Ben! I can spell!]

Anyway – there was a hidden/secret door through from the master bedroom into the gym – and opposite, through the outside wall, a bridge across the delivery space behind the utility rooms to a separate squash court... How *ridiculous* was that?! And the court was all perfectly air-conditioned – not at all stinky – I had no idea you could do that.

Maybe you'd expect it... All those big windows – even the master bedroom and gym – could be opened by motors – remote controlled... Insane! Thankfully they could also be shoved open.

===========

Monster house like that – her clothes were – *incredible* – of course. *Beyond that*... What would you expect?

The sort of couture that *doesn't* have labels.

All way too big for me of course – but it was terrific to quietly sit and feel the fabric – and see the way it was made – had to be hand-made – *beau-tiful*... Luxurious...

It wasn't a whole new world for me – it was a different cosmos. You see pictures in the celebrity mags and all that – but – to sit there and feel the material in my fingers...

I've never been into make-up – but when you saw and smelled the cosmetics she had – well... It could make you think at least... And the bathroom – bathroom suites – Master-Suite-Bathroom...

The whole place was far beyond credible... But – still – empty – barren – but – inconceivable anyway... You'd have imagined a fantastic life...

Except that none of the *loads* of pictures of her made her look remotely like happy... She'd have made a Wicked Witch look giggly.

No! That did not make me feel good. That would have been totally mean of me.

No-way I was going to feel sorry for her either... I don't do "feel sorry" – not for anyone. (It's bullshit). I felt... Well – all that excess just left me empty about her – and him... How they looked – how it looked like they felt... *What-the-fuck was the point???*

I mean – we all know that there's been loads of times since the sickness when we've ground to a stop and asked ourselves "What was it all for?". We've all had discussions about "What was the point...?" But... When you think about how many people had sod-all and struggled... Even when in our lives "sod-all" was the height of luxury compared to most of the world... And our "struggle" was often pretty soft... Well – with our dreams of how wonderful a huge lottery win would be... Just *what* was the point of fabulous wealth – when they looked so grim?

He didn't seem to be so cheerful in any of his (about a tenth as many) pictures – more like he was thinking about business and money all the time. How can a picture make you look like that? Even if you are wearing a suit that would buy anyone else a car? A top-of-the-range, superb car. (A stack of them – with trimmings – in the underground garage...)

Actually – the place had "Bespoke" cars... Their stable wasn't simply air conditioned – it was filtered... Not a speck of dust... Until I got in there – probably...

I had not been overwhelmed with jealousy or outraged at the wealth of the place. I really hadn't. It seemed farcical to me. After I might have been too busy being blown-away by it all. I mean – it was way beyond any reality I had ever imagined. You knew that the magnificent film sets were cardboard cut-outs. This was solid – genuine, authentic... REAL.

Plus – I was actually there – walking around. (Still no boots – not even on the garage carpet)...

And there were all those framed pictures. Not just pictures but those weird special wall lights over a lot of them. Those brass-coloured tube thingies... That's right – "brass-coloured"... **Bonkers!**

So? Okay, meeting The President – Presidents... That could be awesome – yeah. You probably would want a picture of it. Mum and I – maybe Gran and Gramps might... Greg might have done – could have done... You know who'd have slobbered... Wasn't one with the Queen – so they can't have been that fantastic can they?

But – *please!* One A4 in a frame would be enough!

Her ladyship's smile always looked like a cat that had just had its temperature taken.

The nasty, horrible thing?

They had a daughter (Stacey) – would have been about thirteen to fifteen at a guess... You can't ever definitely tell (as Greg *always* complained).

Okay, once I'd actually found a picture of her – after I had found her room – she did look sort of happy – probably on mood-medication or plain stoned... Somewhere in America by the look of it with a woman who, when you figured it, was (under all the surgery) much more Timothy's age...

So – <u>no</u> – I wasn't jealous or outraged – I damn near surprised myself by feeling sad... *Almost* sad for them... More like depressed... All that luxury – and they clearly didn't have what I had... What I had – had... So I hid in a corner of the staff room and wept for a bit...

===========

I no-way thought about it – honest – but – when I identified Stacey's room as I searched the house a third, slower time – she had a whole mass of clothes. Kid had way more than I'd ever done in my whole life – loads of it never taken out of the bags or parcels... And – she was my size...

I <u>had not</u> gone looking to find clothes for me.

I mean, outside of her room it was not exactly as if there was any sign that she ever existed or had been in the place. I reckon her step-mum shut her out about as completely as she could have done.

Poor kid. Yeah, poor kid – all that money. Living in the USA and all that... She never had a Bodger, my Mum, Gran, Gramps or Greg – people that showed that she was important...

That *was* depressing... Except... It kind-of cheered me up as well... All the shitty bits of my life, all the times I might have wished for her world... I'd actually been so much better off... It's not mean-and-horrible – that that cheered me up...

Yeah, yeah... So it made me go all weepy as well... What d'you expect?! Except it was some kind of "happy weepy"... For a change.

When I did find an album in her walk-in closet (well hidden away) most pictures were of places, other people and events. Whenever she was in one she was sort of on the edge – looking like she didn't belong, didn't want to be there...

I figure a lot of people would have thought she was sulky, a stroppy teenager, maybe sour and difficult. I wondered though. If anyone had taken many pictures of me – I wondered what I would have looked like... Unless I was with Bodger – and didn't know I was having a picture taken. Maybe with Greg too. Never with my Mum!

I don't think there is a single picture of the two of us. That is awful – horribly sad... But we both hated having our picture taken – I mean we hated looking at the camera, smiling and being "nice".

(Yeah – so? That's so *really* going to surprise you?)

I guess, though, that in the end there must have been loads of pictures of each of us at parties, festivals and things like that. Things where we would have been in a crowd – people around us – all happy and laughing – not aware that someone was aiming a phone at us.

We probably looked wild – crazy...

I have endless pictures of my Mum in my memory though. Mum – well, Mum simply being my Mum – all the way from when I was little and she seemed huge and tall.

I never caught up with her – never got beyond 155 centimetres.

Sorting clothes had always been a pain before – I've mentioned the horrors that came with travelling and raiding ...

Don't get the idea I ever went short. That never happened (Mum made totally sure of that)... Truth was – I wasn't that interested. Yeah, I liked to look okay... Good for special occasions... Was only that... I never saw any point in working myself up about something that was never going to happen. Trailing round a mall (probably followed by security) with a bunch of girls wasn't my idea of entertainment.

Clothes for me were – well – just practical. Including when I started college and had a brief urge to attract a nice boy... Well... I wasn't ever going to compete with some of the girls was I?

(So I found me a *total* Donut didn't I?)

Okay – maybe I copped out on that – a bit... Told myself there were more important things... Practical...

Greg insisted on being "practical" and got me one of those massive Puffa-Jacket things from America... Said he couldn't-be-arsed with messing about if I went and got a massive cold or pneumonia and couldn't look after Bodger when he needed me to...

So that was practical – hilarious. It nearly doubled my size. It was warm though – steaming if I kept it closed when I went up over the hill.

By the time I reached the big house I had essentials... Good gear to keep me going – assorted T shirts, jeans, and the biggest pile of panties I could hoard. Like I said – practical. Plenty of socks – to go in the boots – fleeces, hoodies – and a couple of good (breathable) waterproof sets.

The things Shania had found me were long gone... You don't stop to do a load of laundry when... Well – I guess you could almost say "when you're on the run"... I went on about that didn't I? Oh well...

I don't think I was weird or crazy to try stuff on... It made a glorious change to stop sleeping in my clothes. I'd been doing that about all the time – you need to when your kind-of "on the run"...

Never thought of it that way before now – but those first weeks were much like that... It got natural to always keep a low profile and be ready to bugger off as fast as possible at a moment's notice...

Even in the big house I always had my stuff ready, knew exactly where it was... Well, almost always...

So I hadn't been taking a shower morning and evening and changing into jim-jams...

Hey! No! There will never-be a way I don't keep spotless after the sickness... You know that if you got through...

At least one thing with the big stores – they didn't originally get cleaned out of wet-wipes and baby-wipes... Food, often, yes – some places (later ones to get hit) people went frantic about that – and bottled water... But – well – we had no idea what it would do to us did we? We had no idea how immense keeping clean would be...

Wasn't like anyone was passing on tips once they'd gone down with it.

So, anyhow, looking at Tracey's Step-Mum's collection was – well – it wasn't weird... Kind-of dreamlike? Fascinating I suppose. The fabrics were – hard to believe... People truly wore this? Went to sleep in it? Didn't just pose for catalogues and magazines in it?

Right... So – truth was – I took a bit of a mini-holiday... I damn sure needed one! More than my body, my whole being was desperate for a break...

Okay – so I found a digicam and charged it up same as I was able to do a laptop. Was top-of-the-range as you'd expect... But easy enough to suss for "Auto" and selfies... So – I played "model" for – um – a few days – not all the time though... Only a bit between eating and sleeping a lot.

On the sensible side there were good things from Tracey's hoard I put together – and a suit. I would have felt extra confident going for an interview in that... Except (of course) you then have to wonder if you haven't over-dressed... But Mum would have been *so* proud of me... When she got over the shock... I'd have loved Greg to see that...

Oh shit! – Crying again...

"Ahem"... Do I need to mention that most of Tracey's clothes were <u>not</u> what you'd call "practical"? Stylish, fashionable – some designer's idea of – "cred"... Lace panels do <u>*not*</u> go with cammo and combat! Then again – you want hard-wearing cotton rather than satin... You want proper button-shut pockets not Velcro or poppers.

I did not have to learn this!

Life around town before the Hermit's place taught me well – long before...

Anyhow...

Out of the nightmare it was so good to dream a bit... Like fantasise that there could ever be a job interview to go to...

Pretending like that... Kind of let you chill – forget "reality"... For a bit... You had to watch that fact didn't creep up on you and crack you up... Smash you in the face... Set you howling and falling into a black pit...

I reckon we all know how come some people only made it so far.. Before...

Once I'd checked everywhere around the place I zoned-out a bit – maybe quite a lot... Probably... There was plenty of food, a whole lot of space to dance around in...

===========

I didn't give up on my plan to get organised and prepared. For a short while it didn't seem quite so important. At least, it didn't seem it with all the stuff already there... And that did include the wine cellar.

Although I knew a bit about it, I'd never been much into wine. It did seem, though, that I should least see if I could educate myself a bit more – practically...

So I confirmed that red wine can give you a blinding headache – when you wake-up/come-round – and Brandy does a banging heap worse... I didn't go near the whiskies and hard booze like that – except the vodkas...

One thing that stopped me from progressing my plans – gave me an excuse at least – for not doing much – was that I couldn't quickly figure how to get the big front gates open. So the van had to stay hidden in the trackway outside. That was hard work.

Backing in once hardly showed... The more trips I made the harder it got to not display my activity. The bushes were soft enough to bend and not break but, wet or dry, I had to watch that the earth didn't streak out onto the hard road. I also had to find a way to not leave fresh tracks in the grass... I was never comfortable that I succeeded.

Having to cart things in from the van all the way round the back was exhausting – and put me outside where I might be seen more than I liked.

You might have thought that I would be screaming out for human company by then.

I had seen what? Maybe thirty – possibly forty – could be going on fifty people up close...? Living people that is... At least half of which I did not want to see again – at least half...

Maybe, could be, two or three times as many more at a distance – the further the better sometimes.

Don't ever go there on how many stiffs... ***Ugh!***

Anyway – apart from Mum, Gran, Gramps, Greg and Bodger I had never had a lot of people in my life. Hardly anyone you would safely call a friend at school. (That word "friend" was so over-used and totally misused!) Kids, that's "social-relationships-people", would always drop you and buddy up to whoever they thought would do them good as soon as it suited them... College – well – that wasn't for so long. (Never would have been either).

Didn't matter how "real and forever" things looked/felt (people declared) – a lot of college was "fleeting" wasn't it? That's including the significance of the wonderful qualifications – and any prospect of getting a good job – *regardless* of all that their glossy sales brochures told us.

Whatever they sold us – we all knew that. We spotted the truth – unless we were totally gullible. We had eyes and ears didn't we? We just needed to keep away from the benefits system all we could – like the government intended... Couple of years being "improved" in college neatly massaged their statistics didn't it?

Okay – so, "relationship wise", Mum and teachers saying that "Expecting it and holding back didn't do me any favours" could have been true – didn't stop it happening though did it?

I can't explain the opposite though. I have no way to say how come Greg and Danny – and Shania – (and – say it quietly – Ben and Beth) were always different from that...

Bodger – Hey! He's easy! He simply liked you – accepted you – no questions... Then again – there's no way that great pudding liking you could be accounted for – it just happened.

Huh! They do say that "kids can be cruel" – so why'd they expect them to be all lovely all the time? It's safer to be your own person.

Bodger was good at scaring the life out of people (like I said) but he wasn't mean. He didn't like you one minute and tell everyone lies about you the next. He took you for who and what you were – didn't have a list of what you should be – no list that changed as the wind blew...

And Greg? Well. So long as I was just me and up-front/honest – then he was cool about it. I could get moody – so long as it wasn't at him – or, if it was – so long as I told him what it was... Which near always turned out to be some stupid idea I'd got muddled into my head and got all wrong.

Don't get the wrong idea. Greg wasn't Mr Perfect – not even in my bright-shiny eyes when he let me stay in my outhouse and offered me the jobs. In fact he told me to expect him to be "mean, horrible and nasty"... He was, as he said, "a male of the species"... So there was *no- way* he would ever be good or sensible and "certainly never anything that I, as superior modern woman, would expect to just come naturally to me"... Which (of course) was pretty much correct.

I had a kid's wisdom full of expectations by then anyway – so everything I saw and did got filtered through those...

Listen to me! He was right again! I was "a kid" and hadn't had time to learn a whole load... Masses that I had no clue about at all... "Knowing everything" is so easy when you know nothing!

Like things you'd gone through definitely could have you waking up screaming...

===========

4 – 3

So – FOR ALL I thought with my teenage wisdom... All that had gone on in school, town and shittyness around the Estate and the Village... The truth was, that I had totally had a soft life... Before...

(Well... When I'm honest about then... My life was easy compared to so many people in the world... Definitely compared to how we are now... But – so long as I don't think about the people I lost much... I prefer now – most of the time... Not when any of us are being shot at though...)

After...

I can't sensibly say – I'm still too close to it... I think that when I landed in the big house I wanted a bit of a "time out". I needed recovery time and to figure a few things. At the very least I needed to eat the good food, exercise and get myself a bit like fit again.

So I ate – didn't stuff my face – I knew all-too-well what effect that would have. I had been lucky to get away with it the first night. And I slept a load. And exercised...

You could probably have run long distance that house was so big – but I settled for the gym and watching my scrawny carcass in the mirrors... Plus I could look out over the balcony away over the far end of the pool and miles into the distance. I told myself that I could watch to see if anyone did move out there, while I waggled my muscles about a bit.

So I wasn't doing nothing...

I began to keep a bit of a log-book of where I saw movement. That would be anywhere I thought I saw it more than a couple of times. I couldn't find a map though, not a single one in the underground garage (the curse of Satnav). I had to tape sheets of paper together and construct some kind of map of my own... Which was *so* not-easy!!! (I never showed it to Danny).

Like I said, I did go raiding... I got diesel for the little emergency generators that ran the fridges and very-basics. (Nosing around I'd sussed that they must have cut-in when the huge main back-up dried-out its vast tank and failed). I also got some of those patio gas heaters and a bigger camping cooker.

My big aim was to avoid running into any of those "active" places – and, *far* more, to not lead anyone back to my hide-away. Not even give anyone the least idea that I had a place.

Rolling full cylinders from the back of the van left way-too-much of a trail – so I got a wheelbarrow – plastic as that was lighter. Places like garden centres were good for things like that. They didn't have a whole lot of food but they usually did have useful stuff. Most of them were a bit remote – out-of-the-way... More important – people weren't looking at them early on. So I didn't get bothered, yelled at and (best of all) I didn't get anything nasty aimed at me.

I did have the sense to think that I should be finding seeds to begin growing fresh food – for later – but didn't get round to it then. (Having no idea how to grow anything was a significant reason for putting it off...)

Ummm... I did get round to clearing out their stocks of chocolate – and their good, healthy nutrition bars – (second choice).

The big house had miles and miles of grass lawns – all going long and tatty after the spring got going towards summer. No! I was not planning to mow them!

The thing was... It wasn't like the old-fashioned country houses you saw in TV dramas with their own veggie gardens and glasshouses. In fact a lot of the labels in the kitchen and pantry showed that the posh people had had a load of their ordinary food flown in privately. (Danny said the massive room was *"the pantry"* – all snotty-voiced and taking the Mickey). There were files and files of waybills from international couriers on a shelf in the staff room – *invading* the staff room, I thought. (Keep the kitchen all neat and shiny and dump on the staff).

(Have to explain Danny sometime...)

Anyhow – I did have some sort of organisation for myself and I was beginning to think a bit more practically – if not much... But – starting to think first, instead of reacting on the fly, was significant progress...

Well? What was I supposed to think? Where was I supposed to start? Where would you have started? Where did you start?

===========

Being practical, getting my act together a bit, I also gained myself a little fast car – for going on fuel raids. Thing was, I still wanted the van for a load of reasons but it was way too visible and slow if I needed to get the hell out of it. It didn't happen much – but anytime I was swiping fuel I was not going to hang around when I heard any human movement..

From round about then people would shoot at you on a petrol station! Even if you had a can with you on the street! How stupid was that!?

Doesn't matter a toss if it's only one time in six that you get shot at... It is NOT fun!!! It is not confined in a screen! Digital doesn't snap past you nor ping off things. Digital doesn't make you poo your sofa. Real sparks off real concrete can ignite any fuel vapour...

You recall that bullet that killed Daz? Well any shot that can do that can just as well penetrate any other car – and probably more than one can of fuel inside... You do not want to be driving around in a box full of petrol fumes – even if there is relatively little chance of ignition – unless someone uses a tracer... You want to gamble on the risk???

You do? Let me know *before* we go raiding... 'Cos otherwise *you will* be walking back!

So I got into looting-and-scooting whenever I wanted fuel. I would drive the van down to where I'd hidden the car, shift cans across, go raiding and do the opposite returning... *That* was the plan – it worked far better than using the van the whole way. The best part was that I was only a little terrified until I was nearly home with a load in the van.

Approaching home (the mansion) was *not* the time to relax – I knew that – but – well – I had a good idea of what should be where – I felt that I would notice anything out-of-the-ordinary – and that would warn me – as long as I stayed alert...

I had figured out that I would always be needing some fuel at least. Building up a bit of a store while I could made sense...

Thing was – when I first arrived at the Big House I didn't have clue-one about the electric... Once I found them I tried to make sure the little generators for the fridges kept going. Seeing as I'd stumbled on a good food supply I was determined to make it last as long as I could – and have a bit of a break from always scavenging.

I did figure out that I didn't need the water chiller though – so risked it and swapped a tablet onto the plug to charge. When that didn't knacker the system I did a laptop as well – and then the famous camera....

That meant that I could at least play myself some music or DVDs – quietly of course – before Danny arrived and sorted things. (Had left my player behind hadn't I? Silly me!!)

I thought that sorting the music was neat of me. It meant I could keep doing dance exercises – which was more fun – so I would do it more... I'd sometimes put on a long tune so that I'd push myself that bit more.

Always had to keep it low though – so that I should hear if anyone got to creeping about. So they wouldn't hear me either. Much like old times...

Another thing... I knew that if it did ever come to moving I was going to need fuel (obviously) – but that it would be harder and harder to get.

A thing that bugged me – not being able to start the bigger power I worried about how to restart the little generators if I ever let them run out. I had no idea at all how long a tank-full would last. I also never knew how long I might be away on a raid for– either by choice or necessity. So I kept them topped up all the time.

I took to getting more cans whenever I got the chance. (Garden places). They had to be good, strong unused cans – clean – no smell to them. I couldn't say where I learnt that – but I knew to not risk contaminating any fuel with any liquid or bits I didn't know about in a dirty can. Not even flakes of rust – that can clog filters – all too easily.

(Wasn't there a bother about a load of cars getting damaged by bad fuel some time?)

Whenever I could I got proper steel jerry cans. Plus spouts for them. (So! This is <u>not</u> a thing I only "have a fret about" now... I've worked on it for ages!)

By then I knew way-too-well that pouring fuel into any vehicle without a spout is a bitch of a disaster – unless you're an octopus. Anyhow – it takes all of my strength to hold up a full can with both arms – so there's no way I want to juggle with a funnel in one hand and a can in the other.

It was definitely idiotic – you are NOT supposed to fill up a generator – *or <u>anything</u> else* – while it's running... You have heat – hot exhaust, cylinder head (spark-plug and leads, if it's petrol) and so on... It's DANGEROUS!

It's not the liquid that burns – it's the fumes coming off it and mixing with air... So – any time there's heat you can get fumes... Least spark and...

Do NOT be there!!!

I did know all that... I tried to figure out how to start them up – but didn't want to risk turning them off in the first place... (Turned out it was infuriatingly easy – once you knew how).

Anyhow I figured the best thing to do was to have a small, very flat-bottomed can to transfer into from the big cans. Little can on the floor is so much easier to fill. Shift the closed big can well away... Then pour the little one through the biggest funnel that will fit – and fit securely – not wobble. You do NOT want the least spill!!!

I did want the fire extinguishers ready to hand. (They were already in the brick hut)... After a bit I also had a fire blanket from the kitchen all set-up ready... To grab and roll me in... Thoughts of what could happen if I screwed up were totally freaking me out... So much I almost gave up on the whole fuss... But then Danny turned up and sorted all that.

I did not tell him what I'd been up to... I let him be impressed by how careful I'd been....

I'm sure (enough) he didn't suspect...

If he did – he had the sense to keep quiet... UNLIKE some people! (Who will remain un-named – just bruised...)

I used the small can trick for the van as well.

Load of messing about? If you get in a tangle and drop the small can you don't lose so much – and you don't splash a load all over yourself.

Obvious? Yeah... Right...

How long did it take you to sort the fuel business once you realised you weren't casually popping into the garage and filling up? Yeah?

(Small can still wants its own spout).

Neat trick... Did you think of this? When you have the sense to hide the big can before pouring into the car – you can make out that the little can is all there is – all you've "acquired"... Acquired someplace else!

And another... Putting a small can into a car you are a bit more safe – like filling the generators... Which means you're a tiny bit more okay leaving the engine running – when you're worried about the battery being knackered or – and – when you're bricking yourself because the place feels threatening – so's you want to leap back in and get the hell out of there as fast as you can, if the shit does hit the fan.

So... All that adds up to... *Grab fuel fast and get out faster*.

Later shift your hoard from the car to the van somewhere nice and quiet and out-of-sight... Cover the cans in the back of the van and secure them tight... Make the effort and put them under the "shopping" you raided before... 'Cos you don't want to mess around stopping at the shops with a load of fuel on board... Someone might get more pissed-off if they check you out... You have got to be able to play "innocent..."

Including with (apparently) nice people.

You do not want anyone figuring out how organised you are – or that you have a good place sorted.

So... When I'd done all that, I would trundle home nice and quietly – with eyes peeled all the way. I'd only stop and back into the track beside the property when I was totally certain that nothing had changed – any other time – I'd have gone on by.

I was lucky. I never had to slide-on-by. That was so much of a relief! I was always completely knackered by then.

"Trundle" because "empty roads" are NOT safe. Other idiots than you, before you get the idea, think they are "empty"... Okay – so swap the "you" for "me" in this case... I did learn this one FAST.

People wanting to check me out could catch up with me faster?

Hell of a lot better than me running full-tilt into them! A load of shopping whacking you in the back of the head when you slam on the brakes is not nice... Bits of hedge poking in the window lash you – if they don't take your eye out.

Taking it steady means you can play all cool, confident (as appropriate) and even "a little bit lost"... Bullshit "femininity" beats male brains – often also the nasty ones... Mostly...

Anyway – going steady is safer for loading any gun you have... Do not drive around with it loaded and not on safety! You end up in a ditch – it makes a different noise from the airbag going off...

Was not me...

He died...

I was lucky again... I'd parked the van up before the engine cooked... I'd totally overheated it... Not knowing about water for the cooling... BUGGER!

I knew I'd knackered it... Horrible noises, sudden cloud of stinky blue smoke and then CLUNK!

I reckoned – definitely DEAD.

Totally.

A temperature gauge? A warning light? *Now* you tell me!!!

Before that...

Soon as I ever got backed into the track, before I had any way recovered, I would scrub out any tracks and hide the van. Then I would split round the back and get inside quick – because the whole thing was always physically knackering as well as a ton of stress...

So – after as short a time as possible – but usually at least a day to get back some strength and chill – I would shift the cans deep into that trackway and hide them in the hedges. I used the plastic wheelbarrow. I no-way wanted to prove what a single, tiny, spark can do with any spillage.

Green or black cans were the best of course but I had got some thick green plastic sheet – patterned... Camouflage – so I used that... And when I'd got more strength again I would do all I could think of to hide the cans short of burying them – like painting them dark colours – anything better than bright red. I did not want them to rust and leak. The whole business wasn't perfect – but – well – it made some sense...

Once the van was knackered I switched to using the little car. As it turned out, that wasn't for long...

With the van dead the walk to the car did take long! Practically a whole day. Why the hell didn't I think to find a bike? Except... Finding a bike would have been yet another thing to mess about taking time and energy to do... I knew where the car was. Soon as I got to it I went to sleep – under a cover.

So – I was working – okay? Fuel was a clear need right then. Great thing was, scary as getting it always was, I did not have to go looking in houses or stores. That was a ginormous improvement. I was not sitting on my arse though. Without fuel – how would I go get anything in the future?

Once I'd got a big map book from a garden place, plus worked out where I was, I set-to to sort out where the lights I could see at night were located. Figured I'd get a better idea of where people were that way... It was extremely difficult. Wasn't helped by trying to do it in the dark while not showing out any light of my own. I didn't give up on it – I just never made much progress...

The big hope was that I could work out where to avoid running into people – or (later) to at least get a good idea where we should take a look at what was going on. It was always hindered by people relocating. Working with Danny at one corner of the quarry support wall and me at the other, we would just about fix where a cluster of lights were a few nights running – and then they'd vanish. Frustrating!

We tried to "triangulate". I got that idea from the "Dam Busters" film... (Watched with Greg's crazy mates singing along to the music – as you should expect by now). Fixing what was where might have been a whole load easier with a plane... Except it could hardly have been discreet could it?

I wonder if there'll ever be any proper planes back in the air again?

Drones are a whole different thing... But that would be jumping my story forward a whole load. I don't think anyone got round to clever tricks like that for at least a couple of years. There was far too much other stuff to sort out first... Like just staying alive and getting some strength back.

===========

Ben's caught a slap...

Not for doubting my efforts – but for a smart-arse remark about "Oh; so you didn't ever find some nice people? You fought everyone off... Or knocked them cold..."

Just because that's how we met...

Yes Ben, I did meet some okay people. Briefly. A few times. Wasn't anything special, "note-worthy", about that was there? You wouldn't write much about a good commute to your office would you? A bad or crazy incident on the way? You remember that don't you?

Yeah, yeah... You <u>would</u> recall seeing a young lady's nice bum on the bus... *<u>You</u> would!* Did you talk to her bum? Did this wonderful experience last more than a few moments...? Do *not* answer that!

So as to shut him up...

There was a good – better – thing...
When I'd gashed my arm climbing in a window...

Almost anywhere else (except your back – naturally) is nowhere near as damn difficult to sort out. You need both hands for any bandaging, or whatever else like that, you need to do.

Bad gash – you can see by my scar that it was serious... How I missed the artery I have <u>no</u> idea – I'm <u>very</u> thankful...

A bad gash should have gone to hospital "of course". Like antibiotics, that was not going to happen. That house was wonderfully clean and sorted though... (I *really* appreciated that!) I grabbed fresh tea towels fast and got pressure on the cut.

Then I got the question... How to keep them there – and tight...?

That's ignoring the "How not to pass-out, chuck-up or plain scream" question...

Answers... Bite lip. (Not too hard). Press arm hard into ribs. Open every drawer and cupboard in sight until you find a roll of food wrap. Later progress to gaffer tape...

Ever tried sticky taping a parcel one handed?

You probably have the picture...

So... Where this got good... (Out of being lousy...)

Pain and being frantic meant that my guard was down. I didn't vanish when the next person showed up. This was only an hour or two later – which was probably as well...

I'd not lost a lot of blood (missed the artery like I said) but – I probably was in shock... I suppose... Anyhow – it hurt enough to make me nauseous... Clearly I wanted an ambulance and a paramedic...

I got lucky. The person was a First Aider bod (badges and all). So he knew first aid. (Duh! Obviously!) He actually had antiseptic and a suture set. All very good. Pity he didn't have anaesthetic... He didn't do a bad job of stitching my arm up... Even if it made me faint.

Yeah. So that was good... I was grateful. I am grateful. But it didn't mean that I wanted to stay around Derek. I'd probably have ended up braining him with his own frying pan.

Put it down to "different personalities". Yeah?

===========

Meanwhile... Back at the " working and sorting"...

I'm still kind of pleased with myself. (Beth says I'm smug). I'd figured out I should get vitamins and iron supplements as well as everything possible to settle my tum... (Would be the polite version). Gran's usual recommendation of "get a cork" was *not* appropriate! (I might have shot anyone behind me... Or myself with a ricochet).

Quietly looking around on a trip (still in the van) I spotted one of those superstore small-satellite places.

They could be good but they were very risky. Other people could always be about and reckon that they "owned" them. There was less of everything. Especially the significant things – like place to hide the car, ways in, somewhere to hide inside – and – most-of-all – exits to bug out of...

Like with the car-keys thing – with so few people around/surviving... How come they always seemed to manage to pop up where I wanted to grab something? (Seemed like that anyhow).

This place had clearly been broken into already. That could have been in passing, though, or mean it was wrecked... But it was syling with rain at the time. That shortened the odds on anyone being out for the fun of it.

(I was already on the move when it started). So I parked round the corner and ducked inside.

As always it was gloomy and dark in the place. Okay, I'd got used to that... I'd learned that you had to go in *extra* carefully because there was usually broken glass all over the floor for a metre or two inside.

Boots protect you from cutting your feet but you could easily go skating if you didn't watch out. Tiny bits of glass are worse than marbles – more like ball bearings. Far worse than puddles – and ice. I'd smacked down on the floor or into shelving a couple of times. So I'd got well into looking first and moving cautiously.

Another fact to learn – it's enough trouble getting good boots – you don't want to go shredding the soles of them. More than that – a bit of broken glass stuck in the sole can cut/slash before you know it – bags of rice, car mat/carpet, anyone you kick (not always such a bad thing) – but – worst of all – it can cut you – your other leg – or your hand when you take the boot off... All little details that you learn – I had to learn – usually the hard way...

I sneaked into this place alright though. It didn't look too bad – and at least I could be confident enough that the trail on the floor was dried-up blood not shit. So things should be okay...

I followed the trail from a stain to where the medicines and plasters section was – which reminded me to get vitamins as well as ointment for my arse while I was about it... You survived – you do not need that explained! Pity sorting our throats and stomachs weren't so easy...

I filled up a big "for life" thick bag and began looking to see what else to get.

The trouble was that in the chaos at the end a whole load of stuff got cleaned out of places (like a hyperstore at Christmas) and then, when any had been raided, more would be gone – so you couldn't easily plan what you would get anywhere. It was always sort-of Lucky-Dip.

This time I struck gold. The place hadn't been cleared out of bog roll or kitchen roll. (Again – you survived – you know what I mean!). They even had the soft and absorbent types. ***Great! Eldorado!***

(Wasn't remotely thinking about tampons and the like around then – never dreamt any of that would ever happen again... Nor that there would be any reason. My body was doing better but it wasn't exactly "fun" – not yet... It needed "waking up" I suppose. I *was* making sure I kept myself clean – and didn't get any sores).

Another thing to get *whenever* you could – skin cream – any sort – to try and see if it worked for a start... Got to be *soooo* careful... But – always grab a pile – because, if it did work, then you didn't want to have to go back for more...

Second visits were always more dangerous than a first look... And first looks soon got so they could be more than dangerous enough – especially anywhere you'd not been before – new places on your travels. Anywhere new on your own, it got to make sense to try to sit around and observe for a day – half a day at least.

Anyway – in that store I filled more bags and, working to not to drop any of it, moved toward the door. By then I'd got used to the idea of not having to go through the checkouts – it didn't feel weird any more – and I didn't look for the security cameras... But the big dish mirror at the exit saved me... I saw movement...

No decision to be made. Quick and quiet as I could I shoved my loot into a checkout position and shoved the swivel chair in front of it. Next I looked around *(frantically)* and spotted a janitor's store... Despite the rain pissing down, I could hear people arguing by then. Loading my revolver and checking the safety was on was natural as I sprinted for the little door.

Turned out to be one of those tiny places for mops and buckets – but I could just about squeeze in...

I spent the next fifteen minutes (that seemed like a week) balancing on a bucket, clutching a mop and hoping that I wouldn't sneeze, cough, fart or anything else.

Why do all those things *always* want to happen when you're hiding?

Three or four lads and a couple of lasses clattered around looking for chocolate, crisps, booze, fag papers and *maybe* even some food for a party – another party by what they were saying.

It sounded like they were right outside my cupboard more than half the time. Had me worried that they'd seen me and knew where I was... So – reliably – I got an itch... I am not telling you where! It was *not* my nose...

At least three of them wafted marijuana around – don't know if they were smoking or carrying a bush or three.

At first they didn't sound too crazy – maybe only a little pissed and not as if they were very stoned – although two of them kept on about "having to get some *good-shit*". Then there was a crash. The shouting and laughing told me one of them had dropped a bottle of whiskey – and that another one objected. Two more bottles smashed – more cursing and shouting. Then three more. Someone else decided it was a joke – it sounded like they shoved a whole line off a shelf. One of the women cut in then, screaming at them to stop. "***Stop*** being so fucking stupid!"

I agreed with her! Finding a whole shelf of any goodies didn't happen often. (Even when you don't want them yourself spirits of any kind are always good for a trade – or a bribe...)

That woman sounded like she could be alright. I couldn't tell for sure though – didn't know about the others at all... Plus – my legs were beginning to cramp up, so I didn't figure I would be able to run for it if I needed to. I had to keep switching the gun from one hand to the other – to give the arm holding me wedged a rest. Each changeover was a super tense juggle for speed and balance. I did *not* want to tumble out – or make the slightest sound.

So, although I might have eased out of hiding and (smiling sweetly) said "Hello", I decided to stay where I was – so long as I could... Especially as, if they were armed and didn't like me, two whole bullets in my gun wasn't going to do me much good if things went wrong.

Around when my left ankle thought it would explode they suddenly shoved off. So I shifted my weight more onto my right leg and stayed put for a bit... Which was as well – yet again experience saved me – from running straight into two of them that came back... Still arguing...

Did I say that they spent the *whole* time they were there quarrelling? It was another reason I kept quiet. I had no doubt at all that a bunch of Muppets, acting like students-on-the-piss, would drive me crazy much worse than being quiet on my own... And I definitely did *not* want them back at the house! I didn't want them to see my van.

They were one of the few bigger groups that I saw at that time... Which did make me wonder about how many people there could be that had made it through – except – I didn't wonder a lot – as it was far too frightening...

Anyway – I waited some more – until I couldn't perch any longer and then – shuddering and wobbling with pins-and-needles in both legs and even my bum – I got out and went and hid for a bit in a checkout... Until my legs were okay again.

Well... I hid after I'd hobbled back to the medicines shelves and found myself a very specific cream... And bagged <u>every</u> bit of it. "Just in case".

By then it was late evening, becoming dark – so I only got my hidden goodies to the van and decided to settle there for the night. It was well out of the way and didn't show up.

So that all sounds very practical and sensible...

I was "flying by the seat of my pants", as Greg would have put it, to be honest... But – I did feel that I was doing a passable job of it. In fact I kidded myself that I should get an "A Star" in surviving,

===========

That night I took the opportunity of being some place with parked cars to swipe as much petrol as I could for the van.

Yeah, okay, I *know*... I'd hardly got any "shopping" so it was backwards to how I said it should be done... I got bored sitting on my arse listening to the rain... Nothing on the radio was there?

I got soaked doing it, but – apart from bashing myself about a bit as well – it was a lot less panicky than doing it in daylight.

(Soaked with rain not petrol. I'm not that silly!)

It was so quiet that night – plus there was still some light rain. I reckoned that if anyone else moved I should hear them... And I would definitely see any lights moving about. So, despite the downside things, I had a productive night...

Oh Yeah – All the time I was creeping about I had my fuel can all wrapped up in a towel and a jumper so that I didn't clatter it. Reckoned I should definitely get my A Star for thinking of that.

When I eventually finished and climbed in the back, the van's sliding door clattered like thunder. It startled the life out of me! I stayed frozen still (and wet) for as long as I could stand it – in case anyone had heard and came looking... But – there wasn't a sound – so – extra carefully and quietly I changed into dry things and got a good sleep – I was shattered by then.

Having a dry change made things a whole load more bearable though... I was getting some ideas right – which was because I'd spent a whole previous night shivering and sore. (Yeah, well... A lousy mistake like that gets the point across far better than any book or DVD...)

===========

I got moving early the next morning. The neighbourhood looked nice and quiet but you never knew. It wasn't like I could check every house. Being around anywhere in town was creepy for me.

Other people couldn't stand being out and "exposed" in the countryside... Crazy! In town there were far more places close up to you – and above or below you – that people could at least be watching from – or planning more – scheming worse.

So, as I near always did, I shifted myself as soon as the lovely birdies woke me – by kicking up their racket. I'm convinced that they yelled at each other much louder once most people were gone – and a lot of their cats had gone with them quite soon – when the cats' soft lives and ready food ended and they had to go back to being serious hunters – or starved. Loads of them failed to make the transition... I reckon that they'd only ever been pulling a fast one with gullible suckers... But I'm biased...

And right.

At a time like that, when it was so quiet you could hear the sparrows coughing and farting between the thrushes yodelling, I would drive by the noise the tyres made on the road. Whenever the engine drowned them out I would usually slow down. I didn't go by the speedo. (I *do* know what that is!) The dial meant taking my eyes off the road – and everywhere else around me – especially behind. (Mirrors – you are *supposed* to use them!)

See! I was putting my act together.

No-one can be frantically alert all the time, though. No-one has the physical energy for that – and it does your head in at least as fast as it drains you.

You have to – well – you have to work out patterns – ones that work for you. You have to manage to be as relaxed as you can – but awake... Pretty much essential – saves you driving into things like walls, hedges, cows – basically everything that can go and get itself in front of you... And you have to be very, very aware.

Anyhow, heading for a long way round so it wouldn't be too obvious where I was finally going, I circled well out into the country. There was also a chance of finding some other garden centre or, I'd started to think, one of those farm-supplies places...

Farms... Animals... Cows...

I managed to miss a couple of hairy cows. *Why* do they *always* have to munch just round a sharp corner or at a junction? (Not only the hairy ones). I suppose they can't see where they're going... (The hairy ones).

Next thing – I'm swerving hard around a car with a flat tyre.

It's flat! You're not going to get it repaired now! *Don't* stop any-old-how as soon as you notice it! *Don't* stop right round a sharp corner! And *move* your arse out of the way at least as fast as the cows do! *Don't* stand there gawping at me!

I might have stopped... I had all that fuel though. I was thinking – "Could she be one of the women from yesterday?" Maybe she was a decoy? I didn't know... I was at least a bit paranoid – especially when I had fuel. So I kept going. Her gob was still open and she hadn't even raised a hand when she vanished from the mirrors.

Yeah, yeah. Funny! I still had mirrors – three of them. I was getting good. I was missing things... Mostly...

So, whoever she was; she was another mystery person.

Okay – confess – I had visions of her being another Carrie... Useless. Stood where she was, gazing blankly at the wheel without any jack or spanner in sight... She had to have been there some time – maybe all night – or I would have been following her – would have seen her.

You don't think for one moment that Mum let me start driving lessons without first making me change every wheel on her car do you? I kind-of forgot to mention that I'd already changed the wheels on Greg's big beasty...

Quietly looked smug enough to wind her up when I'd done hers all faster than she could have changed a single one. Well? What did she expect? I'm her daughter aren't I?

(Was...) *(SHIT!)*

Anyway... I had to decide *fast*. Instantly, while I was not hitting the car, the Donut-of-a-Woman or the ditch – *and* a tree. By which time I was already passed by quite a way... And still yelling and cursing. ***Stupid woman!***

No I am *not* sympathetic! Not of things like that. I've had far away too many frights – smashed up too many cars, vans – one truck... And they were *not* all of them my fault! *Do not go there!*

It would be so *pathetic-irritating* to be another Muppet killed in some stupid, avoidable road accident!

So? I had speeded up some. I was not going that fast... As far as I could tell... Still not looking at the speedo... Probably checking my mirrors – possibly admiring the sunrise... Only possibly though...

I missed her and her car didn't I? And – shows how much better I'd got – missed the tree too... Ditch was full of mud – but not very deep... Added some camouflage to the van didn't it?

Apart from the drumming of my heart the rest of the trip was quiet. (You DO NOT say one word like that while it's happening). I gave-up on the raiding – and got home okay.

===========

4 – 4

So... Danny...

One morning in the big house I had woken up, stuffed food in me, had a drink. (No idea what it was now – probably some (long-life) fruit juice from a carton with a bit of vodka in it – or – honest – a vodka with a bit of juice in it... Well – I figured alcohol would kill off any contamination... Seemed like a sound idea...)

Anyhow, I'd got into doing routines to a video. No idea if it was bullshit but it was a system... At least better than my own random wigglings. Figured it should be a better way to build my strength up – get some shape back – maybe make me look a bit less of a wreck...

Wasn't planning when I began – not the least thinking beyond the moment – not remotely thinking about anyone else. Did want to look and feel at least vaguely human – reasonable... Now that I was starting to feel a tiny bit like I ought to again. Some stamina was returning. I'd stopped wheezing and going to jelly after a few minutes.

I was getting some shape back. I had a tiny-bit of muscle definition – something between my bones and my skin. My breasts looked better. Okay – so I'd given up on the whole "body-hair thing"... Now we all figure that it was a load of self-imposed nonsense anyway...

Actually – we're all getting used to beards as well.

Watch it! *I do mean the men! Behave!*

My "styling"? Coiffure? *(HUH!).* Scragged back into a ponytail – much as ever in my life – if more tatty-ended.

I really could have done without the fresh bout of grumbling guts I'd just got over... Hadn't sussed the full significance of that just then...

Must have felt very good that morning because I extra got into it. I was working little aerobics dumbbells – a bit... Exercise and fitness is so much easier when you feel good – and I worked up quite a sweat in the gym, working to the video and looking out over the balcony at the miles of nothing-happening all the way to the horizon.

Out there was all bathed in lovely sunshine – with a few puffy clouds... It looked wonderful – glorious... Like the world is supposed to look ...

Well, it must have been getting into summer by then – an "English summer" of course. Always hard to tell which is Spring rain and which is Summer rain... They seem at least as wet. No idea what day of the week it was – so no chance of what the date would have been.

The weather hadn't been too bad and a short dry spell was making it beautiful.

The outside looked terrific – gorgeous – and the trees weren't being blown around – they were hardly moving at all... I had this idea...

And then I met Danny – that is – Danny arrived at the big house...

Can't tell you about that – not – yet... Okay, I was going to... But...

We met by the pool. Okay? Later that day I did stagger into the kitchen and scrape a weird mixture of what came to hand together onto a couple of plates. Wasn't too bad with what was left of the vodka. (I left out the anchovies).

Not that I was going to suddenly go all domestic... I was *ravenous* – and he was – What do you expect?

Whatever you expected – he was – *sound* asleep.

===========

One thing, I suppose – we all looked as frightful as each other in those first months.

So – from here, now, it looks utterly stupid the things that seemed important... When you look back and see what had happened, what was happening to us – the – complete mess – the problems – the dangers... We had no idea...

But – that was it – we couldn't start to take on what had happened.

Get our thinking round all the mass of things we needed to do? *No* chance!

I "regressed"...

So?

Give me a break!

Regression... I got a sudden real interest in how I looked. Spent half the night awake frantic about what I could do – would do – what would he want? *What* should I do?

At least I was clean... Not just from the swim – and – and our efforts had removed any chance of pool-water smell... He smelt delicious – musky... Luscious...

What did I smell like? Look like? I shuddered...

I leapt.

He'd reached up and brushed my shoulder as I sat on my heals beside him. "You're – stunning – beautiful..."

No I wasn't! I was a mess! Worse than an anorexic Emo-Goth after puking up a long weekend's booze and greaseburgers...

But he grabbed me – and held on, cuddling me, saying nice things, stroking me a little – gently – not sex – more – making me feel good... So I started to cry... Because my hair was a complete mess...

===========

I said that I'd coloured my hair red didn't I? For the Christmas parties? Before everything kicked-off – fell apart... I'd forgotten all about that, until that night...

Well, naturally, it was growing out – but – there had been no way I thought about doing anything about it. It was all different lengths and – a *mess*... I just kept it tied back. Kept it from flopping across my face. I couldn't begin to get a fringe right – so I didn't begin to try the back. What did it matter anyhow?

I kept myself clean; tidy... We all do – everyone. Washed all of me (often more than once) every single day. You've been in a mess like that – like we all had – well, you can get totally obsessive about being clean... But – well – that's about it really... At least. It was at first... I mean – there was no thought about anyone looking at you.

Yeah, yeah... So I go on about it... Only someone a few generations on from now is not going to know why... Precisely why...

Well, anyhow – the idea of someone "fancying" you would have been – *ridiculous*... Everyone was a wreck. A physical mess... Everyone had lost a whole ton of weight...

It's weird. If you think about it. Why did the not-so-fat people make it through? I mean, seeing as we all ended up so – so... "Gaunt" – is the word Beth uses. Everyone is skin and bone... So – why didn't the fat people make it? You would think that they had more going for them. I'd have thought? Wouldn't they have more "stored fat" – "reserves"? They should have had a better chance shouldn't they?

Alright, so I'm mithering (Ben's word) – fuss-potting... Sometimes though it drives you nuts... "Why me?" Why us? What was different? Is there a reason?

So – um – where was I?

Oh shit – Uh, right... Fussing about how I looked...

(Beth sneaked a look over my shoulder. Says it was because I kept muttering and scratching out bits with a cuss. She says 'not to worry about "Why? Or "How?" and to go on to writing about Danny and me').

So – okay...

(So ... I'm "displacing" – like at school – I sodding know that...)

It seems so crazy looking back... Insane that I was fussed about how I looked... *Go away Beth!*

(She says that it shows how important Danny was for me... I KNOW that!)

[Next part scrubbed out]

Okay, so she's right... And, now I've admitted that, she's gone across the room...

But – how I looked "looks wise" around then was all SO unimportant when it came to simply staying alive...

Except that Danny suddenly made it worth being – no – more than that – far more... (***Fuck it!*** I'm weeping again). It made being alive ***im-portant***... It made how I looked important... It did!

So? It's stupid, *pointless*... But... It *mattered*...

===========

Start again...

Soon as he saw the dumb-bells he was really impressed. That made me glow – all warm inside... He did that to me – a lot...

Crazy! I never saw it before... I never, not for a single moment, thought about how scrawny he looked... Which was skin and bone – of course... Everyone was at that time... But... I don't have words for it...

He was – was – just... Danny... Just – right... "Mr Right" if you want... Soppy of me. Stoopid – maybe... I can say that... You know what'll happen to you if you...

Right – so... No! I did NOT think about how he looked! I... Simply got the ***total-hots*** for him.

Alright? Does that say it? Happy now? He – hit me – BOOM! Right in my head – in my guts – in my heart even. *No!* Muppet! He *did not* slap me! He... He made me go **"POW!"** and "**FIZZ!**" – and – and...

Well – if you don't know what he did to me – you're missing out – and I hope you get to know one day... That's all I can say.

Love at first sight? ***Way** more* than that... No idea what you call it... No-one's invented a word for it...

There is totally no way ever I could begin to explain it...

Why-the-fuck should I?!

So... *Cool* it... *Okay*...

He only made 1.825 metres... He blushed about that – grinned – silly grin... Said it was not quite six foot... ("Real money" like Gramps would say). Said his brothers teased him endlessly about him being a "short-arse"... About not even matching his sisters' two metres... He never said a word about being so much taller than me... Did say that his brothers would flatten his hair right down when he grew it long to look taller.

Suddenly I wanted to be human – to *feel* human... To feel real – to be a real woman... *Don't* dare laugh. I wanted to be "attractive"...

Well, I knew that had me well and truly stuffed didn't it?

But – later that morning he sat me down and made me tidy...

I'd found me a budding stylist. In all that mess – how crazy was that? He was at college – in a crowd of girls... But there was no way he was Gay or the least effeminate... (Why-the-hell do I think I have to tell you that?)

He simply *loved* styling hair – making it right for a face... Anyone's face – whoever they were – right for them – an individual...

My face, for me... I'd never thought about anyone still making a proper living doing hair all fancy – that was something people like Gran's Mum did – ages ago – back in the last century...

Danny thought that was hilarious. Who did I think made royalty or all those film stars look good? That was his ambition... And (I punched him for this) now he'd got the perfect model to practice on.

All I'd ever done was keep it tidy, tied back most of the time... Never spent money on expensive stuff – not even on colour – which never had the effect it was supposed to anyway.

He made me feel so – *fantastic* though. He got my hair *so* right – with the different colours as well... Even with me being all – "gaunt".

I felt human again – maybe – for the first time... Like I could belong at least... In the real world. His making my hair right – and right with the ultra smart clothes – made me feel that I could walk into anywhere. Walk in as though I belonged and no-one would imagine to ask a question...

But – the thing was – if people looked at me – and didn't have to ask questions... That would mean that they saw me...

When I told him that (the first bit) he laughed a load – said that he could turn me into a terrorist then – make me invisible... I refused to tell him why "invisible" upset me, why it made me shudder... But I got round that by telling him about Greg – and that led to Bodger of course – and the village, the Estate, Mum – and college...

All that was gone of course... Everything. Good, bad – everyday and ordinary... All gone...

It set us thinking... We both cried... Wept. Sitting, holding each other... That was a bond... The fact that everything was gone – just – gone...

===========

But – *sex wasn't!* If bunnies are a tenth as good I *know* why there are so many of them. We did it everywhere – every way (almost). We got the giggles trying it in the walk-in freezer to find out what the Swedes and Norwegians found so good... Played silly games... Laughing while shagging gives you an ultimate, *incredible* orgasm... Well – one of them... Gave us...

Uh-Oh!...

Had to take a break...

I'm going to write some of it somewhere else – hidden – about Danny and me – how good it was – what we enjoyed...

All I'm going to say here is...

Well – I don't know...

Was not only physical. Why should I tell you that? 'Cos I want to. That's why. I want to put down, make a good account of the physical – not here... But – seems that men like to see sex – see it in a mirror – when their doing it... I was told it kind of makes it more; more real... And, no, I don't think it's weird or kinky – never did... If they like it... Fine... I like certain pleasures... That I am *not* going to tell you about here!

But... I want to make a record of – of – how ***good*** our time was... Good? A trillion, trillion "EXCELLENT"s wouldn't tell it right...

Like I said though – there was far more than physical. Something – "electric?" Maybe "telepathic?" I can't explain it... "Nuclear" maybe – like in parts of an atom... We – we – span around each other? Yes? We attracted... Completed a wholeness?

Does it hurt an atom when it sheds a bit of itself? Is that why or howcome it gets hot? Is it angry? Furious? When it burns up – is that the evidence of what it's feeling? I could understand that...

I can understand the holding on. The working to keep the circle spinning. The effort to make it work... The tearing apart struggle when it goes out of balance – when you know it's going wrong – something pulling it all out of shape... The struggle to somehow keep it all in there – to hold it together... Then the ripping and shredding when it's inevitably going to come apart...

Not that, that was me and Danny...

That wasn't the way it was at all...

===========

Anyhow... You could say we answered the question – the one about "Where do things go after they've gone to bed?" (Been at the poolside in our case – and then bed... Ummm... After a few other places...) Well – they go to bed again – and then the kitchen – the en-suite (massive) tub – the balcony over the main room – the... Virtually everywhere in the huge place... And a huge place – means – well you figure it...

None of that sounds right though – doesn't explain a single thing – not adequately... Yeah – being made to look and feel good was – superb – especially then – after – everything...

Thing with Danny though... Well...

How should I know?! I'd never experienced it – haven't experienced it again – since... Not sure I could – would want to...

Alright – so I <u>know</u> anyone – *every-fucking-one* – says "Give it time" and all that ***crap*** – but – it feels like it would be a – a *betrayal*...

<u>**I *do not* fucking want that!!!**</u>

===========

Alright... Get my shit together...

Got my shit together...

We – we – just – fit – like bits of a puzzle – or gears – or bullets in a revolver cylinder... Sort of like we were made for each other...

Totally weird thing – <u>way</u>, far-beyond anything Greg had told me of – *warned* me was maybe what he should have done...

I think he knew – had known... I think that was maybe what made him so sad at times...

Thing was – Danny and me... We didn't need to talk... It was – special being together... Even when we weren't together... That sounds stupid!

Only knowing he *was* – was like – like – sitting in sunshine... That sounds *so* pathetically wet!

But it's kind-of how it was... Extreme – total... Outside of explaining...

Even if I went on forever about how we talked – and didn't talk...

It's easier to go on about the sex...

So – okay – we kind of went crazy – for a day or two – um – at least... There was all that good food and booze there... I have no idea where I got the energy from – not-to-mention how he did...

So? What would you do? Your whole world suddenly wiped out, everything gone... Robbed by gulls. People ready to shoot at you... *Being shot at! In England!* ***OUTRAGEOUS!***

Danny had seen and heard all sorts of crap as he came down the country – it sounded much more scary than I had experienced. He wouldn't say much. I could tell though... Hope I could have told – even without the couple of recent scars and the way he'd flinch from a deep-bruised bone...

I reckon people reacted badly – ***wrong*** – because of how he looked... (Not going there).

He didn't/wouldn't talk about that... Said hardly anything about his travels...

But then; I wasn't saying so much about what I'd seen recently either... We – kind of – played safe...

He reckoned that it was more dangerous for a man anyway – people were more ready to see them as a threat and shoot – usually without any warning... He didn't say – I reckon he had been seriously frightened – to put it politely... He'd probably had a dangerously bad time... Which sort of explained some of how he'd taken so long – being *so* careful – all the way back to the big house – and then he felt safe, stripped off and dived in...

He was a bit hurt when I laughed about how "dangerous" that had been with me there.

(Got his head banged on the grass didn't he?)

So – anyhow – after all that journey – and then – a secluded, quiet, safe place. (Massive, yes – but not stand--out. More discreet – sort of snuggled into the hill – it hardly showed at all from down below)... All that food, clothes, wine, spirits... and – best of all – a sexy man... Er – other way round – for him – a randy woman.

What *would* you do?

So? You might prefer one of your own kind. (*Whatever*! Hell! I've been "PC trained" – conditioned – like potty-training. *Good grief!)*

Okay; I'd still have to admit that he'd be nuts, *have* to be nuts, to fall for me... But he did... Danny... Well...

Maybe that explains why eventually I woke one morning and I felt – sooooo good... I wouldn't say "unbelievable" – because about everything I wanted to do was – to *believe* it.

I felt *SO GOOD* – Not just before I opened my eyes – but when I kept them tight shut... And I did that for as long as I could – until – until I began to wonder if this was only some dream...

I could feel him all warm and breathing next to me – except he hardly made any shape on the mattress – was that, could that – be real? *Must* be a dream...

Suddenly desolate I opened my eyes... Where was I? Not my room. (Never let any boy go there anyway...)

Where? E-norm-ous ceiling. Massive! *Dazzling* white walls and ceiling... Couple of vast mirrors. Deep cream curtains – those weren't curtains – they were what the Yanks call "drapes" – real quality – thick – heavy

– you could feel how good they were ten metres away – just looking at them... Sort of made you want to roll up naked in them...

Which I was...

Not rolled in the curtains!

Buck naked on this vast, E-norm-ous bed – satin sheets, massive head-board/canopy-thingy and everything... More like a monster wedding cake than a bed – a mythical cloud-palace to shag yourself silly in...

Yeah well... "Make love" might sound kind-of nicer – but that wasn't what we'd been doing at all...

Except that – it was... Only; way, way *outstanding* better than "just" making love...

No thinking "what should I do right?" "How's this supposed to be" or all that fuss... Far, far less all the horrible "What's he thinking?" 'Does he think...?" "What's he going to tell his mates – especially if I...?" None of that... We DID IT! Wonderful! – No... ***WONDERFUL!***

I don't think there was much we didn't do – er – well there were a couple of things – but not anything we didn't know about (that would be "think of") at the time... Makes me blush to think about it now... But – it was *SO GOOD* – ***AMAZING***...

So – when I woke up that morning, feeling – SO ...

Feeling so incredibly... Amazingly... What's the word for it? (I think I'll go and think about that – maybe ask – discreetly...)

(Okay – got some words – that'll do – if I put them all together...)

Satisfied. (Definitely the first word).

Fulfilled.

Sated. (Never heard that before).

Well-shagged.

(Yeah right! *Never* heard *that* either Phil – you *Muppet*! – except – he's right – it's *exactly* what I did feel)... (And no – he has no idea what situation I was asking for words to describe... Although I did go bright red when he suggested that).

Maybe all the best things we ever feel get to be compared to how good it feels when we've had the finest sex ever – and slept on it...?

I mean – like Greg told me – the sex itself can be FANTASTIC – doesn't matter what position, where, what he looks like – anyhow...

All that belly turning inside out – your toes popping off, headed to outer-space – and stars bursting like bubbles all through – everything, everywhere – not just in your head... *Yeah.* **Nice!** *Totally-shagging-amazing* isn't it?...

Then it can be that some great big lunk goes and farts, calls out the wrong-damn-name... There's a zillion ways of screwing it all up... The build-up was good. The shag was good – nice cock, touched in all the right places, screaming good orgasm... Then – *soggy-flop!* Emotional-wet-dog-turd... Total *WRECK...* Want to get out of there – and cry – probably howl... So that could probably be where saying that something wrecked has been "shagged" comes from...? Maybe...

Yeah? So this bit is only guess work isn't it? Rumours I've heard and all that...

I fucking wish!

Anyway... Back to – cheerful – where was I...?

Oh – right...

Waking up that first morning...

How many "first mornings" are there? (Um – Would be best to not go there...)

No – wasn't the first one... Was – one of the early mornings... But – I'd slept so...? So totally out-of-it that I kind of had to swim back – surface – and didn't connect where I was in the now with – well – anything... Except the lovely warmth of Danny beside me... That felt good. I knew what that was. Kind of "visceral".

Sometimes, times, him being there – next to me... In the room... On the planet...

Didn't have to be him – just his scent... The dent he left in the pillow...

Good grief!

There could never, ever be enough to explain it though...

Pooh!

First thing I had to sort out was – *where* I was...

Would have had to have a massive head to get it round that room... But – BIG house equals BIG bedroom doesn't it? Right? And BIG, BIG Bed... Reckon *she* must have designed that... Great design... "Bespoke" they call it...

I figured "She" must have been taller than me – a lot taller – or had arms like an Orang-utan... (Danny hurt himself laughing at that). (Then he got slapped for noticing the red still in my hair – but we "kissed-and-made-up" – guess how?)

Yeah? So I'm "tiny" (Don't push the point)... Hardly five foot if you *really* must know, skinny, not big at my most – and there was nothing of me at all then – Bum's always been good and tight – because of all the bike riding... So – that *is* all you need know... *Right?*

She must have been well over six foot – I worked that out – experimentally – “empirical research” – when we figured that the strange shapes in the massive headboard/canopy thing were hand-holds – I couldn’t reach some of them... With assistance – that proved – interesting... Had to find a way to support me... (Says she *smugly...*) Was a bit of luck he was still strong...

And, of course, he already did know how tall “She” was... But I’m glad we worked it out the practical way – before he admitted it...

I couldn’t say why we – kind of – straightened out – why or how we got serious... How we ever got round to it... Not gloomy-serious. Just – practical... Thinking about “significant” issues – like food, fuel – and making sure we were safe – secure...

Naturally – I (always) wanted to do it all again... Didn’t think for one second more about how scrawny and awful I looked. Wasn’t bothered – he wasn’t exactly a rock star – would never have made a magazine cover – probably not even a Horror Comic... He was all ribs and jutty-out bones – except for the bit that wasn’t bone – of course... And that was what I was most thinking about... (No! I <u>don’t</u> mean his nose!)

Somehow – when we cuddled (after) – we both started to get practical... Well, kind of sensible – thinking forward – er –- if only in some ways...

I hurt myself a bit – elbows or shoulders – because I was so scrawny... I think Danny was more upset than I was... I’d definitely given up worrying about what he thought I looked like. I had no reason at all to worry about that!

===========

<u>Practical</u>... Danny knew the alarm and surveillance systems of course. You’d expect it to be elaborate in a place like that. Once he’d topped-up the

back-up batteries he set it all back up to monitor the outside for us. We had no-idea how-come it had all been left switched-off.

We never got the main generator running. He could have – except it would have used far too much fuel – after we started to re-fill the drained-out tank (as storage). Anyhow... We didn't need lights – and, more, wouldn't have wanted them to show...

Loading that tank was one thing we worked <u>really</u> hard at... Made it a target to get at least four jerry-cans each trip out. Exhausting!

Anyhow – with the security back up and running we could be more free than either of us had been for weeks. With the system scanning all round we could play music, dance, talk – yell at each other if we wanted to. It was a magic freedom.

I hadn't noticed how much I missed music. He hadn't either.

Thing was, had been, that any sound could both give you away and, at the same time, hide things around you. Most people learnt that – one way or another... For some the lesson was fatal...

Terrible thing.

Another thing I go on about? It was important... And pervasive.

Having music again was like getting our lives back...

===========

4 – 5

It wasn't long after he got there that Danny showed me that he knew the water heating was gas – and how to get round the electric bits – a bit dangerous but he would watch it until there was enough hot and then shut it down...

Which would sort of ask how he got to be there... He'd started out on an apprenticeship in plumbing and maintenance – because he didn't dare tell his Dad and brothers that he wanted to do hair... So once he'd got out of that and he was at college with the girls he could still make money on the side as the "pool boy" and general maintenance at the big house and grounds – which he said were about fifty acres – however much that would be.

The couple were about nothing but money and "tight as a duck's arse". (So that was no surprise!) Every way they could they avoided any kind of tax. Danny was paid in cash. He wasn't sure if the Estonian maid-cum-house-slave and chauffer-cum-general-dog's-body were. Possibly the questions of immigration decided that. They were on minimum wage at best. Would have been on zero hours if the woman could have got away with it. They were the only staff/slaves on site – "on call" 24/7. Danny had no idea why they didn't tell her to shove it... Most people did – often after the first visit... Sometimes in the middle of it... Which suited her – because she refused to pay them.

Everyone that worked there loathed "His Eminence" and "Lady Disdain".

Despite all that, everyone that stayed a bit, easily worked out how to cream extra incomes from the job. She made it easy for them, she was so obsessed with impressing their "circle" and because everything had to be "exactly so". Her waste of perfectly good things was disgusting. That was why Danny stayed around – quietly "recycling".

He reckoned she always watched "vulture style" from a high window while he worked in the garden. She would scream threats at him if she thought he dipped a toe in "their" water.

"Completely insane!" He laughed. "If she could have been she'd have been a mad Transylvanian Princess locked up in a castle on her own to scream at the wind".

I protested that she looked fantastic though. (Why'd I do that?) – and slapped him for telling me it was all the blood of maidens that she drank... I <u>do not</u> believe what he said about some mad Transylvanian actually doing that – all some kind of Horror Movie rubbish... Made the big bed seem a bit weird though...

But we soon found ways of distracting ourselves...

Why wasn't Danny there when I got there?

He'd spent New Year at his Gay brother's place in Newcastle... Out of the way of his Dad. Who was still raging about his brother coming out, "bringing disgrace on the family", dumping their trade – and leading Danny astray into "women's work" when he should be studying for his proper qualifications in a real man's job... "Things are hard enough for our people"...

Danny's Dad sounded like someone out of one of those old films of the middle of the last century – but I'd seen crap like that myself, around the Estate...

And Danny said (I think he was right) that all the Political Correctness only drove a lot of the crap underground. Nothing anywhere ever stopped the undertow of homophobia or racism – or any crap like that. Like with drugs, more and more laws didn't mean that anyone shifted their thinking out of the nineteenth century – so long as "old ways" suited them...

Being rational, at least "reasonable" was never a choice anyone was going to take against decades or centuries of family tradition... Especially when the whole family was "right" – for generations...

A load of people wanted to get back to the Middle Ages... Naturally – it was them that were going to be the Lords of the Manor – at least... (Like I said). No-one stopped thinking the same traditional rubbish – they just bottled it up – hid it – and got more angry in secret.

It seems that humans need someone, some slight "difference" to hate... So long as it isn't them being singled out and rejected – victimised – it makes them feel bigger, stronger – safer... No modern science, not even anthropology and definitely no politics, ever got past the "I'm bigger and better than you" or "I have a better claim than you" – or the other side of all that... "You're not as good as me" and "you shouldn't be taking that away from me – even though I don't want or even need it..."

You <u>can't</u> make everyone appreciate the wonders of being "Multi-Cultural" by legislating it...

People, homo-sapiens, just love to hate and fear – to fear and hate... Fucking idiots are <u>*still*</u> doing it now – when what everyone totally needs is to get on and work together.

Whatever...

I <u>*knew*</u> that Greg would have liked Danny so much. Mum too... It made me cry that I'd found him and couldn't take him to meet them... Show him off... Makes me cringe – *me* thinking *that?*

But – that's what I <u>wanted</u> to be able to do...

And I never could...

===========

Anyhow...

Between us we got sensible... After a day or two more – maybe three or five – we *were* sort of "busy"... We kind of edged our way around to "reality" slowly... With plenty of breaks – to restore our good feelings...

And feeling *was* good – *extremely* good...

He was way more impressed than I was with my revolver; but showed he had some real brain, by not wanting to be the one who had it. Not that I would have minded so much. It was a real pain to lug it around. His man-jeans and a big leather belt made it so much easier – for him... Me? Yeah; right...

Like with the warmer, hot, weather and being with Danny I was wearing cut-offs – shorts and Ts. (When I was wearing anything at all...) *Where* to put a heavy gun with that?!

Yeah; I did have to have a belt – there was so little of me (no bum at all) that I even thought about braces... Danny smirked – and suggested suspenders – yeah – right – he did *so* mean the American version... Not.

If I'd put any weight on the belt – just a gun – my denims would have been round my ankles in no time. Not that he complained about my proving that point... So that was fun!

Anyhow, Danny arrived with his own weapons. (Guns!). By then everyone that had any sense and could do so was finding some kind of defence – if it was only a big kitchen knife or a carving fork taped on a stick. Most had progressed well beyond that.

For a country that was supposed to have so many gun laws and be so safe; there suddenly seemed to be a hell of a lot of things that went "bang" around. Okay, so they were mostly shotguns at the start and like Danny said, about the two he had, they had been mainly for rabbits or rats... But there were unquestionably a whole lot more around than I would have thought. (Especially as I'd not got my hands on much at all...)

Worst thing was – not the guns – but the idiots waving them about.

Greg had never shown me a gun but he'd nagged it into my thinking that if you didn't handle them right you were more of a moronic danger to yourself – and your mates. He told me stories about trained soldiers managing to shoot themselves and each other. His descriptions left me with no doubts about why "civvies" and most of the police shouldn't ever have them either.

I go on and on about safety? Remember Daz? I so wish I didn't!

I'd been right about the owner of the place being into shooting. He was into the right image and his "rights" – Danny confirmed... With his ego he would have shot at trespassers if he'd reckoned he could get away with it like he could have done in America or South Africa. (So that told me a whole load more). Thing was though, that he wasn't allowed to keep them at the house here in England. Danny made him sound like a total nutter – at the least about his "property rights". So that was probably a good thing!

Danny was certain that his lordship must have had at least some guns hidden someplace around the house. Said that it just wouldn't be like him not to – no matter what the law said... The "shit" reckoned that his money made him an exception – or – just plain far above the law – that had to apply to "ordinary people" – who "couldn't be trusted"... Like? Breaking the law qualified him to be trusted?

We did search – a bit... I ignored it (discreetly) but I wasn't so daft that I didn't notice that Danny sometimes did some extra rummaging when he reckoned I wouldn't notice... I don't blame him. It could have been useful... Except...

No idea if it had been his Dad's doing or not but Danny at least had some idea about keeping his two guns safe – a little double barrel ratting gun and a monster pump-action – that only held three shots unless he had one loaded – which I wouldn't let him. (I know now that it was made legal – and a twelve gauge... I know a whole load more now than I did then!)

Anyway. British people think that the most a shotgun has is two barrels – so a third shot is like a bonus... Not that you go banging off unless you have to. It makes way too much noise that tells people that you are around.

When there's only two of you and you're not stupid you go as quietly as you can. If/when someone does have a go at you it's often best to not shoot back. Let them see the gun – but – conserve you ammunition. You can't pop to the shop and get some more –- like you can't with most stuff.

Talking of which... Danny knew where all the big stores were locally, the petrol stations and other useful places – which did *not* include video/ game shops! Leastways – not that he ever admitted... We had ***much*** better ways to relax anyhow.

===========

Going raiding – "salvaging" – "liberating" – whatever you called it – wasn't always bad. A whole load of the time you could wander around with hardly a care in the world... Like I was doing that first time I got shot at.

That was it of course. You got shot at the once – it "woke you up" – FAST... So long as it didn't kill you.

Until you caught on it was bizarre finding a stiff almost anywhere except in a house. The vast majority died at home – where they'd run to. Some that couldn't make it died in their cars.

Naturally you expected corpses around hospitals – not so much medical centres. It took no time at all to keep well away from anywhere like that. Apart from disgusting they got to be an attraction for anyone freaked-out-of-it enough to go looking for drugs. Pharmacies started to get smashed into almost immediately. No subtlety there. Ram, grab and run was most people's way – it seems. Certainly, move fast and clear-out got to be the rule – if you found one not already gutted.

It was *not* nice falling over somebody in the dark of a store. Could be a whole lot less nice if they weren't dead.

Ummm... I started out to say that it wasn't all bad... You simply learnt the important lessons fastest when it was. You didn't get cautious – you got jittery as a cat that heard the word "vet" and saw the basket put ready.

"Ordinary" raiding for basics wasn't anywhere near as horrific as going for fuel, though...

Well... It could be – or worse... The different raids would compete for diabolical. You frequently figured that the last one of them *had* to be the worst... Then you'd prove that wrong... Often (it seemed) right after you'd achieved an excellent raid with no hassles involved. And, no, it wasn't because you had relaxed... Which meant that even when you should feel good you kept getting the jitters.

The thing that utterly freaked me... There was one night before Danny appeared when there was an almighty roar and "Whoomph!" way over in the distance from the mansion. It lit up the sky for ages and I could see smoke for several days and still see flames at night. It didn't take much figuring that something big had gone wrong – or that no-one was sorting it out. Then (of course) knowing that there was no-one to stop it... The facts were getting real – sinking in – getting beyond the first inability to catch a hold on what was going on.

I thought at the time that maybe it was some army place and someone had exploded all the ammunition – like a disaster that would have been on the news.

But when Danny looked out the way I pointed he said it had been a petrol station in a village – and that he'd come through there on his way... Everything was burnt out – everything. I didn't let him tell me any details – although – being a boy he wanted to of course. (*What* is so fascinating about being gruesome?)

Petrol collecting was frightening enough – with the way people could be. Between the fear of being burnt and getting caught it was always a freaky experience – but – to know that if a fire did start there was nothing to stop it – no-one to come and put it out... That was drastically un-nerving – freaking...

At least with two of you one can keep a watch for trouble. We didn't know if it would do any good – but we figured we could at least give a fire extinguisher a try if fire started – maybe at least get ourselves out of there... We hadn't thought about what to do about burns though...

The worst of that (thank God – or whatever) came later... (After Danny ...) When I was with other people...

I said – I was extra careful from the start. I'd seen cars burn...

So – anyway... I'm still supposed to be telling you about what happened – the better times...

Danny was good – that was for sure. I do not just mean the sex! Although that was... Oh – that's me is it? You weren't reading it that way... Yeah! I bet!

So – turned out – Danny could cook – nice, proper meals. (No burnt bits). Even with the lack of basic essentials – like eggs and milk – practically anything fresh... He knew so well how to make good meals with the heaps of catering-type stuff already there. (Frozen milk defrosts weird).

I could heat basics up – a microwave isn't the only way to do that... I *did* know that! I'd not only got, but been using, that camping stove thingy hadn't I?!

Didn't burn my fingers that often... Was a pity I couldn't say the same about the food...

I tried – *I did*... Everything stays raw forever – then singes the moment you blink. I still say it's a conspiracy... (Beth rarely trusts me on my own around her Aga...)

Where...?

Oh yeah... Danny... Ever since he was a kid he'd had to go on camping trips with his Macho-man Dad and his older brothers. His Dad had them do all the Outdoor-man Survivalist training – until he got nicked for damaging private property cutting down trees to make a shelter... Danny and his brothers saw the Wardens and Police coming and ran off to hide, leaving their Dad shouting instructions about how to do it. Way he told it (with actions) made me fold up.

Stories Danny told, the way he did, so often had me in fits... Best person like that I ever knew...

Danny could be sad as well. He wasn't horrible about his Dad. He said that his Dad wasn't really bad. Danny didn't explain that his Dad "meant well"... We both knew what that meant about anyone...

He thought that his Dad probably wanted the best for all his sons...

Danny was very sensitive – very aware. He guessed right that I was thinking that if his Dad so much had to do all the big-manly-things, and so totally went off on one about Danny's brother, then he might have been trying to prove to himself that he wasn't Gay himself...

Danny said that could have been true – maybe he was trying to steer his sons away from a possibility he feared.

I didn't comment on his Dad's church involvement. Neither did Danny but I'm sure he had concluded that they were still caught up by some stupid, "religious", bigoted past...

I never felt it would be right to have any sort of go about his Dad... I mean – for a start – I would hardly be neutral would I?

Sometimes, when we stopped laughing about good stories – it *all* seemed so sad...

But – around then – there was *too* much to be sad about – there were far too many people you were never going to be able to go and give a hug... Too many people you couldn't even go and yell at...

You didn't think about it... Still don't – not very much... It's over-big – I guess it always will be...

Wonderfully cheerful aren't I?

Okay. So – Good things – Happy times...

Was great to talk about things Bodger did... A bit – not too much... Danny got that – he wouldn't let me go on long enough to get upset... He was so sensitive – caring... I don't think I hardly ever talked much about Mum or Greg... Couldn't do that.

I told him about Anton... But – I told any man I went with about Anton – kind of a warning I suppose... Sort-of protecting myself... (Okay – so that crap messed with my mind... Wasn't going to have anyone else do that...)

Anyway!

Going on our first "raid" together the first time was good – hilarious... Ridiculous! Well – it ended up good... Makes me curl up to think of the start now...

We took one of the big, powerful *[maybe armoured?]* cars from the house. The fuss to get the garage door open *should* have made us think about the gates at the road of course. Did we? No chance! Had to go to the "Lodge" to find tools.

I couldn't say why I found the Lodge creepy. I mean. Okay, so I knew that Küllike and Üllar were dead in there – long dead – Danny had gone to check before he came for his swim...

There were dead all over the place though weren't there? I'd seen – way-over, more than enough... But I knew that it was Küllike and Üllar in there didn't I? Maybe because they had names it was somehow different?

I suppose this was the first time – first time I had names for them... I'd run clean away from the village – everyone at home... Could be I was freaking out more about that than those two... Maybe they gave me an excuse when Danny came out with hammers and spanners – and I went off on one at him about what he said about the staff...

Wish I hadn't...

Anyway. We sorted the gates – so we could get in again as well – but left them looking like no-one had touched them and the place was all locked up – and (the important thing) that it wasn't worth the effort to go looking inside...

Danny had brought a broom so that we could sweep the dust clear of our tyre marks. He was expert at covering our tracks like that. That was perhaps some sort of positive his Dad achieved? I'd got a bit of an idea from footprints in the snow – but Danny was extra good at it – focussed. (Then again... Maybe it was about what had happened to him coming south from Newcastle...?)

We didn't go to the nearest store – despite I wanted to because that was my favourite**...** Easy to get into, quite a lot of useful goods still – and lots of ways out... But he went on, headed for the next one.

He said it would have more – so – being me – I got into an argument about how could he know that? Had he been inside and looked already? Didn't wait for or listen to his answer to that... Insanely (totally against what I already knew and did) I didn't want to know his ideas about not making it obvious where we were... And I told him that – um – strongly...
Yelled at him to take me back to the first place. When he wouldn't I screamed at him to "*Stop the fucking car!*" I would "fucking-well walk!"

He did stop – but got out and told me he'd find another car – go back to the house and collect his stuff. Get out of my way before I returned...

Thing was – I *knew* he meant it. He wasn't mad at me or yelling like I was. He – was just – just being Danny. Being kind... Giving me – space – I suppose you'd call it...

I felt a real, utter *shit*.

Is the first time you feel that, right in the middle of being mad at someone, a first step of growing up? Like one of those "milestones"?
Jumped out in the road myself, yelling at him to "take your fucking car!" It wasn't that I was scared of being left on my own again...
Not as such...
I didn't have time to think of that.
I'd actually already done that – a couple of times... Then I had cried my eyes out – in the staff toilet behind the kitchen where I thought he wouldn't hear me or find me.
Wrong – the weird thing was – it turned out he had heard me – but left me to do my own thing... And – that was sort of why we didn't take so much of a long time stopped in the middle of the road between the stores... He wasn't kind-of threatening me with going – Silly Sod thought that he was making me unhappy – so he was reckoning that the best thing to do was to bugger off and leave me in peace...
Would have been *pieces* more like.

You'd think that we'd have got it sorted quickly so that we weren't stuck in the middle of the road, exposed, for too long. That would be the sensible thing wouldn't it?

Wasn't being sensible was I? (He was). Maybe, when I'm honest, I was trying to fight my own fear – prove that I was bigger than it... Pushing it – to make it happen – for real.

Like I said though – I suddenly – well – I saw that he wasn't mad at me – wasn't being mean – he was – kind of – sad – unhappy – distressed (but hiding it)... And I felt a total *shit* – nauseatingly mean – moronic, selfish – and – worse than all else – really – really – *"GIRLY"*

UGH! I had so much (self-righteous) contempt for the girls on the Estate and at college that went off like that at their boyfriends – or each other... I *thought* I was so...

And there I was – *exactly* the same...

I could call myself names for what I did... But Danny said I never should. He said – that I was nowhere near as bad as his Dad... (He made me laugh the way he said it...)

[So the page goes all splodgy here... What you expect?]

He also said (right then) as he got back in the car (once I shut up and looked like I was going to bawl my eyes out) that he was "being practical – and getting us out of there..." I had been "making more noise than a fire engine".

I thought that was strong but kept my mouth shut – I knew I'd been stupid – and mean – and that I had – made a bit of a noise... Could have attracted attention... Anyway – I was filled up with feeling pathetic.

Plus – a Big car like that with a lot of petrol in the tank was not a good thing to attract attention with.

===========

We went on to his store... That hadn't been raided. (Hadn't noticed that had I? *Donut!*)

Naturally with all that outdoor training Danny could easily climb in and open a fire door from the inside...

The alarm going off scared the crap out of us!

But the batteries were nearly done in – so it all went quiet (except the ringing in our ears) almost as quickly as we could like.

I was for running away as quick as we could but Danny said not to. We were in – out of sight – we should wait – see what happened, maybe have a careful look from the office windows upstairs (where he'd got in). If someone was watching they'd be expecting anyone to scram right away... So we should sit tight. If it stayed quiet we'd get what we'd come for – but – to do it carefully – stay away from the windows at the front. Like I *knew* that!

I was impressed though... He didn't rate all the "survivalist" ideas – except, he had his act together – and a good way of telling me – so I didn't get mad at him again...

I wasn't good at being told what to do or how to do it...

Yeah, okay – so you probably guessed that by now...

I figure Danny was much like Greg that way... (Looked *nothing* like him). He – sort of... I can't explain what they did... Kind of respected me – took it that I had enough sense to see what and why they were saying... Didn't spell it out like I was stupid... (Not even that "stay away from the windows" thing...) They both said things in a way I could see how, what and why from the start... Plus, they trusted me to ask about anything I didn't get... PLUS – plus – they didn't look sniffy or any other way make out I was stupid to not get it before they'd even finished.

I know *for a fact* that a whole load of people just pretend that they've understood. Some idiot people even try to do that now when you're showing them how to be safe or clear a jam with a gun.

Have you ever noticed how easily some people bruise?

Maybe Danny said something like he'd got to remember to stay out-of-sight... Kind-of putting the instruction on himself... Could be I might have said something like "Yeah! Don't be such-an-arse that you show yourself"... Could be... There's just a slight chance...

===========

Ummm...

So...

While we waited and watched in the office of the store I didn't need for anything to make me feel more stupid than I'd just been – or tell me that I was being stupid...

Which – um – I was feeling. I knew that I had been...

And then maybe I was a bit more – by finding a way to make up with Danny while he stared out the window to see if anyone showed up, looking for what had caused the alarm noise...

But... We got away with it... We enjoyed it... And he only complained a little bit about me sneaking away to get some knickers and bras – I didn't take long...

Hey! Men can "multi-task"...

Just needs the right encouragement...

(Only had to prod him a few times to keep his eyes open...)

Okay – so there were far more than enough clothes already in the house – and it was loads better quality... But – well – I suppose – "rescuing" it from the store was like it was mine.

Maybe it's a crazy "me" thing?

Taking from Stacey's hoard was – sort of – like "only borrowing" it – I felt mean otherwise... She had a ton – far more than she could ever use – but she looked so – miserable – dejected – alone...

In all the pictures of her – she didn't look to me like she was sulking or being a bitch. Kind of – that she was *so* unhappy. Like her whole rich-kid world was actually shit.

I knew that I *never* felt that shitty. Didn't matter how bad the Estate was. The town was dangerous – the skanks hanging around the streets... The Law and teachers were a pain. Anton copping off with the fat slime-ball wasn't that lousy...

I knew that there were pictures of me laughing... Pictures that got posted...

Except of course – I'd left all that back at the village, the Estate – at home...

Which made me go all sad... And stop – right in the middle of picking up important stuff – like rice and more rice.

Danny insisted we had to stock up *every* grain we could find because getting more, later, would get harder – and then impossible. I knew that! Only wasn't so mad on doing a lot of practical about it in a mad hurry. Dance routines with little dumbbells were fine... Humping bags of rice...

He didn't yell at me when I stopped though. And he didn't get all "empathetic" and acting the consoling counsellor. He held my face in his hands and insisted I tell him what was wrong...

I know that Greg never did that... Mum couldn't of course – not once I stopped being "a little girl"...

OH SHIT! I've cried all over the page again!

For all of them...

===========

4 – 6

RIGHT! GOT ME A ROLL of factory wipes so I won't make a mess blubbing. (Practical – see).

Meanwhile – back at the store we were raiding... Danny cheered me up. He went and got a camera and batteries. Before he came back he found out how to switch on the printer-thing at the front of the store... Then, on a later visit, he powered it up with a little generator – that made a *diabolical* racket – but I'm glad of it now... So I've got prints as well as the disc of me prancing around and posing... And NO you are NOT going to see them... But I do have a smile on my face in them... Especially some he took around the house – later... THERE IS NO WAY YOU ARE *EVER, EVER* SEEING THOSE!

===========

We did three more raids to that store – because it was one that must have shut up shop early – so that there was plenty still in it. Repeat raids anywhere got more and more dangerous – but that place was extra good. Others, including the one I had made a fuss about, had been close to cleaned out of most easy food what with the festivities, breakdown in deliveries and the panic that set in... Although, there was very little of the last... Hardly anyone got time to panic.. Not before...

After was a different matter... But there were all sorts of different panics then – and on different scales... Quite often there wasn't energy to panic much. It was easier to go back to sleep. (The dangerous thing was wanting to never wake up...)

On a different trip, someplace else, I got soaked in oil – horrible slimy-gloop. Wasn't in the big store but some small garage place. Danny reckoned we should stock up with oil for the engines, anti-freeze and brake fluid – before anyone else thought of it and made it difficult..

He got the idea from me when I grabbed some oil in the store – but, of course, they didn't have a whole lot... Okay, so, that somehow led to me admitting that I had wrecked a few cars – and he didn't laugh at me – which was fine... He never said a thing about the knackered van. (Was lack of water not oil anyhow!)

We were in this garage place – and I've still got no idea how I did it – but I got covered – smothered – all over – even down inside my clothes – and soaking through them... *Disgusting!* All clammy. *Gross!*

Danny didn't laugh at that at all – in fact he was seriously worried – said that petrol and chemicals like that are bad for the skin...

So I was ecstatic about all the guck I'd got up my nose by then...

Anyway... We cleaned me up as much as possible and stuck me in some disposable coveralls that were about nine times too big for me. At least we could cut the legs and sleeves shorter... Apart from that I was bundled up with string like a bad parcel. Danny had the sense to keep his reaction to a smile – until he thought I wasn't looking... But I forgave him that one. He was doing his best...

He wouldn't have dared not to be...

He did not get to save those pictures!

The real important thing though, was that, when we'd got home, my hair was still all gooed up and stinky – so Danny got some scissors and cut it all off... It was the only answer. Despite washing what was left, I felt yeuky – so he gently shaved my head...

Kinky! Yeah, okay, you *can* think that this time... The whole business – was sort of bizarre... But – well – it was a lot better going all smoochy and turned on, than crying my eyes out about it...

Danny would do that for me...

And he definitely found the shaven-bald thing – um – shall we say "attractive"?

Wouldn't want to be "inappropriate" would we?

So – anyway – back to the "being serious" – while my hair started all-over again – it got quite fuzzy for a bit – Danny loved that...

I could use my sort-of cropped head to brush his back like a massage... We trimmed his hair right down close as well so he could do it to me... Oooh! Strange... But – ***Ooooh!*** <u>Definitely!</u>

I was supposed to be serious...

Well that was serious... Serious fun!

Cropped hair *is* a really good/practical idea when you're running around surviving – just keeping going... Loads of reasons why...

Practical, serious reasons for a crop...

1. If/when your head gets cut (or just scratched) there's less hair (and anything in it) to get in the cut – stop anyone cleaning it up easy.
2. It's easy to keep clean.

3. It never gets in your eyes.
4. It can't be grabbed.
5. Your helmet should fit better. (Don't wear a helmet? You're an idiot!!!)
6. It doesn't get in the way when you're sighting your rifle. (Tying it back only partly works).
7. So long as you don't have a massive bust or arse you can get yourself mistaken for a male-of-the-species. *[Okay – so I've been told this doesn't need the comments about just acting macho and stupid enough...]* Always assuming you wear cammo and not pretty pink... *[Is that "acceptable"?]* I'm not even bothering to go there about perfumes...
8. Earphones don't get tangled up. None of the different straps (binos and whatever) get tangled. It matters!
9. You don't have to wash it when you fall asleep face-first in your dinner...

So... Cropped is <u>very</u> practical!

And <u>Sexy</u>! *[You <u>do</u> want descriptions of that?]*

Yeah – yeah... So I'm "betraying feminism" and all that by getting myself mistaken for a man... <u>You</u> can practice all the feminism <u>you</u> want when some arsehole has a gun on <u>you</u> and/or your mates. Even more when <u>you're</u> caught on <u>your</u> own by nutters.

My "free thinking" and <u>liberated</u> feminism keeps me alive.

Good luck with <u>your</u> old-style snipe-and-whine at every single thing... 'Cos <u>you're</u> going to need a whole load of luck!

Soon after Danny shifted me off my butt and we started to raid we started to see places where there had been some system of a clear-out. Good thing was that these weren't close to us.

First things that always got ripped were the cigarettes, alcohol, sweets; especially chocolate.

The other thing you saw (everyone talks about) – at the start people only, kind-of "went shopping". Okay, so I did this at first as well – we went round selecting what we thought we wanted – or needed...

I <u>did not</u> ever take my "acquisitions" and wait for someone to open a check-out!

Okay... So I was half looking over my shoulder for "Security"... That was pure habit... 'Cos they were always grabbing me! NOT because I shop-lifted! Mum and Gran would have skinned me – long before I'd have got my arse kicked out of looking after Bodger... (It's all called "deterrent value" – like the A bomb). Anyhow – my checking behind me proved to be an excellent habit.

If people were like me – they cussed a load when whatever they fancied wasn't in stock... Me? Doing that? That'll surprise you! Won't it?!

When early raiding we maybe took more than was needed at once – you didn't have to pay for it after all... But then you so easily got cluttered up with stuff that "might be useful".

Another thing we (most of us) had to learn fast – a lot of times you got what you could and scooted. Taking time could make sense – like in being careful where you trod – but – a couple of frights soon taught us that hanging about was <u>not</u> a good idea... (Practical education!)

Me? "Go on about" getting stuff and the stores? *Me?*

So...? Just how "unimportant" a part of your life was shopping before all this? Yeah-yeah... I'll just bet you never, ever even went on line – never went looking anywhere for bargains...

As if...

Later it was Danny who got me being methodical – clearing out all of important things – like rice. (Rice! Rice! Rice!) Loading up trolleys and getting them ready near a back door so we could shove them out, shift a load into any vehicle we were using – mostly our LandRover – and get out quick...

Part of it, though, was that we had somewhere to take it back to. Which (we all realised later) was massively important.

I said somewhere about not taking everything and not overloading the car – but that changed. With more people looking and getting their heads round things, getting practical, sometimes panicking – and increasingly getting self-ish – then stocking up got to be sensible. Which didn't exactly help any of the panicky reactions – especially when people found places totally cleaned out of anything the least useful... Probably everyone's reactions escalated...

However – you can only effectively build up any kind of stockpile if you have somewhere – and that has to be safe...

Which raises the idea of "safe".

It's not much good doing anything if you're not going to be able to defend it...

(Plus – keep it dry, cool and the damn vermin out...)

So how come all those boys video games <u>didn't</u> teach them that?

I suppose a "supply chain" – "logistics" – isn't exactly exciting and "sexy" is it? You don't go leaping around squirting adrenalin through your arteries with a trolley load of – rice. And another of – rice... And another – of...

Danny insisted that the great leaders in history, "Napoleon"... (Whoever he was – history was <u>so</u> boring...) They all knew how important feeding the troops was... Well – who needs history to tell them that? Any Mum with a hoard of kids knows that food is the quickest way (well, the second quickest way) to get boys (all sizes or ages) to do what you tell them.

Yeah, well – that probably answers my own questions doesn't it?

On the other hand – it's useful that some of the donuts learnt from their games to go running around making straight-on attacks, thinking that they could always start another battle after "game over"...

No... That is not how it works... You get shot – shot up bad... Then you do not just start again... If you're lucky you've reached your ultimate "game over"...

I never saw a game where, when you screwed up, you had to wait a whole day, screaming from time to time and eventually dying of thirst, before you could start over and try again to get to the next level...

In the films – everyone you (the good guys) shot at got killed and conveniently out of the way. Same in the games. I must admit though – I would actually prefer that – I would like that. Sorting out the dying is a worse chore than house cleaning – more than disposing of bodies... And we've had to get way more than enough of those out of the houses... (At least they don't weigh so much now). (Still nauseating).

It's sick – but – talking about now – the recent past rather than back-then – [Huh!] – that's little more than a couple of years ago...

Now – sometimes we try to not kill them – attackers – we aim to hurt them enough so they'll go away and not come back – won't think of coming round again...

You can tell real trouble when you find it – they don't bother about their own people that get shot... They keep coming at you. I've seen them shoot their own wounded people dead instead of looking out for them... That could be kind in a way though. You get shot – there often isn't anything much anyone can do for you...

BUT... I'm moving way out front of myself...

[Very briefly – in this "now" – we have our Valley defences organised].

===========

Looking back, there would have been no way that a small army could have defended the big house. All its huge windows would have been no help at all. Okay – we could see gorgeous views for miles (even from our bed) but there would have been so many ways of creeping up to the perimeter unseen. If anyone had come inside the fence the alarm system would have warned us... But there would have been sod-all we could have done about it.

I'm not going to write you a whole lot about how to make a place so that you can defend it. If you've got this far and have time to sit and read this you should know that stuff – at least – some of it – enough of it...

Here in the Valley we had to learn about that...

It is important to make it so that we see "them" first – better if they don't know it – best if we can encourage them to go away without ever getting close... At least show us who they are and what they're like before we need to react.

Anyway – "then" – we, Danny and me, weren't thinking of all of that and we were busy – not just with all the sex – and we were being careful – if not with the sex – which is (of course) how come I've got little Dani...

Which is good... ***Superb! Excellent!***

Even though it was super- frightening... (More like *fucking terrifying*).

Where's those wipes?

You wanted happy though...

===========

4 – 7

How about a nice sex scene? Yes? Does that sound good?

Had better do – 'coz that's what you're going to get! I mean – getting (a little) drunk can be fun – having a good dance is fun – but how the hell would anyone write about that?

If writing about sex is difficult – well... How about "its subtle aroma and deeply opulent texture created a supreme sensual pleasure..."

That sounds plain kinky to me! You've got to be weird to go into ecstasies about food. All that closed-eyes and deep breathing nonsense... Yeah, so some of the food they had in the Big House was incredible – but none of it was going to give me an orgasm... Not even if you rubbed it on me – and that *really* would be kinky!

I don't have any idea how come we were so randy – or had the energy. We weren't the only ones though – so I'm told...

Someone has said that it was probably like nurses and doctors – dealing with bad health and death all day maybe gave them a zest for life – and for making it.

Must have been like that for us – after...

It can't have been looks or physical attraction... We/everyone looked ghastly – *really dreadful.* Anyone (like me) who had started out skinny was hardly more than parchment skin over bones at the start... I had to be extra-careful to not get pressure sores – just from carrying any back-pack too long...

Yeah – okay – so I did think that Danny looked great. Despite he'd been so hammered by the sickness. He must have been superb before... So – – – *don't* go there (grab a pile of wipes)...

He still had such lovely, soft skin – and good muscles underneath – that we seriously worked on building up again...

(Don't blub!)

So – talking about sex – skinniness and delicate skin also meant you had to watch out for carpet burns – off the sheets – except for Danny and me the sheets were satin – and no problem – which was as well – or I'd have had no skin left at all...

This isn't very "sexy" is it?

STOP waffling me!

Okay...

So – Danny definitely loved it when I would wake him up in the morning... He'd point out the huge window at the incredible English countryside view... That was stunning even when it was pouring with rain – which was only a few days – despite it was English summer... Probably didn't rain so much because there was no cricket or tennis...

Anyway... He'd point outside and then at me – kneeling between his legs – and with a big grin he'd say he knew which view he preferred... Was maybe a result of what I'd been doing to wake him up...

What I'd been told about that was *so right* as well... Remember that?... Soft pads of fingers and long, slow gentle strokes do far more to arouse... Okay – So hard finger tips – finger nails at times – but – you want to start your man/partner off in a superb mood for the day...

Yeah well – a coffee and porridge could be alright... Bit kinky I reckon – still... Have to avoid scalding anything important... OUCH!!!

Didn't have any fresh milk for either though... So I got good with my lips and tongue... I didn't start at his toes...

(*Shit!* This could make me cry again).

Anyway... I was sort of working on starting a bit further away from my goal each morning... See how much I could get him going before I woke him up – or before he had to give in and admit that I'd woken him...

It was fascinating seeing what attention did what to him... Seeing him going from "Mr Squiggly"... (He hated that). (I expect all men do... doesn't matter how true it is). As I was saying – going from "Mr Squiggly" to "Mr Lighthouse". (Never objected to that... And no I never said which one – mainly because I didn't know any names – but he'd have qualified for a record size... And, yes, you can make of that the obvious...).

So... Mr Lighthouse would get all big and tall – and pretty hot... So – if the place was on fire – I'd have to find something wet to put it out – or somewhere...

So...

Oh! It makes me curl up writing this... Embarrassment? NO WAY! Ache – Longing – Emotion – Heart-ache – Heart-break...

Fear of forgetting – of losing what it all was...

Fear... They *don't* teach you about *that* either...

===========

You're **<u>not</u>** supposed to sneak preview-reads of bits of this!

And I haven't got round to what he would do kissing me all over – gently – because we had to be careful about my skin. Um – I keep on about that don't I? Well – it was important. *Very* important.

[Like I keep going on about other things – such as getting in and out of places and dealing with stiffs... (I mean the <u>dead</u> ones!) These things took on <u>massive</u> significance for everyone – like we could never have dreamed – before...]

So – we found a brilliant skin cream that helped a lot – and the massaging it into each other did wonders as well... As did having a really nice hot bath with candles and oils and the whole works – with us enjoying more and more of the whole works...

Well? *You* said I should write about the good memories that made me happy (even if it makes me weep now – weep sort-of-happily though... No-one can ever take those memories away from me...)

What's so wrong about writing about sex anyway? Except that it's sort of difficult making touching – anywhere – let alone the good places that make touching an "interesting subject..."

Difficult? Nearly impossible! ...To make it right...

I mean... How many times can you repeat "in, out, in, out, in, out" and keep it interesting – when it's the tip of his tongue gently tickling – your teeth and lips?

I mean! Men want to know what it's like feeling a nice, (obviously big – they're all "big" – at the *very* least) "cock" going into your sex... Want some sort of description... *How* can I describe <u>that</u>? "Fucking fantastic"... When/if it is...

"Fucking painful" if you get it wrong – *you great big Muppet!*

Yeah – okay – so that can hurt him "a tad" too... They're not supposed to bend by *that* much – I do know *that*...

I couldn't ever begin to describe any of it to another woman... *How-the-hell* would we compare notes? I mean, describe the pleasures – not folding him – his "thing" – in half. Umm... Actually – that wouldn't be so difficult... Cruel probably... (Even when deserved...)

So try learning how to touch me – ***gently***!

Meanwhile...

Comparing notes... You want some sort of Richter Scale?

So? Good idea? *Yeah?*

Yeah – Right! What man wouldn't get all moody and pissed-off if every orgasm wasn't at least *twenty* on the scale? How-the-fuck are we supposed to fake *that* every time?

On the other hand...

Doesn't even have to be sex. A light touch – maybe only on the arm... That can send a thrill through you – or a chill. Doesn't just go with who it is – can be when or where... It's all crazy – ***impossible***...

Where was I? Oh – right... Going to talk about the good times...

What should I...?

With all the extra focus we'd gained on keeping ourselves clean and the beyond-counting increase in the luxury of hot water, the bathrooms in the big place became wonderful for enjoying ourselves... FANTASTIC!

You do have to be extra careful about keeping your balance when enjoying sex in the bath... Slipping around doesn't only happen with your feet...

Missionary is very nice but you must make sure you don't slide under (the *water!)*

Because if you shove up and surface like a U boat that's been depth-charged (that was *his* description) – you can smack your lover right in the nose and give him two black eyes in one go... And he talks all funny for days – after you've had all the bother of tipping him over the side onto the floor so that you don't both drown...

And I never did tell him that I reckon it was when he hit his boots that he bashed his nose... It didn't seem so sexy – or so forgivable...

So – standing up with him behind you is REALLY nice... Especially when he is big. (*Precisely* how much description *do* you want???).

Danny was *absolutely no disappointment...* I was *fascinated* by his cock – I could look at it – study it – and (of course) play with it for hours – except he never let me – not for that long at least... **Meany!**

But – it's better before the water starts to get cold – standing up, bending over the end – which was a bit complicated as the tub was huge and round with a surround – but – I guess you don't need the exact geography of it do you? There was plenty of room for candles and huge fluffy towels though... Mmmm. NICE!

So... After I'd got him all excited with some good oral – keeping the bubbles out of my nose – and mouth – he'd make me stand up. Because there was no way he was doing that to me without having a face full of foam – not without me being a contortionist... Unless I sat on the edge – but that wasn't as good – so I'd stand and bend over – which meant that my breasts also hung down nicely. They're not so big but they do have a nice shape – Danny *definitely* liked them – and would... Oh!

===========

Sod it! I'll have to go and get another roll of wipes soon at this rate... (I guess I'll *never* be all cried out...)

Anyway... It was ***FANTASTIC!*** Right?

I still can't tell you how good he felt in all the ways he touched me...

I *can* tell you that it *fucking hurts* if you slip and land on the taps...

You ***cannot*** both of you put a foot up on the side at the same time... It *doesn't* work!

Isn't it weird how we can describe pain so much more easily than pleasure?

That is *so* absurd...

What would anyone prefer? The pleasures of a nice penis stroking in and out (lots more times than anyone would ever write) and stroking around... Those pleasures – *or* – the pain of an arm ripped by a bullet? Even a slight flesh wound... With all the fears of dirt and blood poisoning?

Hey!
You took a quick nose and said I shouldn't get "too explicit" about sex...

Well **....**

Well try this. See if this is "acceptable"...

We (Danny and me)went out on another raid. Further away, new territory – looking for stuff we'd put on a list, things for the future. Like more vitamins and cough medicine for the winter for a start – but bigger stuff as well – like a practical sized generator for a little light inside the house... (In the rooms without windows – remember them?)

In between making wild-passionate love and curled up quietly together we were working on being serious and responsible.

We'd got to always using the LandRover Defender he'd arrived in by then. Big and green with bars across the front and cages on the lights – although we hardly ever risked using lights... They came like that – which was good... Showed that the beast was serious – and it had a tow-bar which Danny put a big lump of metal on. That way, if anyone did try to ram us from behind, they'd smash themselves up more than they damaged us...

Had a huge "NATO" tow hook on the front as well... That came in useful – later... (Much later...)

Crazy, dune racing-machines? Oh Yeah! Like we *really* had time for all that fetish bullshit!

Anyhow – you want to spend all your time cutting and welding instead of kissing and shagging – you're TOTALLY crazy!

You do not want some stupid, open, go-kart thing – even if that bullshit was supposed to be in the desert someplace – like any survivor would be idiot to go there...

How come near every "scenario" was barren-wasteland/desert or near darkness most of the time?

For us – no-one got any time to get round to nuking the world to dust – hardly to even threatening wars or reprisals. (I'm told).

"The End of the World" hasn't changed the number of hours in a day. I said before – it gets dark – when you're away from a secure base you want to be inside, sheltered at least – tucked up safe. It's more-than-bad-enough messing about in the darkness of stores when raiding them. Searching in the dark inside homes... Well... Go figure...

Anyhow... Tatty clothes? NO way!!!

All that leather would be *so* sweaty!

Studs? Spikes? You've *got* to be kidding! Even with some flesh on your bones they'd be a complete disaster...

Yeah – *you* might like that? Probably like posing... I don't reckon you could do much without someone getting injured... (No I have not tried the studs or spikes!)

[Not any time!!]

Desert? That means **grit**... *No way!!!*

Living in smashed-up places? Wrecked factories or houses with smashed windows and totally knackered rooms? For real?

Really? Post atomic? Look at Hiroshima! Look at Dresden even... Coventry... We've got worries about nuclear – but – nothing's gone BANG! Yet... Chernobyl didn't make a bomb-blast – and it took years for the evacuated towns to fall apart...

Yes, we've got weather issues... So we all make ourselves as warm and comfy as possible. We just love reclining chairs and good-firm mattresses at the end of long days. (The TV's as useless as ever – even without repeats...) We're fitting shutters to windows and doors as fast as we can – and trying to fix any loose tiles as soon as we see them. We're scavenging doors, sheets of glass, tiles and even guttering to provide replacements.

It's all like the nice, complete, warm and clean thing with clothes... This isn't some half-hour short film. There's no film-set catering crew... This is *every* day – weeks and weeks... We want to be comfortable – and warm – and dry.

We hunt down every single sandbag too...

Ummm...

Right – So we had this Defender – ex army – hard top. (Best for English summer weather). Was matt black and green – big rear door we could chuck our gains in fast... Oh – and diesel – because Danny had sorted collecting diesel and it wouldn't blow up on us so easy... And the Landy was that anyway...

I don't know how long it had been – must have been a few weeks – I wasn't exactly paying attention... We'd carefully raided most places immediately around us that looked worth paying some attention and moved on to trying to figure out what to do and where to go next...

We were also thinking about getting tools. They were available in the garden places but it could save time if we got them from one of those "sell-everything" places...

By then new territory was becoming a real challenge... Yeah – that's the word – "challenge" – or plain – "fucking-scary-as-hell"... Danny never said much – but I saw that he had experience that made him a whole load more careful than I was – up to then... He never made anything of it – but we both knew what and why...

More than not wanting anyone else to come looking for our "love-nest" we kept clear of other people... Well... Danny did... I knew there was more too it. Hell! I *knew* what. If he wasn't saying I wasn't going digging...

What we had was too good. We didn't need other people... Didn't want other people. That was way more than I wasn't looking to ask questions. Far more than even remotely avoiding issues or trying to get a quiet life.

Just a couple of times we did bump into people... One lot were okay – no visible reaction to Danny at all. The other lot only got embarrassed... More their potty-training kicking in, if they did actually start to think any reaction, than any hint of trouble though... We made sure both lots got no idea where we were holed-up.

We both of us watched out for territory marks – watched hard for <u>any</u> signs of activity. We went <u>*careful*</u>... <u>*VERY*</u>.

I know we were both stressed – and more stressed the further we got from our familiar patch. It didn't matter that the weather was being beautiful – those gorgeous "big-fat-fluffy-sheep" coasting across blue skies days... Perfect nights – just, only just, touching towards a nip in the air at the darkest... *Zillions* of stars – and the crisp, quarter moon heralding its reappearance through the edge of each cloud... Dreamlike...

Too real...

Is this 20/20 retrospect?

The chill of night tasted and smelled good – fresh – clean...

So, eventually, we headed further, cautiously and quietly, further into completely new territory.

"Annoying" thing on the day, was that we couldn't see anywhere that looked promising for a long way.

We had our eyes open, our ears on... We tasted and scented the air for the least trace of exhaust – for – anything...

If you don't understand it – I'll never, ever be able to explain...

We were right on the edge of turning and bolting...

Then... We found a massive, big out-of-town store in an estate but set deep in a huge hollow (maybe a vast sand pit), surrounded by trees. It looked hardly touched... Bit of smashed glass at the front but the doors hadn't been rammed. We agreed I'd sneak in for a quick check... Once we'd checked-out the immediate area. (As always).

The whole neighbourhood all round look reasonable. The road in looked un-scuffed – not tracks in the dust. (Dust was *everywhere* by then – of course). The store didn't necessarily look so good (probably because the doors hadn't been totally done) like, maybe, one of those places that got cleaned out and didn't get another delivery before no one could deliver anything...

We even checked around the few houses in the hollow beyond the store.

The only sign that there had been any activity was that it was clear that the petrol station had been raided – probably completely... But – some while before...

I'm waffling... Okay – "displacing"... This is hard – *right?*

Checking it out we finally moved closer slowly circled the usual massive car park and loading area – near gagging at the reek of baking old-sump-oil patches steaming off the car park. Midday heat striking back off the store front was near blinding.

We wanted out. .

We really needed a few basics.

We were fed up.

We were hot.

We didn't want a wasted trip.

We checked the whole visible perimeter...

We checked the lorry entrance – the barrier wasn't just down – it was padlocked.

We checked everywhere.

We both did – *thoroughly.*

I *know* we did.

In a front corner we parked up close in against the tall perimeter hedge, in shadow under trees – pointing out.

Waiting some more dragged – excruciating...

The blistering tarmac sucked at my boots when I sprinted inside.

A fast look round showed there was some on our lists that we needed now. Better – there were things we wanted – like veg that had kept and would keep and some big drums of cooking oil (rape seed and ground nut... It's less smelly).

Danny gave me an "All-clear" to zip back across into the Landy. (We never, ever, parked right out front).

TOO STUPID to do that!

We felt like we'd been achieving nothing for a whole load of time, effort and fuel. So we agreed we'd raid – put our stress on hold... Even then we didn't want to hang around – wanted to get gone – back to where we had some idea of the territory before dark...

We figured that by parking where we'd checked, round the back out-of-sight, we'd be able to go out a delivery door at the last minute, load up quick and bugger off... With the bars on the front we could risk taking off as fast as it would go – and with only a small raid-load on board it could be fast enough... (That tow-hook was evil).

Once we got round there and tucked in between the skips and cardboard baler we confirmed that there was a back way in for deliveries... We'd bring trolleys out that way – well tucked away from view. It looked good...

We ghosted back around and in the front... Eyes, ears, noses – taste buds searching the whole time...

Maybe we put feeling creepy down to the heat? To being soaked with sweat...

[I <u>don't</u> *know...]*

By then it no-way felt unusual for us both to be carrying guns... The pump action and revolver...

Okay... So you've got the picture?

We found enough good food stuff for three big trolley loads – but couldn't open the load-bay door... Decided to forget getting any more.

Wasn't so bad because a fire door we'd spotted was very close to the back at one side – no alarm went off – and we wheeled the first two trolleys out and round and loaded up – no problem... Did the veggie oil first – large items – fast to shift – firm on the floor hard up against the front seats. Packed them tight with blankets – then a couple of large net bags of onions... Sacks of (more) rice. Being sensible, practical – and careful. We had our ears <u>wide</u> open. We watched like falcons. We both <u>*double*</u> checked before going back round the corner and inside for the last trolley...

I ***know*** this... I've gone over-and-over it in my head... I could tell you the *exact* labels on stuff – the number of clouds in sight...

The third trolley was heavy and had gone wonky so we both went in for it. Pulled the door shut so as not to show...

The trolley was a mega-bitch. One wheel jammed up completely with a tiny bit of cardboard. Once we'd sorted that Danny put the pump-action safe in the middle of the stuff so that he could wrestle the stupid thing better. Damn trolley was so mean-awkward that we thought about dumping it or changing to another one. We were taking way too much time, though. Didn't want to delay. We ended up struggling on.

Now here is where we get to the "other option" to writing about lovely sex...

[Soon as I get my shit together... This is so fucking hard... I ***know*** *we were being careful...]*

Shoving the trolley as hard as I could, with Danny more kind-of walking backwards at the side trying to steer it, we got back out the fire door – then round the corner...

There they were – instantly right in our faces – crashed the trolley right into one big, tall guy's nuts. Didn't mean to – the trolley suddenly decided to take off like a rabbit down a slight bit of a slope at the same moment he rushed at us.

I'd started to haul back when "BANG!" The trolley stopped. He'd have tumbled into it – instead he caught a smack in the face from stuff piled on top – and I got showered with stuff as I tumbled back – shocked – a bit stunned – winded.

The confusion gave us a moment – not that it exactly did us any good.

The folded-up-on-the-trolley-guy's gun – massive thing – bounced down beside me – fired three or four shots – scared the crap out of me... Windows away behind me shattered... But scrabbling half to my feet, I managed to grab it – by the safe end. Stopped it – didn't know how. Could be that it stopped itself – it didn't jam...

Kind of crouched I rolled and twisted around to see Danny and another one had got into this face-off. Right up close – **screaming** at each other.

I guess maybe the other people didn't see me...

Huge man... Towered over Danny. Screaming ***"Fucking Looters! We're going to hang you from that fucking lamppost and leave you for the crows! Set an example to you stinking scum and all your fucking kind!"*** Back of him his people are howling like piss-head hooligans – cheering him on...

Danny's not backing off one bit. There'd never have been any point... Behind him he's got our pistol out of his belt – all two bullets worth of it – but without moving he's too close to the man to do anything – except he's working the cylinder round to get a bullet up and into place.

I see that the trolley-man might see what Danny's doing any moment. He's grabbing for our shotgun. I get against the trolley with my shoulder and shove with everything in me. Trolley man's feet still aren't on the ground so the trolley takes off down the slope – distracting screaming-man... He steps back – enough for Danny to get the gun round...

Fuck-up is – as I stand up straight from the shove – they must have both fired at the same time – they blow each others' head apart...

I got splattered with my lover's brains... That's how I got my scars...

Isn't like that in the videos is it?

I have the whole thing in my head like a Super-HD DVD. Played it all over-and-over-and-over. The seconds of it... Minutes – seems like ages of going careful – then...

Less time than it takes me to write a line here...

We screwed-up.

***I** fucked-up.*

===========

Even in the latest films, the girl would often stand there squealing and looking stupid...

This scene in my head...

A sudden silence. Only two shots – nearly together – but – in the new, silent, world they're like a bomb's gone off... Everyone stands gob-open for a fraction – there's the smell of cordite – and blood and brains on the hot tarmac – before the yelling starts – maybe their shooting...

Trolley-man's trying to balance, get his feet down – still grabbing our shotgun.

All that happened in seconds. Parts of a second... Way, way less time than it takes to tell it.

I went mental. Dropped myself flat. Pointed the big gun. Pulled the trigger. Shot a load of tins and stuff in the trolley first – stuff exploding all over the place – then got through to the man – ripped him apart – up from his balls, through his belly and chest to his face... Shred him to pieces. That gun throws out bullets at a hell of a rate...

I *can't* stand the smell of tinned apricots.

Didn't know it then. It's "an early, standard issue Soviet Kalashnikov AK47". Evil thing. Big "seven point six two" Russian bullets – from a drum... Then... None left now... Don't recall who told me all that technical bullshit. Don't care – about who or the BS... The thing did its job – killed them and kept me alive...

Not so brilliant – when I didn't want to be...

I fired loads of the bullets in it right then – trying to get some sort of control of the big, heavy brute – screaming, cursing, trying not to get battered by the kick-back (recoil). It sort of – snarled – *Bang!Bang!Bang!Bang!Bang!* Faster than you can say it – bashing me. I didn't care – not sure that I felt it... Had hardly got hold of it – not properly back into my shoulder – bruised the bone – right through. It hurt like hell for weeks – not that I gave a toss. Didn't feel it at all...

Danny was dead. No question. No doubt. No chance of doubt at all with half his head gone – splayed, flat on his back in the bright, bright sunshine.

They were going to pay – whoever they were – however many of them there were. They were going to pay – PAY! Said they'd lynch us for a little bit of food – tons of it around – must have been thousands of tons of it rotted before anyone got round to it... ***Bastards*** killed Danny for a few vitamins and tins of stuff...

Trolley rolled away with its shattered, headless, dripping corpse – blood-and-guts literally sizzling where it splashed. Stinking.

The others stopped, jaw-dropped – gawping at it all. Then they saw me... Fired wildly at me – but – it *can* be a good thing being small – much less to hit... Sod-all tits meant I got real flat.

And they were pulling triggers without aiming. Lucky for me – specially with those that had shotguns.

I've got a better hold on the gun – I roll over (like in the lousy, poxy, movies) fire some more – roll again. I know not to let them work out where I am. I'm terrified one would get it right before I got them. Each time I sprayed at them – pulling the barrel down – cutting their legs out first – so they fell into the spray of bullets – got their *ugly screaming faces* ***smashed*** through their skulls. One-by-one.

They killed my Danny!

I ***smashed*** *every one of their hideous, red, bug-eyed screeching faces...* ***I fucking killed the lot of them!***

It went quiet... Quiet like you've never heard. Quiet that hurt your ears. Heat still sun-burning up off the freshly marked-out parking bays.

There was one then – off to the side a bit... Threw down a gun – the bullet that went off near hit me... So I jumped up (like in the poxy games) and shot the coward running for a big 4x4 pick-up. (I ***hate*** big 4x4 pick-ups)... I cut her to pieces too... And the bullets that missed her hit the truck – hit the petrol tank or something – something in the back...

Before the woman behind the wheel could move the whole thing just went "WOOMF"! Vanished in a massive fireball... She fell out – howling – on fire before she hit the ground.

Burning flesh stinks... If you didn't know it... (You'd never get the stench out of your sofa).

I was kind though... Got as close as I could and killed her – was difficult with her rolling around screaming. I only winged her with the first two tries. She was yelling (between screams) *"I surrender!"* and *"Don't kill me!"* Would have been a lot more cruel to let her live... What was I going to do with her? Take her to hospital?

So they paid for Danny. All for a couple of trolleys of food...

Might feel bad about it.

But I don't. Never will.

Never imagined for one second I'd ever kill anyone... There they were – seven of them...

I already knew there was nothing I could do for Danny – didn't need to look... I was wiped out – maniac-horror eating me away – and I could hardly begin to move him on the ground – I'd never have got him into the Defender... And – I had no idea what being smothered all over in his blood could mean... I didn't care – but – I was held back somehow...

Something else was telling me I had to get the fuck out of there – right now – FAST.

So I used two big cans of petrol from a second truck they had... Backed it up, adrenalin-driven, dragged the cans out and poured half of them on Danny before I tipped them over – with rags in the tops... I didn't want the crows getting Danny... So I chucked a light out on him as I spun the Defender round... He got a good pyre...

Left the rest, them, for the birds – don't know what the crows did to deserve getting that – probably made them vomit...

Never looked around to see if anyone else was rushing to see what all the noise and smoke were about. I drove like a maniac – fast as the voice inside told me...

Was that? Could that have been Danny? Still looking after me?

Was no-way running-away that time... I was keeping me alive. Like the voice in my head kept telling me to.

Wasn't until I got home that I found my face was bleeding badly. I had a gash across my forehead and a chunk of shattered bone in my cheek... I think it has to be part of Danny's skull... So I keep it... A bit like keeping little Dani's baby teeth...

I'll always have the scars. They didn't heal up right – should have gone to hospital and had them stitched and all that of course... Should at least have found a first aider...

Yeah... Right...

I like them – *my* scars – they remind me of Danny all the time...

And scare the Holy-Crap out of people.

===========

So? How's that?

Which do you prefer now? Me and Danny making love or Danny being murdered – and me going crazy-insane?

You know that store we'd gone in – gone through the hole in the front door?

Well – right inside they had racks of DVDs and games – loads of "Shoot-em-up" stuff, horror, torture, poxy-zombies, cannibalism... CRAP! All that sort of shit – with "content warning" little stickers on a few of them... *Only a few*. Nothing to stop kids seeing them as they strolled past – or browsed... Wasn't a single boy's wank-mag or pair of tits in sight anywhere – no-one in a swim suit – they'd been self-censored from the Women's mags and diet and fitness lifestyle stuff... All properly PC... No incorrect "skinny" super-models at all.

===========

Yeah well... The old way of things wouldn't like what I was writing about being happy and things being good... It wouldn't be "proper"... And you managed to drop yourselves right in it by "suggesting" that I shouldn't be "too detailed"...

How'd you like the contrast?

All those poxey games and films... Why was anyone ever "so shocked" when kids out on the piss stabbed each other?

How-the-fuck-many people got murdered, killed, "blown away" on the TV every single day of the year? Including Christmas Day? *What* was so "Normal" about that???

No-one ever made themselves blind from wanking did they? Okay – there was some sick crap on the net – alright – ban that... But there was definitely some lovely stuff – well made – nice, sexy men and women – being – sexy – being nice with each other... Gentle – loving – passionate.

Wasn't all "Porn". Shouldn't have all been wrapped up and rejected in one bundle... Which is better? More natural? Some bloody murder or a ripping-good orgasm?

Making it all "procreation-in-holy-matrimony" and everything, *that's everybody*, else is "SIN" is BOLLOCKS! Social control BOLLOCKS! Prohibition-style BOLLOCKS! Money-making *SCAM* – BOLLOCKS...

All the moral panic, social concern and medical-alert-crap politely discussed on TV... They should have put love, tenderness, good orgasms – *and* Sexually Transmitted Infections – *up-front-and-centre* on the school curriculum... *And* – *done it **nicely***...

Shown kids how good being loving and tender is. Plenty of them needed that in their lives.

Kids needed to know that their bodies were natural and okay. They needed to know about the changes that would happen in their lives – the confusions hormones can create – *before* they kicked in. They needed to know about what alcohol-in-excess does to livers. They needed sensible information about drugs – medicinal as well as leisure. They didn't need body-shaming, taboos, secrecy and smutty jokes. They didn't need Medieval or Victorian social mores. They didn't need politicians and religious leaders talking bullshit to prove how good and righteous they were.

They didn't need endless marketing, excess sugar in their food and cheap, extra-strength booze – made available 24/7 by the government removing the restrictive laws...

Do I go on? Do I rant?

The kids needed to know about emotions, about getting hurt and about feeling great. They needed to know – sensibly – about mental health – and physical health... Dietary stuff especially... Gran said that one time, way back, schools taught proper cooking "domestic studies" or something... Okay – so that should have been for everyone – not only the girls... Except of course – that wouldn't have done the sales of microwave meals and fast food any good would it... Kids needed to learn basic sense about child care – instead of "expert opinion" and social services interventions – and "shock-horror" headlines when the system fucked-up and yet-another baby got killed... Instead of fussing about under-age pregnancy the experts should have shown the kids how diabolical a night in with a screaming kid can be when all your mates are out having fun...

Like I said... Kids do not have a script. What they see is all they know.

So... You want a "Better Society"... Fucking well show them one! Do not tell them how evil and dangerous things like alcohol, fags, drugs and sex are – while you're so clearly thoroughly enjoying them yourself!

Mr and Ms Politician. Mr and Ms Educator... *Don't be fucking moronic!*

Maybe the boys should have been encouraged to go home and have a nice evening's shagging instead of the girls pushed to go out, get pissed-out-of-their-skulls and copy the boys getting into fights...

Wouldn't have been so much money for the brewers and "hospitality" chains to make then would there? Wouldn't have been so much tax for the government either – or "cause" for the police... Or "moral panic" about all the dreadful things happening in society... That the government was supposed to be running... The government that relaxed the licensing laws...

The government that cut police and council budgets... The government that kept telling teachers how to teach...

So? Exactly what were they doing???

And I **never** got a blinding hangover from sex... Not even if I might have been too knackered to stumble out and get to college on time the next day – just a couple of times – or more...

Even the *poorest* shag – I *never* got off-my-head so's I couldn't stand up, so's I puked in the street or in a cab... I never even got into a fight because I was pissed. I never booted someone on the pavement in the kidneys or face. I was always careful about hygiene, STIs, getting pregnant...

Well – *almost* always for the last one...

Okay – so that did make me chuck-up... That was different!

===========

Box 1
File 5

5 – 1

So... Deep breath... What did Eli do next?

I went back to the house. Didn't know what else to do... Wasn't thinking... Don't think I was on the planet.

I guess that if anyone had happened to drive out in front of me I'd have smashed straight into them... Straight through. Wouldn't have stopped.

I'd grabbed stuff from their second truck before I torched it. (No idea why – was barely functioning. Maybe ran on automatic...) That gave me some ammunition for the guns I'd policed up from the tarmac as well... Provided me with rags to wipe the blood off...

Never thought of it before... I suppose I must have spent some time going round – clearing up – guns – mainly shotguns – making them safe – putting them in the Defender... Not much ammunition. They'd probably fired off a whole load at me... I kind of recall skidding and nearly falling over on a spent case. Why do I remember that? Sharp stab of pain in my ankle – then smashing my knuckles down on the ground...

I guess – I suppose I was sort of – dazed... Just knew (somehow) I shouldn't leave weapons or bullets laying around... It must have been another thing that Greg had drilled into me... Yelling at the TV movies probably...

Didn't know what the AK was – but figured out how it worked – detached the drum (it fell off – on my foot) – cleared the "chamber"... I know all the technical words now... Wasn't much left in it anyway – and the rounds are early, became non-standard (important to know that)... Although it turned out I had got two full magazines from the truck in the pile that I chucked in ours.

Where-in-hell did anyone in England get that from!?

But I keep it – sort of a memento...

Some arsehole tried to take it off me – later when it was little use because it was empty... He *wouldn't* listen – so it worked damn good as a club when I smashed him in the chest with the heavy wooden butt... Helped get me my nickname... "AK"... He was lucky I only broke a rib and didn't smash his jaw...

What next?

I suppose I was "traumatised" whatever-the-fuck that would mean.

Was plain dazed, was about all I knew...

Didn't sort my face, didn't get out of my clothes and clean off – for I have no idea how long – days – two at least – could be three. Didn't have the energy to move on from the house – not right away... Don't know why I went back there.

I've no recall of the gate, shutting it – anything... Must have been on auto...

If I'd known how haunted with absence it was going to be...

Except – that was where we'd agreed to head next... (Always have the next place planned... An RV point at least). We had our stores collected there... Our "future"... We'd been starting to think forward – beyond the summer – hardly properly beginning again... I'd no idea what else to do – where else to go... Must have been some sort of sense... Didn't have energy for anything...

No idea how or when I put the oil tidily in the pantry.

The food, the diesel, the starting over – largely was Danny's doing...

I was way too busy trying to put on some weight and being "In Love"... And yeah – that was *fantastic* – and it did make me smile... Makes me smile... Best thing ever...

Makes me cry my fucking eyes out!

===========

I... I don't know what happened for a while... Maybe I shut down. Maybe I've shut it out... Even now it's excruciating.

Sunrises and sunsets sort of kept happening – some days with lots of sun – some with a bit of rain... Don't know. Sun would wake me up – shining in on me... Sometimes the clatter of rain... Rain blowing in...

I was – numb... Except numb doesn't describe it...

And – there was this great-big-enormous... HOLE in me... Not "in my life" – but in me – right in the middle – where I should be... Where my food should go and my breath should be going in and... There you go again... "In and out"... Except there wasn't even a cuddle – not a touch... Nothing...

So sometimes I got raging mad – and smashed things... Ripped things up – all the clothes I had looked good in – as a start... Never wanted to look even human again – *ever...*

But that doesn't explain a thing.

It was – there isn't a word for it... "Painful" won't do. "Agony" is wrong. You could try "burning" – without any heat or fire... It was like everything was all through – not just my body – but – *all* through – everything – all my life... Everything from waking up to – oblivion...

Not like the sickness burning. Nothing like that... Smouldering chilled. Like nothing ever...

My head scooped hollow – frozen. Cold like an arm been tourniqueted.

Arms and legs that didn't belong. Staring at my hands... My scabbed-up knuckles. Limping on my swollen ankle... No connection to them – let alone "how come?"...

I'd turn round – so stupid – so ridiculous – I'd be surprised that Danny wasn't there... Only "surprised" is not the right word for it either... Confused? Bemused? I couldn't stop expecting him to be...

I don't think I would ever have got to somewhere where I wasn't expecting him to be around if I hadn't moved on...

Once I'd got back and hidden the LandRover in the huge garage I mostly stayed in the house... I didn't need to go out – didn't want to... Saw no reason to... I don't know why I kept – kept doing anything at all... It was sort of – you could say it was habit – like a robot... Programmed... No – not that. Nothing so definite...

Somehow I – didn't stop... I didn't live any more – I just didn't die.

I carried the Kalashnikov around with me all the time... Slept with it... After I'd cleaned it and refitted the drum. It was cleaner than me... Heavy.

I wouldn't have minded stopping – just – not being any more... I don't have any idea how that didn't happen. I kept clean – got back to keeping clean – after the sickness – somehow – don't know how – it's always an effort you make – but I wore the same few clothes all the time – not the bloodied ones – burnt them – even the boots – obeying instructions left in my mind from the last loops on the TV – Cathy's Cabin... I couldn't say

– old information told me that blood would be dangerous – like Mum said that AIDS had been – was – is...

So – I ended up keep wearing the same jeans and T shirt... Dull – nearly colourless...

I missed Danny SO MUCH... Like someone had ripped most all of me that was anything-that-mattered away – and hidden it... I dreamed dreams where I searched endlessly for him... Shocked myself by waking up... Hugging the pillows... Pulling them to me as hard as I could... Almost dry-humping them... Feeling – desperate – gutted – futile...

I miss him.

How-the-fuck did they have all those guns?

It bugged the hell out of me. (Before I started trying to figure where we – where I – went wrong...) How did anyone ever have the big gun? The AK. My AK. Ammunition for it? Sure; I'd thought about a gun, I'd got mine – my ancient revolver. The boys say it's "First World War" – argue if that should be Bore War... Is it a Webley, mark four or five? Who-the-fuck cares?!

Hand guns were *supposed* to be banned weren't they? Maybe that one was someone's heirloom... Fat lot of good it did for the man-in-the-road's inheritance...

The shouting man and one other had "automatics". Big ones. Like my gun for size. That's all you need to know! Where did they come from? Illegal guns?

Then again...

Both Gramps and Greg always said that gun laws meant fuck-all to the illegal market, criminals and terrorists. Seeing him in armour around the Hermitage was totally weird at first – but it got to be plain normal... Like it is for all of us now.

Those two with autos also had a short rifle and a black (police-type) short, pump shotgun. I've no recall of un-slinging them off the bodies – no idea how I *ever* did that. Somehow I even kept the slings... Yanked them clear... Nearly fell on my arse with one... Collected the carbine's clips...

The others had three shotguns of different sizes – all ordinary ones.

Yes; Richard! I <u>know</u> they're "break action"! *So-sodding-what!?*

They'd sprayed more than enough lead at me. Turned out that some pellets had got my shoulder – but I never noticed that until Gill's Ken dug them out of the sores that I'd been ignoring... Could hardly treat my own shoulder could I?

The last one was a big heavy old single-shot rifle. I am not going to give its name, calibre, make, date... <u>*Sod off Richard!*</u> It only had seven bullets anyway. I never fired it... Then again, I never fired the gun that killed Danny – or any of the shotguns except for hunting.

All the shotguns got stolen anyway... But that was way off in the future...

I'll never know where they got their guns from. Not that it matters. Wouldn't make any difference. They probably picked them up as they went around scavenging food, clothes and fuel... Like I would have done if I'd seen what I wanted – *had* begun to look for... Probably like most of us would have done... (Once we started to think straight).

Sorting and cleaning the pile kept me a bit busy. Sort of. Was some weird kind of therapeutic... Like solving a puzzle – how they came apart... Sanitising them...

Mainly...? Mainly I was deadened. Far more blanked-out than the sickness and what it had done had made me...

I think I'd kind of only wandered-on from the sickness.

Danny's murder – that more smashed me in the face. Made me wonder... No, I didn't wonder... I simply didn't know what I was doing. I wasn't asking why I was going on... I just – didn't stop...

===========

Then I realised I'd not had one, maybe two periods...

That was insane.

Just before Danny returning I hadn't even thought anything about a short, weak period. That was nothing more than "normal" lurching back... Was going to happen sometime. Didn't note it as some-kind-of landmark... Didn't think any more about it. Far less of a problem than anything my guts got up to...

Soon forgot all about it... About all of that...

Was far, far too busy with other things...

Crazy? Yeah, crazy absorbed in passion and love... Love – and passion – like I'd never known.

But now...

Could be that the horrific shock of it all had just shut me down again. Could it be that?

Something else was going on though...

Nothing I'd ever felt before...

Was it eight or ten weeks? Since?

Like I said – I was "distracted"... I'd not been counting...

Was the moon that gave me some idea...

Autumn was approaching. The first leaves on the lawns. Danny would have been raking them up – bitched at for letting them reach the grass...

In a previous world. Where I'd probably never have met him.

The beauty of the colours maybe began to wake me up? Maybe a first really chill night – an absolute cloud-free sky – and huge silver moon...

Didn't react at first. Pretty sure I didn't. Maybe – probably – shrugged it off... So what? What did it matter? What difference would it make? Wasn't ever going to need to have any kind of sex life again. Better off not bothering with the fuss. Wasn't ever going to get pregnant...

"Oh shit!"

I had ***had*** a period... Small as it was... Just before...

I "woke up"... I screamed... I'm sure about that...

That wasn't immediately of course – Immediately I was void inside – just – going on – existing – not feeling – not feeling anything if I could anyway achieve that...

Didn't get pissed or stoned though – didn't try that... Kind of would have taken too much energy...

Daylight and being awake was foul enough without a banging head.

Anyhow – I had such good memories of getting lightly smashed with Danny – looking at the wine racks or anything else would set me off... I smashed up more bottles than I opened...

What was the good of all that booze? A few times I got mad and hurled stuff at the racks. Pity really – wasn't as if it did any good... Except – as it turned out – not getting smashed out-of-my-gourd when I was carrying Dani was a good thing...

I was – without sensation – a vacuum.

Smashing things – the place... Explosive rage. Hurt. Frustration... Futility.

Like I said – what was the point of all the wealth – with them looking like that? So... I took some of my feelings out on her...

Which proved interesting... Maybe the curiosity that triggered combined with amazement at my "condition"? I don't know... Somehow my brain began to move beyond numbness. Somehow I began to look forward... Perhaps like getting to be responsible for Bodger – having some kind of future plan beyond more shit school and the dole...?

Whatever crap opinions got put on me "back then" I was, in reality, pretty good at taking responsibility... Even if it wasn't always for exactly legal things...

Okay – so – I wouldn't say I was shocked – not by what had happened – being attacked – not so much...

Bewildered? Stunned? By what *I'd* done... Killing...

Even now – I don't think about that...

Doesn't matter how angry/mad you get. Doesn't matter how much people piss you off. Doesn't matter how righteous you get at bad things you see – all the diabolical shit on the TV news... All round the world...

(*What* were we supposed to do about it all?)

Anyhow – the thing that still bewilders me – is – my reaction...

I – I – lost it... Lost something... I didn't go into a "red haze". I didn't "lose it"... I fucking *aimed!* I pulled the fucking gun down so that I made sure I hit them... One-by-one.

I conserved my ammunition.

There is no way... No way at all – ever...

It's not like that *was* me... It ***is*** me...

===========

I had been, I was, aware of the moon doing its thing – waxing and waning... More aware of that than my body in the first days after...

There were loads of vast, clear nights then... Startling clear – and black – going on forever – so that... I wondered – if I could somehow just fall up there – would I keep falling forever? Would I somehow find Danny up there? Way out in the stars?

I was aware of the moon because we'd been so careful about showing lights. We took all the bulbs out of the Landy except the headlamps and a work lamp on the back. As much as we could we didn't use lights of any sort at all. The summer evenings had been light for longer of course – which helped... But – we could see all lights down below the mansion whenever there were any – so we reckoned that we'd show up like a stadium if we weren't very careful.

Thing was – I'd grown up with street lights hadn't I? Tell the truth – in those (way-back) days I was nervous to be out anywhere where there were no lights at all – and the Estate wasn't so far from college... I never liked journeys in the dark though.

The main road was lighted. I *really* had to push myself the first time I discovered that I was going to be riding the bit between the main road and close to the Estate in the dark... But – there were always houses with lights showing somewhere in sight – and the glow from the main road. Whenever it got cloudy I could see the reflections of the town behind me and the Estate in front. I got quite good at it... Could handle it.

But – once everything ended – and the lights began to go out... If I had let myself think about it I would have freaked out.

I must have said somewhere that by the time it gets dark – before that – you need to be inside and somewhere safe. If not inside, you need to be set up as safe as possible somewhere. I'm sure I've said – you don't go shining lights around – not so long as you don't want to risk attracting attention.

If I'd not been doing that, staying in as soon as it got dusk – not that I was out much in daylight... If I'd noticed what was going on... Then, without Danny, I'd have got back to being more than nervous – probably terrified. (Maybe that was another thing that I didn't let myself notice?)

Like with the Daz business – After the killing – I was freaking that someone would come looking for vengeance... My brain wasn't figuring any logic that, if there even were any others to the group, there would probably be no way that they'd have any idea where we'd come from – nor where I'd run back to... I wanted to hide – and hide – and hide. Millions of empty places – but no convenient Hermit's garden... No home to slip back to and no Mum with a meal for me...

Carlton and his brother had their reasons for coming after me... This time, way more than after Daz, there were reasons – and – I was totally on my own... There wasn't going to be a black crewcab pulling up to check me out... I wasn't swearing and cursing...

Although the way I erupted a few times possibly "suggested" to anyone that did notice that the mansion would probably not be a sensible place to take a look at – unless they could do it in a tank...

But instead of trouble coming... Through the huge window spaces I discovered, rediscovered, that there was this ginormous, sort-of silky-with-spangles of sharp light, vastness...

Just sitting there – blank-of-feeling – before I woke up – before I realised... Numbed – staring over the shards that weren't twinkling in moonlight – because it had gone round again... The sky was sparkling...

To be right – I should say that Danny had shown me – before... Carried me outside in the middle of a cloudless, moonless night...

There it all was...

Wonderful...

Incredible...

Don't know if I forgot that – maybe shut it out – and then sort-of stumbled on it again... I hated, *loathed*, remembering the good things then – the superb things...

Things like making love in the silvery darkness – hardly able to see Danny at all except for the difference where my legs wrapped around him – the dark of his silhouette over me against the sparkle...

Like shattered huge window glass, sprayed over stone and grass, shimmering moonlight...

Not entirely sure I want to remember the stars now – they open up the smouldering crevasse in the core of me...

That night – that astounding night... I wasn't stoned.

Not on any substance anyway...

Well when he showed me – probably off-my-head on him...

Later – all that trauma and crap – all the sickness before that still... Kind of out-of-my-mind...

So... I suddenly knew that the moon had gone round twice – and more... I had to ask myself... Was I? Could I be?

All the times I'd felt Danny come – right up deep inside me – like I *so* loved... Adored.

Every position we could think of to feel SO GOOD...

On about the sex again... Does reading about it seem a bit different to you now?

Still can't tell you properly what it felt like... Having him in me – wanting him to fill me – all the way – rubbing skin against skin – feeling all over – kissing – touching – gripping my legs round him hard as I could – forcing him into me – feeling him swelling – working into my own rhythm – feeling me boiling inside – seeing his cock plunging into me – feeling my tits get hot – my nipples harder – my face flushing... My chest, my sex, my belly – all of me... *Losing it.* *Gasping.* Both of us *gasping.* Feeling him swell. Wanting him to burst. Feeling his strength straining. *Explode* right in me. *Gasping.* *Heaving.* Shagging furiously through massive orgasm... ***Massive!***

Like I'd been told – they could be ridiculously – vast... Fill the whole universe... (When I heard that I nearly wet myself laughing – half with embarrassment).

And that laying there after – with Danny still in me for best... Not having to be or do anything... Yeah – he was right about that too...

Happily looking across the LandRover and watching his face (when we were out raiding). He'd complain like mad if I did that when I was driving... Just fussy...

Putting my hand on the middle seat so that he could put his hand on it.

The buzz of making it away after a good raid with no problems... Real, grin-all-over-the-face and "we-did it!" BUZZ... (Still keeping our eyes open all round – that got so natural).

Hearing him go quietly (so quietly) for a pee in the night – the lingering warmth of him – his deep scent – the excitement of waiting for him to softly return and the bed to move under his weight... Deciding whether to "be asleep" – wondering if he'd cuddle me... What to do if...

Sharing the check-around to see if everything was still safe in the mornings...

The no-need to say a thing – the world of meaning in the tiniest look...

The silly things that became tiny jokes – private to us... Silliness that only needed a word, half a word – a look – half a glance...

The movement of the last fraction onto a touch – the approach not even seen – felt, like electricity – the response – to welcome...

The sound of his breath.

And I knew what killing was like now too...

===========

5 – 2

Sod it!!! Okay! I'll tell you now...

I *want* to write this down. Record it. I'm *never* going to forget it. It's in my head – forever...

Meeting Danny. Danny suddenly being there...

Best thing ever happened to me – not just to then – but *ever*.

You remember that when I was first in the big house I was exercising, using DVDs – trying to get fit again?

Right – so you've probably worked it out by now – I can be a bit sensible – and a bit crazy – completely mad is for real...

That morning in the big house I had woken up, made my usual checks all round, cleaned me up (total compulsion by then), shoved some food in me, had a drink – no idea what it was now – may have been some fruit juice from a carton – with a bit of vodka in it... Or – honest – a vodka with a bit of juice in it...

So, anyhow, I'd got into doing these routines to a video – figured it would be a way to build up my strength – get some shape again – maybe make me look a bit less of a wreck... Was making an effort at least once a day, sometimes twice – after another clean-up – before another – and another before crashing out for the night...

Did I mention obsession?

Yeah, well... We all know...

Anyhow – anything "strenuous" usually meant that some kind of cream needed to be applied some-place... Places...

Wasn't planning – not remotely thinking about anyone else (probably shutting that out) – wanted to look and feel at least passable.

Must have felt good that morning because I extra got into it. I was doing a bit of proper exercise – with small dumbbells...

For maybe the first time I was feeling good – much better at least... I worked up quite a sweat exercising and with the video – looking out from the gym over the balcony at the nothing-happening for miles below. Out there was miles of blue, blue sky; a few puffy clouds. All bathed in lovely sunshine...

It looked fantastic.

The weather had been messing about – typical English – not making up its mind what to do. But it had been warmer at least – and the trees looked as though there was barely any breeze... So I got this idea...

I'd looked at the possibility of a dive from the balcony a few times. I reckoned I could go safely from the top of the balcony wall. So I had worked out the details – like diving from rocks..

Only four, maybe five metres – and the water was deep enough.

God! It makes me shudder now! That water was ***freezing!***

I'd got naked, I slid open the huge glass and dived right from the high edge – *whoosh! Terrific!*

Splat! Blat!

Beyond description. There isn't a word for it... It was like brain freeze when you gulp anything iced – the cold *hit* me – ***Crack!***

All over – all at once. It *hurt* – but – it was – ***Wow!*** Both – all at once. Sort of – shocked me awake – like I'd been daydreaming. Jolted me – alive – more than awake...

Then I was swimming – hard as I could – like it was for my life – hard, fast, harder – determined. *Pushing...*

I raced at one time. So I know how to turn fast – and when I did – it was like my mirror image turned with me – and – then again at the gym end. It felt like – it sounds crazy – but it felt, like I guess swimming with a dolphin would feel – sort of natural – exciting...

By the time I was coming back the fourth time I knew I had a choice – stop and climb out or keep going – and drown... Find a watery end to all this mess... But that seemed – wrong – sacri–thing – like they say something's wrong in church...

So I grabbed the end and hauled myself out – and there he was puffing and spluttering; missing his grip, splashing back in – spraying me.

What!? ***Stunned!***

That would no-way describe it.

He'd been swimming right alongside me?

For real? A dark shape like a dolphin? Was I – dreaming? Hallucinating? Hadn't done any drugs – couldn't be that pissed...

I had to grab for his arm – automatically . (What else do you do?)

The natural thing was to haul him up so that he didn't drown. (Crap dolphin skills).

He sprayed me with spluttering breath – *right* in my face.

Where-the-hell would I grab him? He wasn't all thick muscles – his arms looked like they'd pop right out if I yanked on them. When he next came up I grabbed for his hair before he could slide down again... Missed because it was short and close. So next time I got hold of his beardy chin – lost that – grabbed an ear – at least kept his nose above water... Tried to pull him up again...

What thanks did I get? Half way... He yelled! Howled...

So I let go.

Big splash! Freezing cold! I leapt away.

Thrashing around, he half sorted himself – then managed to swim to the side – to the ladder and climb out – naked – skinny bare-bummed. *Frightening* thin. Tall and beautifully proportioned – but so clearly battered by the sickness...

I *wasn't* like that... *Was I?*

Uh! Oh! I was – leastways – I was as naked as he was – and *scrawny* – *horrible*. I had to hide! I was *ghastly!*

Before I could move a muscle he fell flat on his face. He passed clean out. Splat! That was a "SPLAT!" Like a big wet fish on a slab.

Okay. So I'm going to claim all the club lessons about lifesaving. Right? I started to shift him into the recovery position.

I was *not* kneeling to give him a blow-job when he woke up. Got that? *I had no intention at all!*

"Um? Hi?" That's what he said – all he said... Then I saw his...

It *had* to be his fault! For real! He went from nothing, like a caterpillar rolled up in a ball – yeah – well – you think of a nice description...

Anyway – *you* wanted me to write about what happened, nice things – and the things that changed...

Well this changed everything... *Everything.*

Okay. So I forgot all about "Recovery Position" and "Airway, Breath etc" – and kissed him – there...

Proved that there was *absolutely* no problem with his Circulation...

Don't ask me why!

I just... Well – it wasn't (what I was going to say) that "I just did it"...

No. It wasn't like that... Suddenly – I wanted to... *Wanted to...*

I can't explain it – so no point asking...

I've wondered about it often enough myself.

I've said that three sides of the pool were grass haven't I? (Was how come I fell in, in the first place. You'd expect some sort of edge). So – it was grass where the ladders came out the sides. And the new summer grass was all warm in the sun – and...

Weird how I recall this – but I do – and even now it's kind of all sexy – and makes me shiver--- and – heck! ...

Try again...

The scent of the grass, that hadn't been cut – but got crushed... Wasn't the same as hay in late summer... But sweet, delicious...

The day was so beautiful – like I'd seen through the big glass. Maybe I was already turned on by my exercise session. Maybe all the steamy working out – the dancing – on the soft carpet – with hardly a scrap on...

So, I could see how skinny I was in the big mirrors on three sides – but, when I kept moving to the fast rhythms I looked – lithe – almost beautiful – and not skinny and pale... So – okay – I was feeling – hot – inside... Ready – to be touched – wanting to be touched... Wanting my body to respond – to being touched... I wanted to touch...

And I did <u>not</u> want to break the feeling with the fact that there was no-one to touch me or for me to touch... Looked like there never would be... So – I *knew* that. Couldn't get away from that...

But – I could slide the window open – take a few fast steps; jump up on the bit of wall...

Don't know when I stripped... Yeah – okay – probably while I danced – and – okay... I closed my eyes – half closed them and touched myself – moved closer to the mirror – looked at how my body aroused... I could see all my bones – but my muscles had hardened up a whole load since I wasn't sitting on my arse at a college desk all day – or pigging chips and burgers, curries, kebabs...

Keeping my eyes half shut – I fantasised – wished they were nice hands reaching round and caressing my breasts – making my nipples stand up – ache... I wanted a nice firm body behind me to shove my bum back against – and all that that meant... I wanted exploring hands – other hands...

Nice hands, gentle, friendly hands – a nice scent – warm breath – warm skin...

I frantically <u>wanted</u>...

So – before it all melted away into reality I got the idea of a swim. The thought – the sensation of how nice it would be to dive into warm water... And outside it looked so lovely...

So – as I said – I slid the door open.

The air out there was nicely on that edge between fine and warm and a bit cool – little puffs of air – chilled... Made my nipples shrink at first touch – before they swelled... I *ached*...

The first step or two – I was careful – barefoot from that luxurious carpet onto stone slabs... (I had memories of beaches...) And the air moving around me (instead of the still air inside) caressing me – it seemed... Caressing my belly, my breasts, my nipples... Exploring between my legs... WOW!

So – quick check – nothing to tread on – nothing to hurt me – the water below was reasonably clean... Quick run – explosive dash – leap up – hardly touch the wall – ***fly...*** Fly through the air – feel the air – feel my warmed muscles flex – bring my arms round in front of me – bring my legs together – point my toes – air soothing me...

POW!

That water was *fucking freezing!*

But it was great/incredible/perfect – WOW! Smooth – touching me – all of me... My newly toning muscles... And I was light, I had energy – I... I...

Like I said – after the fourth time round I had to push – make the spring, grab the side, lift out – water streaming from me – onto the slightly warmed stone slabs – not way-too-hot like you'd get deep in summer, later in the day – and no noisy people... For a change it really was superb to be utterly alone – and good to be free to be completely naked – I'd always wanted to swim hard – naked... Just me and the wrapping water...

And ("*maybe*") a nice hunky pool guy...

Yeah well... Who doesn't? Never fooled myself it could ever happen – not a shrimp like me... But – there'd always been closed eyes – a soft exploring hand – the idea of a gorgeous body... Nice, gentle touches – even rough (enough)...

So the sun-warmed stone was nice – like – warm skin...

And there was the walrus!

Startled?

It was like I'd fallen into my fantasy... Me – bikini accidentally falling off – people staring – and a hunk following me... Going to...

Yeah – in front of everyone as well – but – me... Not anyone else... And – Oooh... I was going to soooo enjoy it...

Yeah – right... Like I said – he crashed back in... And that splash *was* totally *freezing*... With a bit more breeze now for added effect...

I think that bits of me shrivelled that other chills don't reach...

But – I had to rescue him didn't I?

Wasn't scared or panicking. Didn't have time to. My club training kicked in. (They always said you simply had to get on and do it...)

So – okay... When I saw him – all curled up there and – lovely... Not caterpillar furry – definitely thicker... Okay – maybe not "lovely"... Sexy – fascinating... *You* think of a description!

I *had* to do it. Had to – *didn't I?*

Oh – the ***"zing!"*** that went through me! Can't tell you... The velvet touch – the – instant – swell... The grunt he made when I tickled the eye with my tongue... The way he – ***rose*** – more...

And suddenly I felt terrific! I glowed – all through – all my skin – suddenly different from the warm air and cold water – feeling – completely...

I wanted to rub myself all over him – him to rub me – to wrap myself around him... Have him in me – where I was suddenly open, pulsing and aching...

I'd never felt it before...

Excited – yeah... Turned on – yeah... *Nothing* like that... Suddenly I'm kneeling there beside him and I'm melting – all through – and – extra – all inside – where I wanted – burst – to feel him – feel it – filling me...

And his hand – touched my bum... Gently – "tentatively" – uncertain... Like – like he needed permission...

I think he figured that he got that when I shoved my bum back onto his hand – wriggled it so that he went between my legs – at the same time that I slipped him in my mouth and worked my tongue round him... Around a whole lot of him... As he cradled me in his palm – holding me firmly... So I had to rock myself back and forward – on his strong fingers that he just kept there...

I'd been on top... I liked that. Never facing feet before. I knew the theory... I'd seen pictures – loads of them – and I'd seen girl's expressions... Well – if I was going to do that... I reckoned that I'd be pulling faces!

But there was a *huge* question...

How to get from here to there? His fingers were stroking me now – ever so gently – searching for me – but – softly – teasing... Although I felt that I'd never swollen so big before – I was sure I must be dripping I was so wet for him... I was going to need to be...

Oh! But it all felt so good! And his other hand felt my tummy and cupped my breasts – and – gently...

And I wanted to feel that strong jerk – *deep* in me – against my thighs – against me... I wanted his hands grabbing my breasts harder – stroking...

I wasn't fighting him to move... Well – I was... I got a bit confused – because he managed to wriggle under me at the very moment I decided that I would have to shift and get upright astride him... Except... Right then his tongue *licked* me!

WHEEEE!

He got the back of his head banged in the grass...

Did I remember to say about the scent of the grass? Good, luxurious, grass... And we were crushing it with our bodies... Pushing out – fabulous scent... Like warm honey – kind of...

Pleasure to float away on – stimulus to forever turn you on whenever you notice it again...

But then – then I'm sixty-nined with Danny, *that* scent, *his* scent – warm sun on my back – his tip right in front of me, his curly hair brushing one thigh and then the other... And coolness breezing where I know that I am open, flowering and excited – probably right in front of his nose...

So I stretch out the tip of my tongue as gently as I can, aiming in below the rim to run softly around – see what effect that has... And I'm almost thinking "his breath is cool..." When he replaces the slight breeze with his hot breath – blowing right into me – and then, softly, around – making me know (as I swallow him) that I am *so* open – and SO wanting him inside me...

But his hands have my hips, the pads of his fingers and thumbs pressing firmly to hold me.

Just as well – because – what he does next...

OH!

Was my turn to yelp!

He was ***wicked!***

And he wouldn't let go Wouldn't stop. Had me trapped. Twisting in his grip. Sitting up. Whimpering. Couldn't have done anything else On his tongue And fingers... Don't care they were only holding me. They were pressing into my buttocks. Holding them. Pulling them apart... He didn't need to hold me down – only still(ish)...

'Fraid I forgot about plans to do to him... I *writhed*...

Don't think I've ever come so soon – so fast... So long. So hard.

Came more several times after... (Another story – or three...) Exhausting! Just right for curling up and sleeping.

If his yell when he fell back in had worried me about someone else hearing – well... I got a *bit* noisy... As things – um – progressed... *His* fault again... He – *did* things to me...

Danny kept me up straight with his hands under my ribs – *ooh* – that *lovely* feeling – sort of – warm – supported – safe – (almost)... But... As I stopped gasping – there was – – a whole emptiness – a yearning... I had to find strength – had to... Well – there he was – standing up big and tall – and wide – and exactly what I wanted to put where he had made all wet – and hot – and open – and aching to be filled...

So – like I said – I had never done reverse cowgirl before... So it felt – strange – very different – very – filling – even with knowing he was big... Lovely... Smooth, satiny, hard (in that weird soft way – no – *flexible* way...) *So* right to glide – glide – glide forever slowly to stop that emptiness – to fulfil me – delight me...

And his hands supported and soothed me...

His moan as I carefully eased, pushed myself down on him – him up into me... He held his hips still as he gasped – giving me time. I needed it! I had never been...

He groaned and shoved the last... FILLED me... I squealed... *Squealed!*

Pleasure-not-pain... Well – a little... Only a little – nice though... Not the hurting kind... Smooth and filling – stretching – touching – everywhere... Making me grip...

Gasping, both of us gasping, he had to lift me upward... Oh! I didn't want him to go... But I did – so I could feel that again... And again...

And *again...*

And *again...*

And *again...*

God! It was ***SO*** *good!*

Made me come so hard I milked him... Felt him swell... Made it more. Made it special. *So very special.*

Maybe – could be that, right then – we made Dani... WE made Dani. I hope so.

Danny always said things were because of me – "'cos I did things to him – so it couldn't be him..." After a few slaps (gentle – in the right places) we agreed on "It was <u>us</u>".

And more and more was good that morning... My shoulders can crush grass too... Amazing – looking up at what we're doing – and at his face – closed eyes and – kind of shocked with pleasure...

Skinny as I am (I couldn't get my legs all the way round him) his hands holding my bum – writhing around on the warm grass – and OH! – It pushes that lovely scent out into the warm air as well... Warm air cooling my burning thighs – and breasts... Ooooh!

Anyway...

===========

Need to get waterproof ink... And paper... <u>*Good*</u> tears, though.

===========

So – what I'd been told had been *right* – even for that first time – after I finished making a lot of noise – we just lay there – beside the water... On the grass... In the sun – out of the breeze... It was – lovely... Gentle... His firm, warm body pressed against me... His scent – our scent – his breathing... The sound and the feel – his chest and belly moving against me... Slowing, settling... Getting back to resting – then – still there... Peaceful...

This is what I want to write down.

So – warm – and – and – <u>fulfilled</u> – comfortable – <u>right</u>.

(Didn't have any energy left to be much else).

It was soooo good...

You know the second thing he ever said to me? You know the oh-so-romantic words he managed?

"Uh? Who are you?"

Isn't that *so* romantic? Just had the best sex of my life – I'm all glowy and warm and happy/drowsy... And he says *that?*

Didn't have any energy to slap him – or get mad... We rested a while... Kind-of snoozy...

Next thing he says – "You live here now? Got any food?"

Hey! Way to go on the "amorous-charm"! How about "Mmmmmm! *That was good!*" Or "Mmmmm! *You're nice!*"

No; Mr Charming wants to know if he can stuff his face...

He did have a point though...

The breeze had got round a bit, was picking up – and there were some real clouds brewing...

So we wobbled our jelly legs round and up the stair to the open door on the balcony – which he sussed was where I'd dived from at the same moment he dived from the edge – which was sort of nice – and he didn't make a fuss to go and get his clothes at that point...

I liked that. I wanted to look at him – his body... I wanted him to... Well – honest?

I told you how things went on...

And I told you that it was *not* that I was suddenly going to go all domestic... And he *was* – *snoring!*

Waking up next morning with him there beside me – finding he wasn't a dream – not a sleeping dream anyhow... Reaching to touch his skin when he'd reassured me... That first morning was *so* special...

Sunlight coming in the big windows – the huge bed – Danny...

I was famished by breakfast time!

Was his turn to do the catering! Definitely!

And he knew how! Absolute bonus!

===========

5 – 3

So – THERE YOU GO... That's what happened. We were so terrible, bad, sinful – and all that *crap*... And writing about it is so *terribly* awful...

Maybe you want to read something cool about some SAS guy in disguise on a Belfast street "slotting" someone – someone who doesn't get to have a face or a name...

Oh sod that! There was *always* way-too-much of all that. The "ordinary" soaps had to have their crimes, their domestic violence and their murders... If they were so "true to life", like, if that had really been typical... Well, there'd hardly have been any population left in no time would there? Who'd ever have been stupid enough to move to one of the postcodes where there was a murder every week – twice a week some "places"...

Stupid soaps might have "raised issues" – like anyone involved in an "issue" wouldn't have been only-too-well aware of it... But – did they "normalise it as well? Gramps said that centuries of history didn't need police, counsellors and social services faffing about with clipboards – the neighbours gave any slap-happy arsehole a good thrashing... Without any chance of getting arrested for it. Caveman treatment for caveman behaviour... That's all some morons ever comprehend.

[Then again... The "equality system" could be worked... Another reason the Principal didn't chuck me out, was because I told her that Anton's bragging in the canteen was sexual harassment – so's she'd have to expel him as well – and his jeering mates... And that would have screwed up her statistics

and targets... Said I'd sue for discrimination if he didn't get slung out too. Would have attracted the media... I got to use both old-fashioned and new. (Anton/donut was lucky Gran never got to know about it. She'd have really got "Old fashioned" with him...)].

<u>It isn't easy</u>... But – it's <u>*much nicer*</u> to try to write about the good times with Danny...

Not only the sex – *fantastic* sex...

How to explain going beyond the exercise videos to dancing together to great music – naked of course... On those incredible carpets, those polished floors – that insane dining table... You can probably get a picture – probably lascivious...

How, though, do I explain sitting out by the pool way into the night... Breeze bringing us the scent of the grass, the wild trees down below... A pair of owls ghosting... Slowly, quietly getting through a nice bottle of wine – sometimes a second one...

Pretty sure we never got to a third... Didn't need to...

We even got to like the hedgehog. Seemed sad it was all alone.

Those big windows faced out west of south-west – so the long summer evenings would have long, quiet (nice quiet) sunsets. The stone would keep the day's warmth for ages... The prevailing breeze came up through the quarry's fruiting trees all fresh and clean.

Under the peak of the balcony it could be good sitting out there watching a thunder storm... So long as it didn't get too close.

Yeah, yeah – so I'm a scaredy-cat... Gave me a good excuse to leap into his lap for a cuddle. If the flashes were nice and big I could need a *huge* amount of soothing...

When we sat on the sun-warmed stone, backs against the fixed glass, we couldn't see the land below except right in the distance. It was like looking across the Channel at the coast of France. So – we could fantasise that the land down there wasn't dark, empty and without all the world we'd grown up with...

Never said it exactly... Was just a common, unspoken fantasy. I'm sure we both knew – didn't want to break the illusion...

We could make like the few lights were ships – dream of where they were going – coming from... Where we would cruise to in our luxury yacht... Mysterious places, golden beaches and ice castles... Crazy, nutty dreams...

Okay... So we'd often not want to think about the last trip out – raiding... More so not the next one... We wanted to chill, forget reality... Lose the emptiness of the roads – even more of the streets... Get away from the un-mentioned knowledge of the houses...

Just – cut free from the reality of the day...

There had been horrible, draining times for me a bit like that when I was at college – more so at poxey school of course...

Difficult...

Two ways...

Meant not only the need for constant caution – the wearing drain of alertness... I've talked so much about things that happened... But – "after" – it was far more the "nothing" that beat me – beat us – beat everyone up...

Means I have to think back to good walks with Bodger... Sometimes in similar long, red-glowing evenings... His floppy tongue hanging out and panting like a steam train... "Steam powered dog"... Such sweet memories...

Such sweet – loss – absence...

I don't think about any of that much.

No-one does.

It's far too much...

Wouldn't ever want to go to drugs or even booze to get that escape now, though...

Wouldn't, couldn't be anything like – like "release"... Could *never* be.

Yeah – I did – back then – of course I did... Before Bodger. What kid "from an Estate" didn't? I listened to the bullshit – wanted my own "piece of the action"... How'd you think I got tangled with the skanks?

So... I only ever delivered leaf – dealer to dealer. I never sold (as such). Never had any money did I? Had to earn my smoke... And had to do more and more for less.

Anyhow – I wasn't so stoned that I couldn't see that I <u>wasn't</u> getting pulled by the plod. Sniffy kept getting yanked back to his van every time I came in view. Doesn't matter how high a chopper flies... Sun will angle off its glass or flicker through the rotor. They were mapping me.

They were all using me. Both sides. **<u>Not</u>** the kind of "accepted" or "valued" I wanted.

The dope was never such a great thing anyhow. Not for me leastways. Just because I wanted out of a load of crap with school. Didn't mean I wanted to be a complete stoner. Pretty soon wanted out of another load of shite around town. I mostly managed to keep all but the routine shit away from the Estate... None of it meant that I wanted a head like spuds boiled to mush around town as a 24/7 stoner or, worse, a smackhead .

No way I wanted to feel like the saucepan had boiled dry on any kind of bad mix of weed, caffeine and booze... I clarified that in one effort. That warned me off all the Class As... Frightened me off.

No proper idea what the shit was, what strength, what it was cut with... Anything...

I wanted to get away to see bigger, brighter things... Expanding my mind meant more – not filling it with fuzzy-shit-cotton-wool on the come-down and desperation for the next fix...

I'd seen more-than-enough mullered crack-heads before the skanks tried to work me onto it.

Okay, so I slipped-up the first time. Carried some A... But swapped my "payment" tabs for grass... Didn't stop the dickheads pushing me though...

Bastards! I said "No" – actually said "FUCK OFF!" – the second time, when they'd switched to powder and rock... Skanks soon got the idea to get nowhere near me with a needle...

That was why I <u>had</u> to fight some more... Fight <u>Nasty</u>.

I had far, far more than enough hassle with the law already...

That shit meant I'd got clean well before the Hermit died though... No way I could smoke in my shed. The space he allowed me gave me the break I needed – and the peace – some anyhow... The smell would have attracted attention – attention he'd have had to sort out. Anyway – he deserved respect – the real kind.

The book reading <u>did</u> expand my mind... It let me travel the world, time travel and even see inside things... Once I could take my time – I was hooked...

Anyhow... Plenty of posh kids at public schools used... Not that they ever made any TV documentaries about that! TSGs smashing in cheap doors on ex-council estates with plenty of "idle" unemployed "yobs" and shit-hole rooms – but never anywhere expensive with huge mortgages. never any banks, trading rooms or corporate offices... Somehow those dawn raids never went into gated estates or the big city banks and trading rooms... But then... All those fabulously rich types never, ever even smoked weed did they? The politicians only claimed (jokingly) that they drank a few pints when they were students – to "impress" and be "one of the people"... Yeah – right...

What did <u>they</u> need to escape from?

I'll "be fair"... Maybe they needed to escape from their own pressures... "Expectations". Could be that being super-intelligent and/or super-successful was as much of a pain-in-the-arse as being convinced you were thick and useless... Did having money help them? It never seemed to for them over in the

Village. I have no real idea... No practical knowledge... But I saw more than enough on my discreet travels around the hedge-ways.

I don't think that (back then) I would have minded having the money to find out... Maybe lots of money meant you could get more smashed – possibly better-quality-shit... Unless you probably got ripped off by it being cut more...

There was never a drug, nor an excellent bottle of wine, that began to come close to how good a wild walk with Bodger felt. Nothing could begin to compare with how superb it felt being there on the warm stone with Danny – gazing out into the dark distance... Didn't need to be touching...

Having to listen hard to detect Danny's breath... Eyes shut or when it got *so* dark... But knowing he was there... Somehow, kind of feeling it... Like – like electricity... More like a radio wave...

I didn't even mind if he farted...

Is *that* the essential sign of "true love"?

He would get so embarrassed... I even stopped teasing him about it.

Truth was – my guts could be worse...

Okay... So the reality was that with our damaged insides and the weird combinations of food we were eating... Things would get powerful... We'd both struggle to not be the first to break "the still of the night". It got *totally* silly some nights. I knew when he was struggling – because he would go so still... Like I probably was... Trying-and-trying not to...

In the end that got to be the safe way to get round to the BIG question... "What-the-hell had happened???"

Like we still do, Danny and I never talked about the "events" of what happened... That was much more "too-close" then than it is now. Too RAW in every sense.

We tried to figure out our own timelines though. What we'd been doing, where we were, when we became aware... Our stories weren't that different. We'd both been "busy"... Wrapped up in our own little worlds. Both at college in our own ways of course... Danny had been engrossed in one competition before Christmas and planning for another after... Travelling up to see his brother...

Danny always skipped over most of his journey back... Never talked about getting home... Nothing about how it took so long. Never said about why he came to the pool... I think I know...

He'd always start to half-stutter, get awkward... Switch the subject to me... To "my friend"... Some reason he hardly ever said "Bodger"... Although, for me, that was some kind of sensitive...

Somewhere around there was always where we put the brakes on... Played safe...

Like we all still do – mostly...

Danny and me would end on a nice chuckle... Then sit quiet... Maybe cuddle up... Probably... Once it was safe...

It's safe to write about not talking about it... Still dangerous to go too far...

We did talk about parties though... Carefully again... Stupid, giggly stuff – not too many names... There'd never be a way I'd ever believe that he didn't have at least half the women on his course after him... No way ever! They'd have had to be stupid! He was wonderfully intelligent. (No BS!) As well as beautiful, sexy, charming, considerate and – and – a bit shy... And that wasn't just me and my feelings!

It was not!

Danny didn't get made more handsome or rugged by the sickness... He got *battered.* A deep-fried sausage looked less battered.

Anyhow... It was sensible (at least) to be discreet about what I had or hadn't got up to... For sure I didn't want to give him any bad impressions... I am <u>not</u> saying if they would have been wrong impressions – or not...

Let's simply say – that, whatever I might write now – there are things you DO NOT mention to your lover... <u>Ever</u>... Not even if you'd have got to a stage of breaking up...

I can't recall to say what we did talk about...

"Everything, anything, something – nothing"... That special, relaxed totality...

Danny didn't merely style hair... Once he had some clothes on – he <u>wore</u> style... Walked with style... If anyone ever could have he'd have (you can guess what) with style...

Effortless...

Except – he didn't do sex with style... *We* did that with <u>passion</u> – mad, insane, crazy – <u>boisterous</u>... FANTASTIC...

Only thing he didn't even try to do with style was to listen... He paid attention. Made an effort with that.

I still can't explain...

Can't put it into words that link with the peace – of – after – and in-between... Of just simple every-day, ordinary. Of no questions, no doubts...

Togetherness doing the crap, boring essentials – washing up, washing clothes, humping rice – and more blasted rice – even getting fuel...

More than with anybody – ever.

Of knowing he'd got my back like I'd got his when raiding...

That's weird... Because I still feel so good about it all... I can smile – and not bawl my eyes out... Good feelings. Warm feelings.

Safe...(I think...)

Danny did talk about his family. Only a little at first – but I was fascinated... I tried to be as subtle – and as considerate as possible... Honestly... I did back-off if ever he began to get upset. I think, I hope, I got that right...

I'm glad that I did though... Pressed him for information. I can pass it on to Dani...

I never, ever, wanted to properly know about any other boy/man in my life... Well – probably except Greg... But there would never have been the least way I'd have been idiotic enough to go sticking my beak in with him...

Greg did tell me bits... Nearly always wrapped up in a story – usually with a jokey part to laugh about... I'm sure that all of them, Greg and his mates, handled what they'd seen – and done – by putting a funny slant on it... Fact is... We're beginning to do that now...

Anyway... I must write down absolutely every detail Danny said – for Dani – for the future...

Isn't that strange? "The future"...

I'll have to do that someplace else for now...

To begin here though – basic... I was fascinated because Danny's life, especially his family, was so totally different from mine.

You know my family...

I've tried writing it down and I still can't figure out Danny's... They'd call it "extended"... I *think* that he had three brothers (all older) and two sisters (one maybe younger). He had cousins though. Some with the same names – to help to confuse me. I think he had fostered kids around him as well... Or maybe just kids that needed somewhere safe for a time...

If his Dad seemed Victorian and (at least) a bit crazy... His Mum sounded like a dragon... A loving dragon... But – definitely fire-breathing. Danny spoke of her with some kind of awe... And deep respect and love... Although I'm not sure he wasn't half afraid of her... Maybe a third?

Their house was massive – had to be. They had two caravans as well at some time. Danny and his brothers slept in them. It sounded chaotic.

The main image I have of his Mum is steam, cooking and a *huge* wooden spoon... Discipline was short and swift – including for his Dad.

They all went to church. Every single one of them – whoever was in the house. That wasn't disciplined. That was strictly what happened – polished-smart – straight back – shiny shoes – shiny fingernails – sharp – on time.

Danny said that it wasn't ever that, if you didn't go to church you got chucked out... Everyone just found that they'd, somehow, arrived in church – along with everyone else in the house. There was no hiding. Anytime his brothers tried it on – the spoon tracked them down...

He said that you had to be very careful in church, when the ladies started to sing – or else you would get blown over... The way he described... I hurt myself laughing...

The pictures Danny spoke were hilarious and awesome... I wish I could quote them exactly. (I'll never be that good with words). He had a fondness and a sweet-horror of it...

===========

Horror... Too much of that...

Way too many questions for anyone to ask from their past. Like the BIG one... What was it all about?

Religion... Okay... That's a subject I can write about...

This is safe for me... I never had any religion/religious-stuff/stuff-like-that... I think I've always been lucky/blessed or something with that...

You'll always get a choice of words from me on this... Because nothing has ever been definite for me.

My whole family were "white-old-style English". Religion did not get discussed. Not even at Hatches, Matches and Dispatches... No time. Not ever. (Those few times I saw the "London Clan" – from the very edge – Mum and I never got involved. Looking back... I wonder...?)

Politics (except for hating Tories and Thatcher in particular) like religion were practically taboo... Way more than sex – more than drugs. (Oh... And "New Labour" were a bunch of "sell-out-opportunists" that it was sensible to not mention... You *know* why!)

Ummm... Bit of a difference... Politics didn't get "discussed"... Did get ranted about – from time-to-time...

Religion? Strictly diatribes only.

I saw my first Bible at Greg's place – and didn't know what it was... So – that means that there can't have been one at school either... Which is definitely a good thing. They tried to shove enough other crap down our throats didn't they?

Oh yeah... There was some curriculum-requirement-thing... I don't remember what it was called... "Multi-cultural" probably... Tiny bits of the externals of all sorts of different things... A HUGE focus on "Being Tolerant" and "appreciating"... Never a word said against anyone – except Christians, Atheists and Agnostics... I know those titles off-by-heart from those lessons... About all I did learn from them... Was asleep as much as possible.

It was all "BOLLOCKS" to me. That'll be no surprise to anyone.

What is the point of being all equality, tolerant and appreciating of absolutely everything when every creed says they're the only correct one...? And the whole educating-works has the one huge implication that it's all bullshit? Agreeing-to-disagree and giving space is a way of being tolerant... Saying everyone is equal is not. Saying everyone is equal from a position of "superior wisdom" is bullshit.

I was horrified to find a "religious" thing at Greg's place. I'd not have been upset by graphic porn (wasn't any – not in sight anyhow) – so long as no-one was getting hurt. I'd seen plenty on the computers at school anyway hadn't I?

Parental control? Farce! We were all supposed to learn programming (Government priority)... Excellent for hacking our way around any controls... (Okay – so one initiative they did get right – for us). Why'd anyone ever think we *all* got so keen on that??? Geeks? No way! Hormones? Go figure...

What has religion got to do with sex anyhow? Shouldn't that be private? Between me and – whoever? Between me and any "deity" as well? What's it got to do with priests? Except... Mum said that sex is the one thing that everybody is interested in... So it could be the one thing that all priesty-types knew they could harangue people about – make them feel guilty about... And, of course, Gran's theory about providing cannon-fodder... Real "universal love" that was – wasn't it?

The priests should have tried blessing condoms instead of guns!

Anyhow... Religion is a safe subject now. Why? Because no-one claims to have any belief now. No-one for miles around here anyway...

The sickness blew all of that away. Nearly for everyone.

So – we do get to hear of religious-nutters around some places. A few people I've met have run into or up against some. All those reported seem to be fanatics – fanatical arseholes... Every case you hear of, they seem to be screaming and raging... And demanding that everyone believes every single thing they say – NO questions – not ever. Somehow none of them agree with anyone else but they all have the "One-True-Perfect" version – and every single group exclusively "Got it from God"...

Looks like they all blame someone – someone else – for the sickness. At least half of them want to eradicate the "evil threat"... And that's usually the people next door... Coincidentally – that's usually people with useful things that they want – like fuel or weapons... Unless it's some "lesser people" that should be enslaved...

Seems like it's more of what Greg said... They all want to prove how wonderful and loving their God is – by killing as many people as possible...

Sodding Terrific!

Well... We're all well armed around here now... We *can* be tolerant... We do choose...

Ghosts? I've mentioned ghosts before... Truth is – I do *not* know... There should have been a title for that. (Not only the God-related "agnostic")... I'm neutral on all of it.

I *don't* go looking... Once he could sit me down and get some sense into my head Greg told me that a good approach was to never go looking for "God"... Because, if you did, then you never could know that what you found was anything other than what you looked for.

That seemed wise and practical to me. Every "obvious" reason I'd ever had shoved at me had seemed to me to be pointless, going round in a circle or plain false.

Anyhow... It's not logical to try to explain with a proof something you believe in "by faith"! That's a contradiction! "Knowing" and "believing" are not the same thing! (I knew that without ever studying philosophy!)

The other thing, for me, was that so many things always seemed to get added on to what was said to be "radical"... "Of the root"... I looked that up at the library...

The meaning of radical seemed to have got seriously ballsed-up, though. Seemed like "radical" had gotten to be another reason/excuse for killing people.

Being a total hypocrite with your beliefs was one thing... I mean, as Mum said well before Greg did, "anyone can screw-up – big time. You don't have to keep screwing up." It cannot be right to distort the words of any religion you choose to use, to justify being a complete scum bag, arsehole and brute. Doing that is plain sick.

OOPS! I'm talking about religion... Can't do that! It's *taboo*...

A few other things Greg said – that I go with...

About ghosts – and all that... I don't go seeing what chemicals will explode... I don't go poking my nose into other phenomena I have absolutely no idea about.

(So – okay – Greg knew exactly what would explode... Bit of a different "empirical" study though – wasn't it?)

Doesn't matter how "loving" you are... If you say that only your version is right – *you* are condemning everyone else... And that is one hell of a lot of people... Well – it used to be...

If there's one, true, absolute-correct version... How come so many people have a different interpretation of it?

If any sort of God has to do everything his/her/its believers pray for... How can that be a God? How can that be "powerful" in any way? That would make any "God" a merely mechanical puppet.

Then again... What's the difference between saying that there is a "cause and effect" between the "mumbo-jumbo" of a magic spell and the "sanctified" words of a prayer book – or, even, the waffle of "extemporised prayer"? Is it just that whoever is doing it at the time has the one-true-correct version – and a "direct line" to "God" – or the powers/spirits?

Anyway... Most of that doesn't mean a thing now... The sickness destroyed whatever belief anyone had.

(I suspect that Beth was "religious" in some way – before...)

The big thing – bigger than before – that people do still ask is "How could a God allow all that awful suffering?" Again – I go with Greg's idea on that... "How come, seeing as we all choose to be so fucking-awful to each other – at least – by far the majority do... Then – how come "God" doesn't say 'Sod this! I screwed up big time!' – and then scrap the lot...?"

There you are... A "safe" subject to waffle on about. Safe now... Now that no-one can begin to figure out some sensible explanation...

Except, of course, the nutters that have their perfect answers...

Question I have no answer for...

Did those maniacs I killed murder Danny because of some insane belief that they, and they alone, had the "One True Faith" – and blamed anyone/everyone else for the sickness...? Or – were they only racists?

What were they? Mad? "Prejudiced"? "Fearful" maybe...? *What* goes wrong with people that they ever begin to think that it's right to go attacking other people? *Any* other people?

Yeah, okay... So *I* killed *them*... That was self-defence. It was them or me. I had a choice... Yeah, I did... Except I never realised it in the heat of the moment... Later, sometimes, wished that (maybe) I had let them kill me – in the pain and the emptiness that followed... That still cuts me to pieces...

===========

Don't know if I'll ever "get over" what happened...

Danny murdered...

Didn't drown myself... Or even self harm...
I did get crazy – a bit... Okay... So – I lost it – a few times...
What you expect? What would you have done?
Yeah?

I said (I think I did) about turning round to say something... To him...

The shock that he wasn't there...
The pain that I'd done it – again – again...
It seemed wrong...

I fucking missed him! Okay?! I felt – ripped... Fucking... Gutted –

He was supposed to be there... **NO!** That's wrong...

There was no way he was meant to not be there. Not ever. Never!
We were supposed to **just be**.

============

Okay... So – Ben and Beth made me take a break... I was cracking up. Losing it. Upsetting Dani.

They say "it's okay"... To give myself a break... I want to write this though... Get it down – get it done...

I never, not ever, felt that he was somehow there... One of those ghosts or... Wasn't that I didn't believe in – the possibility... I simply – never felt that.

It wasn't feelings like that when I knew I had to get away... When I drove blind...

There could be a shock... Sometimes when waking up... A shock of the pain not being there... "The shock"... A horror of not feeling it... Even for only a second of respite...

It didn't make for guilt...

Guilt is bollocks anyhow... It's an excuse for not sorting it... A cop-out for not getting off your arse and either recognising that – when you've screwed-up – there's <u>either</u> something to do about it – <u>or</u> nothing you can do about it... "Feeling guilty" is just a bribe to your own feelings for not acting... It's an opiate for your own feelings...

I was NOT going to do that...

Even when there was no way I could change it I could feel remorse – in a positive way – work to *never* screw up again...

But – to be fair – there was absolutely sod-all I could do about what had happened. I had it easy – in a way... I got no choice.

Danny was dead. That was it. Finished.

Finished.

<u>Finished.</u>

I'd killed all his killers... Did that "do something about it"? If it did there was no satisfaction to it... No "closure"... Anyhow – they were trying to kill me. That made what I did more like self preservation... Except, maybe, the last one – or two...

I do not feel bad about that though... Definitely not the elegant "guilty"...

They all of them got into the fight. None were saying "hold on" or stopping to see who we were... They started it. They lost. All of them.

Stupid, stupid, stupid waste.

===========

After that though... Back at the big house...

Slowly, slowly I was realising, accepting...

I was – if I was...

There was no point beating myself up about where we screwed up at the store any further... Not that that stopped me – stops me – even now – sometimes...

BUT... it was "we"...

I don't want to think what it would feel like if I had to take on board that it was only me...

That would be diabolical... Makes me realise the horror some poor sods went through if they felt that they'd not picked-up-on an IED... That would be *so* horrific...

Another of those things that isn't merely "not talked about"... But can't be talked about...

If I was...

Three bouts of nausea and a good throw-up pretty well settled the question...

I began to realise that maybe those new, different funny-feelings in my tum weren't indigestion...

Ten, eleven, twelve weeks? I hadn't a clue... Hadn't been paying attention to mere time passing... However much I wracked my brain and made charts I couldn't figure out any kind of what and when...

So... Okay. I could be... Maybe...?

Totally despite all my crumbling mind and emotions were doing – I felt – physically – absolutely ***FANTASTIC***... I've never felt so good...

[Whatever mind and emotions were doing then? Near breaks me up <u>*now*</u> *– just thinking about it...]*

It hit me... Mum said that she felt marvellous when she was carrying me...

That spooked me for real!

Maybe I was... *Oh God!*
What was I supposed <u>to do</u>?!

I loved it – one way – I had Danny's baby in me... <u>***OUR baby! BEAUTIFUL!***</u>

But – *HOW* was I ever supposed to have a baby? There was a winter coming... That was going to be problem enough...

Summer – maybe a couple of months, Autumn – was that two or three more? Winter – fuck-knows how long... Mild or diabolical... First time I thought about weather forecasts... First serious time – since...

How was I supposed to get through a winter...
On my own...
Okay – so that was practical...

<u>*HOW*</u> was I supposed to have a baby?
They <u>don't</u> teach you that in college or school either.

<u>*Why the hell not?*</u>

['Cos you're not supposed to get pregnant in the first place? 'Cos it would mean actually recognising that teenage girls <u>*do*</u> *get pregnant?]*

Okay – so they make lessons so boring all you want to do is fall asleep – I suppose that's kind of good training for changing nappies – in the middle of – anytime – when you've been awake most of the night – maybe for days...

Could be that if they taught the sleep-deprivation experience it would encourage the girls at least to not get pregnant! Might cut out the "accidental" pregnancies... Might have... Back then...

===========

I guess there's no real preparing for it is there? I mean – how can anyone explain what "being pregnant" – having a life inside you – is like...? I suppose – for a start – it must be so different, so many kinds of different, for – well – about everyone...

Okay... So – I was dazed... I think that was what I was...

I suppose that I was grieving – "bereft" – "LOST" would be another word for it...

Realising... I could NOT get my head round it. It could NOT be real... But – I WANTED it to be... I DREADED it was real...

Maybe it's like that for lots of women... For all different reasons... That word "different" again... Maybe it's been that way throughout time?

Anyway – I couldn't whiz and get a test-kit could I? I couldn't go to a clinic... So *what* could I do?

Get my head together – just ordinary things for a start... Eat regularly – eat better... Keep a track of myself... Behave myself... Like? For real? Me?

I wasn't boozing, smoking, doing drugs or hanging out with the wrong people... Weren't even any right people around that I knew of...

Get my head together... That was a start...

Good thing – NOT an enjoyable thing – I felt nauseous a few mornings... Before I chucked up – big time... Like I said...

I would have **freaked** if I hadn't been figuring – working out what was going on...

Umm... By then I was on the move again... I can't sensibly explain that either... I'd gone out for a raid – probably an excuse... Probably couldn't stand the emptiness in the big house any more... I'd done that a couple of recent times – short trips but longer each time... More than a couple... This time I never got round to going back...

Wasn't telling myself anything about putting more bits ready in the Landy each time than I was taking out at the end of the raid...

The place was a mess anyway...

I know I told myself I'd go back... I could go back... I would... We had our stock of food and fuel there... It was a good place (well – it was better before I let-loose on it...) It had been good...

I only – wasn't getting round to moving on...
Even though I was loading up the Landy – ready...
(pretending I wasn't).
Ready for...?
Other stuff happened – was happening...

===========

5 – 4

Some days down the road...

I'd already had brief contact with a couple of small groups... Scared the living crap out of them. I guess that I looked a little crazed... That and the way I always had the nasty little black shotgun in hand.

In my thinking, people that were frightened of me on first sight weren't going to be much use – even if they weren't leaping to take pot-shots at me.

I've no idea where I got the thought from... I was wandering and not exactly thinking – but keeping my eyes wide open – being vigilant now... Well, I'd *really* seen what could happen hadn't I? That and I had a whole new reason.

I had a whole new arsenal with me to protect that reason too...

Something in my head changed – changed a *whole* lot...

I think, maybe, I had started to look – it wasn't a spur-of-the-moment thing... I saw this camping/survival/army type shop... I needed fresh gas for my stove anyway.

[NOT your kind Richard! Sod off!]

The area looked quiet – no sign of any of the shops on either side being raided. Everything dusty, rain streaked and clearly untouched for ages.

There were already a LandRover and a van (painted brown and sandy) parked out front of the shop. I took a real-good look at them – not just the glass but the door handles, tyres and the ground front-and-back of the wheels. No-way I was getting caught-out now...

I had totally got my old, pre-Hermitage, head on. My eyes and ears more open than ever... And I was armed now...

So, after I'd gone round the block and then sat and watched for a bit, I gently pulled my Landy up behind the other Landy – neat and tidy – disturbed as little dust as possible – so it looked like it belonged... Very important that – look like you shouldn't just be there – but that you've been there forever.

(Can't fake the dust properly – but some dust is a start. Good excuse for not ever cleaning a car).

Easiest way to get into anywhere? Try the door! It is so bloody annoying to have cut yourself smashing a window and climbing in only to find that a front door is open – not locked at least... Guess how I know that! Uh! You do know...

Didn't know what went on with the shop. I guess I got some clue to be extra cautious when the shutters weren't all pulled down and locked... Maybe that's what caught my eye in the first place? I think that by then I'd started seeing and rationalising bits like that... Despite everything... Maybe – because of...

No tags though – not anywhere... I'd definitely developed being careful. I wasn't numbly strolling round the corner to get an ice cream, a paper and a can of drink without being aware of what's going on at all... Those days were well gone... I'd jumped to far more than the caution that had been mere everyday life for me around the Estate and the village before Greg... That probably helped a lot though.

I'd got my swivel eyes on and my bendy neck engaged – looking all around me at everything and everywhere... If it hadn't been my ankle was still bad, I'd have been turning around every few steps. I had that short, black (handy) shotgun on me.

So a probably useful shop not all locked up? Not smashed in either... It was unusual – but not unique – and the area was smart – good street lights (not working by then – they were off everywhere of course) – no pubs or clubs, no takeaway – well – a couple of little restaurants with small "takeaway available" signs in the corners of the windows – discreet – posh...

Yeah – I was suspicious. It looked too good – and that made me jumpy...

Which was a good thing.

Gun level I shoved the door open with my shoulder.

The owner – or whoever he was – he'd hanged himself inside.

Wasn't much of a smell to warn me by then – and he wasn't near the front where there was still some evening light... Could have scared the crap out of me – but I was becoming well used to things like that. In fact I had got round to moving slowly and looking well ahead – although you usually had to look more at the floor than for anyone hanging around. (Sorry – bad joke).

I did think that topping himself was a bit of an over-reaction to the lack of customers coming into his shop... I mean – it wasn't as if the tax man was going to be chasing him was it?

(Yeah – okay – so Ben says that the English "sense of humour" is what has always got us through... Makes him wonder how the serious Germans and Nordics are managing...)

More practically – no-one was doing that "movie-zombie" reach-through-the-shelves and grab-you-by-the-throat thing. People were learning that getting that close practically begged being stabbed. Even in a confined shop-space everyone (with any intelligence) wanted to keep well outside arms reach by that time. (Anyway... How come those slow-shuffling zombies suddenly had the intelligence, skill and speed to do that?) Whatever... When caught in a shop the first essential thing, was to have one-hell-of-a-good exit strategy pre-planned... Like smacking whoever hard with a can of macaroni cheese and charging right by them... But only if you really couldn't simply slide discreetly out some other door.

The pump-gun gave a whole different dimension... Several different ones...

Always more questions...

Did I actually want to shoot anyone?

When? That's a really tricky one.

How to make a split-second decision? And that could be far too long...

Noise. A whole heap of questions of their own.

What else might I hit?

Ricochets...

I knew the gun worked. I'd managed to not be on the receiving end of it – but – I'd seen the muzzle flash – at least – I reckoned that I had – even in the sunlight...

But – I'd not fired it for myself – I had no idea of its range, scatter – or – most important – its recoil... I would be firing from the hip – my right shoulder wouldn't stand another battering – and the left was sore-as-hell with shot in it.

"Would be firing" if/as/when I made my mind up... Provided I lasted that long...

I did figure that dropping on one knee, putting the butt against my heal and firing up-at-an-angle might work – and would make me a smaller target... *If* I reacted something like right...

Anyhow... With the gun sort-of slung upside down on my front (making my neck ache but clear of both shoulders) I started by getting a bunch of gas canisters for my stove and a stash of freeze-dried meals. Wasn't figuring I'd got too much room to load more – not if I wanted to easily sleep/catnap horizontal in the back.

But – the place had a surplus section. I wandered in there thinking of maybe finding some more fuel cans – maybe a water can – which gave me an idea...

Turning around to go look for water purifying tablets I saw a rack of body warmers – and there were some small sizes – which was an unusual and good start... They turned out to be armour vests, though... Which had me a bit confused. They seemed weirdly heavy.

While I figured it out I slunk out and stashed what I'd got so far. Then I realised what they probably were and went back with a tiny lamp for another look. There were green, cammo and black "POLICE" ones.

Hey! A fashion choice!

Reckoned that some people would be all-too-ready to take a shot at any "POLICE" they saw – so hummed-and-hah-ed about green or dinky patterns for a bit... Which was entirely pointless – because the only thing that counted was finding one that I couldn't walk around in – and wasn't *way*-too-heavy. My injured shoulders did <u>not</u> take kindly to them!!!

I found a good one. It's a black, police one – but I reckoned I'd be able to take the labels and chequered bits off easily. The big thing was that it and a couple of others were for women – and the shape <u>does</u> matter. It matters okay? When you're wrapped up in it all day...

It's like Mum had a couple of fights to get provided with lady-shaped hi-viz vest things... I wonder if the army and people ever properly got their act together on that? Anyhow – I got one that fitted me pretty well. A <u>major</u> achievement! And like I said – I still use it – quite a lot. (When my newer, better one needs a clean). Apparently its more than just a good fit but a good "specification" – so that's neat. Always been a pity it's so heavy!

Putting it on I saw myself in a mirror. Only in the gloom I didn't realise. *Frightened myself silly!* First chance to check the "ready to shoot" reaction... NOT ready... Got in a real tangle... But – <u>didn't</u> shoot myself... PHEW!!!

While I tied myself in knots, this other person was suddenly there and getting my attention by doing a jig... She/he/it leapt out of sight the moment I did... Took me a few minutes to put my heart back in, stop the blood pounding, finish untangling, unclench my arse – and (eventually) work out what was going on...

I think we've all done that... Completely shits you up doesn't it? I've seen some mirrors smashed – and a few shot to bits...

Anyway, while I recovered, I got to thinking about the cammo and all that sort of gear. In with the armour were some covers with nothing in them – and one was small enough to fit over the vest that fit me without being too baggy. I reckoned I might use the pouches in it as pockets – and I could tighten it up with a couple of green bungees if I needed to...

Amazing the useful things you can sort out in a place like that...

Next, I figured that a cammo jacket on top of blue jeans and even a dull red T shirt might have been a style choice for college but it looked stupid now.

I started to look (not very hopefully) to see if they had any green or cammo trousers I wouldn't get lost in like I was strolling in a forest. The light was almost gone by then, though.

I didn't want to get absorbed in sorting out a whole new wardrobe in the near dark – definitely not risking any torchlight getting seen... And I did <u>not</u> want to fall over any more ammo boxes! So (grudgingly) I cautiously went back to the front door.

Turning myself green did, however, seem like a positive plan. So I loaded what I'd already got and moved the Defender around the rear of the shops to a corner of the delivery area. (Didn't risk moving far in the dusk with no lights).

That was an okay place – tucked in, well out-of-sight... I had a good sleep there... After I'd carefully sorted all my ammunition and the small guns into some of the ammo boxes... Which kind-of made up for smashing-in my shins. (Would have loved to have been able to find some proper gun oil...)

Next morning, good and early, I had a discreet peek at what was going on from the end of the block of shops... Nothing.

Quickly along the fronts and inside I nipped through to the back of the shop and opened up the delivery door... (Growing a bit wise). Next I wedged the front door hard shut before finding some good LED headlights to see what I was doing in the back parts where the clothes were – and to take with me of course.

[Note – never miss an opportunity to get good lights. If you can still find any, the chemical light-sticks are also excellent].

Never took any notice of the stiff... He was still hanging around of course. Okay, so I wasn't going near – but – I wasn't in any way bothered. Is that weird? It seems like it isn't. Seems like we all saw way too many bodies and shut it all out – at least shut-down any of the old emotions.

I mean – I'd never seen a stiff – a dead body – before Mum and the neighbours – and Greg...

I'm pretty sure I thoroughly shut it all out. I couldn't cope with it – so I didn't... Simple. (Kind-of...)

[Except it can all be tucked away, down deep... Come back later... So – you're gonna need to sort it sometime. That is – so long as you don't want to keep waking up screaming...]

Beth says that when you think about all the old news film – from all over the world – there could be bodies lying around all over and people just got on with their everyday lives... They went on shopping, going to work – taking their kids to school (passing the bodies – even walking between them...). Seems like dead bodies – human ones at least – get to be normal to people... Then again – we never batted an eyelid at all the murder and mayhem the TV and film provided for our entertainment every day. Christmas would never have been the same without a few good murders and war films... A bit of torture, disasters, train/ship/plane wrecks and terror plots for good measure...

So I ignored Fred – or whatever his name was... That's part of it, maybe; there's no name – that makes it easier... "Nothing to do with me..." Don't suppose I ignored him so much as – just stepped carefully around.

Ignoring dead people, especially the endless parade from all over the world on the news (back in the "Old World") was a load easier than ignoring the

Old Guard snotty/posh people in the village shop... I was from the Estate wasn't I? So, even when I was shopping for odd bits of food for Greg or Bodger – and it wasn't long before all the noses knew that – and I was practically waving a twenty at them as soon as I walked in... I was suspect like a terrorist to them.

I told Greg I reckoned that they made the CCTV camera squeaky on purpose – so as to make sure I knew that they were watching my every move...

Laugh! He followed me in one day – and loaded up his jacket stuffed full of tins and packets – so that he bulged... Didn't nick them – dumped them all out over the counter after they'd smiled and thanked him for buying one packet of gum... Then he told them how stupid and prejudiced they were. Told them that if they had any sense they'd watch the girls from the stables... On the way out he said that he didn't mean the staff – but the stable owner's snooty daughters. "These two" he said as they tried (and failed) to shove in through him like he wasn't there.

Prejudice, it's like racism, sexism, ageism and all the rest – just more varieties. And like that showed – it's usually plain stupid. Goes back to that "seeing what you expect" thing.

Of course (back in the camping shop) finding any clothes that fit me properly was ridiculous – until I sussed out to look in the "cadets" section. (Didn't have places like that in my scruffy bit of the Old World did we?) All the time I was around Greg – and I never thought of doing anything like that... Greg never suggested... Probably figured that I'd kick-off – maybe even walk out on him... (Wouldn't actually have done of course... Just settled for a screaming tantrum).

I wonder what he would say now??? I'd never have imagined me as a soldier – how would he have reacted? (Probably told me not to get my arse shot off...) I think Mum and Gran would have freaked.

Anyway, I got a bit systematic and practical about collecting – decided that I would squeeze a bit more in the Landy. I found good boots, socks (plenty of spares of both) – and about everything all the way to a proper *[Kevlar]* helmet that was only a bit too big...

A helmet did seem bizarre... Maybe even more then – seeing as Danny had got shot in the face... Wouldn't have done him any good...

Oh Bollocks!

===========

So okay! If he'd had a helmet on maybe it would have caught his skull and everything and I wouldn't have my scars...

There – said it.

Fuck it!! I'm just going to keep on writing and dripping all over the poxy place...

Shit!

Don't know why I didn't think of that in the shop... Guess that I was still zoned out... Maybe too busily focussed and listening out for anyone else moving around.

At least I had got practical. I put each collection in good load-bags or backpacks and shoved each pair in the Landy soon as they were full.

After a few I was struggling to decide on bits that would be properly practical and not "just in case". Space on board was getting limited. I spent a few minutes wracking my tiny mind for ideas. I'd taken a couple of looks at some of those load-carrying rigs and assault vests but Greg had never reckoned on them much.

His main thing was that if some prick started shooting at you, then you wanted to get down as fast as you could *and* as low and flat as you could.

You did *not* want to be propped up on a load of junk – half of which would be digging in your ribs.

So – well – he did say that he could see that "chest rigs" could be good in some jobs... He still didn't fancy carrying a whole load of bullets on his chest. He reckoned that, if he was facing the enemy as he should be, that was the part that they would be most likely to hit. He did *not* want to be shot by one of his own bullets being hit, going off and whizzing up his nose. Grenade pouches were worse than silly according to him.

Greg explained in incredibly repulsive detail precisely what wasn't sympathetic about a "sympathetic explosion". He was always extra good at being *nauseating* when he wanted to get a point like that across.

Yeah, okay... So a whole load of ideas he'd rabbited on about were suddenly making real sense to me now... I put off making a decision like that – was going to have to get used to the armour anyway...

I'd put it on and, even without sore shoulders, was finding it a bit cumbersome – not much too heavy (couldn't have done with that) but I definitely wasn't used to any extra weight. Was early-on so there was no issue with my shape – that only erupted later...

(Don't know why I never thought of this before... But – back then, before, I often wondered why Greg was going on about all sorts of odd stuff... At least he made it interesting – often wrapped things up with a joke or a funny story that had happened to him or his mates... He got ideas in my head though... Without me knowing it).

What I can't figure now is – did he see this coming? Did he have a premonition or...?

There's a load of essential information I "just <u>know</u>" now – that I never knew I'd heard... Like about keeping guns clean and all that... Weird. But they're more things I owe him for.

Greg didn't ever lecture me – he didn't talk *at* me – about things I *had* to know. I'd never have taken that then. I'd no way have seen what use any of it could ever be for me... My world was safe – comfortable.

Yeah – I had hassles, had to get out of a whole load before Greg showed up – but... But even bullies and bother can be "safe" and "comfortable"... You can know where you are with them. That's way better than any "unknown".

Once Greg was around most of my worries got to be about stupid exams and CVs. Greg's stories were an entertaining distraction while I wound down at the end of the day – making a fuss of Bodger – or being sat on by him... Bodger that is. Probably the big thug was making sure I stayed and listened... Now that *was* a conspiracy – I'm certain of it.

Like I said, I'd got to the stage of looking around the shop and wondering what else to get...

My mind got made up for me. I was looking around in the front – about the furthest area from the delivery door...

"**THUNK!**" Something struck the front door – like someone had expected it to be open and slammed right into it.

Of course I instantly thought "SHIT!" and froze. Whoever it was booted the door massively hard and went into one big time. While he started yelling at whoever was with him a display cabinet I'd ignored caught my eye. It was "boys toys" – big hunting knives, catapults and things... But – it had been left a little open.

Would never have imagined me with a knife – Mum would have thrashed me. Greg would have – well – I hate to think... Anyway; like I said – I was still sorting my act. All my guns were in the Landy – so's I didn't tangle and shoot myself... Great! Terrific! Useless! *Way* beyond reach... *So Stupid!*

Eyes on the big windows in case they looked in, I felt around and got myself a blade that seemed about right – as in "bloody terrifying". I wouldn't have wanted a blade like that waved at me – which was the right idea.

I slowly sank down low with the blade while a second man came and rattled the door – before they started an argument about who had left the keys behind – but then getting into more of a row about who had locked it – had one of them locked it? *"Who-the-fuck-had-fucking-locked-it??!!"*

I thought a whole load more than "SHIT!" – felt it as much as thought it. Certain muscles were working extra hard... More than my legs as I crawled behind a bigger counter.

I was frantic they would soon smash their way in. They made the whole glass front shake and creak. At least they didn't look close enough to see the wedge I'd jammed the door with.

Soon as they stopped hammering and facing off and turned back to their car (that I hadn't heard) I slid low along the back of that bit of the shop, and into the rear... Moment I was completely out of their sight I shot fast and silent out the loading door – dragging a couple more bags I'd begun to fill. Those bags would have been the only clear sign that I'd been in there. I'd left everywhere neat – not trashed the place like some idiots would have.

Chucked the bags in the back – quietly – shut the door hard – quietly. Shut the loading door – *quietly*. Shoved a big round, steel rubbish bin – not so quietly – against the door and jammed up two of the little roller things...

First question then was – whether to drive away – making a noise and near guaranteed to get seen as soon as I got round the end to the road out front – or to sit tight.

Second Q... Shotgun or automatic? I had both to hand...

However...

I was parked up all the way in the corner and nearly hidden by the other bins, bales of cardboard and junk. From what I'd heard I didn't think that they'd come round where I was...

Even though I was tucked away I had a good view of the only way into the service area. There was a good chance that if I stayed still no-one would notice me – unless they came looking to get in the back door. If they did come I now had far more than those two bullets in one old gun if I needed to kick up a racket. That was as far as I was thinking...

I wasn't sure what to do. I was boxed in. That was my *BIG stupid mistake.* I could definitely scare the hell out of anyone – but if they shot back? There were way too many brick walls, steel bins and angles for crap to ricochet off of. Some of my own shots might come back from off of other industrial bins.

See! I <u>had</u> picked up a whole load of sense from Greg and his mates screaming at the films. But, also – in my survival fight – rounds that didn't hit people went whizzing off all over the place. Windows way off got smashed. I think my shoulder got hit by deflected shot – which was, of course, fortunate – as most of the power had gone out of it... It still fucking HURT! *[What-the-hell it found to deflect off I have <u>no</u> idea!]* One idiot managed to shoot a street lamp...

Hiding behind the surplus shop, I could see that if I surprised anyone I might get out of there while they were busy leaping around... Or I might manage to shoot myself with my own bullets..

Yeah... I didn't necessarily <u>have</u> to shoot... So long as no-one aimed at me... Still not getting my head round the business though...

I *think* that I had enough sense to be vaguely aware that I had no idea how I might react if someone only looked like trouble... By then any possible answer wasn't even "theory" in my head – it was a total unknown. Having my new arsenal and reason was one thing (or two) but – explosive, reactive self-defence is totally different from approaching making a decision to "take some kind of action"... Then you need to have an idea <u>what</u> you're going to do... And not freeze up when you need to do it...

Okay... So I'm sure Greg will have told me about all that... It's still a whole other thing when it gets down to it...

I was still thinking like that then. Waffling around. Well – I still do – kind-of... No, I don't waffle now. I've thought it all through. Most of it... At least about the preference for not having to kill people. Chucking beans at people was one thing – even knocking them out... But shooting people...

I've done a load more shooting since then – and shot people... Killed – again. But I think and plan for the "non-fatal options" first... So long as I can – so long as it makes sense...

As far as I ever can I do that thinking ahead-of-time. That way whenever, whatever, shit hits the fan I have a good idea of possibilities – things to do – more important – things <u>*not*</u> to do... When the shit hits the fan I don't spend time sitting on my arse digging out the philosophy, morality and ethics text books... Thoughts like that at the wrong time can get you dead. Thinking ahead can mean you make a sensible choice to <u>not</u> shoot.

So there I was, back of the shops...

At least I'd got everything I wanted by that time. Then, before I got my act together properly, I heard a massive smash from the front. That seemed like a good time to hightail it. I reckoned they'd be busy – and I was right...

When I came out at the end of the block and looked to the left along the front they'd rammed the window. Done it so hard, they'd got their rear wheels stuck and were busy revving the guts out of the engine – and yelling at each other some more .

My Defender was never going to slip away soundlessly so I turned right and floored it – watching their reaction in the mirrors...

For long enough they stood and gawped. Then they jumped around a bit – but, by the time they were waving guns and yelling at each other more than me, I had reached a crossroads and could get out of the way – *very* fast.

There were no nice square, blue signs with a red-and-white "T"... I *did* look... *Before* I began to turn...

I hauled the Landy round hard enough to miss all the parked cars – both sides. Impressive or what?

I never did find out who they were... You do wonder these things sometimes... They might have been okay. You can never know... After a bit I did get to wondering if Fred had hanged himself – or...

But my arse had done enough clenching for one day – I didn't want to think any more about that. I was simply glad that I seemed to have done the right thing – for once. Well, I'd got some of it right...

I'd also got the idea to have one of the guns with me at all times... *Definitely* got that...

At least they didn't shoot. I have never just shot – although I've been shot at way too many times for no reason other than they've seen me.

Anyhow, I reckon that if I'd popped a shot off in their direction when I came out from behind the shops, then they might well have reacted faster and shot at me – instead of standing there gawping and arguing... Again – that big question – when to shoot or not shoot...

The only time you can ever really know you got it wrong – it would be too late...

So – there's not a whole lot of point worrying about it. Is there?

On the other hand...

Whenever I've been seen enough to get fired at I usually let loose now – make them get their heads down and think twice – at least twice.

Yeah, okay – so do not point any weapon at me... These days I figure that's enough reason/justification to give at least a warning shot – and I make them damn close. There aren't many people can aim straight right after a bullet's cracked by their ear.

So, anyhow, we most everybody play safe. Unless you can check someone out you stay low, get out of there – or do what you can to control the meeting...

Have you protocols down. Planned/practiced/practiced/revised/honed/ more...

Body armour.

Helmet.

Eye protection/night vision.

Good boots.

Loaded weapon(s). Safeties ON – to start with.

Know your weapons.

Light behind you – for preference.

Check who is where – "us" as well as "them".

Check out the ground – falling over is not "control".

Diving in a controlled way – is <u>not</u> a success if you land in a puddle...

That's just for starters...

Then again... Making the "opposition"/strangers fall about laughing can be a good distraction tactic. It can even cool off a dodgy situation...

===========

Once I got some distance away from the shop and slowed down – well... Then I did a bit of thinking and I realised that the *one* thing I should have looked for in all that surplus stuff was some sort of holster thingy that fit at least one of the handguns I had. That and, maybe, some sort of better sling for one of the rifles. Maybe I should have gone with a chest rig?

Didn't think that it would do anything for my figure – joke...

Of course – I had no real idea of what was about to happen to "my figure" next...

Maybe, just maybe, my vast range of ignorance was bliss...

I'd not smoked for years. (Thanks Bodger!) I wasn't on drugs, had never done steroids – no unusual hormones except the odd dose of adrenalin... And the little I had been drinking stopped soon as I was getting sure.

See! I can be good! I do behave!

Probably helped a whole load by no-one being around to tell me a whole load of waffle I had to do. No-one loading guilt-trips on me. Also helped by no-one telling me I was a failure and always would be since Greg came on the scene... I suspect that he had a few of those "quiet words" with school for one thing... Another that I owe him.

Yeah... When I was travelling again there were "certain people", kind and supportive people, I *wished* I had around me...

So *not* going there... 'Cos this would all get washed away...

===========

5 – 5

Those early months, right after the sickness, were all an un-dated, almost timeless blur...

But – once I was sure I at least kept count of the days – although I had neither any idea of when I should be counting from nor the least clue about what was supposed to happen or when. (Guess what I think about that!)

I tried breaking into a newsagent, one of those big ones, for mags on pregnancy, childbirth and all the rest... Can't say that anything really helped... Some articles had a good go at scaring me silly... So I used them as fire-lighters.

Raided a book store – terrifying in town... Way-too-much evidence of people being around. Far too many windows, doors, corners. Too many roads. Grabbed and got out. Managed to keep the speed safe. Slept for a couple of days.

Okay – tell me this... Which book first? Which one do you believe?

On the other hand... Most of them focus on doctors, midwives, hospitals, birthing pools, electronics, drugs – epidurals... Not much use to me in my "New World"... I would just have to be brave wouldn't I?

[Neither Ben nor Beth was stupid enough to come up with any of that sort of crap... I don't think that was due to how we met... I'll give them the credit anyhow].

Maybe I chose the wrong place and/or wrong stuff – but nothing I found (cleared out the shelf) really told me how to identify where I'd got to, what I should feel... Anything I had grabbed seemed to miss the mark... For me at least. So – it was a good thing I found Beth – and Ben... And didn't hit them too hard...

What I should get? Prepare? Well – that was one department of stores that had definitely not been cleared out...

I've kept continued to count the days – religiously (about the only religious thing about me) – religiously counted since Dani was born. I want Dani to know when her birthday is. Regardless that her Dad can't be there for her... Least he has a sound reason...

And Dani knows about him – what he looked like – she's got a heap of pictures. Sylvia has been brilliant and laminated them – everyone here in the Valley said it was a "justified" use of the generator.

Dani knows all about him, stories he told me. What he did... Umm... Well – not in the same detail as I've written here – Not for a few years anyway... But one day she can read this.

Maybe I'm writing for her... This bit at least... I hope she someday finds experiences as good – and better.

I want her to know she was created by love – and – passion. We didn't "want" or "plan" her – she's a marvellous miracle... No! A MARVELOUS MIRACLE!!!

Mushy? <u>No way!</u> When you think of what was going on – what had happened – how we were... She's astounding!

I guess that I'll have to explain Beth and Ben, meeting them – what happened... How we got involved with the Valley... I'd rather get my leg right and stop sitting around on my arse here...

Doing this is good though...

{{Beth note – while Eli's not looking... It's certainly good for the rest of us! A bit of peace! (So long as you ignore the mutterings and grumping...) And Eli's sleeping better.}}

CHEEK!

Pregnancy? You get big. You change shape. You ache. Bits of you ache more than any bits have a right to – and it's not just the bits you'd expect to...

People say some *really* stupid things!... Correction – MORONIC. "God! She's FAT!" is <u>not</u> going to encourage me to not shoot you. "She's up-the-duff you twat." Didn't exactly enhance the greetings either. (Have you figured? Men).

You can guess where "You'll <u>have</u> to stay here with us. So that we will look after you" went...

Not sure which gained the prize out of...

"Which Hospital are you going to use?"

"Are you going natural? I did, it's far superior..."

(Followed by howling and weeping – trying to lean on me and hug...)

"It's like shitting an <u>enormous</u> pineapple! *Agony!*"

Followed by "You'll have one <u>hell</u> of a time without drugs!" Gee! Thanks!

"I'd have a Caesarean if I were you"

I met far, <u>far</u> too many idiots before Ben and Beth. It encouraged me to stop trying to find anyone that I might manage to be safe with. Not that actively looking for people didn't go against the grain... I just had this (probably conditioned – aka "nagged") idea – stupid idea – that it was what I <u>had</u> to do... To "do it right".

On the other hand... I copied Mum. I felt ***fantastic!***

I'm sure that really pissed off some people. Their problem!

Oh yeah... I'm all in favour of women's football – light years better than the prima-donna men... BUT! Dani should have waited until she'd ejected before she began practicing!

Giving birth...

What am I supposed to say?

OW!!!!

Would that cover it?

All the Old World years of hearing women bitching about how awful it was for them Did *Not* Help.

If it was so bad, though... How come so many of them kept doing it? I mean – in our modern (luxurious) world in the West. Three, four or more times? If it was so bad – surely one "baby shower" would have been more than sufficient?

Beth? Baby shower? I/we got a monsoon! *Bless her!* (But – don't tell her I said that).

I am *not* complaining. NO!!! Dani is wonderful – worth every second – helped a whole load by being non-typically fast. (Like her Mum – screwed up the statistics from the start). Fine with me!

Ben's not complaining either... It took him longer to recover than it took me... Ignore anything he claims!

Anyhow... It proved one thing beyond doubt for me. *If* there is any sort of creator God – HE is a male. No woman would ever be so crap at design to come up with such a ridiculous, rotten way of doing it! NO WAY!

===========

Meanwhile...

(stop putting this off...)

Those pictures of Dani's Dad...

I managed to take a few reasonable ones of him...

Okay – so – I'm going to try to explain – kind of "build up to"...

Danny created fabulous pictures of me. Superb. Now that was "miraculous"!

He did a bit of sneaking around and taking the shots when I didn't know... When "I wasn't scowling at him"... I do not scowl!... Well – I don't now – I feel it's part of what he did for me...

So – Mum was right. "Looking like a church spinster that has farted and wants to blame someone else is never going to look attractive"... But I thought I was never going to look attractive anyway...

Like (with or without the "porn") some of the women in some of the pictures we found surfing the net – looked ghastly – and worse than the men – which you could call a major achievement...

There were some REALLY beautiful women though... Absolutely gorgeous... And that *no way* made me a Lezzy! They were – ravishing – dazzling... Even those with a monster big cock sticking in them... And the look on the faces of even those ones – beautiful faces (no zits) – well... You could see that there totally had to be something *fantastic* about sex... There *had* to be!

Back "on about" sex again! Like I said, though... Like drugs and booze – if it was so "bad" that we shouldn't do it – how come the adults were that keen on it? How come they were so determined to keep it to themselves? Was it going to run-out?

So, anyhow, what chance did a short-arsed, scrawny, sweaty, spotty kid with no money like me ever have?

I was never going to get scooped up by some sexy hunk and whisked off to a beautiful room that was bigger than our house; was I?

Then again – fantasising about it – I did learn a few things that I could do – for me at least...

Then again, again... If he "oohed" and "aaghed" so easily – *how* was I supposed to know how hard to hold the thing?

Kathy finding the BDSM sites did ***not*** help! (She *always* was *weird! Humungously!!)*

Mum's suggestion that "when their eyeballs burst out – you're squeezing too hard" did *not* help either!

Then again – Anton's eyes did tell me that I'd achieved a thorough revenge... *Sod Anton!* Stupid boy!

Danny – *he* showed me that I am beautiful. Not competing with some conventional idea of beautiful – some stereotype... Yes – some women are extra lucky – maybe some are unlucky – they do have drop-dead-gorgeous looks...

A load of them did just that of course – dropped dead... No-one looks great then... And no – because I survived doesn't make me any better because the "bar got lowered"...

I look good – because I'm me... I'm "me shaped" with my looks – and that is *perfect* for me... Even my scars are perfect for me... They're part of who I am – like stretch marks – like things that make me smile or make me look sad...

Beth completely confused me – she suddenly went into religious stuff – which always gets me muddled – when it doesn't get me fuming... She said that setting up stereotypes of beauty is blasphemous (thanks for the spelling

Ben)... She said that if God makes a person the way they are then saying that how they are is bad is to say that God is wrong... And so is covering up beauty... Like covering up a beautiful statue or painting – or banning wonderful music... Beth can get going so like Mum sometimes...

Maybe I'll have to find a couple of my pictures to show Beth – see what she says...

So – Danny changed how I see me... I don't suppose it makes any sort of sense to anyone else. Don't get the idea that all the pictures are nudes – or sexy – or sex... They're not... Some of them – are ordinary things like – my ear – my nose...

That one he cropped... From a pic of me naked on the bed – legs all over – and hand between them... I <u>was</u> sound asleep!

Okay – so the full pic looks – lurid... O*utrageously* erotic... So he – he took it looking all the way up me – I'll re-phrase that – he took it from my feet end... That isn't so much better is it? Anyway... He cropped it – so that the picture is looking up, no, *at* my nose...

I'd never have thought it... I have quite a nice nose. Dani has a <u>beau-tiful</u> nose. It was *so* cute when she was feeding... Now it's into <u>everything!</u>

===========

So – it's a couple of days after I wrote last...

Stop waffling...

I've jumped way, way ahead... Stumbled into the present... Jumped from then to now...

There's so much happened in the last couple of years... Dani getting born for one thing. Meeting Ben and Beth. Moving here... Other events...

Definitely not writing some of that yet...

But... Something happened. An important thing... I want to get it written while it's fresh – hot... Get it right...

I picked out some nice shots ("respectable" ones) – both me and me and Danny – and Danny on his own – (my efforts).

Showed them to Dani...

Huge event. Has turned me inside-out...

It's not stupid. (Yeah, Beth and Ben are right). (Stuart doesn't have a clue what-the-hell's going on – poor man).

What happened?

(Find me a sponge someone).

Dani was looking at the pics – again – she adores looking at her Dad – everything by her Dad or about him... (I love that).

(I wish I could take her back to the big house... But I wrecked that. Beth says – maybe I should – one day – maybe when she can understand what happened – why it happened – the house – not... Well... Beth hasn't *seen* it... Only heard... She – no-one – knows that it was me...)

(Forget the sponge – get me a bucket).

So... Dani's looking at pictures. Her Dad and me... Her Dad... And then me – a lovely picture... (*Oh God!* – or whatever)...

Dani touched the picture – ever so gently and said "What happened to your face?" Something like that...

Beth heard – not Dani – me... (Thank God! – or whatever). She shot through from her kitchen like a scalded cat...

It was alright though... I only gasped – covered it as a sneeze...

Dani wasn't fazed at all... She just thought that my face in the picture looked – "funny"...

As in "different"... Because it was before – before I got my scars... She'd not seen that before... Her Mum has always had – the face she has... That's Dani's Mum...

I'd never got that...

===========

I've put my act back together okay now.

===========

I <u>will</u> teach her school stuff – but properly – for her– so she can see what things are about – and why... And numbers – as a language... And a load of other useful, practical lessons...

Like you don't have to have an ultra-sound machine and a hospital and a hoard of medical people in a modern place telling you "You must do this" and "You must do that"... Can you imagine what would have happened with me? Giving birth is <u>not **im**possible</u> without an expensive hospital with all the latest gadgets and theories...

It's an incredible thing... (Greg would have laughed himself silly at this). Humans actually managed to keep going for centuries – thousands of years before they invented all that – and made having a sprogg "impossible" without it...

You'd have thought that there would have had to be a massive maternity unit provided in every country around the planet – every county or city – plenty to go round for everyone – so that women could just have babies... You'd have thought that life couldn't happen without it – the way they went on...

How could the human race ever have survived without that?

Modern women... Other survivors... Do not have to be petrified now because we don't have all that "modern scientific progress"...

Okay – there *are* risks... *Real risks*. Always have been. No hospital or science ever got rid of all risks. There have always been so many risks. **Just be careful. Be sensible. Go for the most sensible, safest things possible. Most of all... *DON'T WORRY!***

===========

5 – 6

MEANWHILE... BACK AT WHERE I was on the move, after the Big House...

At least I had worked out "my condition" before the first time I properly threw up... Would have scared me to death otherwise. But then – compared to what any of us went through with the sickness... Well, the first nausea (while I still hadn't finally accepted it) I hardly thought feeling "a bit yeuk" was odd. Put it down to my cooking... Which wouldn't have been any surprise – like I said – I wasn't exactly living.

My cooking was definitely less good once I got on the move... Strange feelings in my tum were nothing new – and the absolute worst result of my cooking was way better than the sickness any time.

Food was plain necessity that sort of went from outside to inside. So long as it didn't come out again in too disgusting a way I wasn't fussed.

Well... Waking up to what was going on woke me up – woke me up sharp... I was terrified – and overjoyed – all at the same time... Cried masses (I blame the hormones)...

But it didn't take me long to get my act together then...

One thing I knew – *and that one thing before everything else day and night* – I had Danny's baby in me and nothing, ***nothing*** between me and those stars was going to stop me having it and protecting it and bringing – er – him or her – up right...

Whatever this crazy new world might try to throw at us!

===========

The Dark Room

Forewarned by the Aftman's terrified shuffling the leisurers promptly straightened and froze the moment Hiro appeared from the narrow passageway. Correctly he ignored them: creatures at that high level never existed for one such as he. He looked at the darkness beyond the tiny hole they had made in the room's opposite wall. The hole was not correct. There should be the bright light of midday.

'Leave'. He made no contact with them or their aftman. The instruction was relayed. Chins to chest and hands clasped everyone left, swiftly, silently: leaving their tools as previously instructed. At the entrance they were guided to the left to be detained by Hiro's escort of faceless guards.

With the flicker of a glance at Yanis, Hiro barely whispered. 'Stay'. Turning briefly back he murmured 'Depart'. Despite the irregularity (the fact that he looked straight at his escort) they removed themselves with only a minimum of indignity. They had become inured to his peculiarity. They feared the penalty of his pleasure.

Yanis waited (still nervous of a snare that would as surely kill him as any rabbit wire).

'Relax. They all know worse than to hesitate'. Hiro allowed his face to move as he spoke softly. 'Relax Yanis. I am not testing you'. His face above and around his eyes moved from bland smoothness to deep folds. 'Come on! You would be in far more trouble for inCorrectness long before this. You know you should have reported me...' The edges of his mouth curled upward while his forehead smoothed. 'Long ago... To be Correct we should both have been moved on, "promoted" – long since'.

The way that he calmly spoke of the ending of this life, especially the official Promotion, still made Yanis shudder enough to worry that it would show through the thickness of his drover's cloak.

'So? What has been uncovered? How many are aware of it? Will there be a need...?'

'Only those two, but not the aftman, I sent him to the corridor to greet you...' Yanis was surprised at the firmness of his own quiet voice. 'Both leisurers have been corrected before, once each... The aftman has two strokes...'

Hiro's face curved again – and more – so that his teeth almost showed between his lips. 'Good. They will not be unfortunately Correct then. You selected them yourself?'

'I could not be credited'.

The folds of Hiro's brow returned. 'So you did... Alright – keep being Correct – but – stop messing about and tell me what we have here'.

Yanis gulped. He did not know. In his world (even in his outlandish, nearly doglandish, freaky world of attending Hiro) this was essentially in-Correct. Everything that could be was known. *That* was The Sole Correct Way... Whatever Hiro might so faintly imply... Whatever (Yanis baulked at the unauthorised effort of thought) – whatever the insurgents and the terrorists beyond the Doglands might dare to say. *Whatever* things that he would never admit to having the least heard of might suggest.

'So...' Hiro shrugged. 'Have you looked?'

Nearly fainting at the idea Yanis could only gulp repeatedly before managing to shake his head.

'Then, perhaps, I should...'

("Perhaps"!? Yanis' eyes flickered frantically toward the entry and back to the small, dark hole).

'Let's see...' With no sign of hesitation and without breaking into a terrified cold sweat Hiro approached the chisel sized hole in the wall. 'Ah! Good... Do you think those three would be better controlled with the removal or addition of a stroke?' He seemed to be talking to himself. Yanis frantically hoped that he was. (Strokes could *not* be removed – a third meant only one thing – Promotion...) Hiro's mouth curved again when he glanced around. 'Don't worry... We are not here...'

That at least was normal; Correct. At least – it would be in the conventional sense... The sense that Yanis seemed to drift ever further from with each day and each crazy event. However; he could take little comfort before his inferior nearly caused his heart to stop by peering hard into the darkness of the hole: and sniffing.

'Hmmm... It seems to be... dry... not musty... This is good... They have left their...?' He stayed close to the opening but looked around. 'Ah, good...' At least the inCorrectness of his touching leisurers' tools had now become familiar. He didn't hesitate at all before lifting a mallet and chisel. 'Let's see... Shall we?'

An open question? While Yanis rechecked the entry Hiro began to work at the clay of the wall. It seemed to be particularly hard – and to come away in odd, solid, lumps. Peculiarly the wall held no binding wattle.

'Yes... I thought so...'

"Thought"?! He openly and coolly professed to have a thought? Yanis swayed and clutched onto reality as a section of the wall crumbled... And did not (however much he had begged it to) reassuringly expose the calm, real, safe – outside world.

===========

Yanis blinked – focused. The floor appeared to be where a wall should be – and the wall where...

'You really should let go of your conditioning...' Hiro rolled him onto his back and easily sat him up and then back against the wall. 'You have been with me long enough...'

What did that mean? Yanis knew that he was at least Hiro's fourth attender. There was (Correctly) only one thing that could have removed his predecessors... Was he about to be sent for Promotion?

'Stop shaking! Calm down!' Hiro took Yanis's face firmly in both hands and turned it toward where the odd (inCorrect) wall had been. 'Look...'

Yanis groaned. There were shelves. Worse: there were the dark shapes that he knew (inCorrectly) to be books – books other than **The Sole Book**. He shuddered. They had stumbled on another hoard. A hoard that included rare, strange shapes.

Oh how he hoped against hope that they had only stumbled upon it... That there was not some inCorrect manner by which they had been guided to it...

Yanis had no hope at all that Correctness would be observed. The place would not be erased. Its memory would not be ploughed into **The Sole Earth**. The village would not be razed. The land not burnt and salted. The population not Promoted.

In the coming night Hiro's escort would silently (apparently blindly) load the hoard into black carts that would trundle away on cloth wrapped wheels behind their silent footed camels.

Leisuring for a man of no significance at all such as Hiro had always seemed to possess so much promise. His family had been so benign for him...

===========

The monstrously unnerving thing was – that Hiro clearly knew what he was looking at.

Yanis was certain that he had never seen a single thing like the objects before: he didn't really want to be seeing them now. The books were bad enough. The strange things that looked like large books, except that they had clearly once been richly coloured in blues, reds, greens and even yellows... (Books at least had the decency to be grey or brown – and well faded). These things opened like a book – but had metal (metal! Not leather) parts inside that held – Hiro called them "pages"... Yanis thought of them as leaves – and these were larger leaves than he had seen in books... And they were still white – even at the edges... The space, the "dark room" had been exceptionally thoroughly sealed...

Look at this!' Ignoring Yanis' near panic (in his enthusiasm quite possibly oblivious to it) Hiro swung from the table with a wide open yellow book – thing. 'Look!'

Daring to obey and not daring to not obey Yanis forced his eyes to focus on the open pages. They appeared to be covered in dried and flattened, completely flattened, worms – coloured blue... He could not begin to imagine (his shock released him to such sacrilege) what he was seeing.

'This!' Hiro breathed with awe. 'Is an – *original manuscript...*'

27630973R00307

Made in the USA
Columbia, SC
30 September 2018